Praise for the Misch[illegible]eries

"A 1960s Technicolor sp[illegible] com-plete with buoyant teeny[illegible] all of Maureen O'Hara's mournful [illegible], and an Ascot race scene straight out of *My Fair Lady*. . . . The sheer exuberance proves irresistible."

—*New York Times Book Review*

"Emma R. Alban is a fresh, distinct new voice in the genre and her debut gives us all the top-tier wit, spice, and swoons we love in a historical romance. One to watch!"

—Evie Dunmore, *USA Today* bestselling author of *Bringing Down the Duke*

"*Don't Want You Like a Best Friend* is a funny, sweet variation on *The Parent Trap*. . . . The characters and their activities are uniformly delightful. . . . Every time I think of this book, I smile."

—Smart Bitches, Trashy Books

"Sweet, angsty, and ingeniously subversive, *Don't Want You Like a Best Friend* will have you turning the pages and rooting for Beth and Gwen to finally get the happily-ever-after they both deserve. A delightfully refreshing historical romance!"

—Amalie Howard, *USA Today* bestselling author of *The Rakehell of Roth*

"A stunning sapphic Victorian romance from an author to watch."

—*Kirkus Reviews* (starred review)

"Equal parts swoony, nail-bitingly emotional, and sizzling, *Don't Want You Like a Best Friend* sweeps readers off their feet in a wholly new and exhilarating dance. With a beautifully rendered setting, whip-smart banter, and a cast of characters that are so easy to love, Alban cements herself as an instant voice to watch in queer romance."

—Carlyn Greenwald, author of *Sizzle Reel*

"For readers who want tenderness, not trauma, in their queer period fiction, this will hit the spot."

—*Publishers Weekly*

"The sapphic friends-to-lovers romance of my dreams, lavished in ball gowns! Emma R. Alban comes to the page with knowledge, depth, and so much beauty it's breathtaking. *Don't Want You Like a Best Friend* is a skillfully crafted, gorgeous love story wrought with forbidden romance, all the pining, and stunning imagery that will sweep you away. A shining new voice in historical romance, Alban's work is soon to be a beloved staple on bookshelves everywhere."

—Courtney Kae, author of *In the Event of Love*

"Alban's gracefully written and keenly witty romance debut perfectly encapsulates all the hunger, heartbreak, and hope involved in falling in love for the first time."

—*Booklist* (starred review)

"In her historical romance *Don't Want You Like a Best Friend,* Emma R. Alban weaves a delightful tale of hijinks and romance that defiantly declares everyone deserves a happy ending, and reminds the reader that queer people have always lived, and always loved."

—Darcy Rose Byrnes, award-winning
actor, writer, composer, comedian

"If you are looking for a bighearted queer romance with stolen kisses and grand gestures, then Alban's *Don't Want You Like a Best Friend* is the book for you."

—*BookPage*

"Alban's debut is a disarmingly sweet and well-written story that promises two romances for the price of one."

—*Library Journal*

You're the Problem, It's You

Also by Emma R. Alban

Don't Want You Like a Best Friend

You're the Problem, It's You

A Novel

EMMA R. ALBAN

AVON

An Imprint of HarperCollins*Publishers*

This book is a work of fiction. References to real people, events, establishments, organizations, or locales are intended only to provide a sense of authenticity, and are used fictitiously. All other characters, and all incidents and dialogue, are drawn from the author's imagination and are not to be construed as real.

HarperCollins books may be purchased for educational, business, or sales promotional use. For information, please email the Special Markets Department at SPsales@harpercollins.com.

FIRST EDITION

Designed by Diahann Sturge-Campbell

Library of Congress Cataloging-in-Publication Data has been applied for.

ISBN 978-0-06-331203-6

24 25 26 27 28 LBC 5 4 3 2 1

For Dylan,
the best *big brother*

Mischief & Matchmaking Series Family Trees

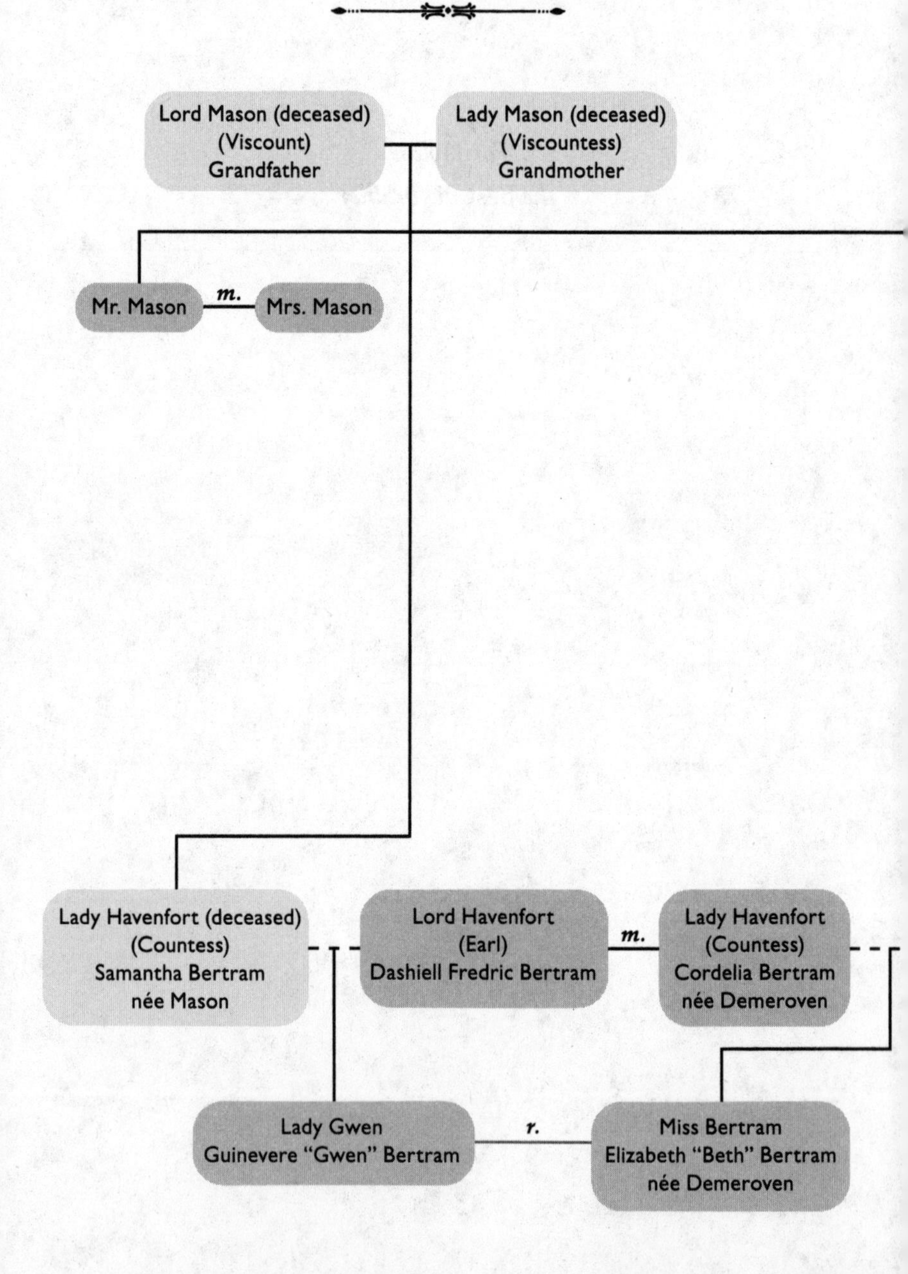

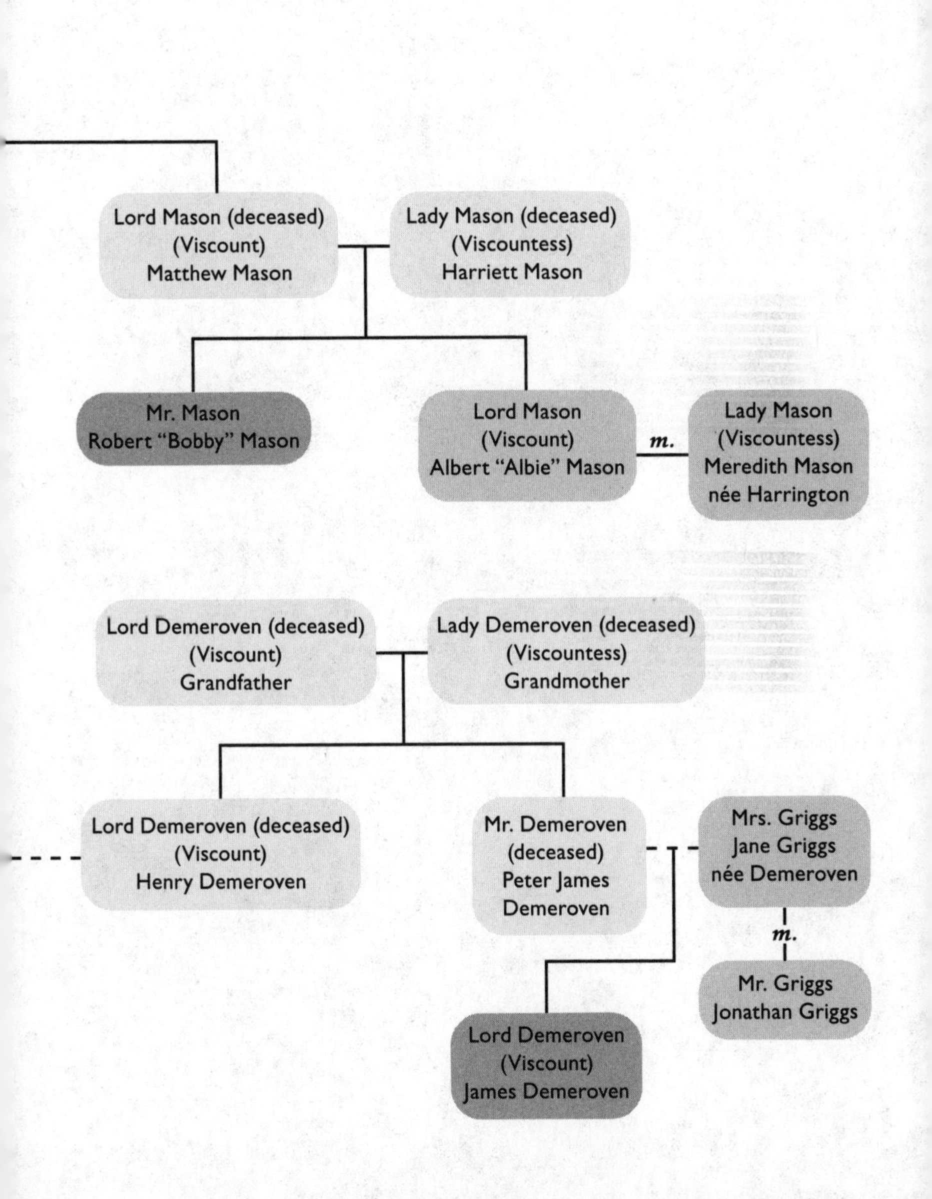

Lord Mason (deceased)
(Viscount)
Matthew Mason
Lady Mason (deceased)
(Viscountess)
Harriett Mason
Mr. Mason
Robert "Bobby" Mason
Lord Mason
(Viscount)
Albert "Albie" Mason
m.
Lady Mason
(Viscountess)
Meredith Mason
née Harrington
Lord Demeroven (deceased)
(Viscount)
Grandfather
Lady Demeroven (deceased)
(Viscountess)
Grandmother
Lord Demeroven (deceased)
(Viscount)
Henry Demeroven
Mr. Demeroven
(deceased)
Peter James
Demeroven
Mrs. Griggs
Jane Griggs
née Demeroven
m.
Mr. Griggs
Jonathan Griggs
Lord Demeroven
(Viscount)
James Demeroven

You're the Problem, It's You

Chapter One

April 1858

Bobby

They haven't invented a liquor strong enough to counteract the absolute banality of an opening-night ball. Bobby Mason stares down into his drink, listening to his brother, Albie, and their friend Lord Cunningham recite a list of debutantes at a rapid-fire pace, all the names swirling into a light buzz. Bobby's not sure how Albie has managed to keep track of this many girls, living up north all year. Perhaps this is what Meredith discusses when they're spending long, loving evenings together.

Guilt overtakes him. He shouldn't think ill of his new sister-in-law, stuck in the country and unable to travel because she's expecting and poorly. If he's being honest, Albie's always the one bringing up engagement gossip, not Meredith. Meredith's a delight. This unending conversation is a pain.

"But I wouldn't put any money on the Steton-Johnson merger," Cunningham says, his slightly nasal voice cutting into Bobby's brooding.

"I wouldn't be too sure," Albie says, chuckling as Cunningham rolls his eyes. "Lady Annabeth goes after what she wants. She already had ten scions last I checked."

"Damn, already?" Bobby grumbles as he looks down at his

own Spot-the-Scion card. He's only managed to spot seven society sons, four of whom include himself, Albie, Cunningham, and his cousin Gwen's partner Beth's cousin Lord James Demeroven.

Bobby glances at Demeroven and finds him staring down into his own glass, narrow shoulders high. Cunningham's apparently betrothed to a nice girl up in the country, so he has no need to make a match this season—the poor lucky sod. But Demeroven, with his new title, will need to think about settling down. Bobby is sure Beth's terrible uncle is eager for Demeroven to pop out an heir.

Of course, that's not a unique perspective in this room. Bobby looks out at the sea of debutantes, mothers, and eligible scions in the immaculate ballroom. It's all swirls of soft pastels, tails, and glittering jewels.

Oh, and there's Mr. Yokely, Lord Yokely's younger brother. "Eight," Bobby mumbles. He fishes the small pencil Gwen passed him earlier out of his pocket to mark his Spot-the-Scion card. He's doing pretty well for having spent the first hour dancing with Beth—another ten eligible sons spotted and he might have a chance at winning.

"You got another?" Albie asks, leaning up to see his card. Bobby's got inches on his older brother now. It's still strange to be able to look down at Albie's light brown hair.

"Not much else to do," Bobby offers with a shrug. He does so love his cousin and Beth for coming up with *something* to keep them occupied.

He really should be trying harder. Beth said that betting rights and gains at the Ascot races would go to the winner of their society sons tournament this year. He's not sure if that prize is just among the extended family, as they are, or if it includes Beth and Gwen's young lady friends too. If so, he's doomed. He can never remember enough of the various heirs to fill out a whole card, and they've added the spares this year too. At least the girls get twirled around the room, giving them a better vantage point to scope out the myriad progeny of the ton.

He notices Albie marking something down on his card. "How many do you have?"

"Fifteen," Albie says, brown eyes twinkling.

Bobby groans. "Demeroven, how are you doing?" he asks, wanting to feel at least a little better about his terrible way with faces and names.

Demeroven looks up, his piercing blue eyes darting about to figure out who addressed him. He looks so uncomfortable. "Um, four?"

"Just us, then?" Albie asks, not unkindly.

"Yes," Demeroven says, sheepish.

"Well, that won't do," Cunningham says, his round cheeks dimpling with a slightly evil smirk. "We'll have to get both of you lads dancing, then, won't we?"

"Oh no. No, no," Bobby says, trying to back away. Albie grabs him about the shoulders, laughing at his expense. "I don't dance."

"You danced with Beth," Albie counters.

"Beth is different," he says hastily. "She doesn't step on my toes."

"I'm sure there are any number of lovely young ladies who can manage a simple waltz without injuring you," Albie says, his grip tightening. "What about—"

"Demeroven's the one who should dance," Bobby says desperately, wincing as Demeroven's head snaps up, a lock of sandy-brown hair falling into those harried blue eyes. "He's new. He needs to meet new people."

"I couldn't, really. I'm sure there must be— Oh, Lord Havenfort," Demeroven says, turning with a relieved smile as Bobby and Albie's uncle approaches them. Bobby thinks he hears Demeroven add a muttered "Thank Christ."

"Gentlemen," Uncle Dashiell greets, smiling down at all of them. Dashiell Frederic Bertram, Earl of Havenfort, is almost a head taller than most of the men in the room and, with his striking blond hair and features, draws every eye his way everywhere he goes.

Honestly, if Bobby's cousin Gwen *wanted* to find a husband, she wouldn't have trouble. She got all of her looks from her father—statuesque, blond, and instantly captivating. Now, if Bobby could only spot her and her partner, Beth, in the crowd . . .

"Bobby, would you mind terribly if I stole Albert, James, and Lord Cunningham away? There are several members of our party I'd like you all to meet," Uncle Dashiell says.

And how can Bobby do anything but nod and smile, watching as his only protection, such as they were, is shepherded away to more important matters? He supposes it wouldn't occur to any of them to invite him along. He's of no political import, after all. But that doesn't mean he can't be interested.

Bobby sighs and swigs the rest of his drink, staring out at the ball. Albie's running the estate. Albie's taking their late father's seat in parliament. Albie's doing everything important. All that's left for Bobby is the social season. He's meant to be making a good impression for the family name, but he'd rather be absolutely anywhere else.

He turns and strides back to the drink station to slug back another whisky. But the burn of the alcohol against his tongue turns his stomach and he only drinks half the dram before placing it back on the table. The doctor wasn't positive it was the drink that killed their father, but it certainly didn't help.

The thought curdles in Bobby's throat and he turns to search some more for Beth and Gwen. He doesn't want to think about his wretched father tonight. Nor the mess he left for Albie to clean up.

He just wants to hide away with his cousin and Beth. Let himself be buoyed by their happiness. Neither Gwen nor Beth needs to think about finding a husband. Uncle Dashiell and his new aunt Cordelia, Beth's mother, have made it quite clear they'd be happy to have Beth and Gwen under their roof, protected and insulated against the ton forever. Two young women, in love, hiding in plain sight.

If only his father hadn't been such an absolute brute, perhaps Bobby could have arranged something similar. Ignoring the fact that he hasn't yet found a man he'd ever consider settling down with, of course.

But now it's no longer a possibility. His father is dead. And he's one carriage accident away from being the reigning Viscount Mason. He needs another drink, sod what the doctors said about his father.

He turns to make for the drinks table again, but finds his path blocked by a deluge of satin and skirts. Lady . . . Chiswith (he thinks) and her daughter have snuck up on him and now stand between him and the sweet relief of alcohol.

"Your father was such a lovely man, Mr. Mason. I know I speak for my husband as well in extending our deepest condolences," Lady Chiswith says, her narrow face crinkled in sympathy that makes Bobby itch.

His father was so far in the opposite direction of "a lovely man" that it's almost comical. "Thank you," he manages, looking briefly to Lady Chiswith's daughter, who's fanning herself with a blue feather monstrosity.

"Miss Chiswith would be more than happy to take your mind off your tragic loss, if you feel as though you have enough strength for dancing," Lady Chiswith says.

Bobby notices Lady Chiswith's daughter paling in mortification. He can relate. No need to put them both through misery. "I'm afraid I haven't the strength," Bobby says seriously, trying to project Albie's pleasant, polite smile at the woman. He's sure it doesn't come off half so well on his face. "Another time," he adds, looking at the daughter.

Her shoulders relax and he silently pats himself on the back. He bows and quickly retreats, striding across the room as if he has somewhere to be. But even with that dance dodged, he sees hungry maternal eyes tracking him from every cluster of attendees. Like he's a piece of fresh meat. Which he supposes he is, though he's hardly a prize.

The second son of a lightly disgraced gambler with an alcohol problem—surely there's someone better for the many daughters at the ball tonight. But the wandering, watchful eyes say otherwise, and, oh dear, he needs to find the safety of his cousin and Beth, now.

He searches for a flash of blond but can't see Gwen anywhere. Beth's far too short to find from this far away. He about-faces again, considering heading out to the small terrace, before he nearly bumps into Demeroven.

The shorter man hovers just outside the hall to the velvet-lined parlor, where many of the gentlemen and parliamentarians have set up camp for the night, far from the fray. Demeroven should still be inside. Bobby can just see Uncle Dashiell's head in the chamber beyond.

Instead, Demeroven has nearly pressed himself back against the wall, blocking Bobby's more furtive path out to the terrace. And though he's not Beth or Gwen, Demeroven is still better than the roving mothers.

"All a little much?" he asks, focusing on Demeroven's discomfort instead of living in his own.

Demeroven's head snaps up, those wide blue eyes staring up at him like he's just appeared out of thin air. "Oh, um, a tad," he says, his voice stiff.

Bobby nods toward his side and Demeroven moves jerkily so Bobby can slip into the gap between him and the pillar that mostly blocks them from the rest of the room. Together they watch the swirling dancers. It's a little quieter here and Bobby lets himself relax.

He's been wracking his brain, but he doesn't remember meeting Demeroven at Oxford, though they were only a year apart. He thinks he would remember if they'd been introduced. It would be hard to forget Demeroven's striking gaze, patrician nose, and the sharp line of his jaw. Though perhaps he's clenching his teeth?

"Anything good on the agenda, you think?" Bobby asks, gesturing back toward the clustered parliamentarians, hoping to put him at ease.

Demeroven glances at him before staring back at the floor. "Not really."

Bobby waits, but the man doesn't elaborate. "I thought the Medical Act sounded interesting," Bobby tries again. Anything but talk of marriage.

Demeroven just shrugs. "It's all a lot of chatter, really."

Bobby stares at him, surprised. "My brother says the briefing Uncle Dashiell gave him was rather interesting."

"I guess," Demeroven says, looking unconvinced.

Bobby clicks his tongue. If he were about to sit in parliament for the first time, he wouldn't be dismissing all the upcoming bills as prattle, but . . . he's sure there's a weight of responsibility that might make it all seem onerous.

He'd rather sit through a hundred boring sessions in the Lords than dance, but fine.

"You know, the Matrimonial Causes Act last year has had a dramatic effect already. Did you see Lady Ashmond earlier? She seems to be much happier as a divorcée."

"Good for her," Demeroven says.

Bobby blows out a breath. This is Beth's cousin. He has to extend him some grace.

"Well, I hope you find an act that piques your interest," Bobby says, forcing lightness into his voice. "I'd hate to think you'd be bored to tears all season."

Demeroven toys with his cuff links, eyes fixed toward the floor. "Every time anyone brings up a point that's remotely interesting, somehow the conversation turns to the events for the season and the racing bets. Endless talk of racing bets. How men who make our laws can be so enthralled with mindless, vulgar gambling, I'll never know," he says in a rush.

The man is certainly making it difficult. "Surely there must be something of interest. I hear the games of whist at the club get rather competitive," Bobby says.

"I don't gamble," Demeroven reiterates.

"You don't have to gamble to play whist," Bobby replies, trying not to take it personally. "Uncle Dashiell says you were good at maths. You must like cards."

Demeroven shrugs again, shoulders slightly hunched. "I'm decent at whist, but I won't abide playing for money, not with them, anyway."

Bobby watches the way his glance shifts back to the parlor, disdain on his otherwise handsome face. That won't do. "You'll have to get better at pretending."

"I beg your pardon?"

"There's no way you'll survive at the clubs with that attitude. Find something, low-stakes games, darts—anything—to make you seem approachable, or you'll be marked for the season."

Demeroven's shoulders stiffen and Bobby winces as he tightens his jaw again. "I only meant . . . Well, you'll need to find a way to survive at the clubs is all. Connections are important. I could suggest a few clubs that are less . . . lordly, if you like."

He starts to say more, but the flat look Demeroven turns his way sours the words in his throat. He was only trying to *help*, for God's sake, no need to look at him as if he's dirt on the man's shoe.

Still struggling for any way to keep the conversation going, Bobby turns at a touch to his elbow. He wilts in relief to find Beth at his side, smiling up at him while Gwen offers her hand to Demeroven.

Demeroven nods stiffly at them. "Lady Gwen, Miss Bertram."

Bobby nearly pushes the man into his cousin's arms, watching Demeroven sedately escort Gwen onto the floor. They make a striking couple once they get moving, his lithe build and her tall, stately frame, twirling gracefully. It seems unfair that Demeroven should be both that attractive and a good dancer, especially when Gwen's always complaining that Bobby's dancing skills pale in comparison to Albie's. He *has* gotten better over the last year; she just refuses to acknowledge it.

"You two getting along?" Beth asks, sidling into Demeroven's empty space.

Bobby looks down at her, rolling his eyes at her eagerness. Always wanting them all to get along, to be happy—dreadfully loving of her. But he can't resist her big brown doe eyes. And with her rich brown hair falling in ringlets from her braided bun, she's almost angelic.

"He's . . . fine," Bobby lies, looking back at the dance floor. Can't miss Gwen, her blond hair styled in much the same way, a head taller than most of the girls, and inches taller than Demeroven, for that matter.

"Do you think you could invite him to visit the clubs with you?" Beth asks.

Bobby turns back to her, eyes narrowed. "Why?"

"Well, he doesn't know anyone. And I remember how lonely I was in the first few weeks of the season. It would be nice for you to introduce him to a few people, help him make friends."

Bobby bites his tongue against the honest retort—that most of his friends have up and gotten married, the poor lads. Cunningham is still about, and Prince, somewhere, though he thinks he's heard that Prince has gotten engaged too.

"I'm not sure he'd like the clubs I attend," Bobby says instead. It's enormously true, but feels safer than baring his own lonely soul.

It's not that Beth wouldn't understand, but she has Gwen. A constant friend, a live-in companion—the love of her blasted life. And he's just . . . second fiddle to his brother, who barely has any time for him anymore.

"I'm sure he'd find them interesting," Beth counters. "Please? I'd hate to see him fall in with the wrong crowd."

Bobby sighs. Albie would tell him to do it—help ensure that Demeroven votes with the liberals, sympathetic to Uncle Dashiell's positions. Help erase the stain of the previous Viscount Demeroven—Beth's late, horrible father. A new voice for a new generation.

And if even Beth—who has every reason to resent Demeroven for coming of age, inheriting her late father's estate, and nearly leaving her and her mother destitute last season—can find it in her heart to help him, how can Bobby refuse?

He spins the new gold signet ring Meredith got him, engraved with his initials, around on his finger and watches Gwen and Demeroven continue dancing into another set. He supposes showing Demeroven the town wouldn't be the worst way to spend a season. He's handsome and learned, even if he seems to be a dour, reticent chap. Bobby has always liked a challenge.

"What do I get if I do this for you?" he asks, looking back at Beth.

"The pride of a job well done and a possibly enduring friendship aren't enough?" Bobby narrows his eyes and she laughs. "How about my undying gratitude?"

Bobby huffs, pretending at greater exasperation just to see her eyebrows crease. He so loves riling her up. Almost as fun as getting Gwen angry.

"Fine."

"Oh, thank you!" Beth says brightly, wrapping her arm through his. "God, doesn't she look beautiful?"

He watches her watch Gwen, her eyes wide, a small smile on her face. Doting, in love, besotted.

Gwen's not the most graceful of the dancers, but there's something in the confident way she carries herself—and maybe a little in the way Demeroven is an actually adequate partner. "She does," he agrees. "And so do you."

"Oh, don't bother—Gwen has been laying it on all night."

"Yes, what a hardship, to be beloved," he says.

She laughs and squeezes his arm. "Shall we find you someone to sing your praises too?"

Bobby fights a shudder. "No, no, turning Lord Demeroven into the toast of the ton is more than enough of a project this season, I think."

Beth hums, giving her attention back to the dancers.

It's not making laws, or making a difference, but shaping Lord Demeroven into a moderately respectable lord is *something*, at least.

CHAPTER TWO

James

He closes the heavy front door to the townhouse and rests his forehead against the cool wood. If he never attends another ball in his life, he could die a happy man. Between the politics, the dancing, and the endless stream of mothers and daughters he disappointed with his utter lack of social flair, he's exhausted.

Dancing with Lady Gwen and his cousin Miss Bertram wasn't terrible, but spending the night surrounded by their chatter, with Lady Gwen's cousins Lord Mason and the younger Mason chiming in, was almost dizzying.

He's not sure if it's the hour, the faint buzz of alcohol in his system, or the lighting, but he thinks his mother may have purchased yet another bust. The statues and paintings all seem to meld together in the narrow, tall space of the foyer. It's oppressive.

But it isn't as if he tried to stop her. At least it gives her something to focus on, now that she's here and separated from her friends back home. His stepfather couldn't wait to get to the city, but he knows his mother took much solace in the community she'd made in Epworth.

She may have purchased herself an entire set of evening ball gowns for the season, but she didn't even make it out of bed today. Her lady's maid, Miss Marina, said it was a headache, but he thinks it's likely just melancholy. They don't deal well with change, he and his mother.

His stepfather, on the other hand—

"'S that you, Demeroven?"

James winces, considering making a break for it up the stairs rather than facing the smoke-filled haze that is his stepfather's study. What should be his study.

But if he doesn't face the man now, he'll be banging down his door tomorrow, bright and early, demanding a full report. So James shuffles across the narrow hall and into the study, coughing at the smoke. The man could at least crack a window.

The space is filled with heavy, half-empty bookshelves. His stepfather brought down his own dark, dour chairs to face the enormous desk left behind by the late Viscount Demeroven. The room has a strange, out-of-time feeling, half full, half considered, half his stepfather's and half a dead man's. There's nothing of James in here at all.

His stepfather looks up from yet another financial ledger. Ever since they arrived, he's been nose-deep in the late viscount's London accounting, not that he truly knows the first thing about managing an estate. Though neither does James, really.

His stepfather's beady eyes peer through the haze, his round, ruddy face set in a scowl. "You're home early," he grunts.

James bites back the automatic retort that he is a man of age now and needn't answer to his stepfather any longer. He's in control of the title now. He's the new Viscount Demeroven. The reign of his stepfather—the gentleman Mr. Griggs—as regent to the estate is over. James is about to sit in parliament, for God's sake. This is, in fact, his house now.

But the words never manage to pass his lips. Instead, he shrugs, like an insolent little boy.

His stepfather frowns and takes a swig of the late viscount's brandy. "Did you meet Lord Henchey?"

James shakes his head. "No. Lord Havenfort introduced me to a fair few, but they were all his lot."

His stepfather groans. "You let that man walk all over you, didn't you? I told your mother you didn't have the backbone for it."

James tries to straighten said weak backbone, curling his fingers into fists as his stepfather slips into one of his tried-and-true rants. James is meek. James is fragile. James is bad with people. James isn't cut out for this life, and if they'd just spoken to the late viscount, they could have ensured that Stepfather maintained official control of the finances once James came of age. But no, Stepfather is saddled with this lump of a boy instead of the man he needs.

"I'll do better," James cuts in, his ears ringing with phantom previous lectures. "Tomorrow. I'll make sure to meet Henchey. Brighton wasn't there, for the record."

"Of course he wasn't. Wouldn't waste his time with something so frivolous."

James yawns theatrically. "Right, well, I'm knackered. I'll see you tomorrow for dinner."

He ducks out of the room before his stepfather can get another word in and pads back across the foyer and down the corridor to the kitchen. He can't face his bed just yet, not with his stepfather's tirade still ringing in his ears.

Instead, he collapses at the long oak staff table in the red-tiled kitchen and lets his head fall into his hands. He just needs a few minutes for the echo of his stepfather's words, the latent sound of the orchestra, the chatter of his cousin, her stepsister, and the Mason boys talking too fast and too furious to fade away.

But as he stares at the backs of his eyelids, Bobby Mason's face fills his mind. His broad jaw, his thoughtful hazel eyes, his frown at finding James as lacking as everyone else always does—

Their chef, Reginald, smacks a plate of scones down in front of James and he jumps.

"Jesus," James says.

Reginald pours him a glass of milk, plops it down beside the plate, and strides around the table to sit heavily across from him. His blue eyes sparkle with interest and James wants to hide his face again.

Reginald has been teasing secrets out of James since he was small and Reginald was just a kitchen hand, plying him with cookies and shielding him from his stepfather whenever possible. Often his only refuge, and friend, Reginald knows every one of James' tells, which is bloody annoying sometimes, even as the smell of the scones does release the tension in his shoulders.

"So?"

James groans and stuffs half a scone into his mouth to stall.

"Come on, tell me. Is he everything you thought he'd be?" Reginald asks.

James feels himself flush. "Shut up," he mumbles.

Reginald grins, rubbing his hands together. His dimples make his smile almost irresistible, but James does not want to discuss this. Not when the night felt like such an unmitigated failure.

"All right. How was the dancing?"

James stuffs another scone in his mouth and Reginald laughs.

"Really? Anyone of interest?"

James shrugs. Lady Gwen wasn't a terrible partner, though she hardly seemed focused on him. Lady Gwen and his cousin, Miss Bertram, are thick as thieves and seem to be able to communicate with nary a glance between them, always laughing and filling out their Spot-the-Scion cards.

"It was fine," he says after he gets the scone down. Usually they're his favorite, but he's parched from all the dancing and alcohol.

He takes a long drink of milk, closing his eyes to hide from Reginald's raised eyebrow.

"Fine," Reginald repeats, waiting him out until he can't drink any more. "You must have met *someone*."

"Lord Havenfort introduced me to the lords," James mumbles, taking another scone simply to crumble it to bits on the plate.

"And?"

"And they were rather boring," he admits, finally looking up to meet Reginald's eyes. "A lot of whose wife was where and which daughter was available."

"Any of those daughters the ones your mother keeps harping on about?"

James sighs. "Plenty."

"And how many did you dance with?"

"Two?" he guesses. He really wasn't paying much attention to anyone but his cousin and Lady Gwen. "The rest were friends of my cousin's, and they're all already taken."

Reginald reaches out for his own scone with a frown. "Your mother won't be happy."

"I went, didn't I?"

Reginald gives him a disapproving look. James crushes a bit of scone between his fingers, agitated.

"There'll be other balls," he says.

Reginald bobs his head. "Of course, of course." He takes a bite of his scone and chews thoughtfully. It almost lulls James into a false sense of security. "And Mr. Mason?"

James groans again and drops his head. "Stop it."

"You've got to give me something," Reginald insists. "All

those summers when you were home from Oxford, waxing poetic, and you never even talked to him. Surely, *surely*, you spoke tonight."

James squeezes his eyes shut, bracing himself, before looking up to meet Reginald's rampant curiosity. "He's fine."

"Fine?" Reginald huffs. "That's all I get? My years of loyalty, my sympathy biscuits, my words of wooing wisdom—"

James shushes him, his shoulders going up as he glances back toward the foyer. But all is quiet, which means, for better or worse, no one is coming to save him.

"Tell me you at least plucked up the courage to talk to the man now that you're tangentially connected."

James blows out a breath and looks back at Reginald. "We talked."

Reginald glowers at him. "Out with it, Viscount."

The title makes him wince and straighten his shoulders all at once. He's a viscount now. He can face his cook's teasing. He danced, he rubbed shoulders, he . . . made possibly the world's least charming impression on blasted Bobby Mason—

"Well?" Reginald prompts.

"He's nosy," James decides, returning to picking at his scone so he won't have to look Reginald in the eye. "And Lady Gwen says he's a poor dancer. My cousin likes him, but it seems he's truly just a pretty face."

He trails a finger through the remains of his scone in the ensuing silence, hoping perhaps Reginald will take that as enough truth for the night and leave him be. Instead, when the silence has lasted long enough that it's uncomfortable, James raises his eyes to find Reginald waiting, entirely unconvinced.

"That's it? The great Bobby Mason, wonder of Oxford, protagonist of half your stories, is just a stuffed shirt? Surely not."

James shrugs. "Don't know what else to tell you," he says,

playing at nonchalance. "He's gotten pretty muscular since school." Reginald's mouth twitches and James hurries to add, "And all he wanted to talk about was the Medical Act."

"That's not enough substance for you?"

"And the clubs," James says quickly. "He kept telling me I'd need to learn to gamble."

Reginald furrows his brow and James works to keep his face blank. He probably didn't need to lay it on quite so thick about the gambling, especially given what Lord Havenfort told him about how the late Viscount Mason wasted away the Mason fortune before his untimely death. But he doesn't want to talk about the clubs, doesn't want to think about having to hobnob with more of these men in small, crowded spaces. Doesn't want to consider them judging him and finding him as lacking as his stepfather does.

And since he doesn't like to frequent the usual clubs, he hardly thinks he'll get along with Bobby Mason, who seems to be all about them. Better that he never discovers how little Bobby Mason could care for him.

Not that he's been dreaming of meeting the man since school, only to find himself tongue-tied and anxious to the point of rudeness in the face of his beauty up close. No. He just simply doesn't care what Bobby Mason thinks. He doesn't care what anyone thinks. It's easier that way.

"Well, if Bobby Mason isn't the catch we thought, were there any other pretty faces to consider?"

James glances back toward the hallway to the foyer again and waits, listening. But they're still safely alone.

"Not really," he says, turning back to Reginald. "Wasn't a lot of time to look or talk to anyone outside of Lord Havenfort's lords, and they're . . ."

"Not who you're looking to meet," Reginald agrees. "Well, Thomas' standing invitation is still there. He would love to have you at the club, introduce you to some nice gentlemen."

James feels his shoulders coming back up. "Right."

Reginald's eyes soften. "It'll be just like back home, only fancier. You'll see."

"I guess," James says, thinking of the small back room at the Inside Inn near Epworth. The comfortable chairs, the worn wooden table, the back door that led out to the woods. Safe, guarded, secluded.

He can't imagine how Reginald's brother, Thomas Parker, could possibly create a space that secret or comfortable in London. His club is supposed to be the safest refuge for men of a certain persuasion in the city. But James doesn't know how that can be true when it feels like there are eyes everywhere.

"Give it some thought, that's all," Reginald says. He pushes back his chair and gets up. "It's not like you're going to meet a nice man elsewhere."

James nods and looks back down at his plate, the crumbs of his scone too closely resembling the shambles of his life.

"What would you like pressed for tomorrow? I'll tell Gabriel on my way to bed."

James lets out a low moan. He'd almost forgotten. "I don't care." He puts his head back into his hands.

"Come now, it's your very first day. We need to make a good impression."

James is tempted to tell him to sod off, but he knows Reginald is right. Even if just to keep his stepfather off his back, he needs to make some effort. "Nothing my mother bought me. Classic, elegant, simple."

"Aye-aye," Reginald says merrily, drawing James' gaze up to

find him posed, hands on his hips. "We'll make you the best-dressed young lord in parliament. On my honor."

"Sod your honor," James says gruffly, laughing despite himself as Reginald lets loose a low, rumbly chuckle. The man's too charming for his own good.

"Get some sleep, yeah? Gabriel will have everything ready come morning."

James forces a smile and watches Reginald head out the servants' door and down toward his room. Tonight was exhausting, and tomorrow promises to be even worse. Him, a sitting lord? Him, making laws? Him, the blockhead who couldn't even be charming to the man he's fancied since university—how is he ever supposed to impress the House of Lords?

He pulls at his collar as he sits beside Lord Mason the next morning. The red leather bench below him is stiff. He stares up at the gilded walls and ceiling of the parliament chamber, trying not to fidget as the lord chancellor goes on and on about the rules of procedure and the order of discussion and votes.

James is stuck between Lord Mason and Lord Havenfort, who both seem deeply interested in procedure, forcing James to at least pretend to care too. It's almost an hour in and they're only now getting to the actual bills on the docket.

"The third act for discussion will be the Medical Act, proposing the establishment of a General Medical Council, which will require and oversee accreditation for physicians, to be added to a public registry of those wishing to practice. Debate will be held—"

The chancellor goes on to the schedule for the debates and someone sneezes loudly across the room. James glances across the aisle and his whole body goes cold. Richard Raverson stares back, giving James a sly, triumphant smile.

Raverson was the most handsome man in his class, with a smile so magnetic he could get away with anything. Skipping classes, a poor essay, stealing plates and trinkets and possessions—he was untouchable. And his way with men . . . no one was immune.

Least of all James, who became Raverson's obsession in his second year. Raverson wooed him with dinners, expensive wines, and outings to all manner of activities. He made James feel like he was the most sought-after, most intriguing man alive. And James fell for it, head over arse.

He was so beguiled by Raverson's affections that he didn't see the true man beneath until it was far too late. Until he'd told his darkest secrets and shared his body with a man who would just as quickly tell him of *other* men's secrets and bodies and prowess. Eventually, Raverson saw a new, shinier young man and left James behind. But by then, it was too late, and James couldn't recapture his safety, couldn't reclaim himself from Raverson.

And now, Raverson is sitting in the House of Lords, surrounded by red leather and gold leaf, with all those secrets, all that information, still at his fingertips. James knew, of course, that Raverson's father had died last year. But somehow in the flurry of turning twenty-one, taking over his own unwanted title, and leaving his quiet country existence behind, James hadn't put two and two together that he would be sitting in the Lords with the man who—

"Absolutely preposterous," Lord Havenfort hisses. "It's 1858."

"We'll join the committee, make sure it's done correctly for a quick passage in the Commons," Lord Mason says across James, his face about as purple as Lord Havenfort's.

James blinks, pulled back to reality as the chancellor moves on to some final announcement. He thinks the last bill mentioned was to create a registry of doctors. Shouldn't that already exist?

"You don't agree?"

James nearly jumps, turning to Lord Mason as he notices everyone around them starting to move. "Beg pardon?"

"Were you paying any attention? Lord Havenfort wants us to join him this week at the club to do research into the independent lists of physicians kept by local hospitals, to prepare to join the standing committee."

James must not do a good job of hiding his confusion, because Lord Mason shakes his head and files out ahead of him. James glances back, but Lord Havenfort isn't even there, already walking out of the room with more important lords.

He tells himself it doesn't matter. No one thinks he's worth talking to, because he isn't. No one missed the Demeroven vote last year, so why does it matter how he votes or participates now? If Lord Mason and Lord Havenfort have already written him off simply for being less invested, then that's their choice.

He shuffles out of the chamber, trying not to look for Raverson while simultaneously searching fervently in hopes of avoiding him. But clearly James isn't a big enough fish for Raverson to trifle with because he spots nothing but blank, monotonous faces on his way out. At least that's one confrontation he doesn't have to face today.

His heartbeat slowly calms as he walks home, passing the backup of hired coaches outside Westminster. Raverson will have other concerns this season. He'll probably avoid James altogether; no need to focus on him or worry about him. Schoolboy fancies are in the past.

But as his panic over Raverson fades, he thinks back on Lord Mason's insulted look. He didn't mean to give off the impression he doesn't care about parliament. But it's not as if his vote will matter, not as if they'll make any lasting change with these acts. The country's deeply unequal. A registration of physicians won't matter to the poor; they'll take any doctor they can get—who cares where he's educated?

By the time he reaches the Demeroven townhouse, James is feeling downright dour. He's disappointed his only real connections in the Lords already, proved himself worthless merely by getting distracted. Some triumphant first day.

Then he pushes open the front door of his townhouse.

"It's not your money to decide!" his mother shrieks from the first landing, glaring down at his stepfather, who's teetering by the base of the stairs, red-faced and already drunk at mid-afternoon.

"You cannot understand the pressure I've been under!" his stepfather shouts back. "Keeping this place running while your disappointment of a son finally grew up. And now—now—you want to tell me I haven't any authority anymore because he's come of age? How dare you—"

"James, tell him, tell him!" his mother insists, spotting him as he tries to quietly slip back outside. She's wearing a dressing gown, her graying hair falling out of the plait over her shoulder.

"Tell him what?" James asks, exhaustion heavy on his tongue.

"Tell him to give me my allowance."

"She's already gone and spent it," his stepfather interjects. "You can't give her more."

"You give him drinking and gambling money, but you won't allow your poor mother an extra few pounds for dresses?" she asks, blue eyes wide and pleading.

"A few pounds—how many dresses do you need, woman? You hardly leave with those blasted headaches. You cannot have any more."

"That's not your decision to make!"

James listens as they continue their argument, the sound bouncing dully around the room. For all that the paintings his mother acquired are horrible, at least they muffle some of the echo.

"Weigh in here, Viscount," his stepfather sneers. James forces himself to shuffle into the middle of the room. "You're the man of the house now."

James rubs at his temples and glances between them. "How much do you need, Mother?"

Her face lights up, all that angry bitterness falling away. She beams down at him. "My son, the sweetheart."

"Your son the weakling," Stepfather cuts in. "Can't even stand up to your own ma, can you?"

"Will another month's allowance suffice?" James asks his mother, ignoring his stepfather's groan.

"That would be wonderful, dearest," she says, nearly dancing on the spot. "Oh, I'll have such lovely dresses, and I'll get you new top hats, and gloves, and cuff links as well."

"That's great, Mother," James says, forcing a smile for her.

She claps her hands and spins to head back upstairs, leaving James and his stepfather alone in the foyer.

"You're pathetic," Stepfather says.

James bobs his head. "All right."

Stepfather glares and then storms into the study to slam the door. It shakes the walls with a resounding boom and James stands there alone in the ringing resulting silence.

Pathetic. That appears to be the opinion of the day.

He stares around at the garish paintings and busts. It seems parliament won't provide any meaningful connection. And being in this house offers nothing more than exhausting arguments, insults, and further wounds to his already minuscule pride.

Perhaps he should try Thomas Parker's club, see if he can't find a single place in London where he can feel safe. Where he can feel like he belongs.

Chapter Three

Bobby

There's a cigar burn on the crushed red velvet siding of their carriage. Bobby stares at the spot as they trundle along, heading to the Kingsmans' for the first tea of the season. He feels his eyes start to go fuzzy and blinks, moving his gaze higher up, only to find another burn.

"I'll make a note to have the interior replaced," Albie says gruffly.

Bobby looks across the cabin at his brother, sitting stiffly in his navy frock coat. Albie messes with his bow tie, frowning. Everything about him is taut these days. Bobby practically had to drag him out of the house to attend this tea.

"Will Cunningham be there?" Bobby asks.

"I believe so," Albie says, fiddling with his cuffs next. "Be good if he were, I can ask about his stepmother's attending physician when she broke her leg."

"Right," Bobby says, looking back at the window. There's a piece of velvet missing along the edging, like maybe a drunken viscount pulled it off.

"Hopefully Lord Bletchle will be there as well. We have Father's debt left to settle there, and if I can find Lord Highton first, perhaps that will cover it."

Bobby rolls his shoulders. There's no escaping the shadow of their father, whether it's his debts or the damage he did to their only carriage. At least sometimes at the balls or the teas he manages to forget, but when it's quiet like this—when Albie's listing off his never-ending tally of tasks—it's like their father is in the carriage with them, drunk and turning yellow while he laughs at a distasteful joke.

Bobby wishes their other uncle was here to help Albie. Maybe he'd actually accept Uncle Jonathan's help. But Aunt Gertrude's gout is acting up, so they won't be down for the season. Which leaves Bobby as the only audience for Albie's tirades about debts and taxes and expenses.

It's like living with a walking abacus.

"I wonder if Prous will have any hunting stories," Bobby says, cutting in when Albie takes a breath.

"Probably not. The Kingsman estate doesn't have the same game as Prous' father's."

"Surely he spent some time at home over the year," Bobby says, wincing on Prous' behalf.

"Lord Kingsman is setting him up to run most of his holdings. I think he was with Lady Eloise the whole winter."

"Dreadful," Bobby says.

Albie laughs. "Being with his fiancée?"

Albie, happily married and disgusting about it, probably thinks it the height of romance. But being trapped beneath a woman's father's thumb in an endless courting ritual sounds like hell to Bobby. And now Prous is in town for the entire season because Lady Kingsman wants to remain an active part of the ton, despite her daughter being happily promised and soon to be wed. Dreadful indeed.

"Trust me, someday you'll meet the right one, and you'll be as soppy as the rest of us," Albie says.

The carriage pulls up to the grand Kingsman townhouse and Albie promptly hops out.

"Not bloody likely," Bobby mumbles as he climbs down.

They're not late, but they're not early either, and the back garden is already teeming with the toast of the ton when they step through the gate. As usual, Lady Kingsman has made ample use of her gardener's talents. The blossoms aren't yet in full bloom, but the hints of color on the green flowering bushes promise a spectacular season.

In and among the greenery, everywhere he looks, there's a nice young lady sitting artfully on a bench, or daintily splayed on a picnic blanket, or fanning herself while standing charmingly by a tall topiary. Dozens of lovely young women, all with slightly predatory smiles, whom Bobby would like to hide from for as long as humanly possible.

Of course, Albie is ready to abandon him as soon as they reach the edge of the patio. "I'll be with the lords. Go have a good time."

Albie pats his shoulder a bit patronizingly and hurries off. Bobby fights a scowl. He has zero interest in finding a nice young lady to chat up. There's more than one nice young man he'd approach were things different, or if he was at Thomas Parker's infamous club.

He catches Jeremiah Prince's eye across the garden. The poor man's gone and gotten engaged to Miss Catherine Langston, a round-cheeked young woman with a pretty smile and lustrous brown hair. Prince raises his glass in Bobby's direction, a hint of a smile playing against his chiseled jaw.

Bobby supposes Prince and Miss Langston don't look terrible together, but it seems an awful waste of a life. Prince is a bright, cheerful man, and a shockingly good kisser. He's made quite a name for himself at Parker's club. And now that's all over for him, shackled to a woman and a marriage and a future Bobby can't fathom wanting for himself.

Bobby notices Prince's eyeline shift and glances back at the gate. Lord Demeroven has entered the party, looking just as handsome and uncomfortable as he did a few days earlier at the ball, and no less indifferent.

Bobby turns back and settles his sights on the alcohol, pouring himself a dram and a half. He may have promised Beth he'd take the man under his wing, but he doesn't have to make the effort sober. He stalls for the next few minutes, painstakingly perusing the finger sandwiches. Crab and cucumber? Ham and cheese? It's an important decision.

By the time he's made his selection and regretfully turned back to the party, Demeroven has been pulled into conversation on the patio, freeing Bobby from obligation at least for the moment. He merrily pops the first of four crab-and-cucumber sandwiches into his mouth and wanders over to lean against the hedge that surrounds the garden, people watching.

Prince and Miss Langston have broken off from the group to whisper to each other on a bench. Across from them, Lady Eloise and Prous are holding court with a group of Gwen's society friends, both of them looking hearty and hale and not at all like Lord Kingsman has held a tyrannical rule over them all winter.

In fact, everyone looks blissfully happy to be here. Prince laughs, that rich baritone bouncing around the garden. It sends shivers down Bobby's spine in a way none of the ladies' polite giggles ever seem to elicit. Bobby's last sandwich loses some of its appeal and he sags against the hedge. It's going to be a long season.

But just as he's contemplating slipping into the house to peruse Lord Kingsman's books, he notices Uncle Dashiell, Gwen, and Beth arriving fashionably late, as always. Finally, some entertainment.

He strides across the lawn toward them, thinking it's a shame

Aunt Cordelia is so heavily with child and won't be attending most of these events. She's a right laugh. Of course, in her absence, Gwen and Beth will suffice, and Bobby grins as they spot him, their eyes lighting up.

It's nice to know *someone* is happy to see him, even if it's just his cousin and her partner.

Uncle Dashiell extends his hand and Bobby shakes it, smiling up at him. Uncle Dashiell smiles back, though Bobby can see there's a tightness around his eyes. Even when he's at something as simple as a garden party, he always has more to worry about.

"Good to see you, Bobby," he says.

"You too, sir. Please give my best to my aunt. I hope she's feeling well?"

"She'll appreciate it," Uncle Dashiell says. "And she sends her best. She was tired this morning."

"Just tired," Gwen puts in. "Father's being overprotective."

Uncle Dashiell frowns down at Gwen, but she's immune to his disapproval.

"She's all right," Beth adds, linking her arm through Gwen's. "But it's probably best she stays off her feet for a day. We've multiple dinners to attend this week."

"Right," Uncle Dashiell says. "Speaking of which, Bobby, may I have a word?"

Bobby nods, surprised, and lets his uncle guide him over to an uncrowded part of the garden. Beth and Gwen meander toward the drinks, deep in renewed conversation. He wonders what they're up to this time, always scheming.

"Is everything all right?" Bobby asks as he looks back up at his uncle, whose face has taken on a more serious set.

"Oh, yes, of course," Uncle Dashiell says quickly. But his blue eyes remain a little distant. "I wondered if I might ask a favor of you."

Bobby straightens his shoulders eagerly. "Of course. Anything I can do to help."

"I wondered if you might be able to help James fit in a bit more."

Bobby's stomach sinks straight to his toes. This is about Demeroven? "Oh?" he manages, keeping his face neutral.

"He doesn't seem to be making many connections," Uncle Dashiell says, glancing back to the patio where, it's true, Demeroven is standing awkwardly alone, sipping his drink while the lords talk around him. "Perhaps if you took him out, introduced him to some of your friends and their older brothers, he might make better acquaintances and feel a bit more at ease. I think his demeanor might be off-putting if he remains so unattached."

"And you think I'm the best person to help him make connections?" Bobby asks, struggling to maintain his poise.

Of course the favor he can do isn't actually about him. Of course it's about babysitting James sodding Demeroven.

"I think you are an affable young man with many good connections, and the kind of poise and demeanor I wish my nephew-in-law to have," Uncle Dashiell says.

Bobby forces himself to smile. He's being very kind, but the message that Bobby's good qualities only matter if they have power attached rings loud and clear.

Still, he can hardly refuse. Uncle Dashiell has been so generous and deeply supportive of both Bobby and Albie. Paid for their education when their father defaulted on payments. Pays for their lodging at events. Takes them out with Gwen. He can't say no. Even if it smarts, he owes his uncle this.

"Thank you, Uncle," he says, smiling and humble. "I'll do my best to make sure he falls in with the right crowd."

"I appreciate it," Uncle Dashiell says, clapping him on the

shoulder and squeezing. But then he turns on his heel and marches toward the patio and the waiting lords, leaving Bobby alone with only his thoughts and his lack of political worth.

It seems his one purpose this season is to make sure James Demeroven makes the most of his connections. Uncle Dashiell *and* Beth are counting on him.

Bobby takes a moment to let himself mourn his own pride, knocking back the rest of his whisky, before he plasters on a smile and turns to find Beth and Gwen—to pretend nothing's amiss.

"I'm just not sure I want to bother," Gwen says as Bobby steps up to her and Beth, idling by the refreshments.

"All right, but the alternative is spending the season with my mother, listening to her talk about her swollen ankles and all the parties we *should* be attending."

Gwen winces and takes a sip of her champagne.

"What are we debating?" Bobby asks, looking between them.

"We're trying to decide on a charity to volunteer with for the season," Beth says, adjusting her pale blue skirt so it's not crumpled against Bobby's leg.

"Oh, that sounds fun. Could I join you?" Bobby asks, delighted by the idea. It would give him something to *do*.

"You can hardly join us at the women's charities," Gwen says archly. "And I'm not convinced. For the first year ever there's no pressure. Why celebrate that by working?"

"Why celebrate it by becoming slovenly either?" Beth counters. "And again, I remind you, the alternative is being with my mother."

"I like your mother," Bobby puts in playfully. He does so love fueling their arguments, like the devious, annoying younger cousin he is.

Gwen sniffs and brushes back a lock of her blond hair. "I

suppose it wouldn't be the worst thing in the world to have somewhere to go on days without events."

"An honest day's work could be rewarding," Bobby agrees, laughing when Gwen frowns at him. She hates it when he plays both sides.

"Speaking of honest work," Beth says, raising her hand and motioning someone over.

Bobby nearly groans. Demeroven's reluctantly heading their way. "That is not what I meant," Bobby tells Beth.

Beth winks at him and offers her cousin a wide smile. Demeroven steps up to their little circle, looking uncomfortably buttoned up in a tight blue frock coat, starched shirt, and black bow tie. Even his hair looks stiff with pomade.

"Cousin," he greets. "Lady Gwen."

"Lovely party, isn't it?" Beth asks.

Demeroven bobs his head and they stand in awkward silence for a disquietingly long beat. Bobby would wait them all out, but he's now promised Uncle Dashiell and Beth that he'll try, and he can't leave all the effort on Beth's shoulders, especially since he knows Gwen won't be the one to break the silence. She delights in awkward pauses.

"Do you remember that strange professor at Oxford, who taught medieval history? Always wore a bright-red bow tie?"

Demeroven blinks, as if surprised Bobby's addressing him. "Professor Marchbank."

"Yes," Bobby says with forced cheer. "Did you hear that he's moved to Stratford-upon-Avon and is apparently compiling a new Shakespearean folio?"

"Really?" Beth asks. "How exciting. That class must have been fascinating."

All three of them look to Demeroven, but he merely offers a bland smile.

"It was," Bobby says after a moment. "You know, Gwen and Beth love Shakespeare."

Another bland smile. Bobby looks to the girls, praying for help. But Gwen's just sucking on her cheek to keep from laughing at his efforts, and Beth is watching him imploringly.

"Did you ever go to that club he liked? The White Rabbit?" Bobby continues, watching Demeroven for . . . *any* sign of engagement.

He doesn't think it was common knowledge that there were sometimes gatherings in the basement of the White Rabbit—he highly doubts Demeroven would know anything about them. But the main club was good for a pint on a cold day, whether or not you wanted to try and pick up a nice gentleman for an afternoon treat.

Demeroven shakes his head stiffly. "No."

Bobby waits, but he doesn't elaborate. It's going to be a long season if this is the only way the man cares to communicate, or . . . not.

Bobby glances at Beth with a small shrug as if to say *I tried*. Beth frowns and then looks to Gwen, raising an eyebrow. Gwen sighs dramatically and swallows the rest of her champagne, unceremoniously handing her glass to a confused Demeroven.

"All right," she calls out, making Demeroven jump, which is, honestly, a little entertaining. "Let's have some festivities," she continues, turning to face the rest of the party and beckoning the young ton to her side.

Lady Eloise leads Prous over, both of them looking dangerously amused. "Are you going to cause a scene at every one of my mother's garden parties, then?" Lady Eloise asks.

Bobby vaguely recalls something about Aunt Cordelia accidentally whacking Uncle Dashiell in the knackers last year with a croquet mallet at the Kingsmans' first season tea, well before they were even engaged. It was . . . probably an accident.

"I plan to have as much fun as possible this year," Gwen replies, winking at Beth.

Beth wraps her arm through Bobby's. "Fun, trouble, they're really the same thing, aren't they?"

"With the two of you, absolutely," he says, laughing as Beth swats at him.

"I think it's time we made use of the lovely lawn-bowling setup your mother so kindly supplied to have a tournament," Gwen tells Lady Eloise.

"Only the debutantes and sons," Lady Eloise says. "My father said after last year the parents aren't allowed to participate."

"That's a shame," Beth says. "Your mother was very good at croquet."

"Yours, not so much," Gwen says. Beth laughs and Lady Eloise gapes. "What? She's my stepmother now—I say it with love," Gwen defends.

"So, lawn bowling?" Prous puts in, before the ladies can devolve into a fast-paced squabble.

"Yes," Gwen says. "We'll play in teams, so everyone gets a turn."

"In couples, of course?" Lady Eloise asks.

"Well, of course. What would be the point otherwise?" Gwen says brightly. "Lady Eloise and Prous, naturally; Lady Annabeth and Johnson; Miss Susan with Haroldson; obviously Miss Langston and Prince; and we'll finish up with Miss Bertram and Mason; and Lord Demeroven, you'll be with me."

The couples pair off excitedly. Beth squeezes Bobby's arm and he meets her smile.

"We're going to wipe the floor with all of them," he says loudly. Beth laughs.

He glances at Gwen, who has stepped up to Demeroven, making equally heckling comments about the other couples, he's sure. Demeroven looks exceedingly uncomfortable, but he hears the man mutter, "Given your prowess at billiards, according to your father, I'm not sure we're giving them any chance."

Gwen laughs and Bobby files that away. Demeroven *is* capable of having some manner of charm, then.

"All right, I believe Lady Kingsman has three sets available?" Gwen says, turning back to the group.

"Yes," Lady Eloise says, her hand threaded with Prous'.

"Then we'll play in groups of four, and then the winning three teams can be in the final tournament," Gwen decides. "Lady Eloise and Prous versus Lady Annabeth and Johnson, and Miss Susan and Haroldson versus Miss Langston and Prince. Beth and Mason, you'll be against us. And we are going to obliterate you, aren't we, Demeroven?"

"Yes," Demeroven says, glancing at Gwen and trying vainly to match her tenacity.

"In your dreams," Beth says, leading Bobby toward the bowling set furthest from the patio.

"Are you any good at lawn bowling?" Bobby thinks to ask as they watch Demeroven stiffly unpack their set of balls.

"Oh, God, no," Beth says brightly. "But I insist we win. We both know she'll be insufferable if we don't." They both look at Gwen, who's practically doing calisthenics to warm up.

"And that's the woman you love," Bobby mutters.

Beth giggles. "With all my heart, the terrible winner she is. You think James has any skill at this?"

Bobby's about to say no, but then Demeroven removes his coat and lays it on a nearby bench. He has a shockingly strong, lithe physique, and coupled with those sharp cheekbones and piercing eyes—

"Bobby?"

"Oh, uh, no. Can't have. Doesn't seem like the lawn-games type," Bobby hurries out, pretending he is not at all feeling any rush of anything at the sight of Beth's cousin's body.

"A friendly family game?" Albie asks, sauntering up to them.

"Perhaps," Bobby says, hoping his voice sounds normal despite the pickup of his pulse.

"Your father told me to come over and referee so we don't have any sort of repeat of . . . last year," Albie tells Gwen.

"Is he worried Beth is going to punt a bowling ball into Bobby's—"

"It's nice of you to join us, Albie," Beth cuts in, rolling her eyes as Gwen snickers. "Perhaps you can keep James and Gwen in line."

"Oh, are you a troublemaker, Demeroven?" Albie asks, tossing the jack to the end of their pitch.

Demeroven looks over at him, startled. Bobby swallows thickly as he rolls up his shirtsleeves. "I . . . endeavor to be very little trouble, mostly."

"Oh, well, we can't have that," Gwen says eagerly, grabbing Demeroven's arm. "We'll take the first round."

"Why am I not surprised?" Bobby grumbles as Beth laughs.

Gwen's two tosses land predictably close to the jack, and Demeroven's balls nudge up against hers. Demeroven might actually end up a fair hand at darts, even if he will refuse to play for money.

"You've a good arm," Gwen says brightly. "And a lot of muscles," she adds as she lightly tugs him out of the way so Beth can push Bobby forward.

Albie passes Beth her two balls, chuckling at Demeroven's

discomfort. Bobby glances back and feels his throat tighten. Demeroven's tugging at his collar, those muscles in his biceps flexing. Bobby does like arms—always has.

"You rowed at school, didn't you?" Albie asks Demeroven.

"I did," Demeroven says.

Bobby splits his focus, watching Beth bite at her lip in concentration, lining up her toss. But he's got an eye on Demeroven as well. He never did bother to attend any of the sculling heats. Perhaps he should have, if all the rowers looked like Demeroven.

Perhaps they would have met before, in better, less socially severe circumstances.

"Yes!"

Gwen groans and Bobby looks over to find that Beth has knocked Gwen's ball out of place. Her blue ball now sits closest to the jack.

"We're so good I'm not even necessary," he crows, laughing as Beth jumps in excitement.

Gwen's glowering, but Demeroven looks nonplussed.

"Think you can beat that?" he asks, looking for any reaction at all.

"Possibly," Demeroven says simply. "Though that was a very good throw, cousin."

Ah, so he can be polite too, when he wants to be. "It was," Bobby agrees, smiling at Beth, who shrugs humbly. He makes his throws, which both land respectably.

"Hardly as impressive as sculling," Beth says.

"They're very different skills," Demeroven allows. He and Bobby trade places while Albie jogs out to send all the balls rolling back to them.

Demeroven makes his next toss, landing perhaps six inches from the jack.

"I don't know," Gwen says, taking her ball and seemingly effortlessly tossing it down the grass to bump into Demeroven's. "They both take teamwork, don't they?"

"They do," Demeroven admits. "Though this has so far involved far less shouting, so I appreciate that."

"Don't count on it," Albie mutters and Bobby laughs.

"Father told me you won most of your races. Do you ever think about joining one of the Henley-on-Thames teams?" Gwen asks.

"Oh, goodness, no," Demeroven says.

Bobby listens as Demeroven, Gwen, and Albie get into a rather in-depth discussion about the odds for each team for the upcoming regatta. Demeroven is rather animated when he's interested in the subject at hand. And the brightness in his eyes, it's almost captivating.

That, and the thin sheen of sweat around his neck, which has him pulling at his collar constantly and making the rest of his starched shirt go taut, giving a hint of what appears to be quite the set of defined abdominals beneath.

"Are you paying attention . . . at all?" Beth asks.

Bobby blinks and looks back at the jack, which he's missed by more than a foot. "Um, of course?"

Beth shakes her head. "She'll be insufferable now, you know."

Bobby shrugs guiltily and steps back for Gwen and Demeroven to make the uncontested winning throws. Beth did a perfectly commendable job, but he's pants at lawn bowling. Which normally doesn't rankle—he's long since given up on any hope of besting either of the girls at sports—but it does make him a little ashamed in front of Demeroven.

He pulls off his coat just as Albie declares them the losers. Gwen whoops while Beth politely congratulates Demeroven.

Albie then leads Gwen, still gloating, off toward the other teams for the next round. Beth looks over at Bobby and shrugs helplessly before she follows them, giggling at Gwen and Albie's antics.

Bobby stretches, shaking his head, dejected. He glances over and finds Demeroven staring at him, his face a bit flushed. Bobby stills, confused, and then realizes he's sweaty and unjacketed himself. And Demeroven is . . . admiring him? How interesting.

Maybe they finally have something in common.

"Would you like to join me at the club this evening? I have a feeling you must have opinions about what sailing bets to place at Cowes, given your background, and I could use some serious help, or Gwen will bet me under the table," Bobby says.

Simple, innocent, but friendly. That's all he's extending. Friendship. He is absolutely not imagining an evening at Thomas Parker's club. At least not yet. They have to learn to swim before he throws Demeroven directly into the deep end. He needs to really suss the man out first.

But all that open regard on Demeroven's face disappears in a single blink. Demeroven hurriedly pulls on his jacket and adjusts his collar, his face flushing. "I don't gamble, if you recall," he says.

"Right," Bobby manages, too surprised by the sudden chill in the man's voice to come up with something more elegant. "I, ah, simply thought it might be fun."

"Well, I don't gamble," Demeroven repeats. "Gambling makes men incautious."

"I . . . suppose that's true," Bobby agrees slowly. "I just thought it would be something we could—"

"I cannot afford to be incautious, regardless of how much our cousins want us to be friends," Demeroven says, his words rushed and clipped. Then he turns on his heel and marches stiffly after Beth and Gwen.

Bobby stands there, totally perplexed. *He* isn't incautious. Was that meant to be a slight against his family reputation? He doesn't even know if Demeroven has any inkling of his father's past.

Bobby hovers for a moment, unsure. He watches Demeroven join Beth, Gwen, and Albie, observing the last of Prous' game. Watches Albie lean down to ask Demeroven something, Gwen listening eagerly beside him. Bobby feels his shoulders come up. He heads for the drinks table, too confused and oddly discomfited to force himself to join the group and cheer on Demeroven and his cousin now.

No matter what they do, there's just no escaping the mess their father left for them, is there? Bobby pours himself another dram and retreats to his original spot against the hedge, the party coming full circle. He watches at a remove as Gwen and Demeroven go on to trounce the remaining competition. There was never any doubt.

Bobby lets the burn of alcohol down his throat mirror the quiet discontent he feels. He's just insulted, that's all. It's not that, for a brief moment, it felt like he might be able to make a friend out of James Demeroven. That he was getting along with Gwen and Beth, that he maybe shares a particular worldview—that he seemed mildly interesting, with his history of sport and his ability to discuss races with Gwen.

He can't be disappointed. So he must be angry. That's what he's feeling. It's the only other option.

Beth breaks off from the crowd to head his way and Bobby sighs. He won't be good company now, and, even though it's sort of Beth's fault for sticking him with the baffling man, he can't be mean to her.

He's only known her for a year, but already she's like the sister he never had. Gwen will always be his annoying, delightful cousin. But Beth is a kindred spirit.

"I think it's going well," Beth says, turning to lean back beside him.

Her blue skirt presses into his leg. She holds out her hand and he passes his drink into her waiting palm. "You do?"

"He and Gwen are certainly getting along."

"That's something," he admits. Gwen is usually a decent judge of character. But this time he's not so sure.

Beth passes his drink back to him and takes his arm. He groans and she laughs. "I've been sent to get you. Gwen wants to discuss our week."

"With Demeroven?"

"Of course," Beth says primly, winking at him.

He really does want to pull away from her, but she's such a petite woman, it wouldn't be fair. And she'd best him in a contest of strength any day, even with all the boxing he's been doing over the last six months.

Gwen, Albie, and a clearly uncomfortable Demeroven meet them by the large weeping willow at the back of the garden. Beth releases him to take Gwen's arm, and Bobby watches them lean against each other, there in broad daylight, with no one any the wiser.

That pit in his stomach only grows deeper as he listens to them plan out his week, and Demeroven's with Albie. Gwen has Beth, the two of them secretly in love and free to spend all their time together as they please. And now Albie has Demeroven in parliament. Where does that leave him?

"I am sorry to hear about your wife," Demeroven says. "Is she feeling any better?"

That pulls Bobby back, forcing him to shake off his melancholy.

"Thank you," Albie replies. "The doctors swear she'll be better in a month or so, but it is . . . difficult to see."

"I guess the registration of physicians might go some way to ensuring your wife has proper care," Demeroven says.

Albie nods seriously. "Speaking of which, we'd best meet those gentlemen Uncle Dashiell told us about before they escape."

And then it's just Bobby, Beth, and Gwen once again. Bobby stands glumly beside them, listening as they make plans to cheer Meredith up, and then move on to what they want to have for dinner, and then something whispered too low to hear. But it makes Beth blush scarlet, so that was probably rather the point.

Bobby leans back against the tree and looks up into its newly green leaves. He closes his eyes and breathes in the damp spring air, running his fingers over the etched initials on his signet ring. Perhaps he should go to Thomas Parker's club, see if he can't build connections beyond his cousin, her lover, her dyspeptic cousin, and his brother. Somewhere where he'll be distracted enough to forget about Meredith's dangerous pregnancy, and his aunt's upcoming dangerous childbirth.

Somewhere where perhaps someone would hold his hand and tell him everything will be all right.

CHAPTER FOUR

James

James sits in his opulent carriage, staring out at the grimy, gaslit street. There's mist in the air, everything has a hazy glow, and his leg won't stop shaking. James balls his fists. He walked into parliament, for God's sake. He can get out of the carriage, walk down the street, and knock on that door. He can.

But now all of him is shaking.

Maybe he should just scrap the idea entirely, in case someone's seen his idling carriage and puts two and two together. But then he contemplates the alternative: a stuffy dinner with his mother and stepfather, listening to them snipe at each other. Or worse, listening to his mother go on about all the lovely young women she's planning to invite for dinner.

That thought is enough to propel him out of the cabin. His feet hit the damp cobblestones and he nearly slips, hanging on to the carriage door. He must look a sight.

But he can do this. He wants to do this.

So he closes the door, adjusts the lapels of his navy frock coat, and sets off with an entirely false confidence. He crosses the street and begins the three-block trek to the alley. He feels like everyone he passes must be able to hear the gallop of his heart. He's been to clubs before; he doesn't know why this is making him so anxious. But when he turns down the narrow alley, marked only by one brass-capped brick at eye level, he knows why he's nervous. It feels like the first days at Oxford all over again.

Except this time, he's not just a gentleman's stepson. He's a viscount, skulking down an alleyway to get to the back entrance of 122. It's an unassuming servants' entrance and he hesitates, fist raised, heart pounding.

He could just go home. He doesn't need to face this tonight.

He glances both ways down the alley, but he's alone in the haze. Home isn't somewhere he belongs. And he wants to belong somewhere. Somewhere could be here.

James takes a deep breath and raps sharply on the door: three raps, two taps, a beat, and one more knock.

And then he waits, feeling like the blurring mist is creeping up on him, hiding shadows. It makes him break out in a cold, clammy sweat, and after a minute he's almost ready to bolt back for the carriage. But then the door slits open just enough for a human head to pop out.

James stares up into the grinning face of a broad, muscular man, wearing an askew, sky-blue top hat.

"Password?" he prompts, that smile mischievous beneath his russet mustache.

"D'Vere is D'Vine," James forces out, his voice hoarse and tight.

"That it is," the man says jovially, opening the door wide and ushing James inside.

James stumbles up the two-step stoop, wincing as the man snaps the door shut behind him. The interior is little more than a narrow staircase lit by dripping candles that leads up to another plain door.

"Thomas Parker welcomes you," the man says, his hand pressing gently against James' back to nudge him up the stairs.

"Um, thanks," James says, taking a few steps before glancing back, just in time to see the man slipping into a hidden door beside the exit. He tips his cap and closes the door. To the untrained eye, it's just a plain wall with fading beige wallpaper.

Secret doors and passwords—he's clearly not in Epworth anymore. He squares his shoulders and heads upstairs, pretending he's not about to sweat through his new white shirt. Because he's James Demeroven, and he can do this.

Far from a cramped little back room at the local inn, the door to D'Vere opens onto an opulent, wealth-laden cigar club. Bright gas lamps and candles light the wide, welcoming space, which is filled with young upstanding men, loitering with cocktails.

The front room is rimmed with deep red leather armchairs and well-stocked bookcases. The wallpaper is a bright blue brocade to match the doorman's jaunty top hat. The curtains are a deep purple, and even the chessboards and checkers on the low tables around the room are royal purple and lavender. Gilded mirrors and beautiful paintings adorn the walls, and the whole space smells of hops and lilac.

James is definitely not in Epworth anymore.

He stares out at the room, intimidated, excited, and intrigued. He's never been anywhere that looks like this, nor that's filled with quite this many men, who must all . . . be of his persuasion, or they wouldn't have found the place.

That nagging voice that always sounds too much like his stepfather's cackles in his head: He's bad with people. He's bad at conversation. He'll be a disappointment here, just like he is in parliament, just like he was at the garden party.

"Ah, a new guest—come in, come in."

James blinks, startled to find his entrance hasn't gone unnoticed. Instead, a tall, willowy man, dressed in a frock coat that matches the blue brocade wallpaper, stands there beaming at him. He's got the same large mustache as the man downstairs, but in a dark chestnut.

His face is familiar. Round and open, with the widow's peak and notch in his eyebrow . . . "You must be Thomas Parker, Reginald's brother," James hears himself say.

"Lord Demeroven!" Parker says, his smile turning somehow more magnetic. "My stars, it is such a pleasure to meet you. Reginald talks about you in all his letters—discreetly, of course."

James feels himself blushing. "Well, he talks about you just as much," he says, taking Parker's extended hand.

Parker gives him an enthusiastic handshake and then quickly slides his hand up to link his arm through James'. "A tour," he announces, spinning them to gesture broadly at the room. "Welcome to D'Vere, where every type of man is welcome, the drinks flow freely, and the secrets stay inside."

James looks over the room again, noting the fine details, like the multicolored glasses and the blue suspenders on the bartender, who also has a large, well-styled mustache. James still hasn't managed to grow a respectable one, and Mother never talks about his father, so he has no idea if his delayed facial hair is inherited or not. Not that he's ever worked up the courage to ask.

"What'll you have?"

"Oh, ah, whisky?"

"Excellent choice," Thomas says, tapping the bar. "Jeremy, the best whisky we have for Lord Demeroven." James fights a wince as his voice bounces around the room. "Don't worry," Parker says, smiling as James looks up to meet his eyes. "Like I said, secrets stay inside."

"Right," James says, taking the whisky from Jeremy the

bartender. He takes a sip, delighting in the smooth, rich flavor and pleasant afterburn. "Delicious."

"Isn't it? Jeremy, remind me, we want to place a standing order with them. It's made at this charming distillery on the border with Scotland, you know?" he tells James as he guides him away from the bar. "Lovely chap by the name of Gaddie. Met him in one of the Edinburgh clubs. Have you ever been?"

"No," James says, trying to keep up with Parker's rapid-fire delivery and also take stock of the second room they've entered, inviting with deep burgundy couches, armchairs, a bear-skin rug, and even more bookshelves. "I see you collect," James says, gesturing with his drink to the shelves.

"Of course, of course," Parker says, smiling fondly around at the books. "I make it a point to worm my way into every salon in each city I visit. These books have seen the furthest reaches of Europe."

"That sounds fascinating," James says, intrigued but unsurprised. It's clear just to look at him that Parker charms each person he meets.

"There's a library upstairs as well, if you ever need somewhere comfortable to study up," Parker says, gesturing toward the staircase they passed between the two rooms.

"How many floors are there?" James asks.

"Three," Parker says proudly. "The library and further salon rooms are on the next floor, and the rented rooms are on the third."

"Rented rooms," James repeats, feeling his back stiffen. He tries to pass it off with a smile, but Parker raises an eyebrow.

"To be rented by consenting men who need a safe place to meet. I'm sure now you're here you realize how few spaces such as this exist." James winces guiltily. "Though, if you are looking for some respectable men for rent, I can point you in any number of directions," Parker continues, that look of reproach melting into a sly smirk.

"Oh, no, thank you," James says quickly. He's so outgunned here.

"Well, if you ever need recommendations, for good houses, good food, good theater, you just come and see me. Reginald will send you to the stuffiest of spots. I'll find you the fun."

James forces his shoulders to relax and takes a sip of whisky. "Thank you—I'll remember that."

Parker walks them back into the main parlor. James can feel him starting to pull away and fights the urge to hold on. It's not that conversation with Parker feels safe, exactly, but it certainly feels safer than facing the glut of intrigued faces milling about the front parlor.

"Now, Viscount, I'll leave you in the capable hands of"—Parker looks around just as Jeremiah Prince shuffles through the door—"ah, Prince, wonderful. I'd love for you to meet—"

"Demeroven!" Prince says, stepping up to them with a beaming smile on his handsome face. "It's been ages, how are you?"

"I'm well," James says, wilting in relief. His old sculling teammate Prince—this night might actually be fun after all.

"Well, I'll leave you two to catch up. You say goodbye before you leave, both of you," Parker says, bowing to them before striding off to mingle. He's greeted with boisterous shouts.

"He's something, isn't he?" Prince asks.

"Something," James agrees, tilting his chin toward the bar.

Prince smiles and walks with him, only to be handed a drink in a bright-green glass before he can even open his mouth. "Jeremy, my good man, always so quick."

"Only for you, Mr. Prince," Jeremy says, winking at Prince before spinning away to help another customer.

"Liar," Prince calls after him before leaning against the bar and taking a sip of the drink. "Delicious, as always."

James watches the bob of his throat, slightly entranced, but trying desperately not to show it. "How have you been?" he asks, a little haltingly.

But Prince doesn't mind. He's always been a kind, lovely man. Never looked at James twice, and now that he's about to be married, James supposes he never will. Though, looking around, he thinks a few of the men in quiet, intimate corners are surely married already.

He's not sure what other course there is for a man of his persuasion. Marriage is the only logical next step, even if it can never be to the object of one's most fervent desires.

"I'm well," Prince says, bringing James' attention back to his bright, smiling face. "Miss Langston and I have planned the most wonderful honeymoon in Paris, and I'm eager as ever for the wedding to arrive."

James bobs his head with a forced smile. He doesn't think he could ever be so jovial about cutting off such a big part of his life. Or at least pretending to. Those two men in the corner are both definitely married—he noticed them at the ball with their wives earlier in the week. But it's not stopping them from sauntering up the stairs to the private rooms.

"Congratulations, by the way. Never got a chance to say," James forces out.

Prince beams at him. "Thank you, thank you."

"She sounds like a lovely young woman," he adds, trying to recall what his cousin said about her.

"She is, at that," Prince agrees. "The most wonderful dancing partner, and sharp as a tack. I think you'd like her, actually. You and that chap . . . Brightley? You used to have those long, convoluted Shakespearean quoting competitions."

"Yes," James says, remembering Frank Brightley, a most pugnacious man. But oh, could he quote Shakespeare.

"Miss Langston might be able to best you both," Prince says.

"Oh?" James wonders. "Well, we might just have to test that, then."

"She'd be delighted!" Prince says happily, those dimples lifting his cheeks. "I'll have her reach out for a dinner. Perhaps the two of you could compete over drinks afterward."

"That would be grand," James says, almost meaning it.

Drinks suggests there would be other people. He's not great under pressure with real eyes watching. His sweaty mates on the sculling team weren't the same.

"But you're happy?" he asks, forcing himself to ignore his unnecessary nerves.

"Very," Prince says. "Really," he adds. James must not have done a good job of hiding his skepticism. "It's a love match, good boy."

"That's wonderful," James says honestly.

"You'll have to come to the stag night as well," Prince continues.

"Of course," James agrees. "Just tell me when."

"Excellent! Oh, good—Cunningham," he calls out, raising his hand.

The Mason brothers' broad friend from the opening-night ball appears from the second parlor. He's lost his overcoat somewhere and is walking around in a white shirt and red suspenders with an undone tie, deep brown hair mussed. James isn't sure why he's so surprised to see him; really, he should have guessed, given Cunningham's dour references to his own fiancée at the opening ball. But James' inattention to signals is hardly his most pressing concern now.

"Another for the guest list," Prince says.

"Fantastic," Cunningham says, blue eyes sparkling. He rubs his hands together and looks James up and down. "You'll do nicely. I think you might be lean enough to stand through the carriage roof."

"Excuse me?" James manages. Cunningham doesn't seem at all surprised to see him, but James feels like the walls are starting to press in. Cunningham is far too close to his world.

"He's kidding. We'll be having Rupping stand and look through the carriage roof to fit everyone inside. He's got another head on Demeroven here," Prince says.

"Ah, well, it is your party," Cunningham says. "Whatever are you drinking?"

"A Jeremy special," Prince says.

Cunningham raises a hand, flagging down Jeremy. He points to Prince's drink. "Add a splash of Gaddie's whisky. Are we running low?"

"Mr. Parker's already planned a standing order. You're behind on the news," Jeremy says as his hands fly around the bar, mixing Cunningham's drink.

"You're writing up the weekly backers report, so it's really your delay, isn't it?" Cunningham asks, laughing when Jeremy just rolls his eyes.

Jeremy glances at James, an eyebrow raised, but James shakes his head. He hasn't even finished his first whisky yet, too busy trying to get the lay of the land.

"You'll learn to keep up," Jeremy says as he hands Cunningham his drink.

"'Course he will. We want Lord Demeroven to be a repeat customer, after all," Cunningham says.

James isn't so sure, but he leans back against the counter, trying to look relaxed. Trying to convince himself that this is D'Vere, and secrets stay inside. He doesn't need to panic. Cunningham clearly has a financial stake in the club. It isn't like he'll be out telling anyone about James, nor will Prince. He's . . . among friends.

Cunningham hails another patron. A tall, wide man with a short-trimmed mustache and a light sheen of sweat on his brow slots into their little circle.

"Demeroven, this is Lord Wristead," Prince says. "Wristead, this is Demeroven's first season. Wristead was a few years ahead of us at Oxford."

"Pleased to make your acquaintance," James says, taking the man's hand. His grip is almost painfully tight. James hopes his palms aren't sweating.

"And yours as well," Wristead says.

"Demeroven will be joining for the stag night," Cunningham says.

"Oh, excellent, excellent. Between you and Rupping, I think we can easily boost Prince back into his room without his father being any the wiser."

James opens his mouth; he wants no part in anything that could upset Lord Prince—

"Father's funding the entire night," Prince says with a laugh. "No need for subterfuge."

"Unless we want to sample more than London's finest liquors," Cunningham says eagerly. "We were just compiling a list of the most tempting—"

"There will be no establishments of the night," Prince says quickly, giving James an apologetic look. "I am very happily-to-be-wed and need none of that particular entertainment."

"Speak for yourself," Cunningham says with another slug of his drink.

"That reminds me, Mary Ann has been asking to see Abigail. Might we schedule that oft-promised visit when we're back in the country?" Wristead asks him.

"Of course, of course. Abs would be glad for the company."

"Shame she couldn't make it down with you," Wristead says blithely.

"It is," Cunningham says. "But her mother wouldn't hear of her being here without a wedding, and I need to get my feet under me with my father's holdings while I handle . . . other matters."

James can't quite tell if it's an excuse or reality.

"No need to leave her on her own for the season if she doesn't have to be, nor under the scrutiny of a prolonged engagement with all these mothers about," Prince says.

"Exactly," Cunningham says. "Though, you'll understand, Prince, why this bachelor party of yours is a bit of my last hurrah as well."

"There's no need for it to be a final hurrah," Wristead says. "Mary Ann and I have an understanding."

"You do?" James hears himself ask, shocked. All three men turn to look at him and he has half a mind to run away. "Pardon me," he says, his voice tight. "I didn't mean to—"

"Think nothing of it," Wristead says. "I'm one of the lucky ones. Mary Ann knew right away I fancied more than women."

"Terrible bluff, this one," Prince agrees. "An attractive man within six meters and his eye is wandering."

"What can I say, I have taste," Wristead says, as if these types of conversations happen every day. "She confronted me about it rather early on. Felt like I owed it to her to be honest. I'm allowed my own life here in the city, and she asks only that it never come home to the country. I find it more than bearable. She is a most excellent whist player."

James bobs his head, as if the arrangement makes perfect sense. But he can't imagine asking his wife to share him that way. Asking her to accept being only half of his life, never mind his heart.

"Have you thought about—" Wristead asks, but Cunningham shakes his head. "You might—"

Cunningham's face turns pinched. "Not all of us are so lucky as to marry a woman as open-minded as Miss Mary Ann."

Prince glances behind him. "Oh, look, Cunningham, Mason just arrived. That'll cheer you right up."

James feels his whole body go rigid. Mason? He glances stiffly over his shoulder and sure enough, Bobby Mason is standing in the entryway in deep conversation with Thomas Parker.

Bobby Mason, who he was obsessed with at school, his cousin's stepsister's cousin—Bobby Mason is *here*?

That means Bobby Mason is—

"Excuse me, I need the washroom," James hears himself say, placing his glass too loudly down onto the bar before stumbling through the group, away from Bobby Mason.

He slams into the small washroom, his heart thundering in his chest. Bobby Mason likes men. Bobby Mason knows Thomas Parker. Bobby Mason is of his persuasion and here and could *see* him and oh, God—

James braces his hands against the closed door, forcing himself to take deep breaths before he faints dead away in the small lavatory closet. Which, even for a lavatory closet, smells wonderfully of lavender. There isn't an inch of this place Thomas Parker hasn't carefully curated.

But that brings him back to Thomas Parker, and Bobby Mason, and the other lords, and how the whole ton could see that he's here, and talk, and it could get back to his stepfather, or, worse, to Lord Havenfort, and his aunt, and—

James slams a fist against the door and forces himself to stand upright. He will not be taken down by this fear again. Thomas Parker runs a tight ship. This is a safe place, Reginald promised.

Expose one man in anger, you risk exposing yourself and everyone else. It's mutually assured secrecy. He is safe here. And if Bobby Mason is here, Bobby Mason will just have to keep his secret as well, just as James will keep Mason's.

James takes a deep breath, and then another, the way Reginald taught him all those years ago. In through his nose, out through his mouth, until he can't feel his pulse against his ears anymore.

This is what he wanted—a group of men who understood. Friends. Possibly more than that. He's never going to find either hiding in the water closet.

So he pushes the door open, forcing himself to move before he's formulated a plan about how he's going to explain this to Bobby Mason. Or face him. Or not just turn bright scarlet now that he knows the boy he used to idolize is someone who thinks like him, could maybe even fancy him—though of course he wouldn't. Someone like Bobby Mason could never fancy *him*.

"Distracted, Viscount?"

James looks up just before he walks straight into Lord Raverson. Just as tall, strong-jawed, and strikingly handsome as he was at Oxford, Raverson looks down at James with a crooked smirk that makes James break out in gooseflesh.

"Raverson," James manages.

Even with their school days far behind them, James finds that now, standing in the hallway to the water closet at Thomas Parker's club, he feels no more a man or a sensible adult than he did at Oxford. Raverson's grin still makes his stomach clench, and he's immediately thrust back to the wretched week Raverson gave him up. It should have only been a relief to finally be out from under his thumb, but he spent that week weeping in his room, feeling worthless and pathetic.

How much has really changed?

"The title suits you," Raverson says, his voice dripping honey. "As do the years. My, you've outgrown that adorable gangly frame, haven't you?"

"Yes," James says tightly, trying not to look like he feels as trapped as he is. Here in the narrow hall, he can only pass if Raverson deigns to allow it, unless he wants to start a brawl.

"And I look as good as ever, don't I?"

"Yes," James grinds out. "But I've actually—"

"Sitting in the Lords is a chore, isn't it?" Raverson asks, bracing an arm against the wall and leaning against it, so he's entirely blocking the hall. "Makes me think of that professor—who was it, Archer?"

James pushes down his old discomfort. Raverson may have held sway over him in school, but his tricks won't work here. At least, James hopes not.

"The chancellor does sound a bit like Archer, that's true," James says, going for calm.

"I thought I might find it interesting, but so far the actual work has been the least compelling part of this season. Did you see that Wristead and Mason are here?"

James forces himself to keep his face blank. "Oh?"

"Didn't think either of them would be here so openly, given their situations."

He doesn't want to contribute to Raverson's penchant for salacious gossip, especially not if that gossip might someday be turned on him. At least Raverson will no longer be trading favors and secrets for social status and wealth. He doesn't need to expand his purse any longer, now that he holds all the strings.

"I was sorry to hear about your father," James says, hoping to divert the conversation.

"Were you?" Raverson asks, his voice morphing from that sweet, honeyed tone to something sharper. "I wasn't."

James fights a wince. Damn. "I remember you weren't fond of him, but still, I extend my condolences. I know how hard taking on the mantle of a title is."

"Yes, that's right. You would remember, wouldn't you? You were in my bed when I received the letter about my brother."

A sick feeling settles in James' stomach. He remembers that morning. Waking in Raverson's bed to find Raverson sitting in his desk chair in an open dressing gown, a letter dangling in one hand, a letter opener in the other. His older brother had died in a carriage accident, and Raverson was now the heir apparent to the Raverson title.

James hadn't known what to do, how to comfort him. How to respond when Raverson showed him the letter, which said only, "Your brother is dead. You are now my heir. I expect you home for Yule."

James had tried to comfort him then—had let Raverson take him back to bed, let him lose himself in James and his body. He thought maybe he had helped, but instead that was the beginning of Raverson's slow dismissal. He had the title and no need for James any longer.

No need for James' secrets after that.

Now Raverson stares past him, eyes fixed somewhere over his shoulder. James can't seem to find his words. Part of him is still stuck in Raverson's bed, staring at the ceiling as Raverson moved on top of him, unsure of whether Raverson was mentally there in the room with him at all.

"So, have you found anyone you might fancy for the season?"

James flinches as Raverson steps suddenly to his side and

wraps an arm around his shoulders, pushing him into the doorway from the washroom hallway so they're left looking out at the parlor together.

"Um, no, not yet," James stammers, his shoulders held tight, stomach in knots.

Between the feeling of Raverson's arm on his shoulders, too heavy and too stiff, and the sight of more than twenty men in the parlor, he feels like his heart might burst out of his chest. There are members of parliament playing chess by the window, heirs hobnobbing by the bar, Prince and Cunningham and Wristead still talking with a larger group, rowdy and boisterous.

If Raverson is here, Parker's world isn't nearly as secure as he thinks it is. There is no mutually assured secrecy with Raverson. His authoritative lies could fool even the most suspicious father at school—get him to pay good money for Raverson to keep quiet without ever questioning *how* Raverson had garnered his information.

James' secrets weren't worth enough to trifle with telling his stepfather. Not in school, when he was just a gentleman's stepson. But now, with the Demeroven title . . .

James feels himself beginning to get lightheaded again, the whisky starting to swirl in his stomach. He needs to leave. He needs to leave right now.

"Ah, would you look at the time," James says, glancing down at his hand as if he has a pocket watch to check. There must be a Demeroven pocket watch somewhere he could start wearing.

"Half past nine, you mean?" Raverson asks, his arm tightening on James' shoulders. "You're not starting to get overwhelmed, are you? I'd have thought you'd have grown out of that."

"I'm perfectly fine," James says brusquely. "I simply have matters to attend to."

"I could always fix that for you. I remember exactly what

used to limber you up at school. Wouldn't take a moment, we're right by the—"

"Excuse me," James says, pulling away from Raverson without a backward glance.

He strides across the room, trying to look like he has somewhere to be. He should find Parker, but doesn't think he can keep his stomach down long enough. Instead, he marches around the bar and pulls open the door to the entryway stairs, only to bump straight into Bobby Mason, who's lounging in the stairwell having a smoke.

"Demeroven? Thought I'd heard you were here," he says, as if everything is perfectly normal. As if it's completely fine that they're both here, and they both know, and—

"I have to go," James mumbles through clenched teeth. He heads for the stairs but trips, groping wildly for the banister only for Mason to catch him.

"Easy, man," Mason says, wrapping his arm around James' back, his grip tight, but nothing like Raverson's. "Let's go out, get some air, yeah?"

James can only nod, feeling like his heart is about to burst out of his chest. His limbs are tingling again, those pinpricks back in his fingertips. But he doesn't think he can fight it off this time. His nerves are going to get the better of him. He just needs to make it outside.

Mason waves to the doorman, who opens the door with a muttered, "Careful, yeah?"

And then they're in the cool night air. James gulps it in, pulling away from Mason to stumble down the two-step stoop and into the alley. He just manages to catch himself on the wall, bracing with both hands as he loses the fight with his stomach.

He vomits up whisky and bile, his back shaking, fingers digging into the rough stone wall. He wishes he could vomit up his past with Raverson, and his fear of being seen, being known, being judged. Wishes his fear would seep into the cobblestones like his sick, and leave him indomitable, instead of this hunched, terrified husk.

"All right?" Mason asks, laying a warm, heavy palm on James' back as he braces himself on the wall, sucking in air around the burn in his throat.

James jerks, Mason's touch as comforting as it is mortifying. Not only does Bobby Mason now have proof that James fancies men, but he's also seen him in an uncontrolled panic, rushing out of what is supposed to be an upstanding, safe, exclusive club.

He's seeing him too weak. He's seeing too much.

"Here," Mason says. He extends a handkerchief to him and James stares down at it, white and covered with little daisies. Dainty, for a solid man like Mason. "There's another pub down the way—we could get you some water . . . or bread, maybe?"

Mason's kindness and soft words burrow against a dark part of him that squirms in horror.

"I'm fine," James rasps, forcing himself upright before he's ready.

He steps back, glancing at Mason, who stands there, handkerchief outstretched, looking too concerned, and too handsome, and too . . . everything.

He can't do this.

It was a far-fetched fantasy—that he'd meet a nice man who understood him, who could know him, who could love him as he is. There is no fairy tale for him in London. Just the prying eyes of the ton, and the lords, and his past, running after him as he tries to stay one step ahead.

"I have to go," he says, lurching around Mason to make for the street.

"You can hardly walk in your—"

"I'm perfectly fine," James repeats, turning to stare just past Mason's ear. It's easier to lie, he's found, if you never meet their eyes, but make them think you have. "I simply have too many important things to do than to waste my time here. Excuse me," he says, shocked by his own poise and pompous arrogance.

He turns on his heel and walks as steadily as he can toward the street. He's left with a heavy feeling as he stumbles back toward his carriage, waiting half a mile away. That life full of love he daydreamed about in Epworth—how can it ever exist when London is just a bigger, darker, wider repetition of his past?

CHAPTER FIVE

Bobby

Bobby bows to the porter at the Steton townhouse and heads around the side of the four-story, white-brick façade that's always covered with immaculate ivy and flowers. Perhaps he should take up gardening, make the yard of their rather modest townhouse into something visually resplendent like the Steton backyard, full to bursting with early flowering trees and bushes. Tables have been laid out throughout the shockingly green lawn. And at the back, multiple badminton courts have been set up to provide the entertainment.

Bobby sighs. There probably aren't funds for new landscaping, not if they're going to refurbish the carriage and consider throwing their own events if Meredith is ever well enough to join them in London. But it would be nice to have something lovely for her to come home to if she does. And maybe he could actually get Albie out from under all his piles of papers and into the sun if they had a nice back garden.

Bobby shakes himself. He can't spend the whole afternoon brooding about his brother; otherwise Lady Steton, already roving about the party in a beautiful and very wide floral gown, will find him and start trying to connect him with her young female relatives. He needs a distraction, and fast.

He spots Beth and Gwen beneath the pink flowering tree by the badminton courts and immediately heads their way. He only hesitates when he notices Demeroven standing on Gwen's other side, as if he might like to disappear directly into the tree trunk.

That image of Demeroven heaving onto the cobblestones fills Bobby's mind again. He remembers how nerve-wracking his own first visit to D'Vere was. If Cunningham hadn't escorted him, Bobby's not sure he would have worked up the gumption to knock. And even then, he spent the whole night sweating through his brand-new frock coat.

The thought of marching up to the club door alone for the first time seems excruciating. Bobby can't blame the man for succumbing to his nerves, nor his anxious, slightly rude behavior afterward. He watches Demeroven shift by the tree now, looking as out of place at the garden party as he seemed at the end of the night at D'Vere.

Bobby feels a renewed sense of purpose bubbling up inside him. The chap's rather moody, but Beth and Uncle Dashiell asked him to help. Bobby's sure it isn't what they intended, but helping Demeroven fit in with London's underground—helping him find his place and happiness in the community—that feels like a worthy use of his time.

Perhaps if the other half of Demeroven's life gets sorted, Demeroven will be better able to focus on his duties in parliament, and hopefully on making amends with Aunt Cordelia and Beth. Bobby assumes Demeroven wasn't personally responsible for Aunt Cordelia and Beth being kicked out of their home when he came of age, or surely Uncle Dashiell wouldn't be working with him. But someone has to apologize for their abrupt eviction, and worse, for Beth's forced almost-marriage into the terrible Ashmond family as a result.

He'll make that his next goal, he decides, before pasting on a smile as he reaches Gwen and Beth.

"You're being rather petty, don't you think?" Beth asks Gwen before Bobby can get a word in edgewise.

"Petty?" Gwen repeats, her face darkening. "That's rich, given you're acting as if there's nothing the matter at all."

"There isn't!" Beth returns, hands on her hips, rustling the skirts of her green dress. Bobby thinks it may be one of Gwen's, actually. "It isn't her fault that I jilted her son. She has money she wants to donate, and time to fill, just like us."

"And you have no qualms about buddying up to her? What, are you looking for information on Montson?"

Bobby would try to mediate, like Albie's always able to do, but he doesn't want either of their furies turned on him instead. So he slips around them to lean back against the tree beside Demeroven, more than close enough to keep listening.

"Have they been at this long?" he asks Demeroven.

"Are you seriously asking me if I have some kind of latent interest in Lord Montson?" Beth demands.

"About fifteen minutes," Demeroven replies without looking at Bobby.

He's staring up into the tree and Bobby follows his gaze, tracking a squirrel sitting above them. He wonders if it too is interested in Beth and Gwen's fight about Lady Ashmond. It sounds as if perhaps she's funding refurbishments at the Foundling Hospital where the girls have just started volunteering.

"I think you have some kind of interest in Lady Ashmond," Gwen snipes back.

"I do!" Beth exclaims.

Gwen huffs and goes to stalk away, but Beth clutches at Gwen's arm. She pulls Gwen in close, exchanging a heated glance that's palpably intimate.

"I'd like to make sure Lady Ashmond is all right. Is that so wrong?"

Gwen sighs and pulls Beth around the tree, removing their argument from earshot. Bobby hopes they'll make up. He does so enjoy their more ridiculous fights, but he knows Montson and the entire engagement from last season remains a sore subject between them. How could it not?

With them bickering on the other side of the tree, Bobby's left beside Demeroven, all the awkwardness of their night in the alleyway pulsing between them. He glances down at the man and finds him almost breaking his neck to avoid eye contact, staring off and up in the other direction. Bobby looks up into the branches, but the nosy squirrel has deserted them.

"Bet it's having a better time," Bobby mutters.

"What?" Demeroven asks.

Bobby winces. "Um, the squirrel. I bet—" God, this is silly. "I bet it's having a better time than we are."

"Too right," Demeroven says, staring up into the leaves with him. "Nothing to do but eat nuts and sleep, what a life."

Bobby laughs, startled, and looks down at Demeroven. Demeroven himself seems a little surprised, but there's a tug at his lips and his shoulders have come down, so that's progress.

"Think he likes one particular type, or prefers to diversify?" Bobby asks before he can stop himself.

"If it's all you can eat, why not a sample?" Demeroven wonders, glancing up to meet Bobby's eyes.

Bobby watches his cheeks go pink before he looks away again. Adorable, really. Bobby waits, wondering if Demeroven might make another joke, but Demeroven doesn't offer anything else and they stand in a growing awkward silence.

"Have you been making morning calls?" Bobby asks. Banal, but it will have to do.

"No," Demeroven says, shrugging. "My mother's made a few, I think."

"Right, right. Mother's prerogative," Bobby agrees, ignoring the pang in his chest. He doesn't know if that's a mother's prerogative, actually, having never gotten to see his mother attend the season. "Parliament starts early too."

"It does," Demeroven agrees. "Bloody early. Makes me miss lying in at Oxford."

"How did you ever lie in at Oxford if you were on the rowing team?" Bobby wonders.

Demeroven glances over at him, a brief look of mischief on his face. "I had my ways."

"Yeah?" Bobby wonders. He could get used to that look. "What, did you bribe the coach?"

"With his very favorite wine, by the caseful," Demeroven says, looking rather proud of himself. "Got every other Saturday to sleep in. It was bliss." Bobby stares at him. "What?"

"You consider having a lie-in every other Saturday bliss?"

"Yes," Demeroven says slowly. "How . . . often do you have a lie-in?"

"In the country? Every day," Bobby exclaims.

"Don't you have anything you have to do?"

"Well . . . sometimes," Bobby says, fighting back a defensive edge. "What, are you up at seven every day on the Demeroven estate?"

"Mostly," Demeroven says, his straight nose rising, giving him an air of superiority Bobby hardly thinks is earned simply by being a morning person.

"And if you ever have a late night out?" Bobby presses.

"Then I'm tired," Demeroven says archly.

"Mmm, all right, now I see how it is," Bobby says, wanting to get the man out of his shell—see that glimmer of someone sly and mischievous and adorable again.

"How what is?" Demeroven asks.

"You must be out late rather often in London, then, if you're always eager for a lie-in," Bobby continues, glancing around. They're quite alone here by the tree. "Have you been to any of the other clubs? There are a few that are quieter. Not quite as open, but nice spots all the same. Might be a good way to ease into the community a bit, you know?"

But instead of donning that playful expression, or some manner of their earlier camaraderie, Demeroven's face goes completely blank. His head twists about, as if they might be suddenly interrupted. "I don't know what you're talking about."

"Well, Parker's club isn't the only place to—" Bobby starts, his voice low.

"Parker? I don't know a Parker," Demeroven whispers quickly.

Bobby stares at him, nonplussed. "You can't be serious."

"You're clearly mistaken. You must have gotten incorrect information at the many *clubs* you attend," Demeroven says, his voice cold, posture going stiff.

Bobby takes a step away from the tree so he can face Demeroven fully. "You're not seriously trying to claim you weren't rubbing shoulders with Cunningham and Prince at—"

"Shut up," Demeroven clips out, his blue eyes darting this way and that. "We are in public. Our maiden cousins are right behind us. How on earth can you be this careless?"

Bobby stares, his mouth falling open. No one can hear them! "I'm being nothing of the sort."

Demeroven pushes off from the tree, stepping close enough that Bobby's nose is almost brushing his forehead. "You never know who could be listening. You would do well to keep your lifestyle to yourself, and protect your cousin and Miss Bertram before your loose lips get them or anyone else hurt."

"I am far from—" Bobby starts just as Beth and Gwen traipse back around the tree, arm in arm.

"We're going to play badminton," Beth announces.

Gwen pulls her to a halt and Bobby and Demeroven step back from each other. Indignation simmers in Bobby's gut, tingling down his arms and into his fingers. How dare Demeroven suggest he would do *anything* that would endanger the girls? How dare he insinuate Bobby's attempt at simple conversation, at trying to help, is somehow—

How can he judge Bobby for doing exactly what he himself has done—attend and make use of one of the only safe spaces in London for men of their persuasion? Like it's something dirty, instead of something to be celebrated?

"Did we interrupt something?" Gwen asks, an eyebrow arched, even if her eyes do look a little bright, like perhaps there were tears on the other side of the tree.

"No," Bobby says, pushing it all down deep into his chest, next to his thoughts about his father and his worries about his sister-in-law. Maybe someday if he pushes those feelings down far enough, they'll simply disappear. "We were talking about which smoking club Demeroven's going to join."

"Right," Demeroven says immediately, offering Beth and Gwen a truly uncomfortable smile. "Badminton?"

"Yes," Beth says, glancing at Gwen before breaking away to take Demeroven's arm. "You'll be with me, Gwen with Bobby."

"All right," Demeroven says, allowing Beth to lead him back to one of the courts.

Bobby forces himself to focus on Gwen, rather than continue trying to figure out what the hell just happened. "Are we teaming up so we'll win and you'll start smiling instead of grimacing?" Bobby asks.

"I'm perfectly fine," Gwen says, her arm tight around his. "Are you trying to distract me from whatever heated moment we just interrupted?"

"Oh, get off," Bobby says, nudging her. "He's a bit difficult is all."

"Seems like it, doesn't it?" Gwen agrees as they reach the pitch.

Bobby stoops to grab rackets for them and they separate to face off against Beth and Demeroven across the net.

"But perhaps he'll grow on you," Gwen says, lowering into a ready stance.

"Like fungus?" Bobby wonders, smiling as Gwen lets out a loud *hah*.

"Like big mushrooms, yes," Gwen says.

"Are you ready to lose?" Beth asks loudly.

"Yeah, right," Bobby says, winking at Gwen. He'll shake off his encounter with Demeroven by wiping the floor with him. "As if you could beat me and Gwen. We've decades of experience."

"Against each other," Beth agrees, serving the shuttlecock. "But James and I are unknowns. We have the element of surprise, don't we, James?"

"Right," Demeroven says, seemingly caught between bemusement at his cousin's competitive edge and pride at being included. "We're, um, crafty."

"Ah, yes, the craft of badminton," Bobby says, returning Demeroven's rally. "Did you study that at Oxford? Learned the art of the shuttlecock?"

He's not exactly sure why it comes out quite . . . like that, but the way Demeroven's gaze darkens begs a challenge.

"Not as well as you did, apparently," Demeroven returns.

Bobby clenches his jaw. The chip on this guy's shoulder . . .

"Is there really a course in badminton at Oxford?" Beth wonders as she and Gwen trade hits.

"No, no. But some colleges were more interested in it than others," Bobby says, watching as Demeroven's face flushes.

"And some halls in particular. Badminton boys had their own little clubs and everything, really," Demeroven says.

"Been to a few of those, have you?" Bobby asks, hitting the shuttlecock a bit too hard so it sails out of bounds.

"Not nearly as many as you. I'm far more discerning about where I spend my time, and with whom," Demeroven says stiffly, waiting patiently as Beth retrieves the off-sides shuttlecock.

"Have we missed something?" she asks Gwen. She serves the shuttlecock across the net again.

"It appears so. Albie's never mentioned anything about . . . badminton clubs."

"He wouldn't," Demeroven and Bobby say together.

Demeroven narrows his eyes at Bobby, almost missing Gwen's volley. But not quite. He sends the shuttlecock careening over the net and Bobby has to jog backward to hit it, only narrowly sending it back. Beth vaults forward and hits the shuttlecock, but tumbles to the ground in the process.

"Must you always be so reckless?" Demeroven exclaims at Bobby as he goes to help Beth up.

Bobby stands gaping. It's not like he meant for her to fall. Gwen hits the shuttlecock over their heads to land in the back third.

"Hah!" she crows.

"That's just low," Beth says, sticking out her tongue.

"I guess Bobby and I are rather unpredictable as well," Gwen says smugly.

"Oh, you're plenty predictable," Beth returns, with exasperated fondness. "Him," she adds, pointing at Bobby, "maybe a little."

"I do aim to be disarming," Bobby manages as she comes back to standing. "You all right?"

"It takes far more than grass stains on my gown to do me in," Beth says, taking the shuttlecock from Demeroven to line up to serve again.

"*My* gown," Gwen mutters. "Mrs. Stelm will have my hide, not hers."

"Oh, posh, she'll be glad to get out from underneath Mrs. Gilpe's and Miss Wilson's word games," Bobby says.

Gwen's housekeeper, Mrs. Gilpe, and her lady's maid, Mrs. Stelm, were a force to be reckoned with before, but with the addition of Beth and Aunt Cordelia's lady's maid in the mix? They're a terror unto themselves now.

"Truly dreadful," Gwen agrees. "Do you like the London staff, Demeroven?"

"Oh, uh, I guess," Demeroven says as he hits the shuttlecock back to Gwen. "Don't know them all that well."

"Except for your cook, right?" Beth asks. "My lady's maid, Miss Wilson, said he's been with your mother since you were small. He has a brother in town somewhere?"

Demeroven's face goes slightly pale. "Ah, yes, he does."

"Runs a club, I think," Bobby says, feeling triumphant when the color in Demeroven's face drains even further.

"Oh, well, you should be a shoo-in there, then," Beth says brightly.

"Perhaps," Demeroven says, his voice halting and high. "Point," he adds, spiking the shuttlecock over the net in a kill shot Bobby can't hope to catch.

"Well, it's one-one, then," Beth says.

"What club have you chosen, Mason?" Demeroven asks, staring pointedly at Bobby.

"I haven't," Bobby says honestly. "Been trying a few out."

"Ah, yes, well, that tracks, doesn't it?"

Bobby hits the shuttlecock across the net, imagining it's Demeroven's smug face. "Wouldn't want to settle on a decision without doing proper research, would I?"

"Even if it could make you look indecisive?" Demeroven returns.

The most infuriating part of all of this is that Demeroven looks unfairly good right now. Heaving in air, all riled up, his face flushed. Bobby feels a flare of want deep in his gut. He bends down and snags the shuttlecock, squeezing too tight against that clench in his belly. He will not be attracted to sodding James Demeroven. He won't. He'll just . . . push that down like everything else.

He lines up to serve. "Actually, bothering to do research makes me informed, not indecisive. You might know the feeling if you were doing even half the work Albie is."

He serves the shuttlecock hard over the net, but Demeroven's ready, rallying it back with enough force that Bobby has to jerk to the side to hit it across to Beth.

"Oh, right, because your gambling and drinking and cavorting is a much better example to the ton," Demeroven grits out.

"At least I'm able to make a decent impression. I'm not the one stumbling out of clubs and running away," Bobby says, feeling a catch in his chest the moment the words are out of his mouth.

Gwen hits the shuttlecock across toward Demeroven, but he doesn't move. It sails over his head as he stares at Bobby, wide-eyed. No matter what kind of arse the man is being, he didn't deserve that.

"Demeroven, I—" Bobby starts.

Demeroven's face shifts, a look of determination falling over him. "No, you've all the arrogance and disregard for decorum of your father, haven't you?" Demeroven says. "Well on your way to being an even bigger disgrace than he was."

Bobby stands there slack-jawed and winded. Beth and Gwen look between them, rackets held awkwardly, all of them still. Demeroven runs a hand through his tousled hair, chest heaving. He meets Bobby's gaze, looking as shocked as Bobby feels.

Bobby would say something back—something cutting, something apologetic, something . . . something—but he can't seem to make anything pass around the sudden lump in his throat. His own words were cruel, he knows. But he didn't think Demeroven's could feel like a knife in his chest like this.

"I didn't— It wasn't—" Demeroven starts, meeting Bobby's eyes, breathless and seemingly horrified. But he doesn't manage an apology. Then again, neither does Bobby.

After a charged, truly dreadful moment, Demeroven cuts his eyes away from Bobby's. He stumbles back and picks up the shuttlecock. "Point," he rasps out, hitting it forcefully across the net.

Neither Bobby nor Gwen makes any move to rally and it glides over them to land in the back third of their court.

Demeroven fiddles with his jacket buttons, glancing among them. "I'll, ah, see you later, ladies. Please give my apologies to Lady Steton. I've . . . work to do. Excuse me."

He drops his racket and walks around Beth, almost jogging out of the garden.

"Bobby, are you—" Beth starts.

"I'm fine," Bobby says automatically, offering Beth and then Gwen a tight, forced smile. "I'll go get a drink, cool off."

"Right," Gwen says. "Bring some back for us, yeah?"

"Yeah," Bobby says, stumbling off toward the drinks, his hands curling into fists at his side.

He came to this tea planning to help Demeroven become more at ease. And instead, it feels like he's been punched in the chest. All he wanted to do was help—to find something in common, to maybe be something other than uncomfortable acquaintances together—but how can he, if that's Demeroven's opinion of Bobby's father—of Bobby's family?

And how could he just let the prick . . . say that? He didn't defend himself, or his father—he just let Demeroven walk away, again. Not only does it seem like he's going to fail Uncle Dashiell, and Beth, but he's failing Albie too, and his father's memory, for whatever that's worth.

CHAPTER SIX

James

"She isn't that bad," Miss Bertram insists, glaring at Lady Gwen as they sit smushed on the opposite carriage bench. They're both in simple work dresses with aprons, ready for a shift at the Foundling Hospital.

James, fidgeting in his stiff suit, isn't entirely sure how he ended up escorting them today, nor how he got roped into speaking with the head physician, Dr. Holting, for the Medical Act standing committee. Now he's trapped in his carriage with his cousin and her stepsister, who have been having a row that he's desperately been trying to follow since he picked them up. Neither has made any comment about his abrupt retreat from the Steton tea at the top of the week, not that there's been a break in the argument to do so.

"My apologies—please, remind me, what is the situation with Lady Ashmond?" James asks, wanting to make at least some effort to add to the conversation. Both women turn to look at him, their frustration cascading around the carriage. "If . . . you don't mind explaining."

"Lady Ashmond is the former wife of Lord Ashmond," Miss Bertram says, nudging Lady Gwen before she can get a word out. "They divorced six months ago."

"And she's your supervisor at the hospital?" James asks,

glancing between them. You could cut the tension with a knife, though he doesn't totally understand why.

"She oversees all the volunteers, yes," Miss Bertram says stiffly.

"And keeps coming by to see how Beth is every single time," Lady Gwen adds. "Hovering."

"Which is kind of her, given I'm the reason she got divorced in the first place," Miss Bertram exclaims.

"Beg pardon?" James asks. How could his cousin—sweet, calm, lovely Miss Bertram—have broken up a marriage?

"Lord Montson is Lady Ashmond's son," Lady Gwen says slowly, as if he isn't actually listening.

"Right," he says. "I know, but I don't under—"

Miss Bertram sighs. "Ending my engagement to Lord Montson rather precipitated Lady Ashmond filing for a divorce," she explains.

"Ah," he says, struggling to follow. "Well, um, it's nice that she's being polite, I suppose, then? Is she otherwise a good manager?"

Lady Gwen opens her mouth and Miss Bertram elbows her. "Surprisingly, yes. She's very dedicated to the work and seems to enjoy it. Perhaps over time we shall get to know her better."

"I don't see why we should even bot—"

"Do shut it, would you?" Miss Bertram says, looking over at Lady Gwen, who glowers back before staring moodily out the window.

They ride in an uncomfortable silence for a while. James had heard rumors of Miss Bertram's rather abrupt refusal to marry Lord Montson, just a day before the wedding. Everything about the previous season confuses him, and no one seems to want to discuss it directly—the engagement between Miss Bertram and Lord Montson, his stepfather's handling of Lady Havenfort's marriage settlement before James came of age, the way in which James, and his stepfather by proxy, took ownership of the Demeroven townhouse—it's all a little hazy.

"Cousin, I wonder if I might impose upon you to discuss—" James starts, hoping perhaps this might be his chance to set the record straight.

But the carriage trundles through the redbrick arch of the Foundling Hospital's courtyard, heading for the tall, three-story maternity wing before he can finish the thought.

Miss Bertram looks across the carriage, but James shakes his head, giving her a false easy smile. He would hardly know what to ask exactly, anyway.

They pull to a stop on the left side of the courtyard, where a cluster of children run about, playing games, tossing balls, and getting fresh air. Lady Gwen and Miss Bertram hop out before he can even think of helping them, not looking at each other. Lady Gwen heads straight for a pack of children, who all beam up at her, inviting her into their game immediately.

"She can be a right brat, but she's very good with them," Miss Bertram tells him once he's closed the carriage door.

She offers her arm and he takes it, allowing her to lead him through the double doors into the maternity wing. "I believe you'll head up to the second floor to find Dr. Holting," she says, gesturing to a broad staircase with windows that overlook the courtyard. "And we'll see you for boating tomorrow with Mr. Mason, yes?"

James forces himself to smile and squeeze her hand, even though the very thought of Bobby Mason turns his stomach to ice. He lets her walk away, watching as she heads for another set of double doors further down the hall. A tall, willowy woman in a voluminous white gown and a green apron steps out and immediately takes Miss Bertram's arm.

"Miss Bertram, do come in. Little Martha has been asking for you. Come this way."

James watches the doors swing shut behind them and stands there at the bottom of the stairs, unsure of how to react to all of it. To his cousin and her stepsister's charged argument, Miss Bertram's history with the Ashmond family—to the strange sense of remove that envelops him as he turns slowly and climbs the stairs.

He should know more about his cousin and her life, about the events of the previous season that everyone seems to allude to but never fully discuss. Why didn't he ever ask his stepfather about his cousin and aunt? Was he so wrapped up in his own impending misery that it never occurred to him to check on the only other family he has left?

Even Bobby Mason has a better relationship with Miss Bertram than he does. But he's not going to think about Bobby Mason today. He's not going to think about the way that cracked, crestfallen look on Mason's face pounded against his chest. He's not going to think about the way he felt every ounce the pillock he's always worried he is as he fled the Steton tea.

He has parliament work to do. Important things to accomplish, even if he didn't volunteer for the duty. So he heads up the stairs, trying to banish all thoughts of Mason, of Lord Havenfort, of his cousin and her mother. And of the way that he feels disconnected from all of them, despite their constant and unnerving forced proximity.

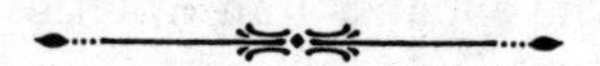

"DID YOU HAVE a good time boating with your cousin today, dearest?" his mother asks, forcing him to look up from his steak across the overlarge mahogany table the next evening.

"Um, yes," he says slowly, grimacing a smile for his mother.

She looks tired, swimming in her ill-fitting gray gown. Not one of those she's had altered so far this season, though she's yet to attend any formal events. He would have just taken his meal in the kitchen, but he had the misfortune to return home just as his mother and stepfather were sitting down for one of their sullen dinners. Now Stepfather's at the head of the table, as usual.

"If you're wasting time courting, you may as well find some women who might actually marry you," Stepfather grumbles around a full mouth.

"My cousin and Lady Gwen introduced me to some of their friends," James says quickly, hoping to stall any talk of courting before his mother can get going on all her plans to have lovely young ladies over for dinner.

"Havenfort's family will do you no favors. You ought to be chumming up to the conservative lords, poaching their daughters. We'll need a good dowry to buy another townhouse."

And now he wants *another* townhouse, not just a different one. London is only sharpening his stepfather's ambitions, and it makes James' chest tight.

"How is Lady Havenfort?" his mother asks.

"She's—" James starts.

"I heard from Lord Constance today that he's making excellent inroads with the railroad companies. You might consider partnering up with him to help improve the legislation for land acquisition. Put us in good stead to get investment stock," Stepfather says loudly, launching into a long rant about railroad stocks, plans, and the expansion in America.

James' mother's eyes lose what little sparkle they had when dinner began, and she looks down at her food, leaving James to hum at intervals for his stepfather. His whole day has been conversations taking place around him, not with him. Why should he imagine it would be any different at home?

It bothers him, this newfound unease with being ignored. In the country, he was fine living his own life, avoiding his stepfather and mother as much as possible while making himself useful as best he could in Epworth. But the way his cousin and Lady Gwen talked around him while they boated today seemed somehow pointed, and it's eating at him.

It's not only Miss Bertram and Lady Gwen who seem indifferent to James, either. The way Lord Mason and Lord Havenfort discuss so much in his presence but rarely actually engage him in conversation about the Medical Act speaks volumes. Though perhaps the information he gathered yesterday at the hospital could help with that.

The only person who *has* actively tried to engage him is Bobby Mason, and James has gone and chased him off. He didn't bother to show for their boating outing, and James can't quite blame him. All he's managed to do is insult the man. But he can't seem to help it.

He knows, logically, that Mason is only trying to find something for them to have in common, but the way he's been prying into James' secrets, trying to get him to admit to things in plain daylight that he's only ever told other men in the dark of night (if they spoke at all) . . . He doesn't want to feel so exposed every time they talk, raw and strangely wanting.

With Raverson roaming around, he can't risk becoming vulnerable or honest about . . . anything. Raverson knows too much already; James can't give him more ammunition. He's sure Mason will give up eventually and let him be.

"You wouldn't believe what some of the men on Havenfort's side get up to. Squiring their mistresses about with abandon—" Stepfather says.

James blinks over at him, unsure of how they got from railroads to adultery. If a public mistress is a bridge too far for his stepfather, what would he think of James frequenting clubs like D'Vere?

No, Mason's cavalier attitude about his persuasion, his penchant for discussing things in public, for trying to be open and honest in a ton that would shun him for far less than buggery—Mason is not the person to befriend. Much less . . . anything else. Better to let him think James is a lout than to court misfortune.

Not that Bobby Mason would ever want anything else with James. He has better options. And they can't get through a single conversation anyway. More importantly, James isn't interested. It was a schoolboy fancy of his, nothing more. The real Bobby Mason isn't someone to pine after. No matter how much those fleeting moments of détente with Mason tug at his youthful crush, James knows there can be nothing between him and Bobby Mason.

"Not hungry, Viscount? Stuffed yourself with free food with Havenfort's daughter? Is she trying to woo you into making a donation to that damn hospital?" Stepfather asks.

James shakes his head. "No, no. Just there for parliament. You know I—" He pauses, forcing a bland smile onto his face. "You know we discuss all the Demeroven donations."

Stepfather grunts and goes back to his rant about . . . racehorses?

James can't keep living like this. At least in Epworth he could escape into the countryside—take solace in his own silence. There, silence was golden, peaceful, and restorative. But more of these dinners, more of the meetings, more of the courting activities with everyone talking around him but not to him . . . Bobby Mason might not be the friend he should have, but James needs to renew his search to find someone he can talk to—someone, anyone, who will talk to him in return.

Chapter Seven

Bobby

"You are being an absolute bore, you know," Prince says, placing a fresh drink down in front of Bobby where he's collapsed into an armchair in the back corner by the window.

"Yes, well, perhaps it's this dreary party you've thrown," Bobby says, enjoying the burn of whisky down his throat.

He looks around the room at the motley collection of school friends, heirs, and spares Prince has assembled for the evening. It's a slapdash, after-the-fact engagement celebration, and, for reasons unknown to Bobby, Prince is holding it in the back room of his townhouse, rather than, oh, absolutely anywhere else.

There's nowhere to hide back here, in Prince's father's over-large sitting room, filled with stuffy chairs and card tables. In a different situation, Bobby might have found a good book to read among the hundreds of leather tomes that line the walls, but it's far too noisy for that.

All of the chaps clustered around the room were a year above Bobby in school. None of their mutual D'Vere crowd is in attendance either. And of course, Albie isn't here. He and Uncle Dashiell are working all night, consolidating their research on the Medical Act. But Albie insisted Bobby attend Prince's party. One of them had to show up.

"Cheer up," Prince cajoles. "You're among friends."

"Your friends," Bobby grouses, hoping it sounds playful.

By Prince's frown, he doesn't quite succeed. "Do we need to get you laid?" Prince asks.

He barely manages to keep from snorting whisky through his nose. "Hardly likely among this lot," Bobby coughs out.

Prince looks about the room. "Touché. Then later this week. We'll give Parker a call. Unless you'd be willing to let Catherine set you up."

Bobby looks over at Prince and plunks his glass down onto the side table. "Do you really think your fiancée can solve this problem?"

"She knows many lovely young ladies," Prince defends.

"If the object is to get me laid, that is not the way to go about it," Bobby says.

"Ah, right, their virtue. Well, I'm sure she knows some women outside of the ton too."

Bobby stares at Prince. It's not their virtue he's concerned with, though of course he would never try to take anyone's. "Prince."

"She does know an opera singer, I think. Or perhaps she's a dancer? I can never keep up, active social life and all."

"I am not interested in an opera singer, or a dancer," Bobby says, watching as Prince continues to ponder. "Prince," he says, waiting until the man meets his eyes. "I am not . . . like you."

Prince considers him. "Open to love?"

"Not the way you've found it, no, I don't think," Bobby says. "Honestly, I'm surprised you have," he adds softly, glancing around. They're in the back corner and no one's paying them any attention.

He wants to understand how Prince went from frequenting Parker's club every night to happily engaged.

"I didn't think I would either, really," Prince says with a shrug. "But I met Catherine and that was it."

"And it didn't matter that she wasn't . . . like your other lovers?" Bobby asks, afraid even with their relative seclusion to say it too plainly.

"Not at all," Prince says easily. "Feels the same. Actually, it feels better. I've never loved anyone like I love Catherine."

"Oh," Bobby says, forcing a smile.

"It doesn't matter, to me," Prince adds, seeming to see through Bobby's curiosity. "I thought it did, for a while, but Catherine was the exception. Or maybe I just hadn't met the right girls before. I don't know. I feel just as passionate about Catherine when I'm with her as I ever did with any of the . . . others."

Bobby looks down into his drink. Is it just a matter of meeting the right woman? He doesn't think so. If it were, surely he'd have felt a stirring in his gut, a tightness, a *something*, when looking at the most beautiful girls of the season. Surely dancing with them would have felt like *more*.

He doesn't know how to ask the question. It feels embarrassing, like laying his heart onto the center of the low table for Prince to see. And especially given that Prince has seen everything else he has to offer, and clearly it didn't stir nearly as much in him as Miss Langston does, Bobby's not sure he could take further scrutiny.

"But that's just me," Prince says.

Bobby blinks and looks up from his drink to meet Prince's knowing gaze. "Sorry?"

"Plenty of chaps have told me they couldn't do it. Or could only marry a woman with the mutual understanding it would be a marriage in name only."

"Oh," Bobby says, feeling his chest unclench just a little. Perhaps it's not just him, then.

"Demeroven said as much, actually. Did I tell you he's coming to the stag night?"

"The stag night?" Bobby asks, feeling the words like a jab to the ribs. Prince asked Demeroven before him?

Prince asked Demeroven to attend his stag night?

"Blast. My apologies, old boy, I guess I took it as a given you'd be there. Just over a month, the twelfth of June, night before the wedding. Cunningham's supposed to be planning it with you, actually. Bugger, man, I'm sorry."

Bobby waves him off, mollified by Prince's polite horror. "Excellent, Cunningham throws a wonderful shindig. Much better than this sorry affair. Where is he, anyway?"

"Here they are now," Prince says, nodding toward the door before he stands and makes his way across the room.

Bobby watches him go. Watches as he greets Cunningham, Demeroven stepping in behind him, all of them jovial and bright. Bobby downs the rest of his drink. Not only will Demeroven ruin Prince's party for him, but now he's here cavorting with Prince and Cunningham—stealing them from Bobby, more like.

He fiddles with his signet ring. It feels like his limbs might jitter themselves right off his body. He's not going to let Demeroven get to him like this. He doesn't owe the man anything, and Demeroven doesn't owe him anything either. Clearly, if his words at the tea party last week were any measure. They don't have to like each other at all. Nor spend any time together, Bobby decides.

He stands, determined to find a group of people to talk to, but he hasn't taken two steps when Cunningham grabs his arm.

"Ah, Mason, excellent. We need a fourth for whist."

Bobby grimaces, but doesn't pull out of his hold. It's one thing for him and Demeroven to behave like cavemen in front of Beth and Gwen. But he can't be that rude in front of Prince when he's invited them both to the stag night.

And so he finds himself seated beside Demeroven at Prince's

small card table, watching Demeroven expertly shuffle the deck. He looks at ease now in an open collar, suspenders, and a loose frock coat. Nothing like the tightly wound prick he traded insults with last week.

Which is a problem, because he looks sodding good like this too. If the man was just atrocious to look at, Bobby might not feel so twisted up. But those damn blue eyes peer up at him and he feels his chest tighten against his will.

"Are you a better whist player than a badminton player?" Demeroven asks, eyes bright, a smile playing at his lips.

Handsome or not, Bobby's not quite ready to make nice. "In a fair game, absolutely."

"Oh, was there dirty badminton at the Steton do? Thought I saw you on the courts," Cunningham says. "What am I saying? Of course there was. Your cousin was there, wasn't she, Mason?"

Bobby looks over at Cunningham. "Lady Gwen?"

"She plays like a demon," Prince puts in. "Beats the pants off everyone."

"Actually, Miss Bertram and I beat Lady Gwen and Mason," Demeroven says as he begins dealing out the cards.

"Really?" Prince asks, glancing at Bobby in surprise. "No one ever beats Lady Gwen."

"Honestly, it's Miss Bertram you should really be watching out for," Bobby says. "Demeroven skated by on her prowess."

"I'd hardly say I skated," Demeroven says, flipping the final card. "Trump is spades, gentlemen," he says, gesturing for everyone to take their cards. "I believe my cousin and I are simply a team well suited."

"Suited, he's funny," Cunningham says.

Bobby turns the first trick, playing his two of diamonds. He tries to ignore Demeroven fidgeting beside him.

"Always was a cutup on the sculls," Prince says.

"I wouldn't have guessed," Bobby says, hearing the snide edge to his voice as Prince plays a five of diamonds on his two.

It bothers him that Prince seems to know only the funny, charming version of Demeroven Bobby's briefly seen in flashes.

"Yes, well, you are fond of assumptions, aren't you?" Demeroven replies. "Isn't he?" he adds to Cunningham.

"I suppose," Cunningham says, glancing at Prince's five and then at his own hand.

"Oh, stop stalling and play, Cunningham," Prince says, exasperated. "He always does this," he adds for Demeroven's sake.

It's why Bobby loves a hand of whist with Cunningham. Gives you enough time for a few sips, and Cunningham's lethargy always allows Bobby to recall the suits. Unfortunately, it seems the same goes for Demeroven, who's lightning fast to lay down a ten of diamonds on Cunningham's six of clubs.

"I was thinking we'd make the stag night a pub crawl, complete with hats," Cunningham says, winking at Prince.

"Hats," Bobby repeats.

"Gaudy ones," Cunningham says brightly. "Not quite sure where to get them, but we could even have letters sewn on in honor of Prince's stag night."

"I don't think we should have any identification on us if it's to be a pub crawl," Prince says while Bobby hesitates to lay down his next card. He has a jack, but has the sneaking suspicion that Demeroven has a king.

"My mother has found a most garish modiste. I'm sure I could persuade her to make them for us if I go in at an off hour," Demeroven says.

"Perfect," Cunningham says.

"When would you have time to visit a modiste for personalized hats?" Bobby wonders, watching Prince mull over his next hand.

They're a contemplative batch of card players, and he can tell it's starting to grate on Demeroven.

"I'll go when parliament's in session, at high tea time," Demeroven says, tossing an ace down on top of Cunningham's triumphantly played king. Blast.

"You're going to skip a parliamentary session for hats?" Bobby asks, indignant.

Demeroven shrugs as he gathers the trick. "There'll be another."

"Yes, another," Cunningham says, glomming on to the last word, as is his habit when he's not really listening. He grabs his empty glass. "Prince, help me get the next round."

Prince holds up a finger to pause their game before following Cunningham back toward the kitchen. Demeroven sighs gustily.

"Why are you here?" Bobby asks, the whisky and his general dour mood leaving his tongue loose and emotions high.

"I beg your pardon?" Demeroven turns to look at him, the two of them sitting close at the far side of the table, pressed up to the wall.

"You should be at Uncle Dashiell's tonight with Albie, working. And instead, you're here, planning hat nonsense."

This close, he's scruffier than Bobby realized, like he hasn't shaved in about a day, his eyes slightly bloodshot. "You seem to think my entire life has to revolve around preparations for parliamentary sessions, as if most of the lords don't spend the entire season drunk or coughing up smoke."

"And you're fine with that," Bobby deduces. "The elder lords don't care, so why should you? All that power, all that money, all that social capital just thrust under your nose and you're happy to let it slip through your fingers because it's too much work?"

"You don't know what you're talking about," Demeroven says, his voice a few degrees cooler.

"I know you're squandering the biggest opportunity—a position most men would kill for. A position your cousin and her mother almost ended up on the street for. And you're going to piss it away. Coast by on the title you were handed and make nothing of yourself."

Demeroven stares at him, his eyes now wide, face curiously blank. It makes Bobby even angrier. "Don't act like you don't understand," he hisses. "You're smarter than that."

"*You* don't understand," Demeroven says, glaring at Bobby before something over Bobby's shoulder catches his eye.

Bobby turns his head, but can't see anything or anyone, and by the time he's turned back, Demeroven's face has settled into that impenetrable mask again.

"You'll never have the kind of responsibility that's been foisted on me, so I suggest you stop telling me how to live my life as if you have any idea what you're talking about before you further embarrass yourself, or your family. Excuse me."

Bobby sits there gaping as Demeroven mechanically stands and walks straight out of the party, like a man possessed by a detached ghost. Bobby stares after him, rage simmering in his chest. The man keeps getting the last word by fleeing. And still, somehow, he's coming out on top every time.

Bobby tosses his cards into the center of the table. He needs a way to forget these wretched weeks. Needs to drown his discontent until he can barely feel it. Until the image of Demeroven's wide eyes fades from his mind.

Forget whatever Uncle Dashiell and Beth want from him. He

won't spend more time on a newly titled viscount who's willing to throw away his power because it's slightly inconvenient.

Bobby marches determinedly toward the kitchen, where Prince has his valet tending bar. In his haste, he nearly collides with Lord Raverson in the hallway.

"In a hurry?" Raverson asks.

Bobby tilts on his feet. Perhaps he doesn't need that third drink after all. "My apologies, Lord Raverson," Bobby says, hoping he sounds more composed than he feels. "And no, just headed for the bar, actually. How are you?" he adds, trying to muster up the polite disinterest a man of Raverson's station deserves. Though in truth, since his arrival last season, from the little Bobby's heard, Raverson's making rather a name for himself within the community. If the rumors are true, he's already slept with a number of Parker's clientele.

Bobby can't blame them. Raverson's striking dark eyes and chiseled jaw would be temptation enough even without the title and all the money that comes with it. The Raverson estate doesn't bring in an immense income, but Raverson's always flush with cash, talking up investments and dividends each time Bobby's been within earshot at the club. And now he's here, and looking at Bobby with distinct interest.

Bafflingly, Bobby thinks for a moment of Demeroven's eyes, softer and deeper and more mysterious than the blatant want in Raverson's. But he shakes himself. He's not going to give Demeroven another second's thought tonight.

"I'm well, I'm well. Saw you were talking to Demeroven earlier. Piece of work, isn't he?"

Bobby blinks. So much for his mental fortitude. "I . . . suppose."

"Hardly worth the effort if you were looking to bark up that particular tree," Raverson continues.

"I, ah, well . . ." Bobby stammers, unsure how to react to Raverson so blatantly discussing not just his proclivities, but in reference to Demeroven, of all people.

"I found him . . . trifling, at best," Raverson says.

"You did?" Bobby asks, his throat dry, whether from the smoldering look Raverson's giving him or the shock of Raverson mentioning his . . . whatever Demeroven is to him.

Raverson inches closer. "Though it was a few years ago. He could have progressed, gained some more experience."

His hand lands next to Bobby's head against the wall Bobby's suddenly backed into. Raverson smiles at him, dark hair swooshed across his forehead, eyes glinting, teeth white and bright.

Something dangerous and wild simmers in Bobby's gut. He knows he should walk away. Raverson's already exhibited more than one danger sign, discussing things so openly here in the hallway, and worse, sharing the intimate details of another man. But at the same time, that edge, and his smile, and his free-spirited openness are appealing.

If Bobby were looking for something to distract him, something to topple headfirst into, well, Raverson just might be it.

"And are you more . . . experienced?" Bobby hears himself ask, his voice deep and husky.

Raverson smiles slyly, his cheeks dimpling in a devastatingly handsome way. He leans forward, putting his lips close enough to Bobby's ear that he can feel his breath. "Experienced enough to notice the bulge in your trousers."

Bobby slips a little against the wall. "Fuck," he mutters.

"That is the idea. There's a closet back this way, if you're looking for something to do."

"Or someone?" Bobby asks as Raverson pulls back.

Raverson's smile stretches. "I like you, Mason."

Bobby lets out a slightly strangled laugh and finds himself

following Raverson down the hall and further into the servants' quarters. And though he knows it's reckless, he lets Raverson pull him into the closet—loses himself in the tug and gasp and heat of a clandestine encounter.

He doesn't think about Demeroven at all, except to note that it's poetic that a man who found Demeroven a disappointment could take such pride in melting Bobby into a puddle of want.

Chapter Eight

James

"They are making a spectacle of themselves."

James glances down the stands through a sea of top hats and bonnets to spot Mason, Lady Gwen, and Miss Bertram. They are indeed garnering a lot of attention heckling Lord Mason, who has the misfortune to be on the field today. James' stepfather insisted they attend the Cambridge vs. Oxford alumni rugby scrimmage, and James couldn't come up with a reasonable excuse.

James doesn't enjoy watching his former classmates and whatever relation-in-law Lord Mason is to him being injured on the field. No matter how much Lady Gwen and Mason seem to revel in it.

So instead of watching, James sits and stews, trying to find the words to ask his stepfather to either confirm or deny Mason's accusation about Miss Bertram and Lady Havenfort from Prince's party, here, where he can't walk away. The thought has left him with a sour stomach all week.

He doesn't know why Mason would lie. And the strained discussions Lady Gwen and Miss Bertram keep having, about Miss Bertram's almost-marriage to Viscount Montson last season . . .

The past two years his stepfather has told him his aunt, Lady Demeroven—Lady Havenfort now—wanted nothing from her late husband and refused his stepfather's offers of funds from James' inheritance while he was acting as executor. But James isn't sure why he ever believed that.

He needs to confront his stepfather, tell him it was craven and horrible to leave their relatives with nothing, to put them in the position of either needing to marry or become destitute. That they owe Lady Havenfort and Miss Bertram a sincere apology, and reparations for their actions.

Because despite not being aware of what happened, James feels guilt burrowing deep into his gut. He should have asked. Even before he came of age and took over the title, he should have pushed his stepfather, should have done *something* to assert himself, rather than tumbling arse backward into his seat.

"Sir," he says, blurting the word out before he can properly brace for the conversation. Thinking about it too hard will only lead him to chicken out, like he always does.

His stepfather lets out a loud whoop when one of the teams scores on the other. James doesn't even remember whom he's meant to be supporting.

"Sir," he tries again, squaring his shoulders. "We need to discuss—"

"Ah, Lord Demeroven."

James turns and feels his spine go rigid. Lord Raverson has vaulted up to scooch into the seat beside him. He's even more resplendent in daylight, and somehow twice as ominous a presence.

"Lord Raverson," James forces out, gritting his teeth against both regret and foreboding.

"You must be the viscount's stepfather—Mr. Griggs, isn't it? I'm Lord Raverson," Raverson continues, leaning across James to extend his hand.

And that, of course, his stepfather hears. "Raverson, did you say?" he asks, turning to take Raverson's hand, further pressing James into the back of the stands.

"Indeed. I believe you knew my father," Raverson says, all charm, flashing those bright, straight teeth at James' stepfather, who looks delighted to be recognized.

It's all he's ever wanted, after all.

"I did, I did," Stepfather says. "Stand-up man, truly fought for his ideals. He and Demeroven's uncle were allies."

"Oh, I know," Raverson says, retracting his hand slowly so it brushes against James' chest. James shivers. "My father spoke regularly of his and the late Lord Demeroven's combined efforts to push through their agenda, and that's exactly how I plan to comport myself in the Lords now. Fighting for what's right."

"Excellent," Stepfather says. "You can help Demeroven here have an opinion. He's always been a bit noncommittal. You knew each other at school?"

Raverson looks to James, all wide-eyed innocence, forcing James to grit out a tight "Yes, we did."

"Splendid. Good to know there's at least one positive influence for the sorry lad. No insult intended, Demeroven," Stepfather says.

James shrugs jerkily, though there was very much insult intended. He should feel more irritated that his stepfather is willfully undermining him in public, but he's too busy fighting the clutch of panic in his chest. His stepfather and Raverson being so close—Raverson being here at all—is terrifying.

"Perhaps I could take you to lunch sometime soon, sir. Pick your brain about the agenda," Raverson says. "I'd appreciate your counsel. I know how much the late Lord Demeroven relied on your sage advice."

What utter sniveling, two-faced drivel—

"Of course. I would be delighted, Viscount. It would be marvelous to discuss the agenda with a man who truly understands. I'll have my valet arrange it," Stepfather says.

"I look forward to it," Raverson says, nudging James.

Stepfather nods brightly and then looks back to the game, immediately engrossed in the intense scrum on the field. Leaving James sandwiched between his stepfather and Raverson, on the edge of a panic attack.

Stepfather hasn't let James get a word in edgewise on the agenda, just barked his instructions, as if James couldn't possibly have any opinions of his own on the matter. And now he's going to lunch with Raverson? James has never been worth his time; it stands to reason he'll be looking for a replacement son while he's here in London. What a happy accident that Stepfather gets what he wants and gets to demean James in the process.

But what does Raverson get out of it?

"What are you doing?" James asks, impressed that it comes out as anything more than a strangled whisper.

"Watching rugby," Raverson says, winking at him.

James clenches his fists and nudges Raverson, forcing him a little further down the bench so James can scoot a few feet away from his stepfather. Raverson shifts without comment, pulling out his handkerchief to blow his nose.

"Why are you inviting my stepfather to lunch?" James demands, watching Raverson meticulously fold the handkerchief into a delicate series of small triangles.

"You must use your contacts, Demeroven. First rule of parliament."

James narrows his eyes just as something exciting happens on the field. A goal, a scrum, a dance break, he isn't sure. The uproar from the crowd is immediate, including Raverson, who shouts gleefully. But the loudest in attendance by far are Lady Gwen and Mason, hooting for much longer than the rest, and then breaking into giggles while Miss Bertram watches them fondly.

James finds his eyes stuck on the three of them, envy gnawing at his gut. There they are, happy and carefree. How is it fair that Bobby Mason gets a loving family, and he has . . . this?

"Awfully conspicuous, aren't they?" Raverson asks, bringing James' attention back to his smarmy, beautiful face.

James feels a frustrating need to defend his cousin, which means he has to defend the lot of them. "They're enjoying themselves."

"Yes, they do like their pleasures, don't they?" Raverson asks, before whipping the handkerchief back out to sneeze.

"You still have hay fever?" James wonders, frowning as Raverson makes a show of folding the handkerchief again.

And then James' blood runs cold. That's Mason's handkerchief. The one he used to try to clean James up that night at Parker's club. White with little yellow daisies. Dainty and lovely, and in Raverson's hand, covered with Raverson's snot.

It could be nothing, James rationalizes. Mason offered it to him to wipe his own vomit; it's not like it's a treasured possession.

But then James thinks of his own handkerchief, the one Raverson kept and used in all of their mutual classes, at all of their social gatherings. A token as if to say: *Look what I know about you. Look how intimate we've been. Look what I could tell all these people.*

If Raverson has Mason's handkerchief—

Mason whoops again down the stands.

"He is loud, isn't he?" Raverson remarks, twisting the handkerchief between his fingers.

"I suppose," James manages, glancing over at Mason. He blinks against an onslaught of images of Mason and Raverson . . . together. It twists something in his stomach, horror and arousal mixing into nausea.

"You know, he's loud during other activities too," Raverson continues, with such a carefully calculated, casual air. Like he lets these things slip in subtle ways all the time. Which James knows he does.

"What are you planning to do with this information?" James asks, wincing at his own lack of tact. But that pressure in his chest is growing larger. If Raverson knows about both Mason and James, the damage he could find a way to inflict on both of their families with just a little more proof—

"Oh, nothing. Yet," Raverson says, shrugging and leaning back against the stands in a stretch that does everything to accentuate the lithe, long line of his body. "But it's always good to have some insurance, isn't it? For when times get lean."

James grinds his teeth together. "You've more than enough to give up these childish games for drinking money," he mutters.

"Oh, but that's where you're wrong, Demeroven. You've always thought small."

"A title and land aren't enough for you?" James wonders, looking up at Raverson to find his eyes sharp and calculating.

"True power, true influence, requires much more than my father's meager estate," he says, leaning around James as Mason and Lady Gwen continue to heckle Lord Mason. "But what you have—the intimate connections . . ."

A chill runs down James' spine at his words. "You wouldn't dare."

"Well, of course I would focus on becoming a formal member of a family such as yours, but given both your cousin and her stepsister seem . . . reluctant to enter into a union, I'm simply making other forays."

"You stay away from my cousin," James hisses.

Raverson shrugs innocently, an infuriatingly blasé smile coming over his face. He opens his mouth, but James jerks forward, his stepfather clapping him hard on the back.

"Lord Raverson, I look forward to our lunch," Stepfather says.

James realizes then that the game has ended and people in the stands are starting to file out. His cousin, Lady Gwen, and Mason have already headed down to the field to greet Lord Mason.

"As do I, Mr. Griggs," Raverson says. "I'll see you both soon," he adds, standing up to button his frock coat before whistling his way down the stands.

James sits there staring after him, panic and terror warring in his chest.

"Now that's an impressive young man," Stepfather says, leaning back in his seat. "You should take after him, watch what he does this season. Might be able to show you a thing or two."

James stares out at the field, refusing to react, lest he turn and throttle his stepfather. Instead, he focuses on Lady Gwen, Miss Bertram, and Mason, watching as they stand chatting, waiting for Lord Mason to gather his muddy things. Mason's laugh carries up to the stands and James feels his ire and panic settling onto Mason's careless shoulders.

They wouldn't be in this predicament if Mason were more circumspect. If he were careful, like he should be. Instead, he's gone and slept with perhaps the most dangerous gossip in the city, who now has evidence of their tryst. Mason has endangered them all. Put a target on their backs and assured Raverson's continued interest in their families.

It's Mason's irresponsibility that's to blame. Mason's devil-may-care attitude.

Mason's the problem here.

And he has the gall to suggest James is the one shirking his duties. Accusing him of abusing his power because James isn't interested in the tittle-tattle of parliament.

Well, no more. If Mason's going to endanger their families, it will be up to James to protect them all from scandal by making himself so useful and well regarded he can counteract any . . . salacious gossip Mason may incur.

JAMES' HAND FLIES over his paper as he listens to Lord Roberts, trying to take down all the notes he can. This committee discussion in favor of the Medical Act has proved surprisingly interesting.

Their collective proposal to work with the few well-established medical institutions to begin their registry with properly accredited graduates is a strong start. They'll then move on to communities using those students as hubs to judge all those privately trained physicians.

Roberts finishes his speech and the lords around James, Lord Mason, and Lord Havenfort begin shifting and shuffling out of the meeting room. James marks down one final medical institution, putting a star beside the University of Edinburgh.

"They do have an excellent program," Lord Havenfort says.

James looks up to find him smiling. His is a handsome face; so much of him in Lady Gwen as well. But the dark circles beneath his eyes are what catches James' attention.

"Thank you," James says, pushing around the lump in his throat that seems to come with addressing anyone of Lord Havenfort's stature. "I have classmates who've gone up for training. I'm sure I could reach out to ask them to begin preparing their rosters."

"That would be excellent," Lord Havenfort says, looking . . . *fond* seems the wrong emotion. Is that—pride? Can't possibly be.

"Yes, Mr. Yorks and Mr. Findlay?" Lord Mason chimes in.

"And Mr. Yorks' younger brother, and Mr. Rilton," James says, glancing back at Lord Mason. "I think you and Mr. Rilton would have played rugby together for a year?"

"We did. He was quite the defense. Once you've written your letters, send me copies, and I'll reach out to Rilton as well, get them all working together."

"Perfect," James says, trying to appear casual. His showing effort is going exceedingly well.

"I'll leave the University of Edinburgh in your capable hands, then," Lord Havenfort says as they shuffle out through the last few chairs and down the steps to the antechamber.

"I believe Lady Mason will have a few wives she can contact for references as well," Lord Mason adds. "I'll write to her."

"How is she?" Lord Havenfort asks.

James hustles to keep up with both taller men as they stride across the antechamber toward the street outside. He still feels a bit like a hanger-on, but they're speaking *with* him, not around him, and that's something. A few more weeks of this attention and he'll be able to prove Mason thoroughly wrong. He'll be irreplaceable, necessary, powerful.

"She's . . . improving," Lord Mason hedges, holding open the antechamber door so Lord Havenfort and James can pass through.

"Good. Remember, I can have Cordelia's doctor sent up for Meredith, all expenses paid. Please don't hesitate to ask."

"Thank you, Uncle," Lord Mason says with a grateful smile.

"How is my aunt?" James puts in, wanting to seem as connected as Lord Mason.

Lord Havenfort's smile falters for a moment before it stretches wide across his face. "She's doing well. I'll tell her you've asked after her. She's been meaning to extend an invitation for dinner, when she's less tired."

"Of course," James says. "My mother is excited for the new baby," he adds, unsure of how else to respond.

It's true, he thinks. Or maybe she's jealous? He's never quite sure when it comes to his mother and her relationship with her late brother-in-law's widow.

"I'll tell Lady Havenfort," Lord Havenfort says. "In lieu of a dinner, actually, I thought you both might enjoy attending the opera tonight."

"I can't this evening," Lord Mason says softly. "My apologies, Uncle, though I do appreciate the invitation. I've a meeting with Cunningham and his father to discuss some property."

"Of course, of course. Gwen and Beth will be disappointed, but they'll understand," Lord Havenfort says.

"I'd be happy to attend," James says quickly, jumping at the chance to make a better impression on his cousin and her stepsister. "I can pick them up, even. I so appreciate the invitation."

"Wonderful," Lord Havenfort says, giving James what feels like a genuine smile. "Seven?"

"I'll come by with the carriage."

"I'll send Bobby along to join them," Lord Mason says. "Make the numbers even and give him something to do. A substitute Mason, if you will."

James opens his mouth, reluctant to be trapped in close, possibly hostile, quarters with Mason for the night, but Lord Havenfort is already handing them both their tickets.

"Splendid. Beth and Gwen will be delighted. Now, I must get home to see my wife. Good day, boys."

James stands stock-still, holding his ticket as he watches Lord Havenfort march away.

"Have a good evening," Lord Mason says, patting James on the shoulder before heading off himself.

James slowly turns to walk home, baffled. How has he just gotten himself invited to an evening full of Bobby Mason?

"PARR IS BY far the best jockey trainer, and to suggest otherwise only shows how little you've been paying attention," Lady Gwen tells Mason later that night as they sit in Lord Havenfort's box at the newly refurbished Royal Opera House waiting for the performance to start.

Mason leans around James to glare at Lady Gwen. His cologne wafts past James' nose and James tells himself staunchly that he detests the scent of sandalwood, even though it's long been his favorite.

"George Abdale is just as good a trainer—better, even, since it was his horse that won last year," Mason counters.

Mason and Lady Gwen have been having this argument now for a solid hour, since James picked them all up in his carriage, and it's beginning to wear on him. Not only does he have exactly zero interest in horse racing, but it's wildly cutting into his efforts to impress his cousin and ignore Bobby Mason. He wants something to come of this uncomfortable evening, but they won't stop talking about the Ascot races, and his opportunity for demonstrating personal growth is rapidly running out.

In a few minutes, the fourth performance of *Les Huguenots* will begin, and they'll be trapped in silence for hours. He's going to have to change tack.

"George Abdale is very good," Miss Bertram says from James' right.

"Don't you take his side," Lady Gwen whines.

"I can have opinions independent of both of you," Miss Bertram says. "And let's not fight across Lord Demeroven all night."

"It's all right," James says, determined to be polite to the ladies, to ingratiate himself, even if it does come at the cost of having done research into his least-favorite topics. "But I am sorry, cousin, it does sound like Parr has the best lineup this season."

"Hah!" Lady Gwen crows.

"I know he's new, but his jockeys have been winning heats up and down the races this season, and Wells is favored to be in the top three by Ascot," James continues.

"Exactly," Lady Gwen agrees. "It's all in the conditioning. Father says Parr has his jockeys doing laps on the field alongside the horses."

"Precisely," James agrees.

Mason stares at him, surprised, and James sits up a little straighter. There, he's not such a terrible social companion after all.

"Shall we discuss something that doesn't leave most of us either yelling or sighing dramatically?" Miss Bertram suggests.

"Fine," Mason says. "We'll see who's right in a month anyway. Care to place a bet?" he adds, leaning around James again.

"I thought Lord Mason got betting rights from the Spot-the-Scion tournament, didn't he?" James asks quickly.

Mason groans and slumps against his seat again. "He did."

"How's parliament?" Miss Bertram asks, overriding some snarky comment from Lady Gwen.

"It's going very well," James says, turning on what little charm he has. "We're organizing to begin a survey of the various medical institutions across the country and in Scotland to form the skeleton of the registry."

"Skeleton, good one," Lady Gwen says with a laugh.

Miss Bertram smiles at him. "That sounds very exciting. We'd be happy to arrange more research at the Foundling Hospital, if you'd like."

"That would be grand," James says, bolstered by the way both ladies are smiling, and how Mason is considering him with what looks like interest. "I've been meaning to arrange to meet more of the physicians myself to discuss their work and any improvements they think could be made with the registry as a reference, now that we have a more concrete plan in place."

"Father might want to join you," Lady Gwen says. "He's eager to pick the brains of the various doctors overseeing the births in the maternity ward."

"I'll be sure to arrange it," James says, feeling a little balloon of pride at the thought. Perhaps the opportunity to cement himself as meaningful to his aunt, his cousin, and their family will come from this Medical Act after all.

"Albie will probably want to attend too. Perhaps you could tag along, Bobby," Lady Gwen suggests.

James glances at Mason to find him watching them all with a strange expression on his face. James doesn't know if it's jealousy, surprise, or even intrigue? But it's a reaction, and that gives him more encouragement.

"Yes, Mason, you could join us. I'm sure your brother would appreciate another set of eyes and ears, so the two of you could strategize afterward."

Mason's eyes widen a little and he bobs his head, almost smiling now. "Perhaps."

"Lord Mason has a whole running list of physicians and former classmates to contact," James continues, looking over at the girls. "We're breaking them down by connections and preparing to send letters. Hopefully they'll get back to us quickly with recommendations of private physicians we can contact too."

"That sounds wonderful," Miss Bertram says.

"Yes, it sounds like you're really making a solid effort for the act," Mason adds, leaning in so he can hear the full conversation.

James smiles at all of them just as the lights begin to dim, pleased as punch. "I find it's quite rewarding to do work that could make so much social change. If we succeed, Lord Mason and I just might save the family reputations after all, and do something of import. I think together we've already attended more sessions this season than either of our drunken predecessors, and we're already making such progress."

James takes a breath, feeling a little manic. He rarely speaks for so long and—

Miss Bertram rises abruptly and hurries out of the box. James blinks, confused, jerking when Mason shoves his shoulder. He watches Mason rise and march after Miss Bertram, leaving James and Lady Gwen alone in the box.

"What happened? Did—" James' words catch up to him then as Lady Gwen stares at him, incredulous. "Oh, God, I didn't mean— You must know I didn't mean to insult— I only— Lord Mason and I actually are doing rather well by the families, and I just meant—"

Lady Gwen turns to watch the curtains below them begin to rise. "I'm not the one you need to apologize to," she says curtly.

Shit.

Chapter Nine

Bobby

"You shouldn't be in here," Beth says, looking at him over the hand towel she has pressed to her face.

Bobby lets the door to the women's water closet swing shut behind him and rummages in his pocket for his handkerchief, but comes up empty. "And leave you in here to cry alone?"

Beth rolls her watery eyes, blowing out a breath to try and calm down. Bobby plunks himself down on one of the overstuffed poufs that are, for some reason, just in the middle of the room. There's much more to the outer chamber here than there is in the men's water closet.

The walls are a deep pink and made of what looks like crushed velvet. There's gold-tassel trim along the molding, and the wash basins are set beneath a row of mirrors lit with gaslights. The whole room is a tad hazy, but inviting.

"It's all right to be mad, you know," Bobby says, watching as Beth tries to shake her tears away, flapping the towel in her hand.

"I don't want to give him the satisfaction," Beth says tightly. She then raises the towel and blows her nose with a sound like a foghorn.

"Then give me the satisfaction of listening to you rail against him, and we'll go out and be all prim, proper, and disgustingly stiff-upper-lip about it," Bobby entices.

If she keeps bottling it all up inside, someday she'll explode, and he doesn't want to see her hurt, or see her have to live with having hurt someone else. On top of that, he needs to hear that it's hurt her too, otherwise he'll feel irrational and oversensitive. James bloody Demeroven is an unmitigated, pompous arse.

"I would be angrier if he wasn't right," Beth says, meeting his eyes with a look of such exhaustion that he instantly rises from the pouf to wrap her in a hug.

Beth presses her forehead into his shoulder with a huff and he stares at their reflection in the mirror.

"Are you angry?" she asks.

"Yes," he says instantly.

"But?"

Bobby sighs. She's not wrong. Demeroven's comment bites not simply because it was a wretched thing to say, but more because it's annoyingly true. His and Beth's fathers were lazy, thoughtless men, who threw their money at everything but their families, and ascribed to the most power-hungry, self-serving of politics.

And they both treated their children like utter filth.

Still. "He shouldn't have said anything," Bobby asserts.

"Bobby."

"Especially to a lady."

"I'm not a lady," Beth says, pulling back to look up at him.

"Sure you are. Best lady I know," he says, releasing her to wipe away her tears. "And even if the arse is entirely right, and Albie's done more for my family since my father died than my father managed in two decades, and he's managing even with Meredith trapped away in the country, it's still wrong for your cousin to treat you that way."

"It's wrong for him to treat us both that way," Beth agrees, squeezing his hands before stepping back from him.

He watches as she shuffles close to the mirror to tend to her lightly melted makeup. "You're right," he says. "And I'm sorry you have to deal with him so much."

Beth turns to regard him, lip between her teeth. "I wish I was only angry at him."

Bobby blinks. He lowers himself down to the overstuffed pouf again, settling in for a good talk. As much as he knows Beth loves Gwen and Uncle Dashiell, the circumstances of her arrangement must make it difficult to talk about the time before—those awful months when Beth was set to marry Lord Montson so she and Cordelia would have somewhere to live.

"I find I'm angrier with my father than I . . . thought I was," Beth admits.

"Me too," Bobby hears himself say.

"Watching James take his seat, I—I didn't think it would be this hard. His attitude notwithstanding."

"He's certainly not making it easier," Bobby agrees.

"And I'm happy, you know?" Beth says, her smile brittle, but clear. "So happy with Gwen. And my mother and Dashiell are so in love, and the baby—" She breaks off to swipe at her eyes again. "Damn."

"I feel kind of helpless," Bobby says, offering her a sad smile, hoping that somehow baring his own broken soul might make her feel less guilty for her completely understandable emotional upheaval.

"You do?" Beth wonders.

"Albie's doing all this work—all these important things—and I'm attending teas and pretending to look for a wife."

"Not trying too hard, are you?" Beth asks with a little laugh.

Bobby smiles, mission accomplished. "I wish there was something I could do that *meant* something. And then there's Demeroven, and he's such a—" He pauses, not wanting to malign the man too much in front of Beth. There is some language that's unfit even for her ears.

"Yes, he is," Beth says, raising a brow, a look she's learned from Gwen.

Bobby sighs and fiddles with his signet ring. "Why do you keep letting Uncle Dashiell invite him to things?" he asks in lieu of getting up to face the literal music that seeps in under the door.

"I don't have much choice, do I?" Beth asks, adjusting her skirts. "But I am sorry he was cruel to you."

"You do not need to apologize on his behalf. His actions are not your responsibility," Bobby says, standing up to mark his point.

"I know," Beth says, waving him off. "Still, perhaps it was wrong of Gwen and me to insist you try and get along with him," she adds, her eyes going distant for a moment. "Maybe we were wrong to think he might be different from my father and his stepfather."

"You're different," Bobby says, forcing some cheer into his voice. She may have asked him to help, but Uncle Dashiell is the one who laid down the decree. "You're the best Demeroven-turned-Bertram I know. Don't tell Gwen."

Beth laughs. "Thank you. But I'm not the one with the legacy. He is, and it just—" She searches for a moment but doesn't seem to find the words. "I'll meet you back in the box," she says instead, squeezing his arm.

She walks past him and out the door. It swings shut behind her and Bobby stands there in the middle of the women's water closet, feeling deeply adrift.

Demeroven's right. Albie will repair the family legacy. And Bobby? Bobby will simply . . . exist. Leaving no legacy behind, nothing of value or substance. His only meaningful contribution could be children—little spares of spares who could someday inherit if something terrible happened to Albie and his family.

But if he has children, he wants to have children for them—to give them the life and love that he and Albie never got. But how could he do that if he couldn't be the right husband to their mother?

And if he can't even bear children, how can he ever be more than a man who "wouldn't understand" what true responsibility is in Demeroven's eyes?

Bobby stares at his reflection in the hanging mirror. Wallowing in the ladies' water closet isn't going to get him anywhere, other than in a potential run-in with the authorities. With a sigh, Bobby straightens up and pushes through the door back into the dim corridor off the box seats. He hesitates, wondering if perhaps he should just set up camp here and wait out the rest of the performance.

But then, if he doesn't go back, will Demeroven think less of him for it? Think he's won, again, in this bizarre battle of painful family histories?

"The tenor is off pitch, don't you think?"

Bobby jumps, a hand to his heart. Lord Raverson seems to appear out of the darkness. He grins slyly, looking Bobby up and down, and Bobby struggles to regain the little poise he has.

"He is," Bobby agrees, though he honestly has no idea. "On your way for a smoke?"

Raverson shrugs and steps up to him, placing a hand against the wall behind Bobby so they're close enough to speak at a whisper. He supposes it's not the most indecent of poses, but surely more intimate than two men would normally be in such a setting.

The fact that they've been as intimate as, well, as Bobby's been with anyone in a good long time stirs hot in his stomach.

Flashes of that night a week ago in Prince's pantry fill Bobby's mind. He feels his cheeks flushing as Raverson continues to peruse his figure.

"Did I see you come out of the women's water closet?"

Bobby swallows a slightly strangled laugh. "My cousin's stepsister, ah, needed to talk."

"Oh, are we thinking of trying to cross the family trees? I didn't think you were so inclined," Raverson says, his eyes seeming to sharpen.

"What? No. Miss Bertram is a dear friend. She was upset. It was nothing untoward, I assure you."

Bobby doesn't know which unsettles him more: the idea that anyone might think he was trying to seduce Beth, or that Raverson might have gotten the wrong impression about who Bobby would like to have trying to seduce him. But he really can't think about much beyond the way Raverson's biting at his lip.

"Would you like to be a little untoward tonight?" Raverson asks, his voice a husky whisper.

And though he knows it's beyond foolish to consider, given where they are and who's waiting for him, Bobby finds himself agreeing. A few minutes of hungry kisses and a good grope with Raverson sounds infinitely more appealing than sitting beside sodding Demeroven or pretending his cousin and Beth aren't upset.

So he lets Raverson lead him past the water closets and into a curtained alcove against the wall behind the box seats. Raverson pulls the curtain around them, plunging them into complete darkness. And then it's all lips and tongue and firm, squeezing, broad hands. Raverson hitches him up so he's straddling the man's thigh, his back flush to the wall.

He grinds down on Raverson, nearly whimpering. All his

pent-up frustration surges through his body in an intense arousal that makes him feel like he's sixteen again. Bobby bucks against Raverson as his hand starts to work the buttons of Bobby's pants. He bites back a curse.

Then someone stumbles into Raverson's back.

Raverson's knee drops, and they cleave apart. The curtain wrenches back and Bobby feels his throat constrict, terror coursing through him. He's about to be sent to jail. His family—sitting not twenty yards away—is about to be disgraced. Albie will never recover the Mason name—

Uncle Dashiell blinks at them in the dim lamplight. Backlit by the gas lamps, he strikes an imposing, dour figure, and Bobby feels himself shrinking down, in multiple ways, horror giving way to keen embarrassment.

"Ah, Lord Havenfort," Raverson says, straightening his lapels and stepping around Uncle Dashiell, out into the hallway like nothing's happened. "How good to see you."

"Raverson," Uncle Dashiell says, glancing from Raverson to Bobby and back.

Bobby ducks out of the alcove as well, adjusting his jacket to hide the evidence of what must be a horribly shocking discovery for his uncle.

"I was just coming to collect Demeroven," Uncle Dashiell says after a beat of the loudest silence Bobby thinks he's ever heard. He knows there's still an opera going on, but he can't seem to hear it.

"Of course, of course," Raverson says smoothly.

"I was . . . going to ask if you would see the girls home, Robert," Uncle Dashiell continues, eyeing Raverson before looking to Bobby. "But if you are otherwise—"

"I would be happy to see the ladies home, my lord," Raverson cuts in.

Uncle Dashiell looks back at him and Bobby tries to see a way out of this situation that doesn't mean his banishment from the family.

"For a small price, of course," Raverson continues, flashing Uncle Dashiell that winning smile. "All nice and respectable. Keep the rumors at bay."

"The—" Bobby starts, something heavy and frantic settling in his gut.

"You've heard the rumors, haven't you, sir?" Raverson asks, ignoring Bobby. "About Mason here, and Demeroven, come to think of it. I wouldn't want any of that chatter to tarnish your daughter and stepdaughter, given what they're already up against."

Bobby stares, his mouth hanging open. Uncle Dashiell slips a hand into his pocket and retrieves a stack of bills without even blinking. He counts a few off and hands them over to Raverson.

"Your silence would be most appreciated, though the girls will get home without your assistance, thank you, Raverson. Good evening."

Raverson dips his head in a bow as he pockets the money. "Good evening, Lord Havenfort. Mason, it's been a pleasure," he adds, winking at Bobby before he turns and saunters away.

Bobby stares after him, horrified. Was this his plan, the entire time? Did he come here simply to trap Bobby, to use him as a means of blackmail? To humiliate him *and* take his uncle for a ride? Is Bobby so naive, so starved for affection, that he didn't see a con man right in front of him?

Good God, he let the man— The man's seen him—

"Have you completely lost your common sense?" Uncle Dashiell asks, his voice like a muted whipcrack.

Bobby nearly jumps. He's seldom seen his uncle this angry, staring at Bobby like he's never seen him before.

"I—" Bobby rasps, trying to find some excuse to defend his irredeemable loss of sense.

"You are in public. What if I hadn't stumbled onto the two of you? What if it had been one of the other lords? Or worse, one of the ladies? Do you have any idea how much money, let alone political capital, your brother and I would have to use to get you out of prison? You'd never recover. *We'd* never recover."

"I know," Bobby says, his voice cracking.

"Do you have any idea how hard your brother is working, right now, to salvage your family name? How hard we are both working to make sure there is something for his children—for your future children—to live on, and be proud of?"

"I know," Bobby says, a little louder, stronger.

He knows how hard Albie's working. Of course he knows. It's like he's lost his brother as well—like he's disappeared and left only a husk of himself behind.

"You've a poor way of showing it," Uncle Dashiell says, a bite to his cold words that makes Bobby flinch.

"I didn't mean to—"

"What, did you fall down onto his mouth?" Uncle Dashiell asks.

Bobby bristles. "It was just—"

"Stupid," Uncle Dashiell supplies.

It was stupid. It was reckless, and irresponsible. But it was just—it was just— "You wouldn't be acting this way if you'd caught Albie with Meredith," he says, a strange hurt surging up his throat.

"If I had caught Albert with Lady Mason before their engagement, I would have dragged him outside and shouted until his ears rang, and then he would have proposed to her on the spot," Uncle Dashiell says, his face still that stone mask, shoulders tense. "But that would be the end of it. Your indiscretion here could cost all of us our livelihoods, let alone our reputations."

"But it's fine when Gwen does it?" Bobby hears himself say.

He clamps his lips shut and glances around. He needs to stop digging this hole before he reaches the other side of the earth. But how can his uncle act this way when—

"My daughter is protected, Beth is protected, and you know it is not in any way the same. Do not try and slander them to save your own skin."

"I didn't say there was anything wrong with it!" Bobby snaps. "But if you're willing to accept her, why am I— Why won't you—" To his horror, his throat is starting to tighten, his eyes stinging.

"Because I do not want to see you thrown in prison," Uncle Dashiell hisses back. "I do not care with whom you get your pleasure, though I suggest you take better care not to find yourself in dark corners with young men so eager to extort your relatives."

Bobby curls his hands into fists. He is not going to cry, not here, not now, not in front of the uncle he's already disappointed.

"You must keep your activities private, for all our sakes," Uncle Dashiell says, staring him down until Bobby manages to nod. "Now, can I trust you to see the girls home?"

"Yes, sir," Bobby whispers, struggling to breathe through his nose without sniffling.

Uncle Dashiell steps around him to head toward their box. Bobby stares at the empty corridor, trying to keep from letting his shoulders shake, his breath rattling.

"Robert."

Bobby sucks in air and turns to find his uncle right behind

him. Uncle Dashiell places both hands on his shoulders and Bobby lets out a very quiet sob.

"It isn't fair. You're right. And I am sorry this is the world you must live in. When we are both less emotional, we can discuss this."

"Okay," Bobby mumbles.

"Go get yourself cleaned up," Uncle Dashiell says, squeezing his shoulders before releasing him to walk over to his box.

Bobby nearly throws himself into the men's water closet, unable to face seeing Demeroven off to do important work—off to impress *his* uncle after Bobby has so disgraced him.

He stumbles to the water basin and stares down at the water. What if his father was just the prelude and it's Bobby who's finally going to sink the Mason name, and bring Albie, Gwen, and Beth down with him?

Chapter Ten

James

James pulls at his cravat as he follows the porter through the Oxford Club. It's been two days of shallow breaths and the horrible sinking realization that he deserves every unkind word that's ever been said about him, and then some.

Neither Lady Gwen nor his cousin would look at him for the rest of the performance, and he didn't even see Mason as Lord Havenfort escorted him out. Then he sat with Lord Havenfort and Lord Mason at the Havenfort townhouse, listening to them detail all the work they've been doing, and he felt like more and more of a cad with each passing second.

And now he's here, at the viscount's club, and he feels like his stomach would escape up his throat if it weren't so tight. How can he face Lord Mason after he treated his brother and family so callously? Surely Mason has told him about James' behavior. And if Mason didn't, Lady Gwen must have. His cousin's disappointment was a quiet simmer, but Lady Gwen's was outright defiant—a curl to her lip and a darkness to her eyes that didn't let up through the whole performance.

He reaches Lord Mason's corner, surrounded by tall bookshelves with one high, narrow window letting in the dreary daylight. The room is hazy with cigar smoke. There are two finished cups of tea on the table surrounded by all manner of papers covered in ink stains and cramped, small writing.

"Thank you," James tells the porter. The man bows and hurries off with a mutter of bringing more tea.

The viscount looks as bad as his work area. His narrow face is drawn, bags under his bloodshot eyes. James watches him run an agitated hand through his hair. He gestures without a word for James to take the opposite seat.

James sits, trying to gird himself. He's good at being dressed down, has lots of experience. And at least this time, he deserves it. But as he waits, and waits, the viscount offers nothing, simply turning back to his papers, riffling through them and muttering to himself.

"There's a page over there," Lord Mason says after an uncomfortably long minute.

"What?" James manages, his voice a squeak against the silence.

"In that stack. Has notes from Lord Hirsmith about his wife's palsy. Find it and pass it here, would you?"

James straightens up to page through the stack. His hand twitches and he knocks another stack of mildly organized pages across the table. Lord Mason drops the paper he's holding to rub at his temples.

"Sorry," James says meekly.

"No, no. Hardly ruining a system here. My apologies, Demeroven. How are you?"

James pauses in his nascent search to meet Lord Mason's eyes. "I'm well. How are you?"

"Exhausted," Lord Mason admits, stretching his arms over his head. "Was up half the night trying to collate these, and then a letter arrived from my wife and I—" He pauses as the porter arrives with their tea.

The man places down a fresh pot and china set with nary a blink as he moves papers around to make more space. James wonders if Lord Mason has made a practice out of working here. Wonders if the staff is as worried as he is.

"Thank you, Lars," Lord Mason says. Lars bows and then fades away. "Good tea," Lord Mason adds, pouring cups for himself and James.

"How is your wife?" James asks, holding his teacup on the saucer. He's a bit worried if he picks it up, he'll shake the tea right out of it.

"At her wit's end, honestly," Lord Mason says, taking a gulp of the scalding tea as if it's lukewarm. "They've tried everything to get the vomiting to stop, but so far, she can barely keep anything down. I'm worried that—" He presses his lips together and sets down his cup. "Hirsmith's notes had something about the antiemetic properties of some herb. I've been trying to find it, but my system is . . . dismal, to quote my brother."

James shifts uncomfortably at the mention of the younger Mason, sure the viscount is about to start in on him. But Lord Mason only scrubs at his face.

James scans the table, realizing that each paper is a different set of notes. He knows they've been asking prominent families to refer them to physicians for further discussion, but this is extreme. "How many husbands have you interviewed?"

"Twenty?" Lord Mason wagers. "I've done a lot of ancillary research based on each conversation."

"I see," James says, nudging his teacup over so he can pick up a few of the pages.

Perhaps the viscount's been too preoccupied with working up the Medical Act and simultaneously trying to find cures for his sick wife to actually talk to his brother and discover what a lout James has been.

"I don't have many contacts in the city, but I could work on organizing these, and meet with you twice a week to keep it going, if that would be helpful?" James suggests, hoping that making more of an effort will quell the burrowing feeling in his guts.

Here he's been so obsessed with his own reputation while Lord Mason is clearly killing himself to do this research for his desperately ill wife on top of his parliamentary duties. The least James can do is help with the parliamentary business. And perhaps if he organizes it, he can be seen as a little more useful to the effort—earn the good reputation he waved beneath Mason's nose at the opera. Because if Lord Mason is Mr. Mason's standard of work, no wonder he finds James so lacking.

"That could be—" Lord Mason starts.

"Hand them here," James says, sitting up straight and reaching out for the stack furthest from Lord Mason. "Do you want it by specialty, region, or surname?"

Lord Mason's lips turn up, the closest to a smile James thinks he'll get. "Region, to start."

"And then subcategories for specialty. Good thinking," James completes.

Lord Mason's shoulders droop in relief and James vows silently to show up three times a week to help from now on, whether Bobby Mason sees him do it or not.

JAMES LEANS BACK against the wall, watching the swirl of dancers on the floor. He's been loitering at the edge of the ballroom for over an hour, and not a single person has stopped to greet him or say anything at all. Granted, he's mostly hidden behind a large floral arrangement on a plinth.

He should be concerned, but the reprieve of being unnoticed is a relief. A moment's escape from the endless rounds of notes and organization he's been doing with Lord Mason. He misses the silence and solitude of the country keenly at balls like this. But as the minutes tick by with nothing to occupy his hands, James begins to get antsy.

He spots his cousin and Lady Gwen across the floor, standing with a group of pastel-clad debutantes. His cousin is wearing a lovely green dress, and Lady Gwen complements her in a deep blue, the two of them clearly the center of attention in their little circle. But though they look beautiful, unlike normal evenings, when it's almost impossible to get a word in edgewise between them, it looks like they're barely speaking.

He watches Lady Gwen bend down to say something softly in his cousin's ear, pointing to someone on the floor. His cousin huffs and takes Lady Gwen's arm, looking up at her to snip something back, before hauling her out of the room and toward the lavatories. Concern slithers into James' chest. He hopes they're not fighting about something he said.

But that's rather self-centered of him. His cousin and her stepsister have their own lives that have nothing to do with his poor behavior. He hadn't been planning on approaching them, still searching for a polite way to apologize for his deplorable words at the opera. But James feels a pang of regret as they disappear from the room. Now even if he does work up the courage to apologize, he can't even manage that.

The antsy, unsettled feeling in his chest starts to crescendo and James gives in to the pull of the drinks table, venturing forlornly out of his little hidey-hole to cross the room. He notices Mason and Cunningham ducking out to the patio and thinks for a moment of following them. Mason deserves an apology too, especially given the nights they've awkwardly avoided each other at Lord Mason's townhouse. For all he knows, Mason hasn't even been home this week. Chasing the man out of his house certainly wasn't his intention in trying to help his brother.

But the thought of Mason being out all week brings deeper, darker thoughts to the fore, and James sighs. He reaches the drinks table, and the bartender's already pouring him another whisky.

"These things are such a bore, aren't they?"

James winces. It's as if he's conjured Raverson out of thin air.

"Almost worth avoiding altogether, but then we wouldn't get to keep our connections warm, would we?" Raverson continues, following James away from the table.

James has half a mind to simply run out of the ballroom. But that would be far too conspicuous, so he leads Raverson over to a high top. He tries to school his features into something other than panic or dread, and takes an overlarge sip of his drink.

"Your stepfather only had wonderful things to say about you at our lunch this afternoon," Raverson says.

That pulls James from his internal struggle, and he looks askance across the table at Raverson's handsome face.

"Well, no, not truly. But he did say you weren't doing the worst job possible. *Middling*, I believe, was the term he used."

Middling is perhaps one of the kinder adjectives James' stepfather has used to describe him over the years. But the idea of it being said directly to Raverson in some intimate conversation makes James' skin crawl.

"Shocking, the entire affair with the Ashmonds, wasn't it?"

James stiffens. "Pardon?"

"Miss Bertram walking out on Lord Montson and the ensuing fallout with Lord and Lady Ashmond? Your stepfather said Lord Havenfort arranged for the woman's attorney and everything. Took Lord Ashmond for a song in the divorce."

James doesn't reply, deeply unsettled by Raverson's gleeful tone. What's more, Raverson knows things even he doesn't.

Lord Havenfort was the one who arranged for Lady Ashmond's attorney?

"And the whole ugly business with your aunt and Lord Havenfort," Raverson continues.

James blinks. "There's nothing ugly between them."

"To hear your stepfather tell it, your aunt was trying to extort money from him for a year before she found Havenfort. Havenfort clearly caved."

James keeps his face carefully blank, but internally, he's reeling. Not only has his stepfather told Raverson more than he's ever discussed with James about his aunt and cousin's situation, he's gone and twisted the story. Lady Havenfort was hardly trying to coerce the Demeroven estate into giving her money. Instead, with James underage and none the wiser, his stepfather refused to give his aunt any help at all after his uncle summarily wrote them out of his will. Left his own wife and daughter to fend for themselves with nothing.

"I'd imagine Lord Havenfort is desperate to see the two young ladies married. The stink of that whole debacle must be hard to fight."

"I believe they're all doing just fine," James says, hearing the tightness in his voice.

He hates that Raverson makes him so off-kilter. He should have a better bluff than this. Should be able to stand tall against this man, defend his family. He's a viscount, for God's sake. But the idea his stepfather might prefer this vile man to him stabs at his innards.

"Thought I might make a call, get to know one of the young ladies after all. Do you find Lady Gwen or Miss Bertram more approachable?"

James opens his mouth and Raverson leans in uncomfortably close.

"Well, Miss Bertram, obviously. Lady Gwen has such a . . . reputation. I wouldn't want a tarnish on my name. And I don't really like to double-dip, as it were."

James blinks. "Excuse me?"

"With Mason. Might be too conspicuous with Lord Havenfort as well. Did Mason tell you that Havenfort caught us at the opera?"

James's heart thuds in his chest. "I beg your pardon?"

"Mason was clearly having a poor time, so I offered to entertain him for a bit, and Havenfort bumped right into us. He was more than willing to pay for my silence. And surely he'd be interested in continuing to keep all this . . . information in the family. Of course, my being in line for the lion's share of the Havenfort fortune wouldn't be a hardship either," Raverson says slyly before knocking back the rest of his drink.

"You're vile," James spits out, too shocked and horrified to mince his words. "Neither of the girls would ever have you."

"We'll see about that," Raverson says breezily.

"And Lady Havenfort is—"

"There's no surety in that child surviving," Raverson says. At what must be the revolted look on his face, Raverson rolls his eyes. "Oh, don't be so sanctimonious. Her age, the likelihood of childhood mortality, I'm not saying anything you don't already know."

James grits his teeth. "Your games won't work. I'll tell Lord Havenfort—"

"What, that both of his nephews are poofs?"

James hesitates, a deep mortification and shame rolling through him at the idea of disappointing Lady Havenfort and Lord Havenfort—at explaining why he needs to tell them, why they'd be forced to reckon with such a heavy secret.

"And how will you prove that?" James asks, pushing the

thought out around his panic. "Going to tell Lord Havenfort you've slept with both of his nephews? Are you so self-hating you'd risk your own reputation?"

"I don't know what you're talking about," Raverson says, that glint of a scheme coming into his eyes—a tall tale about to be expertly told. "You both came on to me. You at school, and Mason at the opera. Simply grabbed me and groped me." He holds up his palms in feigned innocence and something gold glints there on his pinky. A signet ring with the initials RJM—Mason's signet ring.

James' stomach plummets.

Raverson smirks. "I was too polite to fight either of you off, but you both understood that it wasn't to occur again. I'm far too much of a gentleman to try and take either of you to the authorities. I wouldn't want to sully your cousins with such news."

James stares at Raverson, rage, revulsion, and disbelief at war in his chest. He cannot let this man take them all down just to slake his perverse need for power, for control. James isn't sixteen anymore. He won't let Raverson see him scared, even if everything about this conversation has terrified him to his very core.

"Go and get your sick pleasure and power somewhere else. Or better yet, leave these atrocious schoolboy schemes in the past."

"You're so naive, Demeroven," Raverson says, smirking at him. "School was just the start."

James squares his shoulders. "Stay away from my family, or you'll live to regret it."

Raverson just winks at him. "We'll see, won't we?"

And with that he turns and strides away, slipping Mason's ring into his pocket, looking confident and entirely unruffled, while James stands there, thoroughly shaken.

He has to stop this. He has to figure out a way to outplay Raverson at his own game. A way that will keep his and Mason's reputations intact, keep his cousin and her stepsister safe, and keep Lord and Lady Havenfort out of all of it.

The very last thing his aunt needs right now is further stress.

He knocks back his drink. He'll need reinforcements to fight this, and that means teaming up with Mason—who's caused this problem in the first place.

What was the man thinking, messing around with Raverson at the opera? Did James' words really— But no, Mason wouldn't be so affected by anything James has to say. He's sure Mason rarely thinks of him at all, other than to bad-mouth him to his cousin. And it's not as if James is spending all his time thinking about Mason.

Yet, when he sees him alone, leaning against the railing of the patio, smoking, looking devil-may-care and aloof, James can't quite halt the familiar nervous flutter in his chest. But no matter how attractive he is—no matter how much James envies Mason's relationships with his cousin and friends—no matter how much James wants to be like Mason, Mason has put them all in danger. And now Mason must help him fight back against Raverson.

But just as he steps onto the patio, still formulating the proper entrée into this . . . presumably horrible conversation, Mason spots him, sneering in dislike.

"Ah, there he is, the golden boy."

James bristles. "Excuse me?"

"Been off hobnobbing? Gathering votes? Playing nice with the lords you hate so much? Are you humbled?"

James stares at Mason, indignance flushing through him as the man pushes upright, teetering a little. "Better than skulking in the shadows downing whisky like a dilettante," James returns, even though that's exactly what he was doing up until a few minutes ago.

"Charming," Mason says, taking a long drag of his cigar. "I hope you've had a drink to drown your pride. How low you must feel to be doing Albie's busywork."

"At least I'm living up to my obligations," James hisses, stepping forward so there's only a foot between them. "Instead of getting caught being buggered behind curtains at the opera."

Mason's sneer drops and he stares blankly back at James. "What?"

"What were you thinking?" James continues, all thoughts of a rational, reasoned conversation flying out of his head. "What if you'd been caught by someone else? Someone with the power to ruin us all? It's bad enough Raverson thinks he can milk more money from Lord Havenfort without you making it easier for him. Giving him your ring—what were you thinking?"

Mason gapes, glancing down at his hand in confusion. "I didn't—"

"Your need to get whatever you want, whoever you want, whenever you want could ruin the entire family."

Mason looks up, his lip curling. "Oh yes, because denying myself and pretending I'm someone I'm not forever would be better, so I could end up bitter like you, lying to myself and everyone else about who I am."

"At least I care more about my family than my own cock," James spits back, pushing through the hurt that gathers in his chest. Is that really what the man thinks of him?

"How dare you?" Mason's voice is a sharp rumble. He steps forward and James instinctively steps back. "How dare you pretend to know how much I care about my family?"

Up close like this, Mason is broad, and tall, and James feels unease creep over him. The need to make himself small, to cower away, is too strong to fight. Like he's back in the barn on his stepfather's estate, waiting for a lash.

Mason steps forward again and James stumbles backward, his hands coming up of their own accord. And then his foot hits the corner of the railing and suddenly he's falling, tumbling down the rough stone steps to land in a heap on the patio below.

Pain blooms across his cheek, at his elbow, flaring out from his hip. He sucks in air, taking a moment to brace himself. He doesn't think anything is broken, other than his pride.

But before he can gather himself, or figure out a way to rise with a shred of dignity, Mason's hand is on his shoulder, his other coming up to brush the hair out of James' eyes.

"I'm so sorry, Demeroven. I never meant to push you onto the stairs," he says, genuine remorse and deep concern etched across his face.

That hand slips down to cup his cheek and James blinks up at Mason. His head is backlit by the lamps, giving him an almost ethereal glow. It makes James' chest clench in a way wholly unrelated to his recent fall, and there's that damn familiar bubbly feeling zipping over his skin—sparks and excitement and hesitation swirled into one. But he's lying on the ground after a bout of nerves so insistent that he fell down the stairs, all because Mason raised his voice.

The shame of the whole evening closes in on him, and he shuffles out from beneath Mason's hands, pulling himself to standing without even a grunt, though pain screeches across his skin.

"Don't touch me," he gets out, his voice wobbling and low.

Mason rises slowly, hands held up. "All right. I'm sorry."

James searches for something to say—some way to come back from this. From their fight. From the blackmail. From his fall. All that rises is a gripping nausea, and he cannot stand for Mason to see him vomit, again, like a weak little boy overcome by emotion.

Instead, he turns on his heel and marches haltingly off across the grounds.

"Demeroven," Mason calls, but James continues on, refusing to look back.

He holds his head up high until he reaches the side of the ridiculously large townhouse. He turns the corner and limps down the narrow alley until he can collapse against the granite wall, heaving in air. His eyes are leaking, his nose is running, and everything hurts more than it has in a long while. His pride most of all.

How could he let himself get that panicked? Mason isn't his stepfather. Though, in truth, he doesn't really know what kind of man Mason is.

The back of his mind taunts him with the feel of Mason's hand on his shoulder blade in the alley outside D'Vere, the caress of his fingers against James' cheek just now. With the way Mason has tried to engage him in conversation at every uncomfortable event. With the way Mason smiles and laughs with his cousin and her stepsister, how he clearly loves them so hard and so fiercely. James doesn't truly think Mason would intentionally have put them in danger, and insinuating as much . . .

Got him bruised and humiliated.

If he'd simply told Mason about Raverson's designs on the girls—on the family—after the rugby match . . . But who's to say Mason would have listened anyway? All the ifs and maybes of what he could have done are irrelevant now.

Slowly, he hauls himself back to standing, unwilling to stay still long enough for anyone to find him. He limps his way off the property and down the street to where he thinks he'll blend in with the surroundings should anyone be watching from the great house. He hails a passing coach and overpays the driver, sinking into the worn cabin bench with a groan.

How on earth is he supposed to find a way to save his family's reputation, to protect his cousin, her mother, her stepsister, and Lord Havenfort—the only adult to show him even an ounce of kindness—when he can't even face Bobby Mason without having an attack of nerves?

CHAPTER ELEVEN

Bobby

Bobby cracks his neck, overwarm and slightly sweaty. There on the inner green of the Ascot racetrack, the sun beats down on crowds of merry spectators. It's a sea of hoopskirts, linens, and top hats. This year they're pressed up to the whitewashed fence and he feels more claustrophobia than excitement. He squints across the track toward the royal Ascot enclosure and spots Raverson right away. Hard to miss the man—inches taller than most—but still the sight sends a shiver up his spine.

He goes to spin his signet ring and clenches his fist. He hadn't realized it was gone until Demeroven told him Raverson had it. Now he feels its absence keenly, and whatever attraction Bobby felt for Raverson has been replaced with a pulsing, shameful hatred that has him fidgeting. As much as he wants to pretend Demeroven's tirade the other night was out of line, Bobby knows he's to blame. He entangled himself with the wrong man, and now the whole family will pay the price.

Finally, he has a true purpose for the season, and he wants nothing to do with it. How is he supposed to prevent Raverson from revealing his secrets? How is he supposed to protect his cousin and Beth? How is he supposed to stand tall, knowing Raverson's seen him at his most vulnerable, and has turned that vulnerability into a weapon?

"Miss Wilson wins every game of whist. There's no way

Mrs. Stelm has been, what, holding out for a year?" Beth asks, indignant.

Demeroven sighs beside him and Bobby rolls his shoulders. He loves his cousin and Beth, he really does, but even without his other preoccupations, they're a bit much today.

"She's playing the long game," Gwen returns. "Lulling them into a false sense of security."

"And Mrs. Gilpe?" Albie asks, leaning around Beth where they're all pressed up to the fence.

"Has never been able to beat Mrs. Stelm at whist as long as I've known her," Gwen insists.

Bobby hasn't figured out quite what to say to Demeroven, even on the slow carriage ride to Ascot. It's just the five of them; Uncle Dashiell and Aunt Cordelia stayed in town. Aunt Cordelia is too far along to come with them, and Uncle Dashiell far too anxious to leave her. Bobby hasn't spoken with his uncle since . . . Raverson, but he sent him to Ascot, so that's something. Humiliation and shame ripple through him at the thought and Bobby shakes himself, trying to pay attention to the conversation.

"What if it's in fact Mrs. Gilpe who's been playing the long game, waiting for the right bet to take you for all you're worth and run off with Mrs. Stelm?" Albie goads.

"For my entire life?" Gwen asks. "Oh, now, don't you side with him too," she says to Beth, who laughs at her and then leans around Gwen and Demeroven to catch Bobby's eye.

"What do you think?" she asks.

"I think you're letting Gwen distract Albie from the fact that he has yet to place a bet, and it's going to mean no one gets any money," Bobby says, rallying as Albie gapes at Gwen. "You hadn't put that together yet?" he asks, laughing. Albie glares over at him.

"I have decided on Gildermire, thank you," Albie says primly, adjusting his tall top hat. "And I'll not be talked out of it."

"Are you sure?" Gwen needles, that lilt in her voice that always means a protracted fight. "Because I think I can convince you into Fisherman."

"Fisherman's lost his last two races."

All four of them turn to look at Demeroven. His cheek is a livid purple from where it smacked the patio only days earlier, and the poor man's been limping all day. Albie keeps looking between them at intervals, as if trying to decide whether or not Bobby finally hauled off and punched him.

Bobby's been replaying that moment before Demeroven fell over and over in his head—the terrified look of panic that came over his face before he toppled backward down the stairs. The sound of him hitting the ground still makes Bobby wince.

"I think Lord Mason's got it right—Gildermire for sure," Demeroven continues.

Albie preens and then sticks his tongue out at Gwen, who glowers first at Albie and then toward Demeroven. "Fine. But I want ancillary bets."

"That's not part of the bargain," Albie says at once. "I won the tournament, I set our Ascot bets—those were your rules."

"Well, this is boring," Gwen exclaims loudly.

"I suppose I could go in with you on a small bet for Fisherman if you'd like, Lady Gwen," Demeroven says. Bobby turns to look at him, shocked. "What?"

"You don't bet."

Demeroven shrugs. "If it will make Lady Gwen happy, I see no reason to withhold."

"Yes!" Gwen says, her exclamation drawing looks from the attendees around them. "All right, Demeroven, how much are we talking?"

"Well—" Demeroven starts, shifting to stand up tall with a groan. "Given the previous four races—"

"Let's not," Beth says, stepping back from the barrier to maneuver herself between Gwen and Demeroven, her face pinched.

"Why not?" Gwen demands, nudging her, which jostles Beth into Demeroven, and Demeroven into Bobby.

Demeroven lets out the smallest *ouch* and Bobby hesitantly steadies him. Gwen pays them no mind, glaring down at her partner while Beth shakes her head.

"I don't believe any of us need our reputations tarnished by a loud round of betting. Albert will place the bets today and we can all simply stand miserably in the sun, all right?"

The group stares at Beth, who looks resolutely across the track, chin held high.

"A good idea," Albie says after a moment. "Gwen, perhaps you can simply bet against yourself."

"What fun is that?" Gwen grouses, slumping against the fence.

"Fun that can't be misconstrued as anything less than innocent," Beth says.

"I'm sorry."

Bobby starts, looking down at Demeroven, who's looking at Beth.

"What?" Beth asks, inelegant and surprised. Even Gwen looks taken aback.

"If you're refusing to take part in some low-stakes betting on my account, it's unnecessary. My remarks at the opera were . . . indelicate, to say the least, and the words of a cad to say more. Please, do not hold back on my behalf. I—I meant to say I was impressed by the work your cousin is doing, Lady Gwen, and that I hoped I too was making some effort to improve both our families' standings. I did not mean to disparage our predecessors, nor to speak ill of the dead."

Bobby knows there's commotion around them, but he thinks you could hear a pin drop among their group.

"Thank you, Lord Demeroven," Beth manages, a tight smile on her face as she looks up at him. "I appreciate it."

Demeroven rummages in his jacket, pulling out a few bills. "Please, have a wager on me, would you both?"

Gwen snatches the bills before Beth can say anything, winking at Demeroven. She pulls Beth close. Beth's gaze lingers on her cousin for a moment, and then that smile unfurls and she lets Gwen draw her into a quieter, but no less fervid, discussion of bets.

Demeroven looks back across the track, his face a bit less tense than before, and Bobby feels it all click horribly in his head. Bobby can't take Raverson down alone. The only other person who knows about Raverson's extortion plans—the only person Raverson has said it to outright—is Demeroven. Which means he has to accept Demeroven's apology. They'll need to work together to thwart Raverson's scheming. It's not as if anything Demeroven has said—at all—has been wrong. But Bobby's wounded pride still flares bright in his chest.

Unfortunately, he no longer has the luxury of pride. Not with Raverson loudly making jokes and further connections across the track in the royal enclosure. Not when Raverson looks directly back at them and has the gall to tip his bloody hat in their direction before turning to chat with some dignitary Bobby can't name.

Demeroven shifts closer to him, stretching uncomfortably. Bobby takes a deep breath. Demeroven offered an apology. He needs to make the next blasted move. So he reluctantly lowers his head to whisper, "We have to stop him."

Demeroven startles, then glances briefly up at him. "Agreed."

Bobby lets himself lean against the fence. He looks down at Demeroven, the man's cheek such an unpleasant shade of purple that he feels some of his guarded pride slip away. "I'm sorry for startling you the other night."

He sees Demeroven start to fight the comment before his shoulders slump. "I'm sorry for accosting you instead of having a simple conversation about Raverson. My . . . temper was already high; I shouldn't have approached you that way."

Bobby forces himself to nod. He has to meet Demeroven halfway if they're ever to work together. They watch as the horses finally approach the starting gate, the crowd raucous around them. Bobby can hear Beth, Albie, and Gwen discussing something, their chatter fading into the sound of the crowd as the jockeys get into position.

"So what's your plan?"

Bobby stiffens, glancing at Demeroven to find the man watching him carefully. "Why do I have to have the plan?" he asks.

"Because this is your fault," Demeroven replies, his face closing off again.

"Well, if you had just told me Raverson has a habit of extorting his . . . connections," Bobby counters, the indignance he's been trying to ignore rising fast.

"How was I supposed to know that you'd go and dally with the man again?" Demeroven hisses.

"I did not— It wasn't that—" Bobby begins, glancing around them.

The starting gun goes off and the horses charge out of the gate. Bobby watches the race, his pounding pulse having little to do with Gildermire's immediate lead. They can barely get through a single discussion without devolving into an argument. And yet there's something simmering in his stomach about each conversation. They replay over and over in his head, and he wishes he knew why.

Why does this man's opinion of him sit so heavy on his shoulders?

Gildermire wins by two lengths with Fisherman just behind. Gwen and Albie whoop while Beth jumps in place excitedly next to Demeroven. The man himself barely moves, staring broodily across the track. Bobby reluctantly follows his gaze and finds Raverson standing amid a cluster of dukes, shaking hands and grinning that irritatingly straight grin.

"Bobby, escort me to the water closet before the next race?" Beth asks.

"Demeroven, you escort me," Gwen adds, grasping James' arm before he can protest and yanking him toward the exit that will lead them across the track and around to the back of the pavilion.

Bobby sighs and takes Beth's arm. "She's a menace, you know," he says as they follow sedately after Gwen and Demeroven.

Gwen does slow down when it becomes apparent Demeroven's limp hasn't quite loosened up yet. The sight makes Bobby's throat tight with regret and he tugs Beth closer.

"She absolutely is," Beth agrees. "You and James getting along a bit better now?"

"What, now that he's offered a perfunctory apology for making you cry?" He glances down at Beth and finds her frowning up at him beneath her lace bonnet. He sighs. "We're . . . finding things to—"

"Bond over?" Beth suggests.

"Don't get your hopes up too high," Bobby cautions, pretending he hasn't noticed the way Demeroven's pants fit quite snugly in the rear.

"Well, I'm glad you're getting along a little better at least,"

Beth says as they head toward the shaded pavilion where spectators are hurriedly purchasing refreshments before the next heat.

"Why?" Bobby wonders.

"Well, Dashiell is adamant we all get along and work together. He's very impressed by James' new work ethic."

"And neither you nor Gwen has bothered to tell him that he's been an arse to all of us?" Bobby asks, ignoring the pang that it's possible Uncle Dashiell now prefers Demeroven to him—especially as Demeroven hasn't gotten him recently blackmailed, that Uncle Dashiell knows of.

"It's made him so happy, working with Albie and James. He's so big on family, and with Mother so close to . . . I couldn't bear to take that from him," Beth rushes out, her hand going tense in the crook of his elbow.

"Right. Of course," Bobby says quickly. "Of course he is. He's a happy expectant father, no reason to tarnish that. I can—I'll get along with Demeroven."

"You will?" Beth asks, looking up at him with such bright hope, he can't help but nod. "Thank you."

"Beth," Gwen says.

Bobby blinks, surprised to find them already at the outer wall of the water closets.

Beth pats his arm and then lets Gwen pull her away into the lavatories, leaving Bobby and Demeroven loitering outside. Hardly a picturesque location, but at least it's cool. They stand in the shade beneath the white tarps, awkward and alone.

"Blistering hot out there, isn't it?" Demeroven offers, scuffing his good foot against the packed dirt floor.

"Damn right," Bobby agrees, shaking his hands out to pump himself up enough to continue his and Demeroven's charming conversation.

"Perhaps you and the girls could arrange an event, or ensure Raverson is invited to the next tea," Demeroven says quietly.

Bobby jerks his gaze to meet Demeroven's. "Excuse me?"

"You could use the opportunity to suss out his plan, try and understand all the angles."

Bobby would rather fall down his own set of stairs than approach Raverson at a tea. "Why? You seem chummy enough—can't you do the digging?"

"Lord Havenfort has my days planned out down to the hour," Demeroven says. "You've the time, don't you?"

Bobby bristles, hackles rising fast. "I have better things to do."

Demeroven considers him and Bobby tries to keep his shoulders back, chest out. "Do you?" Demeroven asks.

He hates that Demeroven can do this—can ask questions, make statements, make note of things just as they are, no artifice, no sugarcoating.

No, he doesn't have better things to do, but he surely doesn't want to admit that to Demeroven, the frustrating—

"I'm absolutely parched," Gwen announces as she and Beth emerge from the lavatories. "You boys can fetch us some refreshments, can't you?" she prompts.

Bobby would argue, but there's a sheen on Beth's eyes. No matter where they go, or how busy Uncle Dashiell keeps them, nothing can truly distract from the impending birth and the danger Beth's mother will be in when the baby comes. That worry is ever present.

"Of course," Bobby says, even as Demeroven frowns at him. "Come along, Demeroven," he says, taking Demeroven's arm to turn him around and steer him toward the far side of the pavilion where the drinks and food wait for sale.

But Demeroven has other plans, veering off to the right once they've passed the lavatories. He haltingly marches them toward a deserted corner where they can duck behind a tent flap, leaving them in the meter-wide gap between the tent and the side of the whitewashed pavilion.

It's cooler still in this little hideaway, and everything's tinged with an off-white light from the tent above them. If Bobby weren't so uncomfortable in such close quarters with Demeroven, he might be relieved.

"We need to make a plan," Demeroven whispers, glancing up at Bobby before running his fingers through his thick sandy-brown hair.

"Look, if you're going to have me doing investigative work, why don't you tell me everything you know, since your reticence is what got us into this situation," Bobby returns, clenching his jaw the moment the words are out.

He used to be good at hiding his resentments. But it seems like lately all he can do is spew them at anyone willing to listen, whether they deserve it or not.

Demeroven pinches the bridge of his nose. "Why do you have to do this?"

"What?"

"Keep pointing fingers when I'm trying to stop?" Demeroven says, scrubbing his hand down his face before meeting Bobby's eyes.

Bobby feels his defenses rising again despite himself. "Stop? You're the one accusing me of knowingly endangering the family, when it was you not telling me who Raverson was that put us in this position."

"Only because you can't seem to properly vet your paramours," Demeroven says, stepping toward him.

Bobby steps back, trying to put space between them as their animosity swirls around them, feeling less like animosity and more like something else he doesn't quite want to name.

"Raverson was hardly a paramour. And he came on to me," Bobby says.

"And you had no control? Couldn't take even a moment to study his history before you let him into your pants?"

"What, do you vet all of your . . . engagements before having a go? Pause the action to go and interview people about them?" Bobby asks, glancing toward the flap of the curtain, but he doesn't see movement on the other side. "You'll barely discuss D'Vere, let alone anyone else. Do you expect a man to wait for you while you poke about in his life?"

"If he's truly interested, he would wait," Demeroven says haughtily.

Bobby feels his chest tighten. He's so unnervingly smug. "Right. Because you're such a prize, any man would fall over himself to wait around until you deem him worthy."

"Any man worth my time would be doing his own research," James insists.

It burrows against Bobby's gut; no one has ever been willing to wait for him. If they had been, perhaps he wouldn't have snuck into the curtains with Raverson. Perhaps one of his lovers would have stuck around, instead of going off to get married. No one has ever wanted him enough to care about the repercussions, because it's always just been one night, if that.

But Demeroven is staring at him, his eyes narrowed, like he can hear Bobby's pathetic thoughts. He's not going to let this man think himself *better* than Bobby, just because he's clearly met better men.

"So you'll do your research for a paramour, but can't be bothered to step in when your aunt and cousin are being treated abominably, is that it?" Bobby spits out.

"Shut up," Demeroven hisses, his eyes darkening. Bobby

takes another step back, surprised. "I didn't know. If I had, I would have fucking done something."

Bobby can see the truth of it on Demeroven's face, can see anguish and anger and self-loathing. But he can't seem to stop his mouth. "Would you really? Or would you just have let your stepfather—"

"Don't you say a word about my stepfather," Demeroven snarls, stalking forward again. Bobby's back hits the pavilion wall with a light whump. "You couldn't understand what it's like, having so much responsibility heaped on your shoulders all at once, when the year before they told you *nothing.* You think your life is hard: 'Woe is me, I'm a second son, I'm bored and have nothing to do.' You cannot fathom what I've dealt with, the lengths at which I need to go to protect my family, to rehabilitate my name."

"Goddammit, Demeroven, we're aiming for the same thing," Bobby manages, holding back a plethora of ruder responses.

He hates this. He hates that Demeroven is right. That he's seeing clearly while Bobby's been oblivious. And more than anything else, he hates how sodding good Demeroven looks all hot and bothered.

"You accuse me of making this into a competition, but you cannot stop yourself from reminding me that you are more important. And yet you want the responsibility of this blunder to be mine alone. You slept with him too," Bobby says roughly.

"Before I knew better!" Demeroven exclaims, the sound ringing around them.

They both glance toward the tent flap, but there's nothing but the stuffy air in their little alcove and the distant roar of the crowds.

"I could have known better if you'd bothered to tell me," Bobby says, his voice low.

"When would you have listened?" Demeroven mutters.

"If you'd tried even at all to get to know me, we could have been friends," Bobby hears himself say. He's hot, and he's frazzled, and he's getting so tired of fighting about this.

"I know you," Demeroven counters.

"You don't," Bobby insists. "You could have. Instead you've concocted this idea that I'm some kind of sex-crazed deviant determined to ruin you."

"I'd never let you ruin me," Demeroven says and Bobby feels himself flush.

"Right. Right, my mistake. I'm sure I would never pass the safe paramour exam," Bobby grits out. "Or would I just be refused the test altogether? Too lowly for you to trifle with," he hears himself say.

His chest is heaving in tandem with Demeroven's. Demeroven's face is flushed, his eyes suddenly a little wild, his hands balled into fists.

"It's not a question of your status or . . . political value," Demeroven says rapidly.

"What, then it's my personality that's so abhorrent?" Bobby asks, wondering when his mouth got so fully away from him.

"Have you lost your mind?" Demeroven exclaims.

"You're the one that dragged me in here. If it's so difficult to be around me, why don't you just—"

Demeroven steps forward, his hand sliding around to the back of Bobby's head to pull him into a rough and sudden kiss. All that animosity, all the anger, all the hurt boils between them as Demeroven leans forward, trapping Bobby against the wall, their bodies pulled flush together.

Bobby groans into Demeroven's mouth, surprised and aroused and strangely delighted to discover that Demeroven feels just as chiseled beneath his linen coat as he looks. Better than that, Demeroven can bloody kiss. It's all fierce, needy lips and groping hands, and Bobby gives himself over to the physicality of it.

Rough, and hot, and heady—is this what was coming for them the whole time? All the fighting and petty words, was it really *this* beneath the surface, all along?

Demeroven sucks on his bottom lip as he palms Bobby's arse, grinding them together in a press that's delicious friction and frustration and utter glory—

Until Demeroven suddenly pulls away, the two of them left gaping at each other with kiss-raw lips, hair mussed, bodies heaving.

What the actual—

CHAPTER TWELVE

James

Hell.

Oh, hell. What did he just do?

He kissed Mason. Bobby Mason. Bold, fearless, reckless Bobby Mason.

Bobby Mason, who's been beautiful since they were young. Bobby Mason, who wouldn't have given him a second look at Oxford, is now standing debauched and winded, watching him hungrily as if he might like to—

Oh, *hell.*

James can't seem to make . . . any part of himself work. Can't move, can barely think. All he can feel is the heavy drum of his pulse and the tightness of his midsection and his—

Mason reaches out as if to pull James back into his arms. James almost goes, staring at Mason's reddened lips, thinking of the snag of his light stubble and how if James pushed him up against the wall at the right angle, he could wedge his thigh in tight and—

There's a great cheer from the stands far beyond them.

"We can't," he croaks, stepping back from Mason's reaching fingers.

"We absolutely can," Mason counters, pushing off from the wall.

"I—I heard someone."

Mason pauses, listening. James tries to breathe steadily against his racing pulse. He didn't hear anyone. But he could have.

Mason pulls back the curtain and peers out into the tent. James stands there, mind whirring as blood slowly makes its way back into his skull. Mason turns back to James with a sly smile and drops the curtain, sidling forward.

James is so paralyzed by indecision and arousal that he doesn't move. The feeling of Mason's broad palm skating along his jaw to cup his neck makes James shiver. His thumb rests right at James' earlobe, stroking gently.

He could melt into a puddle right there, just collapse into Mason's arms.

"Funny how we've spent so many weeks sniping at each other, when we could have been doing this instead," Mason says huskily, leaning in to glance his lips off James'.

It takes everything James has not to chase his mouth. "We shouldn't," he mumbles, the words bubbling up from the depths of his mind even as the rest of him strains toward Mason.

"We're fine here," Mason assures him.

James so wants to believe him. He hasn't felt anything like the passion or fervor of their kisses in so long. Possibly ever. Mason may be onto something about the fighting turning into ardor.

But Mason's assurances give him little relief from the growing anxiety that's rapidly clawing through his lust haze. Mason's been caught before. Worse, Mason has never been careful. Has never had to be.

Mason's family loves him, clearly. Lord Havenfort caught him in a tryst and still sent him to Ascot with his daughter and stepdaughter. If James' stepfather ever caught him in the act, James isn't sure he'd live to tell the tale, much less be protected.

Mason isn't an option. No matter how much these kisses—the ardent look on his beautiful face—stir something deep and young inside of James, Mason is not the golden boy of his Oxford days.

Mason is a risk—one James can't stand to take. Not now. Not with Raverson looming. Not with his title at stake. Not with his fragile pride and anxiety.

"We can't do this," James says, pulling back with purpose this time.

Mason's hand glides across his cheek as it falls away. James forces himself not to mourn its loss. This was a onetime occurrence. A fantasy, nothing more.

"We could," Mason says, remaining still, his eyes beckoning just as much as his hand did. "Surely this is safer than the alternative. We have credible reasons to see each other, and ample opportunity. Even if we spend half our time bickering, wouldn't it be better to—"

Mason peters off and James realizes he's shaking his head. He can't listen to this—can't let Mason lay out anything close to a reasonable plan for a . . . dalliance. Because it would be reckless, and foolish, and too close to something James never even knew he could consider, or want.

"If you'd just think about, for a moment, the implications of—"

"No," James says, his voice high and tight. "No. We'll—we'll discuss the problem—Raverson," he corrects. Mason snaps his mouth shut, frowning. "Later. I must be going."

He turns and pushes through the curtain, away from Mason and his potentially enticing offer—away from the fantasies of his youth—away from his own desires. Mason is pompous, and reckless, and handsome, and an absurdly good kisser, and James needs to get as far away from him as physically possible before Mason's impulsivity spreads.

"Demeroven."

James keeps moving, limping as quickly as he can back toward the lavatories. Their little hidey-hole was further from the crowds than he thought.

"Why are you always running away?" Mason demands, too close behind him.

James hurries forward, only for Mason to grab his arm just as James goes to swing around the corner of the lavatories.

"For Christ's sake, just talk to—"

James crashes into someone, Mason's hand wrenching off his arm. But two strong hands catch him, and James closes his eyes. He'd know that overtight grip anywhere. It belongs to the very last person he wants to see.

"Afternoon, gentlemen," Raverson says, his voice lilting.

James scrambles back, nearly knocking into Mason, who quickly steps to his side so they're facing Raverson together. James watches Raverson take in their appearance—Mason's ruffled hair, James' askew tie, both of their reddened mouths.

"It seems I might need to pay a visit to the house of Havenfort sooner than I'd planned. How interesting," Raverson says.

James feels his heart rate kick back up. How can they play this off? He'd tell Raverson he's seeing something that isn't there, but one look at Mason proves that there's no denying it. What was he thinking, just walking away without settling himself first? Allowing Mason to traipse after him like an advertisement screaming *Look, I was just nearly shagged.*

"Lord Havenfort has nothing more to say to you," Mason says.

"Oh, I think he will," Raverson says, looking significantly between them.

"You're seeing things, Raverson," James pushes out. He just has to be like Mason—collected, and calm, not visibly panicking out of his mind.

"I don't think I am, little Demeroven."

"Shut up," James hears himself say, a knee-jerk reaction to that honey-tinged tone in Raverson's voice. The one he always used when he would tell James he was being *silly.* Was upset over *nothing.* Was being *immature.*

"Ah, yes, a little romp does tend to make you brave, doesn't it?" Raverson returns.

"You're far off base," Mason says, glancing between them.

"Oh, but you forget, Mason, I know what you both look like when you're freshly . . . debauched. And you've done little to hide it."

James clenches his jaw, looking around, but they're thankfully alone. Just Raverson, Mason, and James here in the dim tent light by the overscented lavatories. And even still, he wants to hide, wants to shrink away. But Mason is tall beside him, strong, and James reminds himself he doesn't have to take this lying down. He doesn't have to let Raverson have this kind of sway over him.

"You're making dangerous assumptions," James tells him, curling his hands into fists.

Raverson meets his eyes with that damn languid smirk. "And you must have gotten better in the sack, then, Demeroven, if you're able to entice Mason. Though Mason is slumming it a bit for you, isn't he?"

He doesn't know quite why he does it. But something inside him snaps and James finds himself rushing forward. His fist collides with a solid, painful thud against Raverson's jaw.

Coming at him from beneath, given their height difference, the impact sets Raverson off balance and James watches in astonishment as he tips backward and lands sprawled on the packed dirt ground, a hand to his jaw.

"Damn, Demeroven," Mason says, whistling as he steps up to his side, a hand out to stay James should he feel like going for a second hit.

But James isn't sure what even got him to the first. He's never hit anyone before. But it—it felt good.

It feels good, staring down at Raverson as he glares up at them, indignant and flattened there on the ground, his white linen suit covered in dust. It makes James feel just a bit powerful.

"You're a dead man, Demeroven. I'll tell the whole town about this—let them in on your precious secrets—the both of you," he spits up at them.

"Oh, yes, and what credibility you'll have. Uh-uh," Mason says, stepping in front of James to kick Raverson's raised foot away.

Raverson must have been trying to strike James in the knee. Perhaps James is not so powerful after all, but rather in shock. He should have seen that coming.

"Who do you think they'll believe—you, or lords in good standing with high morals and good families? You've yet to even claim a party. You're a joke," Mason says, his chin high, looking rather imperious.

Raverson glares at Mason as he slowly sits up. Mason stays that step ahead of James, in a sort of ready stance, like a boxer. James wonders idly if Mason boxes. It would account for the sinuous muscle he felt when—

"I'll tell your stepfather," Raverson says.

A surge of shame washes over James at the clutch those words have around his heart. But no, he will not let Raverson believe he's found James' soft underbelly. He will not let Raverson see an ounce of the hurt and confusion and shame he's brought on James by becoming close with his stepfather. He won't give the man the satisfaction.

"You may think you've charmed my stepfather, and perhaps you have," he says, holding his chin high, just like Mason did, forcing his voice to be steady. "But we're not at Oxford anymore, Richard," he says, his false bravado giving way to something deeper as Raverson stares at him in shock. "Running to a boy's daddy to tell him what he's done won't get you the power or standing you had at school. You'll need to be cleverer than that. Handkerchiefs and trinkets aren't enough anymore. You've no popularity. You're nothing."

Mason glances back at him, looking rather impressed. Raverson struggles to his feet, glaring. James reaches out and tugs on Mason's arm, yanking him back. He thinks there's a glimmer of doubt in Raverson's cold dark eyes as he rubs his jaw.

"You'll both be sorry," he says, disdain and threat dripping from the words.

"Go find some icc," Mason says.

Raverson stares at them for a long, uncomfortable moment before turning on his heel and stalking off. James watches him go, his knuckles almost numb where he's clutching at Mason's sleeve.

The crowd roars distantly and he shakes himself, releasing Mason's arm to run trembling fingers through his hair.

"You should have broken his nose," Mason says, turning to regard James as they stand alone at the back of the pavilion.

"My aim was off," James agrees. "Wasn't thinking straight."

"Fair," Mason says, looking over his shoulder to ensure Raverson has truly disappeared. "How's your hand?"

James shrugs, flexing his fingers. Reginald taught him how to swing a proper punch when he was a boy, but no one ever told him how much it hurts to collide your knuckles with another man's jaw. "I'll be fine," he says, noting the way Mason still looks a little bit impressed.

Men.

Yes, men. He, normally a completely rational man, just had a tryst and then socked a peer. A lord who's currently blackmailing them both.

"Well, this seems to have solved our problem, at least momentarily," Mason says, reaching out for James' hand.

James hastily shoves his hands into his pockets. He can't let Mason touch him again. He doesn't know what he'll do. He doesn't know himself today. And he doesn't know if that's Mason's fault, or Raverson's, or his stepfather's, or if perhaps beneath the surface this is who he's always been—dangerous, reckless, and thoughtless—and he's just been suppressing it with anxiety and fear all this time.

"That's not the last we've seen of Raverson," James says, trying to rein in his swirling thoughts. "We'll have to come up with something better, get your ring back."

"Of course," Mason says, stepping closer. "You know, it's rather attractive, this unguarded side of you. Very bold, very brash. I like it."

James swallows against the look on Mason's face—sly, attractive, hungry. "I—" he starts. Mason's boxing him in against the wall of the lavatories, out in the open, where anyone could see.

"Demeroven, consider—"

"No," James says, all that bravado and bravery and action slamming back into wherever it's been hiding. All he can feel now is the panic of his reality—the sheer number of ways everything could come tumbling down. "No. I told you; we cannot do this. We are partners in preventing blackmail, nothing more. Now please step back."

Mason stills, staring at him. "Come now, we've taken care of Raverson—"

"We haven't," James says, Raverson's threat about his stepfather still ringing in his ears. "There is too much at stake to give into this—this—"

"Angry attraction?" Mason suggests, looking far too mischievous, far too handsome, far too tempting.

"Absurdity," James returns, trying not to care when Mason's smile dims. "I have to leave."

"Leave," Mason repeats, his smile disappearing altogether. "You mean run."

James shrugs—can't deny it, really. He needs to run away, before Mason talks him into anything else. Because he's not sure he has the resolve to stick to his decision. Not with Mason there, rumpled and wanting.

"Please apologize to Lady Gwen and Miss Bertram, would you? We're quite delinquent in bringing their drinks," he says, and his voice sounds foreign, formal.

"Tell them yourself," Mason says, an aloof look falling over his features. "And I'm walking away first," he adds, turning on his heel to stomp off toward the drinks, leaving James alone by the lavatories.

He watches Mason until he fades into the crowd by the refreshments, his thoughts whirring so fast he's not even sure what he's truly thinking. He scrubs at his face, wincing. His knuckles flare with dull pain. He looks down to find them red and already a little swollen.

He should feel proud for having taken Raverson down a peg.

But somehow all he feels is hollow, like today has been some strange, broken dream.

Bobby Mason kissed him. Bobby Mason . . . wants him.

After years of swooning over him at school, of butterflies and late-night fantasies, here it is, his dream come true.

Bobby Mason offered to be his lover. And James said no.

Chapter Thirteen

Bobby

Bobby downs his current drink, relishing in the warmth along the back of his neck. The stag party is clustered at the back of their first pub of the evening, packed into a raucous booth beneath dripping candles. He's trying to focus on the tipsy discussion Cunningham and Prince are having about the upcoming cricket match, but he keeps getting distracted.

There's a light pink flush making its way up Demeroven's neck as he sits between Rupping and Wristead on the opposite side of the booth. His sandy-brown hair is curling adorably with the humidity and sweat, and his eyes are a little big, trying to keep up with their motley group.

Bobby wants to be so insulted, so angry, so over Demeroven. But the man looks entirely out of his depth and it does something to Bobby's stomach. Something swirly and swoony. He raises his glass, trying to flag down the beleaguered barmaid to get another scotch.

Prince's stag night is off to a very successful start, and Bobby might die before the evening runs out.

"Here you go, love," the barmaid says, leaning across the table to pass Bobby another glass.

She has a pretty round face and very ample cleavage, rather on display. Doesn't do much for Bobby, but Prince's eyes glide over the barmaid, his rattle of cricket statistics trailing off, and Bobby hears Demeroven snort across the booth.

"And some waters," Bobby says, meeting her eyes. "If you've got them. Otherwise, some weak beer, please, if you can." They need to pace themselves.

"And all the bread you have," Demeroven puts in.

The barmaid laughs and gives them both a wink before straightening up and sashaying away. Bobby's and Demeroven's eyes meet briefly and then skid away. He forces himself to turn back to Prince, who's still ogling the barmaid's luscious figure.

"I see love hasn't tamed your roving eye, man," Bobby says.

Cunningham snorts while Prince gapes at Bobby, his brown hair flopping into his eyes as if in admonishment. "I admire a lovely lady," Prince says innocently.

"And a lovely gent, if there's one around," Cunningham adds, reaching around Bobby's back to flick Prince's ear.

Bobby notes Demeroven glancing around. But the dim, crowded pub is more than loud enough to drown out any secrets they may reveal in their drunken revels. It's why he and Cunningham picked the Thirsty Pig as their first spot. And they'll only get more rowdy from here.

"It's my stag night. I'll ogle anyone I please, thanks," Prince says haughtily, before letting out an enormous belch.

The whole table laughs. "And does your fiancée enjoy seeing you this sloshed?" Wristead asks merrily, his face already flushed, hair plastered to his forehead.

"She does," Prince says easily. "What about Mary Ann?"

"She's such a lightweight, we've never managed," Wristead admits. "But she mixes an excellent cocktail. Could give Jeremy a run for his money."

"We should get her together with my cousin and Miss Bertram," Bobby says. "Lady Gwen has developed a keen interest in mixed drinks over the last year."

"Has she?" Demeroven asks, blinking at his own question.

"She makes a mean sherry cobbler," Bobby finds himself saying. Nothing strange about them discussing Gwen, when they've yet to speak a direct word to each other all night. Let alone about anything . . . important.

"Oh, that could be dangerous territory," Rupping says, his voice loud and scratchy already. "Lady Gwen gets ever so competitive."

"I think Mary Ann can take her," Wristead insists.

"If she's a better sport than you are, Lady Gwen would delight in challenging her," Bobby says as Wristead frowns over at him.

"That's right. Didn't you break your croquet mallet two seasons ago after a run-in with Mason's dear cousin?" Cunningham asks Wristead while Prince chuckles into his drink.

"I didn't break it. It broke. Very different. And she cheated," Wristead insists.

Bobby rolls his eyes. "Lady Gwen doesn't need to cheat to beat every one of your arses at whatever sport she chooses. You're just a sore loser, Wristead."

"Truly," Prince agrees.

"The worst," Rupping says.

"You're making me long for the country," Wristead grumbles. "And I hate the country."

Prince belches again and Bobby glances over toward the bar. He catches the barmaid's harried eyes, her arms laden with orders. She shakes her head.

"All right, lads, I think it's time we hit the next bar, before our groom drinks himself to death at this one," he suggests.

"Fox and Toad?" Rupping asks the group.

"Fox and Toad," they all chorus, even Demeroven.

Bobby gets distracted watching Demeroven slide out of the booth, his slender, muscled frame unfolding as he stands. He's got his frock coat over his arm and his shirt cuffs rolled up to his biceps, tie undone around his neck. Ruffled and sweaty—the look brings back memories of their tryst behind the tent flap and Bobby shakes himself.

It was a onetime thing. He can't let himself become captivated by the idea. The man isn't interested. And he's not in the business of chasing someone who doesn't want him.

Prince pulls Bobby up, leaning into him with a dopey little smile. He was able to get over his crush on Prince, after all. And now he's happy for the man, off to a life of wedded bliss with a lovely young woman. He'll . . . get over Demeroven, somehow.

Cunningham struggles up behind him and Bobby has enough presence of mind to get Prince's arm around his shoulder. He turns to Cunningham and nudges him. "Give her something extra; we're a handful."

"Steady on," Cunningham agrees, pulling a few crumpled notes from his pocket.

They traipse through the crowded pub and Bobby ensures Cunningham runs into their barmaid to hand the money to her directly, before they all spill out onto the street.

Rupping and Wristead are swinging around a lamppost, singing some shanty and garnering glares from the still fairly respectable citizens on the high street. It's early yet. Too early for dirty sea shanties.

Prince stumbles against him and Bobby eyes their drunker friends. "Demeroven," he says, catching the man's attention. Demeroven looks back at him, then glances at Rupping and Wristead. "Take Prince. I'll handle them, and Cunningham will—"

"This way, lads!" Cunningham proclaims, dancing down the street ahead of them.

Both Bobby and Demeroven laugh. Their eyes meet as Bobby passes Prince over to Demeroven and he feels that pull again. He knows there could be something more than animosity between them, if they let it. But Demeroven skirts his glance away and starts guiding Prince down the street, leaving Bobby to corral Wristead and Rupping. A good distraction if ever he knew one.

Four pubs later, Bobby's impressed any of them are still standing. He cut himself off at the third pub, and his buzz is beginning to wear down. But the rest of the gents are still going strong. They've already lost Rupping. Not quite sure where he got off to.

Wristead's starting to nod off against the wall as they stand at the entrance to the Pewter House, waiting for Cunningham to close their tab. Bobby wonders idly how much Prince's father provided for this evening.

"On to Twildings!" Cunningham decrees as he guides a stumbling Prince out of the pub. Demeroven brings up the rear, hands out to catch Prince should he fall backward.

"Wristead, you should take a coach," Bobby says.

Wristead startles and starts to fall sideways. Demeroven runs up to catch him, buckling under his weight. Prince turns to help, slipping out of Cunningham's grip, and Bobby rushes forward to brace him.

He and Demeroven exchange a glance. They're reluctant partners in keeping their friends alive tonight, it seems. He supposes that's nominally better than being partners in evading extortion.

"I'll get Wristead into a coach. Cunningham, help me, would you?" Demeroven says, beckoning Cunningham over while Bobby steadies Prince on his shoulder.

He jerks his chin toward the end of the block and Demeroven nods, ushering Wristead and Cunningham toward the curb. Bobby helps Prince begin to shuffle in the opposite direction.

"My lover's eyes are the sea. She walks on air and clouds to me. Each morn I wake I feel a glow, her skin like cream and hair like . . ." Prince hesitates, tongue poking out of his mouth in concentration.

"What are you doing?"

"Sonnets," Prince says, as if it's a normal pastime. "What rhymes with *glow*?"

"*Snow*," Bobby suggests, laughing as Prince gives him a truly affronted look.

"Her hair is brown."

"Sorry. Um, *know*?"

"Why would her hair be like know?" Prince demands.

"Poetry is not my forte, Prince. But, oh, easy there," he says as Prince trips over an askew cobblestone.

"Catherine's like poetry," Prince says dreamily. "You should find a woman like poetry."

"I wouldn't even know where to begin," Bobby says honestly, guiding Prince over to a stone wall they can lean against until Demeroven and Cunningham catch up.

"But it's so nice to have a lady. She's so smart and pretty and nice. Ladies are so kind, Mason."

"I'm sure they are," Bobby agrees. Beth is, at least. Gwen is . . . something.

"You need a good woman to love," Prince insists.

Bobby sighs and looks over at his friend, who's leaning against the wall at an absurd angle. "Prince."

"You never know who will light up your life," Prince says, his gaze suddenly serious. "Sometimes they just stumble into you when you're not looking."

"Whatever you say," Bobby agrees, his head a little heavy—with melancholy or alcohol, he's not sure.

Prince smiles blearily and opens his mouth, but whatever he plans to say is drowned out by the sound of Cunningham falling against a bush, heaving his guts out.

Demeroven stumbles back from him, checking that he made it out of the splash zone. "Wristead's gone home."

"Just us left, then?" Bobby asks, trying not to look at the mess seeping out from the roots of Cunningham's bush, or at Demeroven, who looks even more beautiful under the lamplight. Frazzled and frustrated suits him. Oh, Lord, no wonder he's become . . . infatuated; he frustrates Demeroven every time they speak.

"Perhaps we should think about ending the night before someone winds up sleeping in the gutter?" Demeroven suggests.

"Nonsense," Cunningham says, straightening up and wiping his mouth. "We've three more pubs to hit before dawn."

Prince sags against Bobby's shoulder, and Bobby and Demeroven exchange a look. "Cunningham, if we take this man to another pub, he won't make it to his wedding tomorrow. Look at the poor sod."

Cunningham gives Prince a once-over and sighs dramatically. "Fine, fine. Put him in a coach and we'll drink to his honor."

Prince hiccoughs and wraps his other arm around Bobby's stomach. "Nighty-night."

"I think I'll see him home," Bobby says, glancing from Cunningham to Demeroven.

Demeroven jumps in. "And if the groom is leaving, I think I should—"

"Nonsense, Demeroven, we've hours left!" Cunningham insists, reaching out to take Demeroven's arm.

"I see only the strongest have survived," a voice calls out.

Bobby looks over as Thomas Parker strolls across the street with Jeremy the bartender in tow. They're a pair of grins with matching mustaches and overeager eyes. Cunningham whoops in excitement.

"The club's gone quiet without you lot, so we thought we'd come and join the party," Parker continues, glancing among them. "Cunningham show you the spots I recommended?"

"And then some," Cunningham says brightly. "Just about to take Demeroven on to Sloughthams. Mason's making Prince pack it in."

Demeroven meets Bobby's eyes, terror on his face. Cunningham, Parker, and Jeremy would eat him alive, and possibly get him tossed in jail. Bobby can't leave the man alone with them.

"Demeroven, help me get Prince home? Cunningham, gentlemen, we'll see you in the morning. Early, remember?"

"Of course, milords," Cunningham says.

He sweeps into a deep bow, belches, and then turns to Parker and Jeremy. He merrily wraps his arms about their shoulders. Parker and Jeremy salute Prince, Demeroven, and Bobby, and the three of them saunter off, exchanging shouts of delight.

"If he makes it to the wedding in proper attire, I'll be shocked," Bobby mutters.

Demeroven hums exhaustedly. He steps up on Prince's other side and gently tugs Prince's arm from Bobby's stomach. Bobby tries not to watch the way Demeroven maneuvers Prince's arm over his shoulder. Tries to ignore the little smile he gives Prince as Prince blathers something about Demeroven being the best. Bobby's focus needs to be on getting everyone home safely; that's it.

"Think they'll all even be alive by daybreak?" Demeroven mutters, shuffling under Prince's weight as they head for the next coach stand. Their height difference definitely isn't helping.

"Alive, yes. Functional, debatable," Bobby says. "Cunningham's beyond drunk."

"What can you do with a drunken sailor?" Prince sings hoarsely.

Bobby and Demeroven both laugh. Bobby looks across and catches Demeroven's eye, smiling.

"C'mon, Demeroven. We sang this every practice," Prince whines.

"For what?" Bobby wonders. It's hardly a good pace-keeper.

"When we brought the boats down to the river in winter. Kept up morale," Demeroven says. "But, Prince, I really don't—"

"Sing, or I'm lying down," Prince threatens, digging in his heels.

Bobby lurches forward, as does Demeroven, the three of them nearly toppling headlong into the stone wall along the sidewalk.

"Weigh hey and up she rises," Demeroven sings gruffly, blushing as Bobby tries not to laugh.

"Weigh hey and up she rises," Prince repeats happily.

"Weigh hey and up she rises, early in the morning," Demeroven continues.

"Put him in the longboat till he's sober," Prince slurs.

"Maybe we should do that to you," Bobby suggests, turning their awkward threesome to approach the curb just as a coach arrives at the stop.

"Put him in the longboat till he's sober, early in the morning!" Prince exclaims, loud enough for the whole street to hear.

Demeroven groans. Bobby digs in his pocket and fishes out

a pound to pay the coachman, hoping it'll cover any damage should Prince go the way Cunningham did.

"My apologies in advance," Bobby says as he passes it to the driver.

The driver just shakes his head and pockets the money. "Where to?"

"Maddox and St. George," Bobby says.

Demeroven hops up first and braces himself in the cabin to help pull Prince up.

Prince mumbles something incoherent and Demeroven snorts as Bobby pushes Prince up the steps. Demeroven gets him settled inside and Bobby vaults up unsteadily. Everything feels a little hazy, though that could just be the hour.

He hesitates, stooped in the door of the coach. Prince has sprawled out on the opposite bench, leaving Bobby no choice but to sit beside Demeroven. And Demeroven is seated ramrod straight, as far to his side as humanly possible. Excellent.

With a sigh, Bobby slides in, keeping as much distance from Demeroven as he can, and slams the door closed. Prince groans and just for that Bobby taps the ceiling hard enough it makes his own head hurt.

The carriage lurches off from the curb, throwing Bobby and Demeroven into each other. They scramble to separate, pointedly not looking at each other. Prince watches blankly and Bobby thanks God that he's not sober.

"Catherine is so pretty," Prince says.

Ah, more than preoccupied enough with his own love life, then.

"I look forward to meeting her tomorrow," Demeroven says.

"She's looking forward to meeting both of you. Told her loads about you."

Bobby and Demeroven do exchange a glance then. "Oh?"

"How you're both lovely chaps who need to get married," Prince says merrily.

"Prince," Bobby whines.

Prince rolls his eyes and looks to Demeroven. "When are you settling down with a nice girl, hmm?"

"Oh, I'm—I'm not even thinking about it," Demeroven says.

"Well, that's not good enough. It's not something you do with your head, anyhow, is it?" Prince says brightly.

"Depends on which head we're discussing," Bobby mutters.

Demeroven snorts and Bobby can't help but grin. Prince looks over at them, puzzled.

"Your heart!" he says dolefully.

"Right, right, the heart," Bobby says, holding up his hands. "My apologies. Demeroven, what does your heart say?"

Demeroven groans. "That it's been fed too many poems and sonnets, and had too much fish and chips, and now it burns."

"My heart burns for Catherine," Prince says.

"I'm sure it does," Demeroven says primly. He then glances at Bobby and blushes, running a hand through his hair. "What do you think it'll be like, marriage? I know you love her, but the marriage part's a whole other thing."

Oh, he's clever. A bit of a treacly question, but Prince does like to pontificate when he's drunk.

"I think it'll be glorious," Prince says, his indignation falling away to that dreamy look Bobby finds both endearing and annoying. "'S like living with your best friend for the rest of time, isn't it? What could be better?"

Neither Bobby nor Demeroven seems to have a good response. Prince begins to wax poetic about Miss Langston's various attributes as they turn down the long avenue that will eventually arrive at Prince's townhouse. Bobby can't bring himself to look at Demeroven.

He hasn't hated tonight. Taking care of the group together has almost been . . . fun, in its way. And Demeroven makes a good teammate. Are he and Demeroven friends? Would they really have enough of a foundation to build something more? And does that matter, really, if Demeroven's unwilling to even consider it?

CHAPTER FOURTEEN

James

Prince eventually trails off, falling into a light doze across from them. James looks to Mason, to share in the humor that is Prince mumbling while he sleeps, but finds Mason dozing too. Which leaves James alone in the very loud silence of the coach, with nothing but his feelings.

And that certainly won't do, given that this whole night has turned his staunch decision on its head. Instead of spending the evening squabbling or trying to one-up each other, they've simply . . . worked together in a détente that's frighteningly comfortable. Mason's calm, easy attitude all night has put him off-kilter. He hasn't pushed, hasn't prodded, hasn't tried to entice James into anything.

Instead, Mason—irresponsible, reckless Mason—has spent the whole evening making sure everyone had food and water. Making sure Prince was always having a good time. Cajoling Cunningham (quite a feat in itself) into changing pubs the moment the groom-to-be was less than amused.

He cares about his friends. He cares about his family. And he's quite responsible when it suits him. Which makes the narrative James has been clinging to, one of immorality and danger and disregard, feel all the flimsier. This person he's concocted in his head, so brash and prideful and confident—maybe he's not real. Maybe he never has been.

Perhaps James is the brash one. Perhaps Mason is as lonely as James himself feels, and that's what's driven him into trysts and casual flings. Perhaps it's not ego, but a want for intimacy.

Which is exactly what he asked of James at Ascot. A formal, steady, understanding arrangement, which would include the intimacy, of course, but would probably also include a lot of . . . this. Working as a team. Sitting together and sharing jokes. Camaraderie. Safe and secure.

And why wouldn't Mason feel comfortable asking for that, with a group of friends like Prince and Cunningham around him? Mason fits in with these boisterous, unguarded men. They're all making their own arrangements, going after their own happiness, in whatever way they can.

But no matter how entertaining they've been, or how eagerly they brought him along for this celebration, James knows *he* doesn't truly fit in here, not really. He's not, he can't be, like them—like Mason. Hell, he can't even get his shoulders to fully come down now that they're safely in a coach. He's spent the whole night watching the corners, peering down alleys. He can't help but worry someone is there, just beyond sight, watching, listening. Someone out to ruin them all. He'd give more than Prince's father paid for the whole night to feel as relaxed as Mason seemed tonight.

"Do you think it would be like that?"

James startles, looking over at Mason. "What?"

"Like being married to your best friend?"

James knots his fingers together in his lap. He wishes he knew what to *do* with all this newfound perspective, other than sit there anxiously as Mason shifts in his seat, his hair falling into his eyes so prettily.

James can't imagine marriage to be anything less than a painful lie—an extension of the life he's already living, hiding all the various parts of who he is, but from someone with whom he's supposed to share a bed.

Physical intimacy aside, he's not sure he's actually had a best friend before. Reginald's been like an uncle to him, but it's never been—it's not what Prince is talking about, he doesn't think. He wouldn't know what to do, how to be one. He's terrible at most things that have to do with other people, after all.

"I don't think I could find someone who would fully understand me, and accept me, without hurting them in the process," he says.

At Mason's surprised look, James realizes he's already said too much. He fights the urge to shrink back against the seat and simply lets the discomfort sit.

"Don't think much of yourself, do you?" Mason asks archly.

James blinks back at him, feeling a bit too raw to come at that head-on. "What, and you do? Sleeping with Raverson?"

That was uncalled for, even for him. But Mason just shrugs, which is infuriating.

"I don't define my self-worth by who I take to bed," Mason says.

James feels his eyebrows go up. He doesn't believe that. Mason's intelligent; surely he understands that paramours reflect on each other, well or poorly. Mason tips his head back to stare up at the ceiling, avoiding James' eyes.

"All right, fine, maybe we're both worthless, then."

James squirms in his seat. Nothing about Mason fits tonight, and it makes James uncomfortable. He doesn't like to be wrong about things, let alone to be this *completely* wrong about someone.

"And you?" James asks, going straight to deflection. "Do you think you'll ever get married?"

"I don't know," Mason says slowly, peeling his gaze from the ceiling to look over at Prince. "I certainly don't think I'd be as excited as Prince is, at any rate."

"That makes two of us," James agrees.

Mason tilts his head back again and closes his eyes. James can tell they're nearly there. He gives Mason about forty seconds, and then kicks him lightly in the shin.

"Oi!" Mason says, glaring over at him.

"I'm not hauling his prone body out and leaving it on his father's doorstep alone," James says.

Mason huffs, but waves a hand in acquiescence just as the carriage comes to a halt. Prince jerks awake and stares at the two of them.

"Wher'we?" he slurs.

"Home. Time for the groom to go to sleep," Mason says, moving across the cab to prop Prince up while James opens the door and hops down.

Together, and with no small possibility for injury to person or pride, they manage to get Prince out of the carriage and up the steps of the Prince townhouse, which could easily fit two Demeroven townhouses inside.

Bobby raps on the door, and they hover there, keeping Prince upright. They're all going to be trashed come morning.

The door opens and a tall butler with a broad face takes one look at Prince and lets out a highly Scottish curse.

"Give 'em here," he says.

James and Mason pass Prince into his care, and he slams the door behind them without even a word.

"Nice chap," Mason says, staring at the door. "Eloquent."

"And loquacious," James says.

Mason turns and James follows, the two of them looking down at the waiting coach. The idea of being inside that small space without the buffer of Prince doesn't fill James with confidence. Mason bumps his shoulder and James waves the coach away.

Then they set off, hands in their pockets, arms brushing. Each slight touch of Mason's elbow sends shock waves down James' spine, which is ridiculous, given they're both fully clothed. But with all the revelations of this evening, all the self-discoveries, all the kindness and honesty, James' body seems to have no defenses.

The memory of their kiss, and the way his hands held James so tenderly yet passionately—it haunts his dreams, and his waking hours, and any moment he so much as breathes. He's never felt something that instantaneous. It makes him foolhardy. His lust has no conscience.

But his head surely does. Doesn't it?

They round the block, approaching the Mason townhome, a modest blue three stories with well-tended ivy on the balconies and a river-stone stoop. James feels like his heart might beat right out of his chest, while his stomach ties itself into knots. He doesn't like feeling so mixed up and unsure.

"What if there were someone who knew all the parts of you?" Mason asks.

James falters but keeps walking, determinedly not looking at Mason. His palms feel sweaty. A person who knew every part of him and, what, loved him anyway? There isn't that person. There can't be that person.

Mason cannot be implying that—

They approach the front stoop, but Mason veers suddenly toward the narrow alley between his house and the next. James hurries after him, just managing to catch him as Mason trips over his own feet. He ducks beneath Mason's shoulder and pushes his thoughts away, letting Mason shuffle them down the cobblestone alley. He can't leave Mason alone, unsteady as he is, and he finds he doesn't quite want to. Unlike the weight of Prince's arm, Mason's arm falling across his shoulders elicits a visceral reaction, like pinpricks of surprise spreading all over his skin.

James tells himself he doesn't like the feeling. Tells himself Mason's waist beneath his palm doesn't feel like a perfect fit. That he doesn't enjoy the way Mason's hand lingers on his shoulder as they approach the door to the kitchen, hidden from the street and out of view of the windows of the neighboring house. They turn to face each other on the worn single step. James tells himself that the somersault of his stomach as Mason gazes into his eyes means *nothing*.

Mason begins to lean forward, the hand on James' shoulder gliding up to cup the back of James' head.

Quite without thinking, James shoots an arm out, pushing Mason gently away. His palm lands right above Mason's heart, and he can feel its thud. Mason stares at him, his eyes shuttering, disappointed.

"I thought . . ." he says.

James shakes his head. Pining is one thing. Intrigue is one thing. Lust and . . . magnetism are one thing. But he's not brave like Mason is.

"We're partners in—"

"Preventing blackmail, nothing more. Yes, I remember," Mason says, his hand falling from James' cheek to clench at his side.

James tells himself he doesn't miss its warmth.

"And in keeping grooms-to-be alive," James offers, feeling like he must give the man something, in exchange for all that he cannot offer.

"We could be more than that," Mason says. His eyes are clearer now. "We have a perfect cover, a perfect situation. Wouldn't—" He pauses, licking his lips. And damn, if that doesn't send a frisson of want through James' body. "Wouldn't it be nice to be with someone who understands, even a little?"

Mason's words land against James' chest like a blow. Of course it would.

He understands, he does, Mason's fixation on this. But that doesn't make it the safe choice Mason thinks it is.

Mason, with his understanding family and friends. Mason with his secure position as the second son, unwatched, unhindered by obligation. He couldn't understand the sacrifice it would be to engage in an affair this risky. With all of London always watching—it would be a scandal of monumental proportions waiting to happen.

James meets Mason's eyes, and his strong refusal dies in his throat. Mason looks so earnest, and so vulnerable.

"We can't be lovers. But we could be friends," James hears himself say.

Mason blinks at him, before a smile slowly stretches across his face. "Yeah?"

James can't help but smile back, even as something sinks hard in his gut. Regret, maybe? "Yeah. We could try being friends."

Mason nods happily and squeezes the hand James still has pressed to his heart. James quickly retracts it, but keeps his smile wide. He knocks on the door as Mason shuffles his feet.

"Try to get some sleep, and eat something, before the wedding," James suggests.

Mason rolls his eyes, opening his mouth for some retort when the door cracks open. Lord Mason leans out in his robe, looking between them.

"You're both in one piece. I'm impressed," he says.

"Demeroven's worried I'm going to faint dead away, though," Mason says, shockingly put together given the previous few minutes.

"I'll leave him in your care. Do be on time tomorrow, won't you?" James says, stepping down into the alley while Mason snorts.

"Thank you for bringing him home," Lord Mason says.

Mason whacks his brother's shoulder. He turns, gives James a wink, and disappears inside.

"We'll see you at the wedding," Lord Mason says, before closing the door with a soft snick.

James stares at the closed door, something strange swirling in his chest. *Friends.*

Chapter Fifteen

Bobby

He can hear his teeth.

He's never been well the next morning after more than three drinks, but this is one of the worst hangovers he's ever experienced. He can literally hear his teeth as they sit inside his head. And instead of spending the morning convalescing in bed, or more likely bent over a chamber pot, he has to somehow survive Prince's wedding. Which means making it down the stairs without breaking his neck.

"You look horrid," Albie says as he stumbles down the final steps, clinging to the banister for dear life.

"Thank you," Bobby snarls, gratefully taking the glass of water their valet Mr. Tilty hands him, and pocketing the scone for later, if his stomach feels solid enough for food. He really thought he'd cut himself off at the right time last night, but God, it's like there are hammers in his skull.

"Did you sleep at all?" Albie wonders, passing Bobby his top hat.

"I think so," Bobby says, looking Albie over.

In his freshly tailored black suit with his top hat, Albie looks downright dashing. While Bobby feels like a well-dressed sewer rat.

"It looks like you slept five minutes, at most," Albie says, stepping up to redo his bow tie.

How could he have slept any more, when his dreams were full of ridiculous maudlin nonsense? Visions of him and Demeroven tandem-riding a horse around the Demeroven estate.

Albie steps back, deeming him . . . as fit as he can be for this morning. Bobby rubs his head, trying to clear it of the image of him and Demeroven sprawled out on a picnic blanket, Demeroven's hand in his hair. But the movement only makes him nauseous, and he follows with a grimace as Albie makes for the door.

Before he can reach for the knob, the front door flies open, nearly knocking them both to the floor. Bobby grips at Albie's shoulder to stay standing, squinting in the bright sunlight. Mrs. Stelm stands harried and frantic in their doorway, eyes wide.

"The baby is coming and you must come to the residence *now*," she demands.

All thoughts of Demeroven or Prince's wedding fly out of Bobby's head.

"Mr. Tilty," Albie bellows. Bobby staggers as pain lances across his skull. "Send word to the Prince residence that we are indisposed with an urgent family matter, and tell any and all callers that we are not at home, and not expected presently. Mrs. Stelm, please lead the way."

Bobby lets Albie yank him out of the house, following as best he can. Each footfall feels like a cymbal crash across his brain, but he cannot miss this. Uncle Dashiell needs them. Gwen and Beth need them. And Aunt Cordelia—God had better see her through, or they are going to have words. What if something *happens*?

By the time they arrive at the Havenfort townhouse, Bobby's stomach is doing battle with his throat. But he sucks in air, willing his nausea down. They don't have time for his hangover.

The front door bursts open as they come up the steps and Gwen, still dressed in her chemise and robe, ushers them in. Her hair has half fallen from the bun she slept in. Her hands tremble when she grips his and Albie's arms, yanking them up the stairs without even a hello.

"You look horrible, by the way," she says instead to Bobby.

Mrs. Stelm races around the corner of the stairwell, and they hurry behind her.

"Thanks," Bobby says gruffly.

Mrs. Gilpe meets them at the door to Aunt Cordelia and Uncle Dashiell's suite. Bobby's never seen her so pale before, and all thoughts of his own appearance disappear. She's never anything but stalwart, Mrs. Gilpe. Tall, imposing, and fair. And today she looks scared. That can't be good.

Mrs. Gilpe hands Mrs. Stelm a bowl of hot water and gently takes Gwen from Bobby and Albie.

"Lord Havenfort is in his study. Mr. Verton is . . . holding him there. See if you can keep him downstairs? It's early yet."

"And—" Bobby says, glancing at the cracked-open door of the suite, where they can just hear Beth muttering something unintelligible.

"Lady Havenfort is strong and doing well. Dr. Brayton is here, and is well qualified, as both you and your uncle have confirmed," she continues, looking to Albie.

But even with that reassurance, Bobby watches how Mrs. Gilpe squeezes Gwen to her, notes the sheen on Gwen's eyes. "I promise. Now keep your uncle company, please."

"Of course," Albie says, taking Bobby's arm.

Mrs. Gilpe guides Gwen into the bedroom and closes the door behind them, leaving Bobby with only a small glimpse of Aunt Cordelia, sitting in bed with Beth behind her, rubbing her shoulders as she groans.

"Albie," Bobby mumbles, turning to his brother. "What if—"

"Aunt Cordelia will be fine, and the baby will be healthy," Albie says firmly.

"But—" Bobby starts, stories of his first aunt's death, of Aunt Cordelia's miscarriages, swirling through his head. And all those statistics Albie's been gathering for the Medical Act—how can he be so calm?

"We need to go and tell our uncle his wife and child will be just fine, all right? We're here to be his confidence, to be his comfort. We—we can have an entire bottle of scotch tonight, yeah?" Bobby groans, his panic giving way to how truly awful he still feels. "Or some water and bread for you. But right now, we need to go be with Uncle Dashiell."

"Yes," Bobby agrees, letting Albie guide him back down the stairs and toward the study.

The portraits of Gwen at all ages comfort him slightly. Uncle Dashiell had a daughter. Aunt Cordelia had a daughter. And they'll all just pretend that Uncle Dashiell's first wife, the aunt Bobby never got to meet, died . . . some other way. Some non-bloody, non-horrific way.

The Havenfort valet, Mr. Verton, is indeed holding the doors to the study shut with his body weight. If he were a larger man, and less of a compact, delicate fellow, perhaps his position would be doing more. As it is, the doors shudder violently behind him.

"We've got him, Verton," Albie says.

Bobby gently guides Verton away from the doors. A moment later, Uncle Dashiell nearly topples through them, just stopping himself with Albie's help.

"I need to see my wife," he implores, looking among them.

"Sir, it isn't proper—"

"I don't give a flying damn what's proper! I'm going to see my wife," Uncle Dashiell insists, starting to push past Albie.

Albie grabs his arms, holding him back. Bobby steps awkwardly into the middle of the hallway, unsure of what to do. Are they really going to bodily restrain their uncle right now?

"You need to stay down here," Albie says calmly. Bobby can't fathom where he's finding his serenity. "Mrs. Stelm, Mrs. Gilpe, Miss Wilson, and the girls have Aunt Cordelia. She is fine and doing well."

"Your presence would only—" Verton starts.

"She's my *wife*," Uncle Dashiell spits.

"And she needs to focus on what she's doing," Albie says firmly.

Albie shoots Bobby a look and he wets his lips. "She can't have a safe birth and keep you calm at the same time, Uncle," he says, and his voice is a shaking thing.

Uncle Dashiell glares at him for a moment before slumping in Albie's arms. "Fine. Fine. Come in."

He pulls away from Albie and tromps back into the study, leaving Albie, Bobby, and Verton alone in the strangely silent hallway.

"Verton, please bring us a small breakfast, water, and the lord's best scotch, would you?" Albie asks.

Verton nods and hurries down the hall and out of sight. Albie and Bobby stare at each other. For a moment, his brother's eyes are large and Bobby feels just a bit better, knowing he's out of his depth here too. But then Albie shutters it away, nodding at Bobby once before ushering him through the door.

Bobby steps into the study and looks around, aghast. What is usually an orderly, large room bordered with bookcases and enhanced by a nice sofa set, Uncle Dashiell's large mahogany desk, and an assortment of knickknacks, now looks like a war zone. Papers are strewn over every possible surface. One of the armchairs by the sofa has . . . fallen over? Or more likely been kicked, given the broken glass baubles by the window.

Uncle Dashiell paces between the settees and a low table, hands fisted in his paisley dressing gown.

"Sit down, Uncle," Albie directs, gently maneuvering Uncle Dashiell into the remaining armchair while gesturing for Bobby to right the other.

Bobby does and then seats himself in it, feeling totally inadequate.

Uncle Dashiell scrubs at his face, staring blankly at the bookcases. Bobby glances at Albie and Albie looks back, equally at sea, until he smirks. Which is very unsettling.

"Bobby's terribly hungover," Albie announces.

"Oi!" Bobby says, flushing up to his ears.

Uncle Dashiell blinks at the two of them for a moment. "That's right, the stag night. How was it?"

From the tightness around his eyes and the clench of his jaw, Bobby can tell Uncle Dashiell couldn't care less, but it's *something* he can offer. "Rowdy. Cunningham throws a great pub crawl, and Prince had a wonderful time. Demeroven and I saw him safely home. Hopefully he feels a tad bit better than I do this morning."

Verton returns with a tray of scones and cream, three steaming mugs of tea, and glasses for the preposterously good bottle of scotch he's brought. He sets it all down on the low table between the armchairs and settee and gives an unsure bow.

"I'm fine, Verton," Uncle Dashiell says, offering a truly unconvincing smile. "Thank you."

"Very good, my lord," Verton squeaks, and then flees the room.

"What have you been doing to the poor man?" Albie asks.

"More likely Mrs. Gilpe put the fear of God into him lest he let me see my wife while she's in labor," Uncle Dashiell says, going straight for the scotch. "Hair of the dog?" he asks, pointing the bottle at Bobby once he's poured his own glass.

"In my tea, sure," Bobby says, holding out his mug for Uncle Dashiell to add a shot.

"That's revolting," Albie says.

Bobby takes a sip, and it is quite disgusting, but better than straight scotch at only ten in the morning. He tears off a piece of scone, dipping it into the cream.

"Bobby," Albie protests, at the same moment Uncle Dashiell is swiping his own dollop with his own torn scone. "You're both terrible."

Uncle Dashiell gives Bobby a true smile and Bobby winks back. At least he's helping somehow. He slowly chews his scone, then nearly chokes as loud groans begin to filter through the ceiling. Albie hurriedly starts listing off all the research he's been doing to drown out the sound.

Bobby knows it's normal, but it sends a sliver of dread through him to hear his aunt in such agony. How can that kind of pain result in anything less than catastrophe?

"I could fetch Demeroven for you, if you'd like," Albie suggests. Uncle Dashiell slowly rips his gaze from the ceiling. "He's been doing most of the aggregating of the various correspondence from the medical schools."

Bobby winces. Part of him is desperate to see Demeroven. Would even appreciate his helping to distract Uncle Dashiell, but . . . "One member of our extended family tree should be at Prince's wedding," Bobby says.

"Prince's wedding," Uncle Dashiell repeats, surprised. "Boys, I am sorry to have taken you from your friends. You can attend.

This . . . will take some time," he completes, just as the first true scream rips through the house.

"We don't mind, Uncle. We'd much rather be here with you," Bobby says honestly.

Uncle Dashiell gives him more of a grimace than a smile, and Albie launches into another round of statistics.

Bobby feels something from the previous night click against his brain. *Friends.* Is that what he and Demeroven really are now, odd family friends? Is that all they'll ever be? Partners in keeping their two families safe, joined by Uncle Dashiell and Aunt Cordelia, and Beth and Gwen? Will they see each other socially, as true friends would? And would that really be enough?

The door to the study opens slowly and all three of them whip around to find Gwen padding into the room. She's smiling brightly, but Bobby can see the tension in every single movement she makes.

"Cordelia sent me to tell you she's fine—this is all normal, and you know she's loud—and she loves you," Gwen says, coming up behind Uncle Dashiell to wrap her arms around his shoulders.

Uncle Dashiell pats at her arm. "Right."

"And that she hopes the boys aren't getting you too drunk, but just the right amount, so you'll be relaxed, but still safe to hold my little sister."

"Brother," Albie corrects.

"Sister," Uncle Dashiell says, squeezing Gwen's arm and shifting so he can look up at her. "You're a wonderful daughter, you know?"

"I know," Gwen says, before kissing his forehead. "Now, I'm going back upstairs, but everything is fine, and we're all happy and—"

Aunt Cordelia's scream pierces the quiet of the study.

"And your wife is loud," Gwen says firmly.

"Yes. That's all it is," Uncle Dashiell agrees. "Now go be with Cordelia, and give Beth a hug for me as well; I'm sure she's terrified."

"Beth is ordering all of us around like a bossy little hen," Gwen says, adoration in her voice.

"And Cordelia?"

"Loving every second of it."

"Good."

Gwen smiles at Bobby and Albie and goes to pull back from her father.

"Gwen," Uncle Dashiell says, turning to hold her arm, so they can't see his face. "I love you, very much."

Gwen's careful smile cracks a little, her eyes brightening. "I love you too, Papa. She'll be fine."

Uncle Dashiell nods and slowly relinquishes her. Gwen hurries from the room, wiping at her eyes. Uncle Dashiell turns back to them, slumping in his seat. He pinches the bridge of his nose, taking a deep breath.

"I hope both of you know the love I feel for my wife someday," he says, opening his eyes to give them both a piercing look.

"I do," Albie says immediately. "I promise, sir, I love Meredith with all my heart, and I'll need you both there to keep me locked in my study when she gives birth."

Uncle Dashiell reaches out and pats his shoulder. Bobby feels suddenly like the other in the room.

"It is a joy to love so deeply that you—that it is this terrifying to have your wife with child. That her health and safety mean the world to you. I did not know I could feel like this, that I could love like this, before she came back into my life, and it is a gift, boys. It is a true gift to be so happy that—that if anything happened to her, I think I would throw myself into the Thames."

"I know," Albie says.

If Aunt Cordelia . . . if something happens—Bobby doesn't think he can stand losing his uncle, and his new aunt, and their baby. Not now. Not after everything—

"I will not actually throw myself into the Thames," Uncle Dashiell says.

Bobby blinks and finds both Uncle Dashiell and Albie looking at him in concern. "Right," he mumbles, horrified to find he's let a tear slip down his cheek. "I'm sorry, I'm—I might still be drunk?"

Uncle Dashiell laughs, surprised, and Albie claps him on the back. Bobby smiles through it, a knot in his stomach.

"Someday we'll find you a wonderful partner, Bobby, and you can take all that heart and give it to them," Uncle Dashiell says. He then turns to Albie and begins what promises to be a lengthy discussion about parliamentary procedure.

Bobby listens to their conversation as though through a haze. Not only does Uncle Dashiell want an earth-shattering love for him, but he didn't—he didn't say *wife*. He said *partner*. Granted, the man is more agitated than Bobby's ever seen him, worrying about the possible death of his wife and unborn child, but still.

If Bobby can have a great love, he wants what they have. He won't be content with trysts in corners, much less a traditional marriage where he has to hide his true desires from his wife, along with the world. He won't survive trying to bury his feelings with propriety. He wants something real.

Around the third hour of pained screaming and Albie's increasingly frantic recitations of cholera statistics, Gwen bursts into the study. Uncle Dashiell stands up immediately, knocking into the coffee table and sending their used cups crashing to the floor.

"Papa, come see. Come meet your son."

Without hesitation, Uncle Dashiell takes off at a sprint, grabbing Gwen's wrist and dragging her along as she shrieks with glee. Albie and Bobby follow, and even after their frantic dash up the stairs, Bobby feels like he can take his first true breath all day when they run into the bedroom suite.

There Aunt Cordelia sits, Beth beside her in the enormous bed, both of them grinning down at a squirming little bundle. All three alive. All three well. All three beaming and beautiful.

Gwen guides Uncle Dashiell around to the opposite side of the bed, and Bobby watches, tears liberally falling down his cheeks, as his uncle carefully climbs onto the bed, weeping, and reaches out to kiss his wife. Aunt Cordelia smiles into his mouth, her brown hair sweaty, cheeks flushed. She takes his free hand to rest it against the crown of the little baby's head.

Bobby startles as a man steps up to Albie. "Thank you, Doctor," he hears his brother say, watches him pass the short, bespectacled man an envelope with payment. Watches the man take his bag of medical supplies and quietly leave the room.

When did . . . How did Albie know to take care . . . Albie wraps his arm around Bobby's shoulders and Bobby decides to forget about the doctor and all the hours of uncertainty that just passed. He leans into his brother, watching their uncle, aunt, cousin, and Beth as they all marvel at the miracle that is—

"Frederic Jonathan Bertram?" Aunt Cordelia asks, looking up at Uncle Dashiell. "For your brother?"

"Perfect," Uncle Dashiell says, so much emotion in his voice that Bobby lets out a quiet sob of his own.

Gwen looks over at him, her arms wrapped around Beth,

chin resting on her shoulder as Beth leans against Aunt Cordelia, Frederic holding her finger.

See? Gwen mouths.

Bobby nods and Albie chuckles.

This is what he wants. He wants a love like this. A family like this. He doesn't know how to have it. But there must be a way.

It doesn't have to be Demeroven, even if he can't stop thinking about him. *Friends* hardly seems like enough now as he watches Beth and Gwen coo over the baby, wrapped up in each other and happy. Beth and Gwen found a way. Surely, he can find a way to make it work for himself.

And though it doesn't have to be Demeroven . . . couldn't it be? Couldn't they find a way?

Chapter Sixteen

James

James slumps in his seat, his shoulder brushing Lord Mason's. Even Lord Mason is yawning, his penchant for decorum no match for Lord What's-his-face and his mind-numbing, unending speech about governmental oversight today.

Unfortunately, without something to actually focus on in session, James can't help but return to memories of Prince's stag night, to his hand on Mason's chest, to their declaration of *friends*. Nor can he forget the way his chest felt strangely hollow when neither Mason nor Lord Mason attended the wedding. And then the further blow of discovering his aunt had given birth without anyone bothering to notify him.

He doesn't know when it started to matter to him what the whole family thought of him, strange unrelated relations that they are. More than that, when did it start to make him antsy to go a few days without seeing Mason? It was his decision to keep him at arm's length, after all. Friends, and nothing more.

But his traitorous brain keeps replaying their kisses, keeps remembering how lovely their easy camaraderie was. He can't focus on anything. He's hardly eating. His sleep is shit. Mason has ruined him, and he's not even allowed him to do it properly.

Lord Mason elbows him, sitting up straight in his seat. James follows suit by reflex.

Lord What's-his-face has finally sat down. And Lord Havenfort now stands tall in front of the bottom row, staring out at the assembly, hands twisting at his sides.

"The right to self-accreditation may have merit when it comes to many trades. Farmers, carpenters, bakers, housekeepers—all these professions may be taught outside of formal schooling without fatal consequences.

"But I ask you, gentlemen, do you want the man overseeing the birth of your very heirs to have been taught by his father, who was taught by his father, and not a one of them ever having received formal training? Who's to say he won't butcher your wife, leave your child dead, and walk away telling you that's the best medicine can do?"

Bodies shift around the room. James finds himself with his hands on his knees, listening, as Lord Mason leans so far forward, he's nearly into the pew below them.

"Proponents of this act do not wish to limit the freedoms of Englishmen," Lord Havenfort says. Lord What's-his-name sighs gustily. "Instead, we want to ensure that all people of our great nation have the right to safe medical procedures. The freedom to know that when they are in a doctor's care, they are safe.

"My first wife died in childbed." This falls like a mallet over the assembly. "I was assured after the birth of my daughter that my wife was well. I held my daughter in the nursery, content, until I heard the screaming."

James swallows hard, Lord Havenfort's face blurring in and out of focus. He struggles to remind himself that his aunt is just fine. This was over twenty-two years ago, when Lady Gwen was born.

"I was later told, by a coroner, that something ruptured on the wall of my late wife's womb, bleeding her dry in a matter of minutes. I didn't even make it to the room for her final breath.

"And her noble physician? Told me there was nothing he could have done. That my wife's lost life was simply a matter of course.

"My daughter grew up without a mother, because the physician I hired to care for my wife didn't know enough to save her. The physician who came heavily recommended. The best I could find."

Lord Havenfort looks around the room, meeting as many eyes as possible as the men sit silent and aghast.

"Twenty-two years later, I have just been blessed with a son, and my beloved wife is truly fine, stable, and happy."

Lord Mason suddenly sits up straight, clapping vigorously. The room slowly joins in. James claps his hands, his fingers numb from where he was gripping the bench.

Lord Havenfort below them offers a small smile. "Their survival is in no small part thanks to a qualified physician, Dr. Brayton, who was accredited at the University of Edinburgh Medical College. I was able to properly vet Dr. Brayton using the meticulous research from our committee.

"But should we fail to pass this act, what becomes of all those without the wealth to hire qualified physicians? Do we not, as Englishmen, as Christians, have a duty to support the poor, to provide them with opportunity? Do we not have a duty to provide access to proper healthcare so that our children survive? So that countless thousands do not die of curable diseases, decimating our workforces?"

Murmurs of assent begin to fill the hall, the lords shifting from awed regard to impassioned agreement. James finds himself exclaiming along with them.

"Were there another way to ensure such a registry, without the guiding hand of Parliament, perhaps I would not feel compelled to speak to you thus. But as it has fallen on our shoulders to protect our citizens, our children, our wives—I call on you to make the right decision. Join us in voting to enact this registry along with the Commons, so that all Englishmen may have proper care, and be safe in the knowledge that their physicians will keep them well.

"I must return to my healthy son and wife now. Thank you."

The room jumps to its feet. The lords clap vigorously. Even those across the aisle, who hate Lord Havenfort with every fiber of their being, can't quite refuse him this accolade.

"I've never heard such a speech in my life," James says, leaning over to Lord Mason, who's clapping so hard his hands are turning red.

Lord Mason only nods, his jaw clenched tight, eyes a little shiny. James realizes then that Lord Mason's wife has not yet made it safely through the trial of childbirth. He knows Lord Havenfort will ensure she has only the best physicians possible, but it cannot be easy for Lord Mason to know what is coming for her, and to be so far away.

James has no want of a wife, but he certainly wants Lord Mason's to be well, and for their child to survive. James follows Lord Mason from their pew, hoping he'll be able to intercept Lord Havenfort briefly to congratulate him on the birth. He really should pay a visit to his aunt as well and give her his felicitations.

Perhaps if he extends that long overdue apology to his aunt and cousin, someday he could become someone they think to call when big things are happening.

As he heads down the stairs at the end of his aisle, he spots Raverson across the room. Their eyes lock and James' stomach clenches. The extended family has weathered one crisis, but there's still another brewing. Raverson sneers at James and James trips, clutching Lord Mason's arm to stay upright.

"Steady on," Lord Mason says, helping James down the last few stairs into the aisle.

James gives him a grimace of a smile, and looks back to where Raverson was. But Raverson is gone. James cranes his neck, but he's fled the chamber, leaving James with no choice but to shuffle out behind Lord Mason. He knows they've staved Raverson off, for now, but can't quite banish the unsettled, panicked feeling in his chest.

He wishes Mason were here to reassure him, or distract him, or— James shakes himself. This is neither the time nor the place to think about that clandestine moment.

But even ignoring . . . thoughts of Ascot, or Raverson, James is surprised to find he just wants to talk to Mason. He wants to tell him about watching Cunningham, Wristead, and Rupping try to keep their eyes open and stay standing throughout Prince's wedding. He wants to give Mason the play-by-play. *Friends*, they said. He's rarely wanted to speak to a friend so badly, now that he thinks on it.

He and Lord Mason make their way through the antechamber, Lord Mason holding on to the cuff of James' sleeve. It feels shockingly safe. Like maybe he and Lord Mason might be something like friends too.

And if he found a way to make himself a greater part of the larger family, he could be friends with his cousin and her stepsister as well. No longer just trying to make a good impression to prove himself worthy, he's rather surprised to find he genuinely wants to be part of all of this. Of the research that might protect the two girls, should they ever decide to settle down rather than making mischief through another few seasons. Of the dinners and card games Lord Mason and even Mason have alluded to.

He . . . wants a family. Not one born of himself, he doesn't think. Though occasionally when he thinks of having a son of his own, one he could love and support, rather than belittle, he thinks perhaps he could survive a traditional marriage. But then all the butterflies he feels for Mason, all the longing and want and—

"Uncle!"

James bumps into Lord Mason as they cascade onto the street in the wave of lords leaving the chamber. He can see Lord Havenfort just to their left, his blond head high above the rest. He stops moving and Lord Mason leads James by his suit cuff to join Lord Havenfort at the side of the wrought-iron fence.

"That was amazing," Lord Mason tells Lord Havenfort.

Lord Havenfort gives him an honest, if exhausted, smile. Up close, Lord Havenfort's eyes are rimmed with purple, and it looks like perhaps either Lady Gwen or Miss Bertram put some kind of rouge on him to make him look less . . . sleep deprived.

"Truly," James adds quickly. "And congratulations on the baby, sir. Please pass my regards on to your wife."

"I will," Lord Havenfort says, reaching out to pat his shoulder. "Thank you both for your hard work. We may just pass this thing yet."

"If there's a single lord in opposition after that speech, I'll eat one of Meredith's hats," Lord Mason says.

Lord Havenfort laughs. "Don't be too hasty with your assurances, Albert. But thank you. Now, I must get home. Be safe, both of you."

With that, he turns and nearly jogs down the street, back to his beautiful family. James looks up at Lord Mason to find him watching his uncle wistfully.

"How is your wife, Mason? I haven't asked in too long," James says.

Lord Mason blinks and looks down at him. "She's doing better, actually," he says with a small smile. "Not quite well enough to travel yet, but hopefully soon. I'm planning to bring Beth and Gwen up to the country for a week's visit on the weekend. As much for Meredith as to get them out of Uncle Dashiell and Aunt Cordelia's hair. Would you like to join us?"

He doesn't even think about it. "I would, thank you. I'll meet you at the Havenfort residence?"

"That would be splendid," Lord Mason says. He and Mason have the same bright smile. "I'll send you the details. Meredith will be very glad to meet you—I've told her all about you."

James watches Lord Mason walk off, a spring in his step. James stares after him, a slow blooming panic coming over his chest. He just— But that means he'll be in the country for a week with Mason, for the first time they will have seen each other since . . . *friends*.

He can't tell if the irregular patter of his heart is excitement or terror.

Chapter Seventeen

Bobby

"You've already had ten minutes—it's my turn."

"Miss Wilson is next, actually," Mrs. Gilpe says, passing baby Frederic over to an already cooing Miss Wilson.

"You're a horrid woman," Mrs. Stelm says, even as she settles onto the arm of Mrs. Gilpe's armchair, the two of them watching Miss Wilson babble down at baby Frederic.

The doorbell rings and Bobby, Gwen, Beth, Uncle Dashiell, Albie, and Aunt Cordelia, seated around the low table, all look toward the hall.

"One of you will have to get it, we're watching the most important member of the family," Miss Wilson says from her seat in the corner by the fire. "Baby Frederic forbids us to leave."

"I'll go," Bobby says, smiling as Beth and Gwen laugh on either side of Aunt Cordelia.

All three women look rather exhausted, even with their housekeeper and lady's maids monopolizing the baby. He hasn't experienced it himself, but he knows babies disrupt the entire house, if you care about them at all. They could be leaving his care entirely to their staff, but in the Havenfort home? Hardly likely. From what he's heard, it's been a fight each evening for who gets to bring Aunt Cordelia the baby to nurse.

Bobby heads for the front door as the doorbell chimes again.

It makes him wistful, all this joy. Makes him wish there had been another little Mason baby, before his mother passed away.

He's decided he quite likes babies, even if they are messy, and sometimes smelly. Sitting and watching Frederic make a small face or successfully wave his fist into his mouth is entrancing.

Bobby pulls open the door just as the doorbell chimes a third time. James Demeroven stands on the front stoop, hat beneath his arm and sandy-brown hair falling into his eyes. He's in a new gray traveling suit, nicely tailored, and he looks at Bobby, equally at sea.

Bobby's not sure why it's caught him in the chest to see him on the doorstep, other than . . . they haven't seen each other in nearly two weeks, not since the stag night, and *friends*.

"Do . . . you and the girls need more time?" Demeroven asks.

Bobby blows out a breath. He was just . . . staring at the man, wasn't he? "Sorry, sorry, they're saying their goodbyes. Please, come in."

Bobby steps back so Demeroven can enter. He turns and closes the door, giving himself a moment. It's like butterflies are fighting with razor blades in his stomach. And if this is his reaction just to seeing the man, how is he supposed to survive a day-long carriage ride with him?

"The family is in the sitting room," he says, turning back to Demeroven with forced calm. "Have you met the baby yet?"

"Um, no," Demeroven says, gesturing for Bobby to lead the way.

Bobby listens to Demeroven's almost mouselike footfalls behind him. He leads Demeroven up the stairs, too many thoughts and questions piling up against his tongue, none of them elegant. They pause at the doorway to the sitting room, glancing awkwardly at each other. He has to say something, anything, just—

Before he manages even a word, Uncle Dashiell is up and ushering them in, clapping Demeroven on the back.

"James, please meet my son, Frederic," he says, walking over to gently take the baby from a pouting Mrs. Stelm. "Oh, you'll have him to yourself once the rest leave."

Mrs. Gilpe laughs and tugs Mrs. Stelm back onto the armchair to begin planning their week. Something about a tournament of cards with the lord and lady.

Before he can listen for details, Bobby's distracted by Demeroven approaching Uncle Dashiell and peering down at baby Frederic. The baby still looks a little squashed and indistinct, though Bobby thinks he'll have Aunt Cordelia's nose, and the light fuzz on his head does look like Uncle Dashiell's blond.

"He's a beautiful baby, sir," Demeroven says.

Uncle Dashiell smiles and goes to hand him to Demeroven but Demeroven steps back, casting about the room for a viable reason not to hold the baby. Bobby doesn't know if it's fear or panic, but he can't leave the man out to dry.

"Oh, is it my turn?" he asks, swooping in to steal Frederic from Uncle Dashiell's arms, cuddling the soft, squirmy little boy close. "Yes, you just wanted your very favorite cousin, didn't you?" he coos down at the baby.

"It is far too early for favorites," Albie says from his seat in the armchair next to Beth. "I shall be teaching him to ride."

"But I'll be teaching him to fence—he'll like that much better," Gwen puts in quickly.

"He'll be an archer, like me, actually," Beth says. "And play duets with me and Mother."

"Well, I'll just have to teach him all the best hiding places in this house, then, won't I?" Bobby says, putting his nose in the air. "We'll share secrets about the lot of you."

"It sounds like he'll have a most wonderful childhood," Demeroven says.

The room turns to look at him and Uncle Dashiell pats his shoulder. "Perhaps you can teach him the manners the rest of your peers seem to lack."

"We are entirely proper all of the time every day," Gwen says.

Aunt Cordelia snorts and Beth giggles, the two of them sharing a look.

"Fine. We'd best be going anyway," Gwen says, standing and shrugging off Beth's arm.

Beth rolls her eyes and leans in to kiss Aunt Cordelia's cheek. Bobby looks down at baby Frederic while Albie and Demeroven speak with Uncle Dashiell. He'd rather like to stay just like this, all of them safe and together in Uncle Dashiell's house.

Frederic meets his eyes, staring up at him with that piercing blue gaze, as if he knows Bobby's feeling vulnerable and wants to comfort him.

"You'll be good for your parents, won't you?" he whispers, brushing his thumb along Frederic's ear. "Don't cry too much, and try and smile. I know Aunt Cordelia would love it if you started making more of your little sounds. Beth and Gwen too. So practice while we're away, yeah?"

Frederic burbles and Bobby smiles, glancing up to find Demeroven watching him. He shrugs, a bit embarrassed, but Demeroven just blushes and looks away.

"I promise, your mother will be fine. I'll take excellent care of her, and Mrs. Gilpe, Mrs. Stelm, and Miss Wilson won't let anything happen to the baby," Uncle Dashiell says.

Bobby turns back to the sitting area, watching Gwen and Beth stand together facing their parents. Their fingers are entwined so tightly that their knuckles are going white.

As much as he might like to stay here with the whole family, the time away will likely do all of them some good. He decides then that he'll make it his mission for Beth and Gwen to have as much fun as possible while at Mason Manor.

"Finally, my turn," Mrs. Stelm says, gently plucking Frederic from his arms.

Bobby misses his warmth immediately. He didn't know he could enjoy holding a baby so much. Frederic has made him antsy for Albie and Meredith's little one to arrive, as much for the joy of holding the baby as for Meredith's health.

"All right, we really should be going if we want to get there before midnight," Albie says, gently ushering Beth and Gwen away from their parents. "I'll send word once we've arrived."

"Thank you," Aunt Cordelia says, standing to hug Beth and Gwen before letting them go.

Bobby wraps his arm around Beth's shoulders while Albie takes Gwen. Together they guide the anxious young ladies out of the parlor, Demeroven bringing up the rear.

Bobby's so focused on keeping Beth from crying that he doesn't really think about the five of them being squashed together in the carriage until Demeroven slides in beside him on the boys' bench. It's a tight fit, Demeroven's thigh pressed hard to his, their shoulders knocking together, as the carriage sets off at a gentle sway.

Bobby, Albie, and Demeroven sit watching awkwardly as Beth and Gwen stare out the windows, their jaws tight, hands still clenched together, both of them breathing very determinedly. Bobby glances at Albie, who shrugs, looking about as helpless as he feels.

"How is working at the Foundling Hospital going?"

Beth and Gwen both turn to look at Demeroven, their eyes lighting up, and Bobby could bloody kiss him, just for that.

"Very well," Beth says, her voice a little wobbly. "It's so interesting, all the medicine, and it's lovely to see so many babies born."

"Professor Martin speaks very highly of Dr. Holting, and he seemed impressive when we met," Demeroven says. "Are you getting to work with him at all?"

"Some," Gwen says, exchanging a look with Beth. "We're not allowed to see any of the surgeries, but he does come to the maternity ward now and again."

"Lady Ashmond has tea with him regularly to discuss improvements to the hospital, though, so we do hear stories," Beth adds.

"And how are things with Lady Ashmond?" Albie asks.

Gwen shifts a little in her seat, pulling Beth's hand into her lap. Beth looks to Gwen and Gwen sighs. "She throws the most amazing salon parties," she says grumpily.

"Really?" Bobby wonders. Beth and Gwen go to salon parties?

"Really," Gwen says, her surliness dissolving as she goes on. "She brings in all of these artisans and artists with wares to sell. Some of them stay for cards, and the stories they tell—"

"She has a whole network made up of all classes; it's really quite extraordinary," Beth interjects.

"She wants to pair up entrepreneurial business owners with peer investors, particularly women and second sons—start creating some independent wealth that has nothing to do with the peerage to spread around," Gwen says.

Bobby glances at Albie, flabbergasted. "That's . . . wonderful," he says. Demeroven's leaning forward in his seat with interest.

"When Mama's out of confinement, we're planning to bring her. I actually think they'd get along now," Beth adds eagerly.

"She's really taken the freedom of divorce and made something of her life," Gwen continues. "Cordelia would definitely approve. And we should think about bringing along Miss Wilson—I think she'd enjoy meeting some new people as well."

"That's a great idea," Beth says eagerly.

They go on to tell Albie and Demeroven about a recent gathering where they all discussed the Medical Act, but Bobby can't quite pay attention. He's still stuck on Gwen's acceptance of Lady Ashmond. He never thought she could accept Beth's former fiancé's mother, especially since he knows Gwen would gladly let Lord Montson fall into a ditch given the chance.

He doesn't think he could smile and be friendly with anyone, regardless of divorce, if their relatives were trying to steal Demeroven away.

Not . . . not that it's at all the same. Beth was engaged to Lord Montson, and Beth and Gwen are actually in love, and in a committed relationship, and he and Demeroven are—

"Perhaps I'll have to drag Mason along, then. I don't think I could weather that kind of scrutiny," Demeroven says.

Bobby looks up, finding the whole carriage watching him. He has no idea what he's missed, only that apparently it involved Demeroven *wanting* to go somewhere with him?

"Right, yes, I am, ah, a great buffer against . . . Who's doing the scrutinizing?"

"Lady Ashmond. As I said, she's quite intent on matchmaking," Gwen says, giving him a look.

"And you want me to save you?" Bobby hears himself ask, gaping at Demeroven.

"Or at least let me use you as a shield," Demeroven says, blue eyes twinkling, a real smile on his face.

Bobby forces himself to smile back, watching as if in a trance as Demeroven turns back to the conversation. There's a swoon in his stomach and a tingle in his fingers at the mere mention of an outing with Demeroven.

There's no denying it. All this time convincing himself it was just the security he wanted in a relationship, not Demeroven himself. *Friends.* What a load of rot. All those things Prince said about falling in love with your best friend, of feeling safe and secure with your partner—has he fallen that hard for Demeroven amid all the squabbling and sparring?

He doesn't know what to do with himself, with this revelation, trapped in this coach. He isn't even sure he knows what to do with himself once they get to the manor. Everything just feels too big and too complicated.

Across from him, Gwen and Beth rest against each other, Beth's eyes slipping closed, Gwen looking peacefully out the window, both of them sufficiently cheered up and comfortable. Beth shifts and wraps her arm around Gwen's stomach and Gwen smiles, bending to press a kiss to Beth's forehead.

Bobby's pulled from his swirling thoughts at Demeroven's sharp intake of breath.

"Just a reminder, we all need to be discreet while we're at the manor. Meredith's mother is staying with us, and she is not privy to our . . . group dynamic," Albie says.

Bobby nods, but Demeroven looks back and forth between them. "Discreet?" Demeroven asks.

"Demeroven is very discreet," Bobby says, smiling at Demeroven, whose look of consternation turns to genuine alarm. "What? You are."

"I don't—I don't understand," Demeroven says, and there's a hint of panic in his voice, all that jovial good humor dropping away now.

"We . . . work as a team to provide Beth and Gwen with

time alone away from prying eyes," Albie says slowly, glancing at Bobby.

Bobby watches Demeroven's eyes dart around the carriage, from Beth and Gwen, to him, to Albie, and back. The look on his face reminds Bobby of his retreat after their tryst at Ascot and something clicks sickeningly into place.

Demeroven doesn't *know*. No wonder he balked at the idea of an alliance! He hasn't even noticed the one staring him in the face. And how could he possibly know how accepting Uncle Dashiell and Aunt Cordelia are if he's never understood that Beth and Gwen—

"You haven't figured it out yet," Bobby says softly.

Demeroven's confused eyes meet his. "Figured out what?"

Bobby looks over at the girls and then at Albie. This isn't their secret to tell, but Demeroven needs to know. Though honestly how he's failed to notice before now is truly a mystery. Especially given Demeroven's own inclination, he must have some sense for when he's in accepting company.

But then, he's always so scared, always so concerned with appearances. Perhaps this really is the first time he's ever been surrounded by safe, accepting, loving people, and he hasn't even known he's had that support.

Surely he won't judge Beth and Gwen. How could he?

They need to make this right. *He* needs to make this right. But he knows that they can't just . . . expose their cousin and Beth like that without permission.

"Would someone please explain what's going on?" Demeroven says.

Bobby huffs, glancing across the carriage to find Gwen looking back at him from where she's been resting her cheek on Beth's head. She gives him a little smile and one bob of her head, before closing her eyes. Bobby looks to Albie, who sighs.

"Beth and Gwen are in love," Albie says, matter-of-factly, which Bobby appreciates. But Demeroven just stares at him. "Together. In love . . . together."

"Surely you've noticed something," Bobby adds gently. Demeroven swings his head around to stare at him, because clearly, he hasn't. "Never wondered why they're both still single when they're so eligible?"

"I don't want to get married; why should they?" Demeroven asks tightly.

Albie laughs and Bobby hears Gwen snort, though her eyes remain decidedly closed. Goodness, they've made a mess of this somehow.

"You're all missing out," Albie says, smirking at them.

"Yes, well, it's a bit easier if you're born wanting to get married, isn't it?" Bobby says tartly.

"I can't help how I was born. Nor can they," Albie says, looking toward the girls. "So I ask that we all simply be careful at the house. Meredith knows," he adds for Demeroven's sake. "And they'd be bunking together either way. But we just don't discuss anything with her mother, all right?"

"Of course," Bobby says, while Demeroven just nods, staring at Gwen and Beth napping against each other.

Bobby sits back in his seat and the rest of the ride passes peacefully. But he can feel every movement Demeroven makes, every shift, every little adjustment. Because now Demeroven knows—now he understands that the family loves Beth and Gwen the way they are. Now Demeroven knows they've architected a situation where the girls can be happy, and together, and in love, without consequence, or pressure, or judgment.

And sure, all four of them could force themselves into traditional marriages, and take their true happinesses fleetingly. Live their lives in bits and pieces, hiding who they are.

But that's not what Beth and Gwen want. That's certainly not what Bobby wants. And he knows it's not what Demeroven wants either. But to take the opposite step—to enter into a true relationship, like Beth and Gwen have—to trust their families to protect them, to support them—

He doesn't know if this is enough to convince Demeroven that it's possible.

No matter how much Bobby understands his own feelings now, no matter how much he actually wants the man beside him, Bobby doesn't know if he can stand to be turned down a third time.

He didn't know until this month how much he truly wants to be loved the way Gwen loves Beth. The way his uncle loves his aunt. The way Albie loves Meredith.

But does Demeroven want the same thing, from him?

By the time night falls and they reach the manor, he's about to crawl out of his skin with nerves and anticipation. He glances at Demeroven as they pull up along the long gravel drive and finds him alert, face pensive.

As soon as they come to a stop, the doors to the manor fly open, revealing Meredith in a house dress, illuminated by the lights in the two-story foyer. She stands with her hands on her hips, red hair in untamed curls that land on her shoulders.

Albie throws open the carriage door and they can hear Meredith's loud "What took you so long?" Albie nearly falls out of the carriage in his haste to get to her.

Beth, Gwen, and Demeroven slowly follow him out. Albie sprints up the grand outer staircase to wrap his arms around his wife. Bobby stoops and leans out of the carriage, watching Albie gently pick Meredith up and spin her around. Her giggles echo across the lawn.

In the dark, Bobby can't see much of the manor, just the light spilling down the long front steps. But he can smell the honeysuckle and hear the familiar rustle of the leaves in the trees above them. It's peaceful, and he tries to let that peace seep into his anxious skin. During his childhood, when his father was gone on business, this was a happy place. And now his father is . . . permanently gone.

Therefore, this should forever be a happy place now, right? Meredith is all right. They should all be happy.

"They're going to be sickening, aren't they?" Gwen asks.

"Absolutely," Beth says, Bobby echoing her automatically. Beth sounds far more charmed than Bobby is, but he'll take it for the relief of seeing Meredith standing.

"It's sweet," Demeroven says.

Gwen laughs and takes Beth's hand, pulling her up the path.

Bobby stays hanging out the door of the carriage. He's incredibly happy to see Meredith up and about, and to see his brother so genuinely excited. They're snogging now, completely enraptured. They're home, and everything is fine.

Fingers clasp his and Bobby startles. Demeroven looks up at him, his soft, broad hand clutching Bobby's, and gestures for him to climb down.

Bobby does, a tightness in his middle that has nothing to do with the hunger gripping at his stomach. They stand for a moment, staring at each other, something crackling between them. Beth's laughter splits the air and Demeroven releases his hand. He gives Bobby a slightly bashful smile before turning to follow the group, but Bobby can feel the press of his skin like a phantom tingle the whole walk up to the house.

Despite their party numbering only seven, the foyer rings with sound and chaos. Beth, Gwen, and Demeroven stand admiring the house while Meredith's mother, Lady Harrington, hugs the life out of Albie, maternal and warm despite her tall, willowy frame and severe gray dress.

"What, no hug for your sister-in-law?"

Bobby spins and finds Meredith beaming up at him. Her face is rounder, but she's still frighteningly thin for being five months with child. He immediately wraps her up tight, pleased to find she smells like lilacs, her signature scent. She'd written that she couldn't stand the smell just last month, so he takes this as a grand improvement.

"All right, let me look at you," she says, pulling back to give him a once-over.

"Shouldn't I be saying that to you?" he asks, laughing as she whacks his arm.

"I see London hasn't made you more proper."

"Perish the very thought," he says, feeling tension lift off his shoulders when she laughs.

"It is good to see you," she says.

"Meredith, you have no idea," he returns honestly. "How are you, really?"

"I'm well, really," she says.

Albie steps up behind her and wraps his arm around her shoulders even as she hangs on to Bobby's hands. "Dr. Morris agrees," he tells Bobby.

"Good," Bobby says, squeezing her hands. "That is wonderful news. And I'm so glad we're here for the week."

"Me too," she says brightly. "Now, Mother's had dinner waiting for over an hour, so we shouldn't keep her . . ."

Meredith trails off and Bobby releases her hands to follow her line of sight. Lady Harrington is fawning over Demeroven, adjusting his lapels and going on about how he's bound to make a killing in the marriage mart. Beth and Gwen stand off to the side, hands over their mouths to keep from laughing at Demeroven's beet-red face.

"Oh dear," Meredith mumbles. "She's been so excited for this visit, and you've brought her entirely fresh meat."

Bobby turns a laugh into a cough and Albie chuckles into Meredith's hair. "I suppose we should save him," Albie says.

"Before she adopts him as her new son-in-law, I think," Bobby agrees.

Meredith sighs when they make absolutely no move to step in. It's not that he wants Demeroven to suffer, but Lady Harrington can be a bit . . . much, and it's nice, for a moment, to have her attention turned elsewhere. And Demeroven's blush is absolutely darling.

Of course, she notices Demeroven looking at Bobby beseechingly, and his reprieve is short-lived.

"Come, let me have a look at you," Lady Harrington says, her melodic voice a booming command that bounces around the two-story foyer.

He can hear Albie still snickering as he girds himself and steps forward to submit to Lady Harrington's appraisal.

She takes his hands, much like Meredith did. "You have grown," she says, looking him up and down.

"I suppose," Bobby agrees with a smile. He always gets the feeling Lady Harrington can see straight through absolutely anyone with those blue-gray eyes. "And how are you, Lady Harrington?"

"I am delighted to have all these wonderful young people here to stay for the week, but famished. Come, come, all of you, into the dining room."

Bobby lets her take his arm, walking her down the hall still decorated with his late father's favorite sailing-scapes and then into the grand dining room. The long, narrow, lacquered oak table is set for a full dinner service, with high tapers and bright floral arrangements. Much more festive than anything they ever had while his father was alive.

But he's thinking about his father too much, when he really should be paying attention to the seating. Lady Harrington leaves him halfway down the table to make her way regally to the head, which suits him just fine. He knows Albie would rather sit in the kitchen than take the head seat.

But that cedes the arrangements to Lady Harrington, who demands Beth and Gwen sit to either side of her, so she can get all the best gossip. Albie hurries to help Lady Harrington get seated. Meredith steps up beside Gwen, forcing Bobby and Demeroven to sit opposite one another, with no hope of interrupted eyelines.

Bobby goes to help Meredith into her chair, leaving Gwen beside her to her own devices. Meredith bats his hands away and pushes herself in, giving him a look.

"I am perfectly capable of normal tasks."

Bobby withholds a laugh, watching Demeroven race to try and push in Beth before she can do it herself. "See? It's only polite."

"Well, Demeroven needs to make a good impression. We already know and adore you," Meredith says under her breath while she smiles at Demeroven.

Beth pushes herself in before Demeroven can, and Gwen snorts on Meredith's other side. Demeroven slinks back to his seat, thwarted.

"Be nice," Bobby finds himself saying.

Demeroven sits primly, listening attentively around Albie as Beth and Gwen fill Lady Harrington in on their work at the Foundling Hospital. He actually looks like he fits there, which does something very funny to Bobby's stomach.

Even though the soup Mr. Brile and Mr. Canton bring out is

his favorite—potato and leek, with the most delicious crusted bread—he finds he's barely able to manage a few spoonfuls. He didn't expect that seeing Demeroven at his family table would feel like this—like a puzzle piece that may have just fallen perfectly into place. How ridiculous.

"I heard that Prous and Eloise were caught at the Yokely tea in the hedges," Meredith says, pulling Bobby from his maudlin thoughts.

"How?" he demands. "You weren't even there."

"Oh, but Annabeth was," Meredith says wickedly.

"Her mother was ready to kill her," Gwen says with some delight. "But I think it had the desired effect of getting Prous' father to finally agree to all the terms."

"So it was premeditated?" Lady Harrington wonders.

"It seems so," Beth says.

"How clever," Lady Harrington says.

Bobby chuckles softly, finally tucking properly into his soup while Demeroven stares, agog. Lady Harrington may look like the portrait of propriety, but she's as wily as Beth and Gwen.

"And you, ladies? Anyone on your horizons?"

Bobby watches Beth and Gwen share a faux innocent look. "No," Gwen says, with forced melancholy.

"But with the new baby, I don't mind so much," Beth puts in.

"He is very cute," Gwen agrees.

"And he's well? And Lady Havenfort?" Meredith asks immediately. "I should have asked first thing."

"They're both doing wonderfully," Beth assures her. "And baby Frederic gets more animated by the day. I swear he smiled at me the other morning; it was the most precious thing."

"He was smiling at me, actually," Gwen says.

"I can't wait to play with your little one," Beth adds to Meredith, both she and Gwen looking a little wistful.

"All the more reason for you two beautiful girls to find yourselves husbands," Lady Harrington says. "I know a number of unattached young gentlemen. Lord Highmore, for instance."

"Who hates Gwen with a passion," Meredith mumbles.

"I believe he's actually getting rather friendly with Lady Liesel," Demeroven says.

Bobby looks over at him, impressed. Demeroven winks at him, which has Bobby sitting up straight.

"Ah, well, that's a pity, though Lady Liesel is a lovely young girl. Lord Ruming, however—"

"Albie, weren't you telling me that Lord Ruming is about to propose to someone?" Meredith interjects.

"I was," Albie agrees. "Nice girl from the country; untitled too, I believe."

"A true love match, then," Lady Harrington says. "Well, good for him. I'll have to think of some other young men to suggest. Once we get to London, I'm sure Miss Bertram's mother and I can sit down and make a proper list. Your father has never been much for planning, has he, dear?" she asks, looking to Gwen.

Gwen holds back a laugh. "I'm sure he'd appreciate it. Though," she says, glancing down the table in a way that makes Bobby want to duck and cover, "I think he's actually been making more plans for Bobby and Demeroven, as they're more valuable to the family, aren't they, Albie?"

Albie glances from Gwen to Bobby, looking apologetic. "I suppose that's true, politically speaking. Though what's most important is for everyone to be happy; no one in this family need be a chess piece."

"Good to know," Bobby hears Demeroven mutter.

"Well, boys, tell me—what outings have you been on, then? Have any young ladies caught your eye?" Lady Harrington asks.

"No one so far," Bobby says slowly, working hard to look

down the table and not across at Demeroven. "I went out once with Lady Annabeth."

"Oh, yes, a big accomplishment, seeing as she and Johnson have been courting for a year," Meredith says.

Bobby only just refrains from elbowing her while Gwen snickers.

"Only Lady Annabeth? Honestly, Robert, you could make more of an effort. You're a delightful young man."

"Thank you," he says, feeling himself blush. "I do think I've actually got Demeroven beat, though," he says, glancing across the table to see Demeroven glaring back. "He's not been on one outing that I know of."

"That you know of," Demeroven repeats, his face unguarded and playful. He's sitting up straighter too, come to think of it. "But in fact, I think I have found someone special this season."

Bobby feels his delight turn to lead in his stomach just as Brile and Canton return to remove their soup and replace it with individual roasted quails and tureens of potatoes.

"You haven't mentioned any outings," Gwen says, a note of accusation in her voice as she carves her bird with a little too much force.

Bobby picks up his cutlery with numb hands. Has he missed something—something obvious—something that would make the last few weeks more than embarrassing?

"I do sometimes like to maintain an air of mystique," Demeroven says.

Bobby forces himself to breathe evenly and begins to nestle his knife into the meat along the breastbone of the bird. He thinks he might know how the poor thing feels.

Beth looks around Albie with a raised eyebrow. "Oh? And what else have you been leaving out, when you know we're always so starved for good gossip?"

"I don't want to besmirch the honor of my paramour," Demeroven says casually, spearing a carrot from his plate.

"Well, that won't do. If Miss Bertram and Lady Gwen are starved for gossip, you can only imagine how much Meredith and I have wasted away these long months. Now tell us, who have you met, Lord Demeroven?" Lady Harrington asks as she daintily carves her bird.

"It's no one titled, but I've been having some fun," Demeroven says, and Bobby feels like his heart has sunk all the way into his guts and gotten twisted. He can't even bear to lift his forkful of quail to his mouth.

Has he been too caught up in his own infatuation to see what's clearly right in front of him? Demeroven has never wanted him; he made that very plain. He said friends, and friends only. So all the angst and daydreaming Bobby's been doing has been for what? Just to break his own heart?

"But the relationship is private, and I need to respect the honor of my paramour," Demeroven says.

Bobby considers simply running out of the room, feeling so wrenchingly mortified he could melt right into the floor. Then something brushes his ankle. He jerks in his seat, only just playing the movement off as a cough into his napkin.

It's a foot. It's a foot very pointedly brushing up against his leg. He blinks and finds himself beneath Demeroven's gaze while Gwen, Beth, Meredith, and Lady Harrington begin putting together bets for who this mysterious paramour could be.

But Bobby's eyes are caught on Demeroven's. Demeroven, who is . . . *running his foot up Bobby's calf.* He can't be—is he—he can't be talking about Bobby, can he? An untitled paramour with whom he's been having fun but wants to keep private? It can't possibly be Bobby.

But that's his sodding foot making Bobby hard *at the dinner table.*

Demeroven smiles slyly and then turns back to Lady Harrington, gamely fending off every name the ladies provide while Albie sits back in his seat, eating with a little smile.

Holy shit. He— How can this man be so demurring and anxious and scared, and simultaneously be this hot and daring all at once?

And what on earth is Bobby supposed to make of Demeroven's foot rubbing against the soft underside of his knee? How is he supposed to eat? What is he supposed to *do*?

Suffer, it turns out. Suffer in agonizing ecstasy, because Demeroven keeps it up all through dinner, long after Lady Harrington and the girls give up the ghost and go back to their normal gossip.

It's only at dessert that Demeroven ceases to torture him, clearly too in love with Mr. Whiley's soufflé to continue his sexual advances. It is remarkably good, and Bobby tries to focus on the decadent chocolate (apparently one of the only things Meredith's been able to stomach reliably, which must be costing Albie a small fortune).

Every glance from Demeroven sends a charge coursing through his veins. Pinpricks of heat are bouncing all over him. Every single nerve is on alert. It feels like he might spontaneously combust.

It's late. They've traveled all day. Meredith is with child. Surely, surely, that means they can end this torture soon and go to bed. And he can somehow . . . push Demeroven up against a wall, any wall, he doesn't care which, and snog the living shit out of him until he's crying with want as payback.

Because apparently they have a relationship, and he damn

well deserves to get some retribution for this dinner. More than that, he desperately wants to talk.

Of course, no one seems to care much about his fried nerve endings. The moment Lady Harrington deems dessert complete, they're ushered upstairs by the whole staff. He tries to keep track of Demeroven in the fray, but he keeps being pulled in multiple directions.

He glances up the stairs just in time to spot Demeroven disappearing around the first landing when their housekeeper, Mrs. Tilty, takes his arm.

"We have missed you and the viscount," she says seriously, looking up at him. "And you've gone and grown again."

He laughs, watching the way her eyes crinkle and noting the few new strands of gray in the curls that peek out beneath her lace cap. "I think it's just the distance, Mrs. Tilty. I'm much the same."

"No, no, there's something different about you," she insists as they mount the stairs. "You look older."

"I'm sure it's just the travel," Bobby demurs, though her words settle somewhere behind his breastbone.

He does feel a bit older. It could just be the time away—he's always surprised by how it feels like the house stands still when they're gone. Though, of course, this time it hasn't. His bedroom corridor has been redone, he notices, taking stock of the new rose-patterned wall etchings in a dusky pink outlined with gold.

"Lady Mason had it commissioned. She's been dreadfully bored," Mrs. Tilty says, her voice low but amused.

Bobby tries to focus on the new wall decoration and not the fact that Demeroven is hovering outside the room across the hall from his.

"How have you been, Mrs. Tilty?" he forces himself to ask,

not wanting to be so self-absorbed he neglects the housekeeper who raised him.

She pulls him to a stop outside his door, glances at Demeroven, and then turns to Bobby, smiling fondly. She runs her aging hand over his door, tracing the faded etching where he carved his name into the wood when he was four. His father beat him, but Mrs. Tilty was impressed he knew his letters.

"I am well, Mr. Mason," she says. "Glad to have you back, and for your company."

They both look at Demeroven, who blushes and then slips into the guest room, the door closing with what feels like a decisive click. So much for conversation.

Bobby forces himself to look back at Mrs. Tilty. "We've missed you too. There's absolutely room for you at the London house, if you're interested," he says, thinking it might be rather nice to have her there.

But of course: "No, no, my place is here. Mr. Tilty has London well in hand. And what would he and I have to discuss when he comes home if I were there to experience it with him?"

"I do hate that we take your husband from you for four months out of the year," Bobby says.

"Oh, goodness. If we didn't have this break every year, we'd surely murder each other," Mrs. Tilty says with a chuckle. "Now, I've laundered your sheets with the lavender soap you like, and there's water and a bit of rosemary bread on the side table if you get hungry."

Bobby reaches out impulsively to hug her. She squeaks and then hums, rubbing his back. He takes just a moment to savor her familiarity, her safety. She feels like all the good of childhood, and he wonders as he pulls back how he survives in London without her.

"All right, all right. To bed with you. Lady Harrington has

all kinds of things planned for the week, as does Lady Mason. We've tried to keep them entertained, but nothing beats young blood."

"I'm sure you've done a wonderful job," Bobby says, taking her hands. "And thank you. I know it is a huge comfort to Albie that you've been here with Meredith."

"It's my honor. I can't wait to have another little boy to chase."

Bobby smiles and lets her leave him after a squeeze of his hands. He stands there, big and small, old and young, comforted and disconnected all at once. He leans back against his door, feeling the familiar solid wood, hoping it can ground him.

Instead, he's left staring at Demeroven's door, all kinds of other feelings rising in his chest until they crescendo. He throws his door open and catapults himself into his childhood bedroom. He strides across the room with practiced steps to launch himself face down onto his bed, feeling the bounce like an old friend, eyes squeezed shut.

He's had many a strop in this room, with its blue walls and cream-colored furniture. He doesn't need to open his eyes to see the tattered lace of his canopy. Doesn't need to look to know there are little horse and knight figurines still on the windowsill. His sheets smell like lavender, and the bed is the kind of soft only an extremely old mattress can be, lumpy in just the right spots.

It's the perfect place to simply dissolve into a puddle of frayed nerves, sexual frustration, and general malaise, and he's set to do just that, rolling onto his back to splay like a starfish, his feet hanging off the side of the bed.

And then the bed moves.

CHAPTER EIGHTEEN

James

He's not entirely sure how he finds himself with a knee on Mason's bed, in what's clearly Mason's childhood bedroom, with Mason sprawled out below him. All he knows is that there was this feeling, all through the carriage ride, all through dinner, like a brightening in his chest. Like someone reached inside him and lit a light he didn't know existed.

All along, he's thought Mason was being reckless, suggesting something that could never be. How could there be a safe dalliance? How could there be protection, and acceptance, and support for a relationship such as theirs?

But here they are, in a house made of three families, where his cousin and her *lover* are accepted, and loved, and championed. Mason wasn't simply talking from between his legs. He knew—he's *lived*—another way.

And yes, in London, it's different.

But James knows the bravery that wormed its way down to his foot at dinner, knows how warm and comfortable and . . . happy he's felt for the last twelve hours. Even if it's just here, just with their weird extended families, all tangled into a protective web of acceptance. Even if they have to hide from Lady Harrington—how much easier it is to hide from just one woman than all of London.

He wants to know, just once, what it would be like to have

this. What it might be like to be as comfortable as Lady Gwen and his cousin. What it might be like to finally reach out and take something he wants—someone he wants.

Mason blinks his eyes open, staring up at James, his mouth parted, chest rising and falling rapidly. He can see Mason's mind whirring behind his hazel eyes. Can see the questions, the hesitation. Can see the frustration too—that look he gave James at dinner, full of heat and future payback and lust.

James doesn't know how to explain what's changed. How he's gone from idolizing Mason, to hating everything he stands for, to being jealous, to wanting more. How much it means, how much it excites him, how much it baffles him, that Mason wants him back.

He can't seem to form the words, and so he falls back on the only thing he knows, and bends over Mason. He dips his head, waiting only a fraction of a moment for Mason to raise his neck, and then their lips collide.

It's soft, and heated, and achingly tender. James slowly straddles Mason, a knee on either side of his broad hips so he can press down, gasping into Mason's mouth. Mason's hands move to cradle James' jaw, angling him so he can better nibble on James' bottom lip.

James groans, heat shooting through him, and Mason pulls back.

They stare at each other for a charged beat.

"Your room is cute," James says, closing his eyes in mortification as soon as the words pop out.

Mason chuckles and brushes his thumb along James' jaw. "Thank you," he says, no hint of derision in his voice. "You're cute."

James opens his eyes to find Mason's sparkling with

something—amusement, attraction, appreciation? "You're absurdly handsome."

God, he's awkward.

"If you think it's not mutual, you're a fool," Mason says and James feels something let go in his chest again. Mason's really here holding him, grinding up into him ever so slightly.

James groans and Mason's little smile turns more predatory. He leans up and sips a gentle kiss from James' lips before flipping them with practiced ease. James' back hits the mattress and he lets out a startled breath, everything tightening. The awkwardness slips away as Mason holds himself above him, hands on either side of his head. He slowly lowers the rest of his body, so they're aligned, head to toe.

"I've thought a lot about this," Mason whispers as he slips his thigh between James' legs.

James bites back another groan and forces himself to make eye contact. "Not as much as I have," he says, fighting the urge to blush.

If they're going to do this, they're going to be equals in it. He's been shy and demurring in bed before. But James is not a fumbling young man any longer, learning his firsts. He knows what he wants, he knows what he likes, and damned if he's going to let his hesitations get in the way of finally being in bed with Bobby Mason.

"Oh yeah?" Mason says, breathing hard as James lets go and rubs against him with abandon. "Jesus, Demeroven."

"James," James pants, regaining enough sense to bring Mason's mouth down to his.

Mason hums against his lips, opening his mouth with a groan when James slicks his tongue across his bottom lip. "Bobby," he rasps some minutes later.

"You're wearing too many clothes, Bobby," James says, his voice a husky whine as *Bobby*'s hand begins to travel down his side, ghosting over too many layers and yet trailing fire as it goes.

"Good point," Bobby says, immediately rucking up James' shirt.

James can't help but laugh as Bobby rears back to work on the buttons, sitting across James' hips. James sits up too, both of them gasping. Bobby wiggles in his lap and James leans forward, working his way down Bobby's buttons while Bobby claims his mouth again.

Bobby finishes first, mostly because the movement of his hips is driving James wild. Bobby's hands glide up his chest beneath his undershirt, soft and strong and spreading zips of pleasure as they go. Bobby tugs James' arms back while slipping off his shirt and undershirt in one go.

Not wanting to be outdone, or to come in his pants from just the friction of Bobby in his lap, James manages Bobby's final button. He nearly tears Bobby's shirt and undershirt in his effort to remove them, tossing them off the bed triumphantly. Bobby mock glares at him.

"Hey," Bobby says.

James kisses him in reply. "Like you don't have twenty in this room," James mumbles against his mouth, leaning forward to press Bobby back against the bed.

Bobby hums in delight, using the movement to wrap his legs around James' waist. James gives himself just a moment, rutting against Bobby Mason, both of them still half clothed, moving frantically. He thinks his schoolboy dreams may have died and gone to heaven.

But they're not schoolboys anymore, and there's no need for this to end in damp frottage, much as the idea sends a juvenile thrill through him. So he lifts himself up to meet Bobby's eyes, briefly entranced by how dark and wide his pupils have gone. By the image of Bobby mussed and panting, with swollen lips and a light sheen of sweat covering his solid, built chest. Like some kind of Spartan god, sprawled out entirely for James' pleasure.

"Trousers," James says, closing his eyes as it slips out without any smoothness at all.

"Definitely," Bobby says, squirming beneath James immediately.

James opens his eyes and laughs at the look of concentration on Bobby's face as he tries to divest himself of his trousers without changing their position. "Want some help?"

Bobby meets his eyes. "Please."

James smiles and shifts to his side to help Bobby pull off his boots, so they can work together to relieve him of both trousers and pants. It takes some maneuvering, and James learns Bobby's ticklish at the joint of his knee. And then it's not so funny anymore.

Bobby lies there beneath him, totally at ease in nothing but his skin, allowing James as much time to peruse as he likes. And what a glorious perusal it is. Every part of Bobby is defined and firm, from his magnificent broad chest to his muscular thighs. And at their apex—well, the man has never had anything to be modest about. No wonder he's got a pompous edge once in a while.

"You're glorious," James says, running a finger from the base of Bobby's throat down to his navel.

Bobby's breath hitches and James looks back to meet his eyes, waiting for Bobby's small nod before he lets his fingertip slip lower. Before he rasps through that dark, curly hair. Before he wraps his hand around Bobby Mason and looks up to watch his head tip back in ecstasy, mouth parted, a little wrinkle of pleasure between his eyebrows.

It's almost enough to make James come right then and there. But before that, he wants to see Bobby come undone. Wants to watch as the movement of his hand makes him twitch and sigh and moan. Wants to learn what rhythm makes him arch from the bed. Wants to keep a steady pace, and then stop to circle his finger around Bobby's head and watch Bobby's eyes pop open in bliss.

"Fuck," Bobby says as James repeats his pattern, adding a little twist. "If you don't stop—"

"Do you want me to? We have all night," James says.

Bobby hesitates and James swirls his thumb through a drop of moisture. He's close. Bobby groans and flops back, biting at his lip and waving James on. James chuckles and increases his pace, leaning down to press a kiss to Bobby's throat. Bobby shifts, reaching out to tug James' mouth to his, sucking on his lip as his hips stutter.

In three short jerks Bobby moans against his mouth. His body goes taut and he comes over James' hand. James slows his pace and Bobby falls back to the mattress, eyes closed, mouth open, utterly beautiful and blissed-out and gloriously all for James.

James gently releases him and rolls, just for a moment, to find Bobby's pants on the floor to wipe his hand. When he turns back, Bobby's eyes are open, watching him, his chest still heaving.

"That was the most spectacular tug I've *ever* had," he says.

James can't help but blush. "Thank you."

"Thank *you*," Bobby says, reaching out to pull James down into another kiss. "God," he mumbles against James' lips.

James lets himself get lost in the kiss, feeling proud and

touched and unbearably horny. But he hates to be rushed when he's post-climax, so he doesn't want to—

Suddenly he's on his back and Bobby is climbing off the bed, then tugging him by his ankles. James slides across the comforter, staring up at the canopy, unable to fully believe where he is.

He rises on his elbows when he hears his first boot hit the floor, his legs now dangling off the mattress. He watches, his pulse in his ears as Bobby makes quick work of his trouser button. He lifts his hips so Bobby can shimmy his trousers and pants down and all the way off. He would feel immodest, but the way Bobby stares down at him and licks his fucking lips—James has no calm, no suave, no nothing left in him. Except one exaggerated gulp, and a twitch in his midsection he can't at all control.

"May I?" Bobby asks, his breath fanning across James' thigh where he's kneeling at the side of the bed.

"God, yes," James hears himself say.

And then it's heat and hands and slippery pleasure that has James' fingers twisting in the comforter below him. He tries to stay on his elbows, tries to watch, but it's entirely too much, and he falls back to the mattress, eyes clenched shut as Bobby's mouth makes stars burst behind his eyelids. He thinks briefly of stopping him—of demanding to be inside a different part of him before he comes, but they have all night, and the idea of coming in Bobby Mason's—

It's too bright and wonderful and intense to even finish the thought. He throws his head back on a loud moan, his hips straining toward the ceiling. Pleasure floods through him, tight and pulsing. His fists clench into the sheets. It's perhaps the most extraordinary thing he's ever felt, and it takes him a long minute to even begin to feel anything but white-hot bliss.

Tingles and zips course through him in aftershocks as Bobby finally releases him. He blinks his eyes open and tips his chin, looking down to find Bobby's cheek resting against his thigh, beside his softening— Lord, that's hot.

"Here," he mumbles, his mouth dry. "Up here."

Bobby smirks, climbing up to stretch himself out against James' chest. He leans down for a kiss, halting just above James' mouth. James can barely move, but manages to raise one hand to cradle the back of Bobby's skull and guide him down so he can give him what he hopes is the most grateful kiss of his life. He tastes faintly of salt and tang and James hums against his lips.

"Spectacular doesn't begin to cover it," he manages to say as Bobby pulls back, still held close enough that he's a little blurry.

"Good," Bobby says, such tenderness in the word.

James can feel a flush spreading over his cheeks. Bobby shifts against him, sinuous and languid.

"I'll . . . need a minute," he admits.

"We have all night," Bobby says simply, sliding down to curl himself against James' chest, his nose pressing to James' clavicle.

James cards his fingers through Bobby's hair. "I've never had all night," James finds himself admitting. "Have you?"

Bobby traces his fingers along James' chest, contact that tingles just faintly, stirring the first inklings of recovery in James' abdomen. "I have, but it didn't seem so—" James can feel his frown.

"Safe?" James suggests, the thought swelling in his own chest.

No wondering if someone will enter the room. No worrying that they need to pay. No rush, no hurry, no sense that time is running out and they need to reach for climax immediately.

"Yeah," Bobby says, his breath warm against James' neck. "And real. 'S nice to know I'll see you again."

James closes his eyes against the rush of comfort that surges over him. "Yeah."

"By the way, you're even prettier in the throes of passion, you know?"

James blinks and looks down to find Bobby staring up at him, chin resting against his chest. "So are you," he says, more comfortable returning the compliment than thinking about the reality that Bobby Mason thinks he's pretty when he comes.

Fucking hell, Bobby Mason just made him come. And by the way Bobby slides up his chest, the way he hooks his thigh over James' hip, the way he leans down to take James' mouth, he's going to make him come again.

And again and again and again this week if James has any say as he loses himself in an absolutely wonderful snog. Because this—the feeling of the two of them together—is more wondrous than anything he's ever felt before. Even discovering the pleasures of the flesh as a young man, he didn't feel like this.

What could be minutes or hours or seconds later Bobby finally pulls back, both of them breathing heavily. James opens his eyes, body straining, and they stare at each other, mouths plump, faces flushed. Bobby winks at him and then rolls to the side.

James admires his nimble, muscular form as Bobby crawls across the bed. James follows enough to realign himself, so they're at least somewhere close to the pillows. He watches in confusion as Bobby rummages through his bedside drawer, and then grins when he returns with a small bottle of oil.

"If you want to," Bobby says, shrugging. "No pressure or anything."

"Give it here," James says, holding out his hand, because *of course* he wants to.

Bobby beams and passes over the oil before flopping down on

his back. James can't help but admire him again, from shapely legs, to hardening cock, up to that eager smile. He'd like to know everything he can about Bobby Mason, from how he feels in hand, to what it's like to be inside of him, to how he looks when he sleeps.

So he lets himself admire. Lets himself take his time, situating himself between Bobby's legs and lifting his hips. Lets himself enjoy the press of Bobby's thighs against his knees as he splays his legs.

James oils his fingers and studies Bobby's every groan and sigh and moan. He makes it languid and takes pleasure in every frustrated look Bobby gives him before his head tips back on another whine. He's beautiful, and glorious, and just the effort of making him ready has James ready too.

"Do you want to be on your back?" he asks.

Bobby blinks his eyes open, staring up at James. "Oh," he says, thinking.

James waits. He's never done anything he truly didn't want to do. But so often there's not time, or affection enough, to make choices just based on taste. He's received often enough to know what he doesn't like, but a coat closet rarely provides enough space to make a real decision.

"I'd like you behind me," Bobby says, and James can hear both that it's what he wants, and that it's costing him something dear to admit to it.

James smiles, shifting back to allow Bobby to turn over. He slicks himself as Bobby rises up on hands and knees. He leans over him, letting every inch of himself wrap around Bobby's body, relishing in the warmth of Bobby's back against his chest, and the way that, like this, he can surround Bobby, even though Bobby has so much height on him.

"Please," Bobby says, shifting his hips in a way that nearly steals all of James' resolve.

James kisses Bobby's shoulder and then straightens up, taking time to allow Bobby to adjust as he presses close and slowly, achingly, enters. He breathes through his nose, following the shallow rock of Bobby's body, listening to his whines and sounds and watching the tension in his back, until he sees Bobby relax.

The tight, hot, gripping welcome of Bobby's body almost makes him black out. He steadies himself in the sound of Bobby's heavy breathing, in the feel of his hot skin, in the light smell of sweat that hangs around them. And then he begins to move. The sound Bobby lets out, low and gorgeous and full, is almost as good as the way it feels to be enveloped in him.

James runs a hand up and down Bobby's back as he angles his hips, searching for the spot he found with his fingers. Bobby muffles a shout and James groans, moving faster. He adjusts to glide his hand down Bobby's flank, curling inward until his hand finds Bobby's cock. But the movement changes the angle of his hips and Bobby grunts.

Then suddenly Bobby rears back so they're both kneeling together, James driving into Bobby as his back presses into James' chest. Like this, with them moving together, everything is deep and tight and warm. James plants sloppy kisses on Bobby's shoulder as he moves his hand in time with his thrusts, using every bit of his self-control to make sure Bobby feels as much pleasure as humanly possible. Because he knows the minute he lets himself go, it'll be over in four short pumps.

"Fuck, fuck, fuck," Bobby says, arching against James.

"You feel incredible," James says, not quite tall enough to reach Bobby's ear, but just right to press open kisses to the side of his neck.

"I— Oh, God, I'm going— I can't," Bobby stammers, rocking into James' hand as James keeps moving steadily, pushing Bobby toward the edge until he comes with a loud groan.

His hips stutter into James', and James keeps going, wringing every last drop of pleasure from Bobby until he feels him go slack, shuddering against his thighs. James kisses his shoulder and guides Bobby back to the bed, so he can rest, spent, face buried in the pillows. James waits, his whole body straining, the angle almost unbearable.

After what seems like a cursed eternity in heaven, Bobby opens one eye and looks back at James. His lips quirk into a dazed smile and he turns his face into the pillows. Only then does James let go, focusing on his own pleasure, and the blazing, gripping, white-hot tautness in his groin that snaps with a ferocity he's never felt before.

He collapses down on top of Bobby after surely the longest, most spectacular orgasm of his life. He rests there, breathing heavily, his sweaty cheek pressing into Bobby's shoulder blade, where nothing but pleasure and Bobby and a buzzing euphoria exist in the world anymore.

"Good?" Bobby mumbles, turning his head to look up at James with one squinted eye, his face still flushed, hair matted to his forehead.

"Fucking brilliant," James rasps without hesitation. "For you?"

"Fucking brilliant," Bobby repeats, a sweet smile lifting the corner of his lips.

James bends his neck to press a kiss to the apple of his cheek and then starts to pull away, only for Bobby to whine and scrabble a hand at his hip.

"Stay," he says.

"I'll be right back," James promises, heaving himself up with regret.

He stands, naked as the day he was born, and thoroughly unembarrassed. It's a new, heady feeling, and he lets himself bask in it while he orients himself to the room he completely ignored when he snuck inside. It's a lovely shade of blue, and somehow already messy. Pride tingles through him—partly his doing.

He spots the wash basin on the far dresser and strides over, quickly cleaning himself up before dipping another cloth and returning to the bed. Bobby's still sprawled on his stomach, but he's raised his chest to watch James return.

James can't help but feel a slight exhausted twitch between his legs at the sight of his . . . *lover*? Bobby is a gorgeous man, and now that he knows the feel of his muscles, the sounds of his mouth, the wonderful undulations of his body, he's not quite sure how he's going to remain proper for the rest of the week.

But they have the rest of the week, and isn't that something?

He sits at Bobby's hip and gently cleans him up, smiling as Bobby sighs and flops back to the mattress.

"God, you're sweet. Hot and sweet. Never known that one before," he mumbles into his pillow.

James laughs and lays the cloth over the hamper with his own, hopefully to dry by the fire before morning. He turns and watches Bobby crawl under the covers, the two of them staring at each other in the soft firelight.

"Come back to bed," Bobby says, reaching out a hand.

He'll have to wake early and slink back across the hallway to his own room, lest Bobby's nosy staff find them entwined together like this. But he can't ignore the pull of Bobby's earnest expression, nor the want to be wrapped in his arms.

Bobby doesn't disappoint, scooting to the middle of the bed so James can slip in beside him. Bobby gloms immediately on to James' back, his strong, muscled arm sliding around James' waist to pull him tight against Bobby's stomach. His leg threads through James', providing a much-needed light stretch of his overused hips, and James turns into pudding.

"This is nice," Bobby says, nuzzling the back of his head.

"Yeah," James agrees. "It is."

So nice he thinks he could stay right here forever, warm and comfortable and . . . something else he's not ready to name. Something glowing and wonderful, but too much, too big, too soon.

The way Bobby's broad hand rests, pressing on his stomach. The way his foot has wrapped around James' ankle, his thigh between his legs, rubbing ever so slightly. The rise and fall of his chest against James' back, easy and even and lazy.

He's never felt this before, not with anyone, much less with *Bobby Mason*, a man with whom he's shared so much in such a small time. It scares him. But at the same time, there's a fullness in his chest he can't fight—a bright, burgeoning security. It pounds against his breastbone. He's never felt this safe before.

And he's certainly never been in bed with Bobby Mason falling asleep behind him, holding him tight and close.

He's pretty sure he's never going to be able to feel like this again, if it's not with Bobby.

The thought should terrify him into leaving, but instead he closes his eyes and lets the warm rise and fall of Bobby behind him lull him into a deep, untroubled sleep.

Chapter Nineteen

Bobby

Bobby leans back on his hands, staring up at the beautifully blue sky. The picnic blanket is a little rough beneath his palms, and his body feels languorous and just the smallest bit sore. It's a relatively perfect morning-after, and he rolls his neck, glancing sideways at James.

His legs are crossed and he's dutifully knotting flowers together for Beth, who takes his strands to weave them into an elegant flower crown. Gwen and Meredith sit on either side of her, handing her leaves as requested, continuing to gossip a mile a minute.

James meets his eyes for a moment, a soft blush flaring up his throat before he looks back at his flowers. Bobby could stay here forever, replaying that little look in his mind. Otherwise, he'll relive moments from last night, and that won't do, as certain parts of his body would hardly behave.

Even the mere thought of what they got up to, again, when he woke for a drink of water in the middle of the night, has him shifting on the blanket, staring determinedly up at the single fluffy cloud lazing across the sky. He will not think about James naked, below him, inside—

He closes his eyes tight and then opens them, desperate to find something to do with his hands, and a better position to hide what . . . might become a problem. Blasted James is just sitting there, kissable and a little rumpled, with delicately knotted flowers in his talented hands.

God, how is Bobby going to survive seeing the man all buttoned up again? How will he ever face James on the street, or in their homes, or at the club, without just jumping him immediately, or having a very noticeable problem?

How are they even going to continue this once they're no longer under the protection of his childhood home, with the buffer of laziness or alcohol or simply good humor to excuse any . . . friendliness? How are they ever going to hide this from the ton?

He doesn't want to think about it, but finds that if he can't dwell on memories of last night, there's little stopping him from obsessing about the hows and whens and whats of their future, since it seems they suddenly have one.

"I certainly think women should be allowed to compete in fencing, even at the casual level," Meredith says.

"Gwen would vanquish them all, no question," Beth says, taking James' line of flowers with a grateful smile. "I think she could probably best you too, James."

James shrugs. "If she's the better competitor, then I'd gladly admit defeat," he tells Beth, smiling over at Gwen.

"When we get back, we should schedule a match. I'm sure my father's suit would fit you . . . if we roll up the ankles," Gwen says.

James snorts and gathers another handful of flowers. Even the idea of James in an overlarge fencing costume has Bobby feeling tight around the middle. There's no way he'll survive being out in public with the man right now. Though maybe another few romps might cure him of his schoolboy hormones, and then he could be reasonable. Because the comfort of James in his bed every night isn't something he wants to give up.

James looks over at him again, an eyebrow raised, as if he can read the thoughts behind Bobby's eyes. Bobby smooths his face and offers a casual smile. He doesn't want to share his concerns about the future. James looks happy, bright, even a little glowing. Bobby doesn't want to spoil that. Why waste this rare opportunity on the future, when he can immerse himself entirely in a wonderfully pleasurable present?

"Demeroven, you haven't seen the lake, have you?" he asks.

All four of his fellow picnickers look over at him, apparently in the middle of a conversation he's been ignoring. Gwen gives him a look while Meredith simply smiles. He doesn't look at Beth, too sure she'll see right through him.

"Ah, no, I haven't," James says, looking befuddled but not disinterested.

"Excellent. Let's leave the women to their gossip and I'll take you on the hunting tour, get you ready for the late summer season."

"Aren't you all shooting at the Havenfort estate? My father's been preparing to stock the lake and the land," Gwen says.

"We'll come here after. Don't rain on my hunting plans," Bobby says, standing up to brush off his pants as if he's being entirely rational.

He'll need to work on his terrible subterfuge, it seems. Though James has risen gamely and stands with his hands on his hips, waiting for Bobby's next move.

"We'll see you later," Bobby tells the girls, nodding toward the trees that will, if they want, take them on the winding path out to the lake.

"I do want to hear about that new cholera treatment you

were talking about later," James tells Beth, giving her a smile before heading out in front of Bobby.

"Have fun," Meredith says, while Gwen just continues to scrutinize them.

"We will," Bobby says cheerfully, setting off after James at a leisurely pace.

It takes all the self-control he possesses not to run forward. Instead, he meanders behind James, enjoying the view. James is wearing just a green vest over his starched white shirt, and the high waist of his brown trousers only makes his pleasing shape more entrancing.

It's a long two minutes until they're safely within the tree line and Bobby approaches James, letting all of his lust and want and frustration show. James leans back against a thick oak just off the path, watching him in amusement.

"Could you have been even a little more delicate?" he asks.

"I could have," Bobby admits, stepping right up to James to press his hands on either side of his head. "But why?"

"So perhaps our cousins don't figure us out, oh, immediately?" James suggests, looking up at him and tilting his head, which leaves the long line of his throat open and available.

Bobby takes his opportunity, bending to press an open-mouthed kiss against James' pulse, reveling in his little gasp. "My focus was on getting you off that blanket, don't much care about how I did it," he says, nosing up to trail his lips along James' jaw.

James raises one of his hands and glides his fingers into the hair just above Bobby's ear. It sends tingles all the way down his spine and Bobby hums, finally pressing his lips to the corner of James', right against his languid smile.

"Well, I suppose we're here now," James mumbles, his hand curling further to rest on the nape of Bobby's neck.

Bobby hums again, and James sucks on his bottom lip just the way he likes. A quick study, James Demeroven.

James suddenly spins them so Bobby's back lands against the tree and James can press up against him. Bobby lets out a surprised huff against James' mouth. The top of his hips grinds right into where Bobby wants him most, their height difference allowing James to press every last inch of himself against Bobby, arching up to continue their fabulous snog.

"We should move further back," Bobby says regretfully a few minutes later, when they're both starting to tug at each other's shirts, hands dipping dangerously toward belt buckles.

James pulls away, looking wonderfully disheveled, his hair sticking out every which way. "Right," he says.

He takes Bobby's hand, and then it's the mad race he wanted to begin with, the two of them running with shirts untucked and kiss-red lips, until they're deep within the forest and well off the path toward the lake. Is Bobby entirely sure he can get them back out? Not particularly.

But with the dappled green light, and the quiet, earthy stillness of the forest around them, and James there with his heaving spectacular chest, he doesn't much care what needs to happen in twenty minutes. All that matters now is letting James push him back up against another tree. All that matters is tripping his fingers down James' stomach to undo the buttons on his trousers.

All that matters is the two of them pressed together, hips moving urgently among hands while they breathe around each other's mouths, groaning softly in growing ecstasy. The tug of James' teeth on his lips, the press of his chest, the steady rock of the two of them into the messy tangle of their hands—it's pure bliss.

When they're both spent and breathing heavily, James resting against Bobby's chest, Bobby can't help but laugh.

"What?" James asks, his lips pressed to Bobby's neck.

"I just didn't see this weekend resulting in the two of us—"

"Coming in the woods?" James suggests, pulling back with a knowing look.

"Oh, I was going to be much lewder. You spoil all my fun," Bobby says playfully.

James laughs. Bobby reaches down and gently tucks James back into place, doing up his buttons. James sucks in a breath but then gets to work on Bobby's trousers. They surely could go for another round, possibly something . . . lewder, in fact. But as he watches James button his shirt and goes to right himself as well, he decides there's more than enough time to fellate James against a tree later in the week.

For now, it might actually be nice to go see the lake, bask in the afterglow together, rather than return to the group sweaty and too obviously sated.

"Come on," he says, taking James' hand to lead him back toward the path. And while they've been entirely more intimate, something about holding James' hand in broad daylight feels momentous. The sound of their footsteps crunching leaves and twigs, the feel of his soft palm against Bobby's, is almost magical.

They walk lazily through the woods until they finally reach the lake. Sunlight glints off the wide expanse of calm water, ringed with vibrant green trees. He can see the family of ducks that regularly makes its home on the Mason lands splashing near the far shore.

It may not be grand, but it's beautiful, and the bank on the southern shore is always the perfect slope for lying down in the soft grass. Which is exactly what he wants to do with James, so he tugs gently on his hand, releasing him reluctantly to plop down in his favorite spot, just past the biggest, broadest rock on the lakeshore. It looks a little like a toadstool, and he's pleased to see the patch of moss on the right side is still there. It's the little things that give him comfort here.

That, and the sight of James sitting gingerly in his linen pants, cheeks still slightly flushed from their endeavors, and looking gorgeous there in the bright sunlight.

"Your manor is lovely," James says after a few contented minutes that Bobby spends staring out at the lake and sneaking glances at his handsome . . . whatever he and James are to each other.

"Thank you," Bobby says, as if it has anything at all to do with him. "'S nice to be away from the city sometimes."

"Yes," James agrees.

He watches the way James stares out across the water. "Do you miss the country?"

"All the time," James says, meeting his eyes briefly before glancing away. "I was very fond of my stepfather's lands."

"Where are they?"

"Near the Peak District, by Epworth," James says. "We had twenty acres of land, and he—well, I—was involved in helping the village and overseeing some of the rents and such."

"Oh," Bobby mumbles, surprised. "You're young for that. What has your stepfather been doing?"

"Helping reluctantly and drinking," James says. "I didn't do *much*. But I helped with some of the trade in town, looked over books—simple things. But it was nice. I felt—" He trails off with a shrug.

Bobby watches James fiddle with his cuffs. "Have you spent much time at the Demeroven estate?"

James bobs his head. "It's big. Lovely, but big. I mostly walked the grounds or stayed in the library out of my mother's way. She redid half the manor. I rather liked Lady Havenfort's style, but my mother . . . Anyway. And my stepfather adored the late viscount's study, almost as much as he loves the one in London."

"Maybe you'll find more to do after the season."

James shrugs. "Not sure I'll spend much time at the manor, or even keep it. My stepfather's been going on about staying in London full-time."

Bobby notes the way James' shoulders have risen, how he's picking at the skin around his thumbnail on his left hand. "Do you want to live in London full-time?"

"God, no," James says, immediate and firm.

That would suit Bobby just fine. Not that they need to think about it this week. At least not right now. Instead of letting that thought fester in his head, he reaches out to still James' hands.

"Then you needn't," Bobby says.

James huffs out a laugh, squeezing his fingers. "It should be that simple, shouldn't it?" he asks, looking over at Bobby. "My stepfather wants to buy another townhouse—a better, bigger one. But the only way we'd have the funds for that would be to sell the northern estate."

That would break Beth's heart, he's sure. More, it looks like it might break James' too.

"Is that something you'd want to do?" he presses.

James shakes his head. "It's a gorgeous estate. I'd be happy to stay there."

"Then can't you?" Bobby asks, not wanting to push, but wondering if anyone has told James that he has a choice yet.

That *he* is in control of the Demeroven estate, not his stepfather. From the way he looks now, tense, and smaller, and uneasy at just the thought of his stepfather, perhaps it never has been a choice before.

James looks down at their hands. Bobby squeezes his and James' cheek dimples in a half smile. He threads their fingers together, loose but connected and lovely.

"If I were as brave as you? I could," he says softly.

Bobby feels his eyebrows crease. "Oh?"

"You're so sure of who you are. You always have been. And here you've gotten maybe five sentences out of me, and you see the whole relationship with my family clear as day. And you know the solution, because it's simple. But every time I'm in front of my stepfather, I . . ."

"You're a little boy again," Bobby completes for him. "God, I know the feeling."

The look on James' face is a brittle thing. "Yeah."

"And I may seem brave, but you never saw me with my father."

James' fingers tighten around Bobby's. "But you were always so confident and sure of yourself at school."

Bobby blinks. "I— We never met. I've been wracking my brain, but I'd remember you."

"No, we never met," James agrees, his cheeks pinking a little. "But I noticed you. A . . . lot."

Bobby stares. "You noticed me."

"I, ah, fancied you," James admits, his knuckles squeezing Bobby's as that blush spreads from his cheeks and down his neck. "But I was a year ahead of you, and I don't know why you'd ever have noticed me. I was pretty scrawny until last year."

"I'd have noticed you," Bobby says immediately. James gives him a look. "I would have! And we were all scrawny in school. I didn't always look like this."

"You were handsome then, and now you're handsome *and* muscular," James says dryly.

"Well," Bobby says, preening a little just to see James laugh.

"I still would have noticed you, and liked you, and probably fancied you back."

James rolls his eyes. "You had much better options."

Bobby frowns. He's not sure how to fix that hurt, which looks like it runs deep. Doesn't know exactly how to explain that while he finds James exceedingly attractive, it isn't his looks that drew Bobby to him. It's— "We're kindred spirits," he decides.

James blinks. "Beg pardon?"

"Whether or not you were scrawny, or spotty, or whatever makes you think you wouldn't have caught my eye, it's who you are that drew me to you, not how you look. You're—steady." He groans as James' eyebrow goes up. "Solid. Fuck, no, it's— Look, it's not your . . . looks, or the fact that it's convenient for us to have a dalliance, okay? I think you're brilliant, and funny, and sharp as hell, and it's more fun to do things when you're around, even when we're fighting. So don't sell yourself short, okay?" he finishes.

It's a far cry from the romantic words James deserves. Especially after admitting that he fancied Bobby, which honestly feels like an expanding ball of warm light in his chest. He's honored that a younger James fancied him, and that despite the ugliness of the early part of the season he still likes Bobby enough to—

James' lips are soft against his. The hand not tangled with Bobby's cups his cheek and Bobby sighs into the kiss, lets himself get lost in its languid pleasure. When James pulls back, Bobby slowly blinks his eyes open, sure he looks as dopey as he feels.

"I think you're smart, and funny, and handsome as hell," James says softly. "And I still admire and envy how brave you are."

Bobby shakes his head. "It's easy to be who you are when there are no expectations on your shoulders. You could be like my father, enjoying all the spoils with none of the work. And instead, you're trying to make a difference. I think that's brave."

James stares at him, lips parted, chest rising and falling quickly. Bobby tugs on their joined hands to bring them both down to lie on the hill, staring up at the sky. It's a lot, this honesty. It's wonderful, but aching. He's never been so candid with anyone he's slept with.

And isn't that a sad thought?

"I want to tell him to bugger off, I really do," James says, his voice a hoarse whisper.

Bobby turns his head to watch as James stares up at the sky, lip between his teeth. "You don't have to do all the big things at once."'

James takes a deep breath and then turns to meet Bobby's gaze. "Oh, no?" he says, and Bobby can hear him rallying. "Don't have to change the world, and have a secret relationship, *and* fight my stepfather?"

"Nah, I think two out of three is good," Bobby says with mock severity.

"I appreciate that," James says, his thumb tracing the edge of Bobby's palm in a way that's more than just pleasant.

Bobby forces himself to look back at the sky. Otherwise, he thinks he'll be on top of James in about fifteen seconds, and it's a little too exposed here for that. Though someday it might be nice.

Whatever someday they have.

"What do you want?" James asks softly, breaking Bobby from the start of another spiral.

"What do I want out of what?"

"Life."

Jesus. Bobby stares up at the blue sky. *You,* his mind whispers. But that's far too bald. This thing between them, whatever this fragile, beautiful thing is, it's breakable.

But he has to say something. And his heart and brain are too raw to lie. "A family" slips from his lips. James stiffens and Bobby squeezes his hand. "With someone I truly love. A partner."

James' grip tightens. "That best-friend kind of love Prince went on about?"

Bobby swallows, gripping back. "Yeah."

"That's a lovely idea," James says.

His eyes blur a little as he stares up at the sky, their hands still tangled tightly together. "Yeah. Yeah, it is."

CHAPTER TWENTY

James

James cracks open Bobby's door, peering into the hall. He clutches his robe across his chest, but there's no one there. He glances back at Bobby, blissfully naked, sheets about his waist, body already curling around James' abandoned pillow. For a moment, James thinks maybe he should just get back into the bed—allow whoever plans to see to his room find him absent—and curl back up against his beautiful sleeping paramour.

But the fear of someone finding them together zips across his skin, and with regret he tiptoes into the hall, closes Bobby's door, and hurries across and into his room. He stands at the threshold, staring around. It's quite orderly, compared to the mess they keep making of Bobby's each night. His trunk is mostly still organized, his bed barely slept in. The staff must think he's a most well-behaved houseguest.

Hopefully they'll never know it's because he's been buggering Mr. Mason all night. James feels an exhausted clench in his midsection at the thought and rolls his eyes. He can't exist on sex and Bobby alone. His stomach rumbles and James sighs, heading for the wash basin. They were up most of the night, and even with his hunger he's tempted to slip back across the hall to lie back down with Bobby when the clock on his mantel chimes nine.

There's no turning back now. While Bobby can lie in until

midafternoon, James' absence would be far too conspicuous much later than this. He has to face the day and return to the real world. Bobby's bed will be waiting tonight.

He stretches as he heads down the empty halls, feeling his back pop, his thighs and arse and abdomen delightfully sore. Much as he's coming to detest sneaking out of Bobby's room, the rest of the days at Mason Manor have so far been quite devoid of anxiety. It's probably all the bloody fantastic sex that has him so relaxed, but it is odd. He's not used to feeling . . . settled. But there's no sense in focusing on the absence of panic. He should enjoy this week as best he can—wring every possible ounce of every type of pleasure from it—before they have to face the world again.

He yawns and comes around the doorway to the dining room, surprised to find Beth still in her seat, a cup of tea in one hand and a book in the other.

"Sorry," he says as she looks up.

"For what?" Beth asks, smiling at him before looking back at her book.

James shuffles into the room, feeling wrong-footed somehow, though he knows he hasn't done anything wrong. He's never been very comfortable in other people's homes. He spoons the last of the porridge into a bowl and pours a cup of tea, then slides in across from Beth and stares down at his breakfast.

He's damn uncomfortable in his own home, if he's honest. It doesn't feel like his home.

He looks up at the sound of a page turning and that discomforted unease suddenly makes sense. He does have an apology to make. An important one. And this might be the only chance he has to make it without an audience.

He bites at his lip. He just has to do it, be brave. He's learning to fight for things; this should be one of them.

"I'm sorry," he says, wincing as it comes out high and a little cracked.

Beth looks up, letting her book slowly slip down to rest on the table. "Beg pardon?"

James picks up his napkin to wipe his suddenly sweating palms. "I need to apologize on behalf of my deplorable family. For my uncle, and my stepfather, and the callous cruelty with which they treated you and your mother," he rushes out.

"Oh," she says, looking as shocked as he felt when he found out all the ways his own silence had punished Beth and her mother.

"And I must apologize too for my own inaction. Had I asked more questions, or taken more initiative, I might have saved you the pain and humiliation of being sent from your home, even if you have managed to end up in a better place."

Beth slowly closes her book, considering James as he sits there, hoping his apology alone can suffice. She and Lady Havenfort will never receive what they're due from his stepfather, but then again, that's not his stepfather's place. James is Viscount Demeroven. It's up to him to make this right.

"If there is anything I can do now that I have my title, and the Demeroven fortune, anything at all, please tell me. As soon as I came into the title, I should have made it right. But I was cowardly and took my terrible stepfather's words as truth, instead of coming to you and your mother. It was wrong, and I want to make amends."

"James," Beth says, her voice soft and a little hoarse.

"I want to make this right," he insists, feeling an urgency and a simultaneous overwhelming relief. He's said what needed to be said, and now he can do what must be done.

Beth stands and James feels that relief flickering in his chest. He watches Beth walk around the table and tries to keep his back straight as she approaches his chair. Beth leans down and takes him by the shoulders, guiding him up so she can wrap her arms around him. James hesitates, and then hugs back, feeling like a giant weight has just come off his shoulders.

Beth pulls back, holding his biceps. She smiles, her eyes shiny. "I cannot tell you what it means to me to have what happened acknowledged."

"I could do more," he insists, shifting to take her hands. "Please. Let me make this right."

Beth shakes her head. "I don't blame you for what your stepfather did to us, nor what my father did to us. That isn't your burden to bear."

"But it is mine to make right," James says, squeezing her hands. "And it's taken me too long already."

"It was a battle between our parents, and we're not responsible for their mistakes. All I ask is that we do better," Beth says firmly.

The way she's staring at him, collected, calm, and sure—she looks so like his aunt. "All right," he agrees, because what else can he do but do as she asks?

Beth smiles and pulls him in for another fast hug before releasing him to return to her seat. He stays standing, watching as she settles herself and picks up her teacup. There's relief and joy and pride humming through him, but it's still not quite right.

"You're wrong, you know," he says, slowly sinking back into his seat at Beth's arched eyebrow. "I may not be responsible, but I need to reckon with the mistakes of my predecessors to make the Demeroven name right."

He winces. How easily he falls into old patterns, letting his words get ahead of him to insult her father . . .

"My father was a complete arse. And let's be honest, your stepfather is too," Beth says easily.

James snorts in surprise. "No argument here."

"But I agree, it would be nice to see something good come from the Demeroven title. Something . . ." She trails off, eyes fixed against the back wall.

"Agreed," he says, the reality of their impending return sinking back onto his shoulders. "Obviously, I agree with Lord Havenfort's politics. It seems . . . inconceivable not to, so I will continue to . . . fight the good fight in the Lords."

"Already an improvement over my father," Beth says.

James raises his teacup and takes a sip, wishing it felt like more of an accomplishment. "Otherwise, I only know I want to put the title toward something good. I just don't know what that should be," he admits.

Beth bobs her head, contemplative. "Whatever you decide, my mother and I will support you."

"I'll try to do the family proud, whatever I choose to do—whatever we choose to do," he says, watching as she smiles. "You may not have the name any longer, but you'll always be part of the Demeroven title."

Beth takes a deep breath, her eyes glistening. "We'll make our own path?"

"Together," James agrees, something like contentment settling into his bones.

"Dream bigger than our parents ever did," Beth adds.

James feels himself smile. "I'll cheers to that," he says, raising his teacup. Beth smiles and does the same. They each take a sip and Beth considers him for another moment before returning to her book, that smile still wide on her face, a little knowing.

And finally, he feels true hunger, and tucks into his breakfast.

CHAPTER TWENTY-ONE

Bobby

"The entire chandelier came down," Lady Harrington says.

They all gape at her, gathered around the card table in the sitting room. Beth, Gwen, and Meredith have made a team of three, with Albie and Lady Harrington, and Bobby and James paired up in what has become a truly competitive game of whist.

"Was anyone hurt?" Beth asks as Lady Harrington takes the latest trick.

"No, but Mr. Pinches' father did have to pay for the chandelier and about seven ladies' gowns, since it came down on the drinks table and sent wine flying everywhere. Your father wasn't allowed out for two weeks after that," Lady Harrington tells Meredith.

"As I recall, he got his revenge by convincing five of his school friends to sneak in, steal Mr. Pinches out of his bed, and float him into the lake in the park on a skiff," Meredith says, playing her ace to take the next trick.

"And he stayed asleep the whole time?" Bobby asks.

"Well, Lord Harrington may have paid a valet to get him drunk," Lady Harrington says with an innocent shrug. "Honestly, it's a wonder we ever got married."

"It did take another season for Father to prove himself to Grandfather after that," Meredith says.

"It's a good thing they were a few years ahead of my father. It would have been chaos," Gwen says, clearly intentionally losing a few low hearts as they go around the table.

"Absolutely," Beth agrees.

"Oh, like your mother wouldn't have helped," Gwen says.

"Lady Havenfort wouldn't have gone that far," James says. All six of them stare incredulously back at him. "Would she?"

"Assume that your aunt has the schemes of Gwen, the calculation of Beth, and every mad impulse of Uncle Dashiell. She just hides them better than we ever could," Albie says.

"Oh, dear," James mutters. He glances across at Bobby and plays his ten of hearts.

Bobby nudges his leg beneath the table in understanding. It's shameful, actually, that they're cheating and still getting beaten. Because of course after Bobby plays his king, Albie has the ace, and takes the trick, winning the round.

Bobby leans back in defeat. "Lady Harrington, is there any mischief you and your husband didn't get up to during the season?" Lady Harrington fixes him with the most sardonic look he's ever received, and he flushes up to his ears. "In terms of pranks, of course."

"I never played any pranks," she says slowly.

"You gave Father all the ideas!" Meredith says.

Gwen and Beth cackle and Lady Harrington shrugs, taking a large sip of her wine. "Maybe," she admits.

James snorts and then Bobby finds himself perfectly upright as James' foot makes its way up his ankle.

"Final round," Albie says, taking his turn to deal out the table. "You'd have to win . . . oh, every trick to overtake us," he tells Bobby and James. "And you three are simply playing for pride," he tells the girls.

"Or we'll just be trying to ensure you get no tricks at all," Meredith says.

Bobby watches his brother try to look competitively at his wife and completely fail. He's just too besotted, and something else behind his eyes Bobby can't name. At least not with James' foot trailing against the most sensitive part of his calf.

He needs to concentrate. He kicks James lightly, raising his eyebrows. James sits up straight. Albie looks between them and Bobby gives him an innocent smile.

Albie shakes his head and turns the trump. "Diamonds, everyone."

James taps his left hand and Bobby sucks on his cheek. They're getting better with their tells. They might just win this hand yet.

Or not. Because despite their furtive cheating, and Gwen's, Beth's, and Meredith's attempts at intervention, Albie and Lady Harrington beat James and Bobby by almost thirty points.

"Well, that was humiliating," Bobby declares as he tosses his remaining card toward James, who's gathering the cards while Albie does their final tally.

"Escort me upstairs, ladies," Lady Harrington says, allowing Gwen to help her up and guide her around the table toward the hall. "Don't stay up too late smoking now," she tells Bobby, James, and Albie.

The three girls follow Lady Harrington out, Meredith turning to smile at Albie before leaving the room. Albie waves her on with a tight smile, and then rises to hover by the mantel, toying with a cigar they both know he won't smoke.

James glances between them while he puts the cards away. "I'm actually rather tired," he says with a theatrical yawn. "I'll see you in the morning."

He stands and comes around the table to clap Bobby on the shoulder. Bobby looks up at him and James jerks his chin toward Albie, who's now staring down at his cigar with a pronounced frown. Bobby briefly squeezes James' hand before letting him go. Brother first, other . . . *matters* second.

James heads out into the hall and Bobby sits in his chair, waiting. Albie usually does best when left to his own devices. He'll talk; he just needs a minute.

But after five, Bobby starts to worry. Albie's simply standing there, slowly squashing the cigar into a mangled tube.

"Shall we head out onto the terrace, light that?" Bobby suggests, standing to approach his brother slowly.

"Oh. Sorry, I, ah, got distracted. You can head to bed. I've work to do."

Bobby plucks the cigar from his hand and wraps his free arm through Albie's. "Watch me smoke this on the terrace, get some fresh air in your lungs. Then you can work yourself to death, all right?"

Albie goes to protest, but Bobby tugs on his arm. The only real advantage of his new physique is his strength. Albie spent the winter months tied to a desk, and Bobby spent those months outside, running and riding and sword fighting. They were both hiding, he thinks.

But his coping method has the added benefit now of giving him enough strength to bodily haul his big brother wherever he wants. Something to keep in mind when Albie isn't quite this pliable.

Bobby gently shuts the patio doors and guides Albie over to the solid sandstone railing so they can look out over the gardens and across to the lake together. They used to sit out here and try to enjoy Father's cigars as boys, hacking up their lungs and snickering. Not so much fun when Father caught them, but at least then they were in for a beating together. The two of them against the world.

It hasn't felt much like that in a long while. Albie behind that desk, Bobby aimless out in the world—they haven't stood still together, outside of being in a carriage, in months.

"Here, sit," Bobby says, pulling Albie down to brace their backs against the railing, like they did as children.

"You're not really going to light it, are you?" Albie asks, looking over at him, his head resting back against the railing, legs splayed out in front of him, exhausted and drained.

"No," Bobby says, pocketing the mangled cigar for another time. "Just thought we could use some . . . air."

"Air's good," Albie says, his eyes drifting back toward the sitting room. "'S been good for Mere."

"She seems well," Bobby says cautiously. "And so happy to see you."

"Yeah," Albie says, his mouth quirking upward for a moment before that all-too-familiar frown settles over his face again.

"It'll be lovely to have her with us in London. Really brighten up the place."

Albie nods, but his frown only deepens. Bobby watches as he balls a fist against his thigh.

"Albie, she's fine. The doctors have said. You can stop worrying."

Albie turns his head, fixing Bobby with a glare that could rival their late father's. Bobby forces himself to remember that this is his brother, not his father. The look still makes the hair on the back of his neck stand up.

"Stop worrying? What if she catches cholera? What if she gets consumption? What if the jostling in the carriage makes her go into labor early? What if someone knocks her down in the street? I could more easily stop worrying if the world wasn't— If she wasn't—"

He breaks off, heaving in air, and Bobby scoots closer, all fear forgotten. Instead, a hollow sadness overtakes his chest. Albie begins to sob quietly, curling in on himself, and Bobby can do nothing but wrap his arm around his big brother and hold on as grief and pain and fear pour out of him. Like they're boys again, but in reverse—Bobby holding Albie together instead of Albie putting Bobby back to rights.

"She's strong, Albie," Bobby murmurs. "We'll take care of her. And Lady Harrington will only be a few doors away, and Aunt Cordelia too. And Beth, and Gwen, and God, even Lady Ashmond might come to help, and bring more doctors with her. She'll have the very best care."

"But they die anyway," Albie says, raising his sniffling head to meet Bobby's eyes, looking so young and vulnerable.

He's been telling himself Albie has the viscountcy under control, parliament, marriage, everything. And maybe all along he's been cracking while Bobby's been falling to pieces. They just didn't bother to talk about it.

"You've been reading too many studies," Bobby says, pushing past the truth of it. "Meredith will be fine. Aunt Cordelia was. And just think, you'll have your own little baby soon, even cuter than Frederic. Though, honestly, that's a high bar," Bobby says, smiling as Albie snuffles out a laugh. "You'll see, it'll all be fine."

Albie sighs, his sobs quieting. Bobby lets him sit, tries to provide what meager comfort he can. He doesn't know that it'll all be fine, but he can't bear to live in the alternative for another four months until Meredith's baby comes. It would kill him.

"I feel like I'm walking around in Father's shoes again," Albie whispers. Bobby looks over at him and he shrugs, working his handkerchief out of his pocket to wipe his face. "When we were small, we used to put them on and race?"

"Right," Bobby says, smiling at the memory. "You always won."

"I had bigger feet," Albie says simply.

"And now?"

"Parliament, and the finances, and Meredith—it's like all of it is a few sizes too big. All I want to do is smash things, Bobs, all the time."

Bobby blows out a slow breath. "If it helps, me too?"

Albie chuckles wetly. "Uncle Dashiell was terrified while Cordelia was pregnant, but he still—he still managed it all, and so easily. And I just want to throw everything through a window the second it gets quiet."

"If it's the difference between punching the wall and throwing one of Father's hideous ashtrays out the window, I think smashing things is the way to go." Albie looks over at him in exasperation. "Beats smashing people."

"I guess," Albie mutters. He wipes at his nose. "I just—I don't know if I can do this, all of it, and be . . . good at it."

Doing this apart, Albie with the title, Bobby out in the world with the family reputation, it's just made them both angrier. "So let me help," he says, shifting to look at Albie head-on.

"I can't put that on you," Albie deflects, avoiding Bobby's eyes to refold his soiled handkerchief.

"I'm offering," Bobby says, nudging his shoulder. "I'm not trained for much, but I *can* help with more than the tea parties. I can do research, go to meetings, and do the social stuff. You don't have to martyr yourself for the family just because the title fell on you."

"Bobby," Albie says gruffly.

"I'll get Uncle Dashiell to give me . . . lordly lessons, or something. James could use them as well. And hell, we'll get Gwen and Beth in on it too, give them something else to do. I'm sure Uncle Dashiell would approve."

Albie snorts. "Planning to overthrow me?"

"God, no," Bobby says, laughing.

"We don't both have to suffer this," Albie says.

"We suffer less together than separately," Bobby says firmly. "And maybe with two of us, it'll be doable, even fun. Give you and Meredith some time together. Actually, Meredith being with us will make the social stuff easier. We can host dinner parties. A team of three, that's what you said when Father died."

"I did," Albie admits, his eyes large and still red-rimmed. But that haunted look has lessened, and Bobby considers it a win.

"Then we're a team. Of like . . . six now. Gwen and Beth can help Meredith, and James can work with you and me."

"It's 'James' now, huh? When did that happen?" Albie asks.

Bobby shrugs as they both haul themselves up to standing. Not quite as comfortable at twenty as it was at seven, but the patio did its job. Still has some of that brotherly magic in it.

"He's not so bad," Bobby deflects, gesturing for Albie to precede him into the sitting room.

The house is still, everyone already in bed, and Bobby finds himself more relaxed after the whole upheaval. Everything out in the air, a real plan for getting themselves back on track as the . . . weird little family they are.

"Oh, by the way, you might try to be a bit quieter tonight," Albie says as they round the second landing onto the third floor.

"What?" Bobby blurts, turning to meet his brother's all-too-knowing gaze. "I don't, ah, I don't know what you mean."

"I heard some things when I came down last night. Couldn't sleep is all. Wouldn't want the staff to get any ideas, though, you know? So keep it down, but good on you."

Bobby stands rooted to the spot, openly gaping at his brother. "How did you— How long have you— What . . ."

Albie smirks, giving him a cheeky wink before he turns to head down his and Meredith's hallway, leaving Bobby standing there, flabbergasted. Albie figured out Beth and Gwen early on. But he's never said anything to Bobby about his—about any of it. Don't ask, don't tell. It's how they made it through life with their father, and they haven't had to discuss it until now. But did Bobby and James mess up somehow, or is Albie just like a bloodhound for relationships that sit . . . outside the usual parameters?

"It was my foot you were toying with earlier, by the way," Albie says.

Bobby jerks, turning to find Albie smirking at him before he enters his bedroom. The door shuts and Bobby groans, dropping his head into his hands.

He stumbles toward his room and then swerves, opening James' door without knocking. James looks up from his book, startled, the most darling pair of reading glasses sliding down his nose. But Bobby doesn't have the words.

Instead, he about-faces and storms back across the hall into his room to flop onto his bed in mortification. When he doesn't hear James following, he raises up on his elbows, watching in amused frustration as James peeks out into the hallway, looking left and right before closing his door and scurrying across the hall into Bobby's room. He shuts the door and spins around, looking at Bobby in confusion. If Bobby wasn't quite so horrified, he'd give James flak for being so overcautious.

As it is, he's just glad they're in this together now. He moans and sinks backward, an arm over his eyes. He feels James sit down at his hip and tries to summon the right words.

"What happened?" James asks, concerned.

"I played footsie with my brother," Bobby says hoarsely, lowering his arm to look up at James.

"Oh, God," James says, his face going a bit pale. "Does he—"

"Know about us? He *heard* us last night," Bobby whines out.

James' face loses the rest of its color, his back going straight, and Bobby internally winces. He meant it to be funny. He didn't mean to put James into a panic.

"Hey," he says softly, sitting up so he can reach out and stroke James' cheek. "Albie's happy for us," he says, surprised by the hitch in his own voice. James' eyes meet his, wide and bright. "Truly. He won't tell anyone you don't want to know. He keeps secrets, you know that." Perhaps he's reminding himself as much as he is James, after all. "Hell, you didn't know about Beth and Gwen until this weekend, and really, *you* of all people should have figured it out."

James huffs out a laugh, his body relaxing just a bit. "I guess."

"Don't worry. Albie's on our side," Bobby insists, scooting forward to press a soft kiss to James' lips.

James is stiff beneath him for a moment, and then slowly melts, letting Bobby lay him back against the mattress. He's already in his pajamas and a sinfully soft blue robe. "If you're sure," James whispers.

Bobby smiles, something bright and warm and free easing softly into his chest. He's very sure. "You'll just have to be quieter tonight," Bobby mumbles as he leans in to take James' mouth and works his hand down the front of his robe.

James snorts and pushes Bobby back, giving him the most fantastic look of consternation. "*I* am not the problem, Robert."

"Who, me?" Bobby asks, laughing as James' look goes from disapproving to predatory. "Am I loud?"

"The loudest," James says, hands already tripping down the buttons of Bobby's vest.

"Well, that's your fault," Bobby says, unashamed to already be breathing heavily and squirming against James' thighs.

"My fault?" James returns, pushing the vest off Bobby's shoulders and then heading straight for his trousers.

"That thing you do with your tongue is utterly incomprehensible," Bobby insists, laughing as James' smile turns into a self-satisfied smirk.

"And you want me to stop, so you're not so loud?" James asks, rucking up Bobby's shirt.

Bobby raises his arms so James can lift it off him, sighing in delight as James sits up and runs his lips down Bobby's newly exposed throat.

"Not on your life," Bobby groans.

James laughs, the sound rumbling across Bobby's body. James' hand slips down his stomach, and Bobby decides he can forget everything else for the night. Nothing matters except for James' mouth, and his hand, and his wonderful body. Not pregnancy, not finances, not parliament, and not the too-big shoes they all have to toddle through adulthood in until they fit.

No, tonight he'll slick his tongue into James' mouth and grind down against the hand toying with him, and forget everything else.

CHAPTER TWENTY-TWO

James

"Do you get the sense that they're onto us?" Bobby whispers, leaning over to James on their half of the badminton court.

James watches Beth and Gwen giggle and sip at their drinks on the picnic blanket a few yards away, taking a moment for "refreshment" before they'll be back to decimate Bobby and James for likely the third time. He and Bobby actually make a decent team, but it's rather hot outside now and they're both down to their shirtsleeves and it's . . . distracting.

"How do you figure?" James whispers back, wiping at his brow. He turns to look at Bobby and finds his eyes dark and wanting. Any concern he had about Gwen and Beth being onto them pales in comparison to the heat that flushes through him looking at Bobby now. Jesus, they're pathetic.

"Switching sides with us every game, forcing us to bend over to pick up the shuttlecock," Bobby says, his voice dipping on the hard "k" in a way that makes James' whole body tighten.

"Oh, so you're blaming that on them?" James asks, looking him up and down. "Just because you let Gwen's serve pass you by doesn't mean you have to wiggle your delectable arse at me when you bend over," he whispers, unable to keep from smiling as Bobby crowds closer.

But as much as he'd like to throw him down and ravish him

in the green grass, he notices Beth and Gwen returning, so he coughs and steps back.

Perhaps a little distance is what they all need, given Beth and Gwen are looking rather handsy themselves, and he and Bobby can barely keep their hands off each other. Lady Harrington is about somewhere. No need to tempt discovery, for any of them.

"Why don't we switch teams?" James suggests. "Give me and Bobby a fighting shot."

Bobby groans while Beth and Gwen consider the offer. "I'm just going to keep losing. I'm the weak link," Bobby admits.

"Ah, but this way *I* can at least win one. Ladies, which of you shall be the bigger person and take poor Bobby?" James asks.

Gwen cackles and Beth nudges her, smiling at Bobby. "We'll beat them, you'll see," she promises. "Go be mean with James," she adds, shoving Gwen away as she continues to snicker.

"It's not mean, just practical," James defends, pleased by how little he has to take her comment to heart now.

Both Beth and Gwen have opened up to him with bright cheer over the past few days, and it's let him just . . . float. Stealing kisses with Bobby, playing cards with the girls, basking in the sun, flirting over croquet and bowling, all followed by endless rounds in the sheets—it's bliss here at Mason Manor, and he wishes idly it could always be this way.

"Ready to decimate?" Gwen asks, tapping her racket against her hand.

"Oh, absolutely," James says.

He didn't expect to enjoy spending time with his cousin's lover so much. But Gwen is vicious and sharp-witted, incredibly quick, and hilarious. He doesn't have to be nice to her for his cousin's sake, or Bobby's sake; he genuinely enjoys her company.

And he thoroughly enjoys beating Beth and Bobby in a punishing 15–2 victory.

"Take that!" Gwen yells, jumping up and down in triumph as Beth and Bobby lean against each other, winded.

"We are the victors," James exclaims.

"Oh, they're both poor winners, that's tragic," he hears Beth mutter.

Bobby's loud laughter rings across the lawn and James can't help but smile, even in his admittedly petty victory.

"We deserve sweets in celebration," Gwen declares, plucking the racket from his hand to toss both of theirs by the net.

She takes his arm and guides him across the lawn back toward the patio where Mrs. Tilty has just finished laying out a magnificent lunch.

"You are an excellent partner," James tells Gwen.

She pats his hand. "I know." He laughs, glancing up to find her looking over her shoulder at Beth and Bobby. "I'm glad you're here," she says, turning back to him.

James feels himself smiling. "I am too. It was kind of you all to let me come. I truly appreciate it."

"I appreciate that you took the time to apologize to Beth," Gwen says, no preamble, no gloss.

James ignores his fleeting discomfort. "Someone had to. She deserves an apology, at the very least. I'd do more, if she'd let me."

Gwen smiles, the corners of her eyes crinkling, and another unforeseen weight lifts off his shoulders. "I've got her covered there, but thank you."

"I wish it had been different, but I am glad that the silver lining of such a horrible year was you and your father. You both make Beth and her mother very happy."

"We try," Gwen says, a little bashful all of a sudden, which is an interesting look on her usually proud face. "You and Bobby make quite a good team as well, usually. Though you're terrible at badminton."

She releases his arm to take her seat at the long table with its flowing white tablecloth, and James stands, puzzled. Do they know about him and Bobby? Or is everyone just glad they're no longer at each other's throats? And more, has he really grown so much that the thought of them finding out no longer fills him with dread?

Or is it more that he feels safe here? That Albert knows, and doesn't care—and all of them, save Lady Harrington, know about Beth and Gwen, so why *should* they care about James and Bobby? He didn't think he could consider being discovered without panic, but there's barely an edge to his anxiety as he rounds the table to sit across from Gwen, leaving space for Albert and Meredith to join them as they stroll out of the solarium.

Bobby and Beth reach the table and Bobby plops down beside him dramatically, feigning exhaustion from having his ego so horribly beaten down.

"You'll have to make it up to me somehow," Bobby declares, looking across at Gwen. He presses his foot to James' beneath the table, requesting decidedly different restitution.

"You'll survive," Gwen says, arching a brow in James' direction.

"Here, have the larger sandwich," he says, shrugging as Gwen rolls her eyes. "What, I'm a pushover?"

Gwen snorts and Meredith laughs. "So we shouldn't leave the babysitting up to you when this one is three years old and incorrigible?" Meredith asks.

James looks over, surprised. "Um, well, I mean, with an

actual child, I would certainly try," he hedges, feeling a flush creeping up toward his forehead.

He watches Beth and Gwen glance around and then share a sticky jam kiss. Watches Albert rub Meredith's stomach as they lounge, rumpled and comfortable together. Watches Bobby laugh at something his brother says, seeming lighter than he's been before.

He feels safe here, he decides. Safe and cared about. And it's lovely.

Lady Harrington swans out of the solarium, waving at all of them as they go to rise and apologize for starting without her. She sits without fanfare and immediately pulls Beth and Gwen into a discussion about this season's gowns.

"Larger than life," Bobby mutters, their shoulders briefly pressing together as he leans across James to snag a biscuit.

"But wonderful," James argues.

"Oh, no denying. But you call me dramatic?"

James meets his gaze. "I call you many things—dramatic is just one of the more appropriate."

"I'll need a list of the others," Bobby says, his voice a shade lower, husky.

James shrugs and forces himself to take a calm sip of his tea. He glances down the table and finds Lady Harrington smiling at him. He smiles back, trying to ignore the sudden gnawing feeling in his stomach. Nothing's changed. Lady Harrington is marvelous fun, and he's enjoyed their evenings playing cards. Why should her arrival unsettle him from the comfortable sense of secluded joy he's been basking in all day?

"We'll have to send a second carriage with all of your things," he hears Albert say.

"Mother can bring them with her. I think she'd like to stay here an extra day or two," Meredith says.

He turns to listen to Albert, Meredith, and Bobby's conversation, that gnawing feeling gripping at him more firmly.

"You could stay with her," Albert says, and even James can hear the hesitation in his voice.

"There's no way I'm giving up a carriage ride with Beth and Gwen," Meredith says indignantly. "You ride back with her, then."

"James and I need to be in session on Monday, or I would," Albert says soothingly. "I want to make this as comfortable a journey for you as possible. And if you want to be squished up with Beth and Gwen, that's your right."

"Yes, and we don't have to wear dress hoops for the journey, that will make it better," Beth chimes in, smiling over at them before turning back to Lady Harrington and Gwen.

James puts down the finger sandwich he'd been keen on eating just minutes ago. That clenching sensation is joined by a sinking feeling. He knows, of course, that they're returning home the day after tomorrow. But up until this moment, he'd been doing an admirable job of distracting himself from thinking about it. It's been a problem for later, for after, for someone less happy, and less calm, and less content. A job for his former self, the one terrified of his stepfather.

A person he's been trying to tell himself he isn't anymore.

But the clutch of panic in his chest, the restlessness in his legs, and the choking fear invading his throat are proof that his transformation is far from complete. He is still terrified of what his stepfather would do if he discovered James' proclivities. Terrified of the ton. Terrified of what happens if they try and keep all of this going—the happiness, and sex, and . . . *feelings* he's not ready to name—and then the end of the season comes and they all have to separate anyway.

Or worse, what if he lets himself fall hopelessly in love with

Bobby Mason, and in a few years he has to shatter both their hearts to do his duty to his title, and take the life they would build with all these wonderful people around them out in the cross fire?

Lady Harrington laughs and James nearly flinches. Everything is suddenly off-kilter, and he wants to shake this off. Wants to hold on to the happiness he's felt here for one day longer, but an all-too-familiar anxiety is roiling in his stomach and he's not sure he can sit here for another minute.

"I'm going to take a walk; feeling a little overfull. I'll see you all at dinner," he says, directing his words to no one in particular.

He rises without meeting anyone's eyes and heads as steadily as possible around the table and off the patio, marching toward the hedges at the far corner of the back lawn. Hopefully he can scurry down into the depths of the maze and find a quiet corner in which he can collapse, far away from prying eyes.

He makes it almost all the way there before he hears footsteps jogging behind him. It can only be one person, and he doesn't know how he can face Bobby right now. Doesn't know how to explain everything swirling through his head.

"You all right?" Bobby asks, catching up to him and lightly taking his elbow.

James forces himself to nod, continuing to walk into the maze. Bobby follows without argument. He's seen James in a state before, after all. But not since they've been sleeping together.

James doesn't want to make this Bobby's problem, but it is. It's all their mutual problem now. He's gone and developed feelings for Bobby Mason, and Bobby's developed some level of feelings for him, and now his anxiety is swirling, and he doesn't know what to *say.*

"James, slow down, hey," Bobby says, pulling him to a stop after they turn their third corner into the maze. "What's wrong?"

James stares down at their feet, trying to breathe through it. Trying to find the words to tell Bobby's he's fine.

"Did Gwen say something to upset you?"

"What?" he says, looking up in surprise. Which is a tactical error, because Bobby looks so concerned, and lovely, and handsome. It instantly cracks something in James' chest. "No," he says. "No, she didn't."

"Then what's wrong?"

James shakes his head. "Nothing. Just . . . a little sun-tired," he lies.

Bobby raises an eyebrow. "Sun-tired? Do you want to . . . nap?" James forces a strangled chuckle. "What's the matter, really?"

"I—I just—" Bobby steps closer, running his hands up and down James' biceps and James loses the battle to keep it all from bubbling out of his mouth. "How can you stand this?" he exclaims.

Bobby's hands go still as he blinks down at James, that sly look slipping off his face. "Stand what?" he asks.

He can see Bobby's thoughts racing behind his eyes, knows he has only one chance to properly explain this. "It's like—it's like there are rocks sitting on my chest, you know?"

Bobby cocks his head. "What?"

"I've— Being here is amazing. And *you* are amazing. And I've tried, really I have, to be like you—to just live in the moment and not worry about the future and not care about the consequences."

James hears his words play back only in time for Bobby's face to darken. Bobby's hands slip from his arms. He doesn't move, but the lack of contact feels like a chasm between them all the same.

"Is that what I do? Don't give a damn about the consequences—that's what you still think of me?"

"No!" James exclaims. "No, I just—I'm not explaining this well."

"Clearly," Bobby says, and there's no warmth to his voice, no teasing.

"I just—I don't know how I can—how we can—just return to London after everything we've done and face everyone. How we—"

"'Everything we've done,'" Bobby repeats. "What, is this a tawdry secret to you? Something wrong and disgraceful?"

"No!" James says again, that clutch of panic shooting all over his body in a tight, pulsing fear. He's messing this up, like always. His mouth running away before he can make sense the way he means to. "No, but my stepfather, and the ton, and—you know they're just waiting for something to use against me—us—and this . . . if it ever got out, what we've done—"

"Stop saying that," Bobby says, his words ringing around the hedge maze. "I am not something you've done. I'm not some boy at the back of an inn or a classmate behind the classics building. This— I am more than that."

That's not what he meant, not at all. "Of cour—"

"I know you feel it between us," Bobby says, and James clenches his fists, trying to control his own breathing. "This is *something*, James. Are you really so afraid of your bloody stepfather you're willing to throw this away on the off chance he finds out? So afraid of him you can't even admit you wanted this?"

"How do you expect us to continue a relationship like this in London? How could we do this in the actual world?" James beseeches, his heart thudding loudly.

"Tell me you don't feel it," Bobby demands.

James steps back, gravel crunching under his feet. "Bobby."

"Tell me you only fucked me because we're in the country. Tell me you don't feel anything real for me."

James' back presses into the hedge behind him, and Bobby

looms over him. He can't lie and tell Bobby he doesn't feel what's clawing up his throat, desperate to be shouted to the rooftops. But he can't free those words from his mouth when he has no plan for how to keep them safe.

When he doesn't know how a *love* could survive beyond the safety of Bobby's family's country home.

Feeling overcome and desperate and pent up, he does the only thing he can think of and lurches forward, grabbing Bobby's face to pull him into a hard kiss. Bobby stills against him for a moment before pushing James back, hands on his shoulders, holding him against the hedge, glaring.

They stare at each other, too much to be said, and then their mouths crash back together. James groans as Bobby rucks up his shirt. The press of his hands against James' skin, the stroke of his fingers, sends shivers up and down James' spine. He clutches at Bobby's neck, sucking on his bottom lip. He bucks into Bobby's hand, already making its way into his trousers.

"Tell me you don't feel anything for me," Bobby rasps against his mouth as his hand wraps around James.

James can only moan, pleasure clenching all over his body as Bobby uses everything he's learned about James this week to bring him to the edge in a matter of minutes.

"Tell me," Bobby insists.

He can't explain, but he could show him. He kisses Bobby roughly, skirting his hand down to fumble with the buttons on Bobby's trousers. He would drop to his knees right here in the hedges, worship at the altar of Bobby's body to say all the things he can't put into words. And maybe if he does, maybe Bobby can understand what he meant to say all alon—

A shriek pierces their hazy frenzy of lust and anger and feelings, and the little control James has over his panic and fear shatters apart.

Chapter Twenty-Three

Bobby

He twists his fingers together, pacing across the faded rug outside the sitting room, and wishes he still had his blasted signet ring. He keeps replaying the horrible sight of Lady Harrington fainting to the ground while his hand was wrapped around James'—

Bobby shudders and rolls his shoulders. If only that were the worst of it.

Because then James ran, leaving him alone in the hedge maze to help the collapsed Lady Harrington. He bolted clean off the estate—left everything behind, his luggage, the clothes strewn between their bedrooms, his books, his money, everything.

Bobby's not surprised. Running is what James does best.

He comes to a halt across from the closed double doors to the sitting room where Gwen, Beth, Meredith, and Albie are attempting to deal with the mess he's made.

Except he didn't think James would run this time. There was a part of him, a larger part than he wants to admit, that thought maybe it was enough—maybe *he* was enough—that what they were building together, through kisses and sex and games of whist and time with his family, was enough to make James—

What? Make him want to fight through the justifiable fear of retribution and prison? Make him want to shout from London's rooftops that he's been fucking Bobby Mason and wants to continue for the foreseeable future? Enough to make him want to forsake all his duties, and a wife, and a family, for Bobby?

Of course it wasn't enough. Of course Bobby wasn't enough. James has a bigger life to build, a viscountcy to honor, political ambitions to achieve. How could Bobby alone be enough to persuade him to forsake all of that?

How could Bobby be enough to love, really? What was he thinking?

He jumps when the doors to the sitting room open. Meredith slips through, giving him a once-over. Bobby stands up straight, tries to look like he isn't completely falling apart. Tries to drum up the words to apologize and explain and promise it won't ever happen again.

"Meredith," he starts, her name a croak out of his parched mouth.

"Come here," Meredith says, stepping across the narrow hall to take his arm and lead him two doors down to his father's old study.

Bobby goes, an old unhappiness rippling in his stomach alongside his humiliation and fear and rage. He can do no more than stumble in behind Meredith as she opens the door and waves him through.

The room is dusty, like time has stood still since he and Albie left for London. The chairs are still covered with drapes, the curtains still drawn. It's close, and a little musty, and filled with the ghost of his father, who would be screaming bloody murder if he had caught Bobby—

"I'm sorry," he says, blinking as Meredith throws back the curtains, sending a plume of dust into the air and filling the study with fading sunlight. "It can't be healthy for you to be in here."

She shoots a look over her shoulder and cracks the window to let the warm afternoon breeze waft through the room. Bobby watches it rustle the remaining papers on the desk, a whisper of years past.

"Sit," Meredith says, turning to look at him with her hands on her hips.

Bobby jolts into motion, yanking the drapes off the two armchairs across from his father's immense desk. They're a faded red to complement the dark wood of the desk and bookshelves, which only serve to make the room seem smaller, taller, and more intimidating.

Though the sight of Meredith sitting down in one of the chairs brings him a little peace. His mother never sat in here. But Meredith is now. And Meredith is not his father.

"I really am sorry," he repeats.

"Bobby, sit down," Meredith insists.

Bobby plops into the opposite chair, coughing as dust rises around him. Meredith waves a hand in front of her face until it settles. His tongue almost feels too big for his mouth, like all his apologies and justifications are ballooning against his teeth.

"Are you all right?"

Bobby blinks at Meredith. "What?"

"Are you all right?" she repeats.

"Am I— Is your mother all right?" he asks. "She fell so hard."

"She's just fine," Meredith says, her voice soothing and smooth. She reaches between the chairs to take his hand. "She was merely startled. But I'm worried about you."

"Me? Why?" Bobby asks, his voice squeaky with nerves.

"Because you look like someone just shot your puppy, and you're jumpy as anything, and the man you—and James ran off, and I want to know how you are, please."

"I'm fine," he says, rough and probably too quickly. "I just hope Lady Harrington isn't too angry. I truly didn't mean to upset her. Or, God, for her to see—I didn't mean for any of you to see—I would never put you in that position. We were being careful, but I just—"

"Bobby," Meredith says, squeezing his hand. "Please. No one is angry."

Bobby's heart stutters in his chest. "You don't need to lie."

"I'm not," she says firmly. "My mother is fine. She was surprised, as I said, that's all. She's not upset, or scandalized. And the rest of us—" She pauses, her grip tight and eyes a bit shiny. "Did you think we wouldn't support you?"

Bobby blows out a breath, feeling his chin start to tremble. He does not want to cry in front of his sister-in-law. She's already dealing with more than enough without him breaking down into the heaving sobs he can feel building in his chest.

"We love you," Meredith says. "No matter who you choose to love, okay?"

Bobby does lose the battle with his tears then, one slipping fat down his cheek. He grips back at Meredith's hand, watching as her smile softens.

"We love Gwen and Beth just the same, don't we?"

"'Course," he mumbles. "But it's not . . . They're—they have Uncle Dashiell, and Aunt Cordelia, and it's *not* the same."

Meredith sighs. "It will be harder, but it's no different to us—to me and Albie. I promise you that," she insists.

Bobby goes to shake his head, knowing any relationship of his would put Albie in danger in a way even Gwen and Beth getting exposed never could.

Meredith squeezes his fingers. "Albie and I will help you make whatever life you want. We get to choose how we spend our lives now. It's us against the world—isn't that what you told Albie?"

He meets her eyes at that, feeling the pit of despair in his stomach start to fill. "Old habits," he admits. "With you here, and Albie working himself to the bone in parliament, it— I haven't—"

"I know," Meredith says, and her voice sounds a little watery too. "But I'm better now. And you and Albie are going to get your heads out of your arses and work together, and we are going to build a life that makes us *all* happy."

"Okay," Bobby says, fighting with his whole heart to believe her, because he wants so desperately to believe her.

"And we'll find a way to convince James that—"

Bobby shakes his head and stares down at the floor, deflating. "It doesn't matter. I don't know what I was thinking," he says quickly. "James—Demeroven—he doesn't want a life like that. It was just a passing . . . something . . ." He peters off. The words feel like thin knives pushing into his chest.

He thought it was more than that. Thought it was—they were—on their way to a kind of everything. But he was wrong.

"That's all right. You both keep running. We'll be waiting when you're done," Meredith says.

Bobby looks up to meet her eyes. "Mere."

Meredith only smiles. "It will be all right, I promise," she says. "Now, I need to go make sure Gwen and Beth have my mother in hand."

"I should come with you," Bobby says quickly. "Apologize."

"It's unnecessary, but you may," Meredith agrees. "She went snooping. What she found is entirely her own fault."

Bobby blushes up to his ears. "We shouldn't have been . . ."

"We've all been there," Meredith says with a coy little shrug that makes Bobby choke out a true laugh. "A few games of whist, she'll forget completely."

"I doubt that," Bobby says, but he rises and helps Meredith from her chair all the same.

"Be glad it wasn't Beth and Gwen—you'd never hear the end of it," Meredith says, leading him toward the door.

"What, you think I will now?"

Meredith looks over her shoulder with a slightly evil smirk, eyebrow raised.

"You're awful, you know," Bobby tells her, feeling himself smile as she cackles.

But his brief good cheer evaporates when someone knocks lightly on the door. Meredith squeezes Bobby's hand and then lets go, opening the doors to reveal Albie waiting there, pulled up to his full height in the dim hallway. Dread creeps into Bobby's chest as he watches Meredith lean up to give Albie a brief kiss before disappearing out the door.

Bobby scuffs a foot against the ground, bracing himself. Albie slips into the room and closes the doors behind him with a light bang. A dressing-down will feel much more fitting than Meredith's soft, encouraging words, and he certainly deserves one, no matter what Meredith—

Albie wraps his arms around Bobby, pulling him into his chest. Bobby exhales in surprise, hesitantly wrapping his arms around Albie in return.

Then the tears he's barely managed to withhold burst forth and he finds himself suddenly weeping into his brother's shoulder. All the pain of the last year, and the grief, and the anger pour out on top of the hurt of seeing James run away—of realizing that he alone isn't enough to make James want an alternate life. Heartbreak, that's what he's feeling. And Albie just takes it all, rubbing his back, a stoic rock.

After what feels like an eternity, his tears finally stop, and Bobby pulls back, blinking up at Albie with hazy eyes. "Sorry," he mumbles.

"*I'm* sorry," Albie says. "We'll find a way for the two of you to be together."

Bobby shakes his head. "James won't want to find one."

Albie sighs, holding Bobby by the shoulders. "Then we'll find someone who will," he says firmly. "I should have said something ages ago, made it clear. I will love whoever you choose to love, and I will treat them like family just the same."

Bobby feels one final tear slipping down his face, his chest expanding.

"We're in this together. Gwen and Beth too. We make a good team, remember?" Albie smiles as he wipes the tear away.

"Meredith reminded me," Bobby says hoarsely.

"Good. We'll be okay."

"Yeah," Bobby says, bobbing his head. "Yeah, we will."

Albie squeezes his shoulders. "Now, Lady Harrington is telling Beth and Gwen about the woman she was in love with at finishing school, and we're missing it."

"What?" Bobby exclaims.

"A schoolgirl fancy, she's calling it. Grew out of it, apparently, but she remembers her fondly. She was just telling us about scaling the dormitory wall to sneak into her room, if you want to get in there?"

"Why are we just standing here?" Bobby asks, wiping sloppily at his nose and smiling tremulously up at his brother.

Albie laughs brightly and takes his arm, the two of them hurrying out of the office and across to the sitting room.

And no, things aren't all right. And no, Bobby isn't sure if they can really make a true, loving life for him the way they're all promising. But damned if he won't try.

And if James can't be part of it—he has nights and nights to weep over that. Today, he's not going to let James steal any more of his joy.

CHAPTER TWENTY-FOUR

James

If every hoofbeat of the massive rented black stallion below him didn't send a jolt of pain lancing through his head, he'd still be crying. He ran from the estate, down the long winding drive, and what must have been two miles to Oswestry in a fraught panic. He left everything behind, save for the clothes on his back and the money in this pair of trousers, which will certainly be ruined by the time he makes it back to London.

And now he's riding into the fading sunset, his head aching, body sore, and lungs tight from tears and panic and heartache. Branwen—his terrifying equine travel companion—keeps the punishing pace he started. It matches the staccato pulse of his heart, which hasn't let up since Lady Harrington collapsed while Bobby—

James fights back a dry sob, forcing himself to focus, lest he steer himself and the enormous horse into a ditch in the dying light. Lady Harrington's horrified shriek won't leave his ears, but it's the image of Bobby's heartbroken face that keeps blurring with the road in front of him. In that split second, as James' fragile peace tore apart, he saw his decision in Bobby's eyes before he made it. In the quick shuttering of his hope, in the tightening of his face, in the way his hands fell away from James and his body stiffened.

Bobby knew that James would run. And James did nothing to prove otherwise.

He was finally surrounded by the friends and family he's always wanted, who accepted him, encouraged him, even. Had seemingly found the one man who's ever fully understood him, maybe even trusted him—and he fled at the very first sign of danger. Like he always does.

He hates himself, and he hates the world, and he maybe hates Bobby just a little for showing him that life could be different—life could be glorious—if he wasn't such a dreadful coward.

He thinks he might actually love . . .

It doesn't matter. In under an hour he'll be back in London. Back in his stable, safe, wretched life. There will be nothing to fear, and no one to ruin, and he'll be able to go back to being exactly who he was six days ago.

The thought wrings another heaving sob from his chest, and he almost loses his grip on the reins. He squeezes his thighs together, holding onto Branwen as best he can. He wants the life he just left. He wants the friends, and the family—his fragile peace with Beth, his camaraderie with Albert, his sporting repartee with Gwen.

And he wants—he wanted—he had Bobby Mason. Not the schoolboy fantasy, not the season's antagonist, the real Bobby Mason. Human, and halting, and honorable. A man who could be—could have been—the kind of partner James has never let himself dream about before. The bloody *best friend* kind of love that Prince talked about. It was new, and tender, and burgeoning, and in one moment it was gone.

Now he's sitting on a massive horse at the servants' entrance to his late uncle's townhouse. He never asked to be named heir to the Demeroven title. He never asked to sit in parliament.

He never asked to be anything more than a gentleman's weak stepson, living a simple life in the country.

He's been fighting all season to prove himself worthy of a life he frankly hates, and for what? He's given up his pride, and his freedom, and now—now he's left everything behind to protect this house, this title, this family. But instead of doing right by the title—like he promised Beth he would—instead of building something new, he's run back to the old, horrible, miserable same he left six days ago.

James clenches his jaw. He can feel the gaping maw in his chest, a gripping grief he knows won't ever be filled by a *title*.

He takes a shaky breath, unsurprised to find he does still have tears left to cry. He's angry, he realizes. Angry at himself. Angry at his stepfather for making him feel so small he's forgotten what it felt like to take up space. Angry at the world for making him choose between love and duty.

He sits there, heaving in air, unsure of what he wants, or how to fix what he's broken. Unsure of everything but the rage rippling through his chest and the grief clawing at his stomach.

Reginald steps out of the servants' entrance, placing down a crate of empty milk bottles. He turns, wiping his hands on his apron, and nearly falls over at the sight of James mounted on Branwen in the little servants' courtyard.

"What the bloody hell?" Reginald exclaims, closing the door with a snick before stepping forward to stare up at James. "Where did you— Why are you— Whose horse is this?"

"Tack house in Oswestry," James rasps out, blinking down at him.

"You're paler than a ghost. Get down from there," Reginald insists, quickly tying Branwen's reins to the tack post in the courtyard. He then steps up to steady James as he slowly dismounts, every muscle in his body screaming out in protest.

James hits the ground and stumbles, trying to get his balance back. He's never ridden so hard or so long before. And the six days of overzealous sex certainly didn't help. His thighs and arse feel like they're made of twisted lead, and he leans into Reginald there in the dim light from the kitchen windows.

"What happened?" Reginald asks, slowly guiding James over to rest against a stack of crates opposite the door.

James struggles to drag his voice up his throat, exhaustion falling heavily over his shoulders, the adrenaline of the five-hour horse ride beginning to wane. He should feel relieved to have arrived. But he doesn't want to be here. He's never wanted to be here.

The only place he's ever wanted to be is the one he just fled.

"James," Reginald presses.

"Screwed everything up," James admits. "Ruined everything, just like he always says I will," he continues, jerking his chin toward the windows to the study along the back of the townhouse.

Reginald peers at him in the dim light, his face tight and worried. "I'm sure you didn't ruin anything. Come inside—I'll feed you, and we'll get you to bed. It'll look better in the morning."

"No, it won't," James says on a hoarse scoff. Things can go back to normal, but they'll never be better.

"Nonsense," Reginald says, hauling him up and shuffling them back to the servants' door.

James lets himself be led inside. What's the use in arguing with Reginald? Eventually he too will see James for the failure he is—the coward. Everyone does. Because he shows them. Because he runs. Because he's *scared*.

"Come on," Reginald coaxes, bringing him into the kitchen.

But before James can protest or acquiesce, there's a loud cough from the doorway. Stepfather steps into the kitchen in a haze of smoke. He's wearing the late viscount's watch, smoking jacket, and, if James isn't mistaken, his slippers.

"And there he is. Back early, yet again," Stepfather says, his voice overloud in the small kitchen, eyes gleaming with malice. "Why am I not surprised?"

James stares up at his stepfather, watching more than hearing as he slips into his favorite familiar rant. *James is weak, James is pathetic, James is unworthy.* He's heard this speech thousands of times; it's almost a part of him. It's his stepfather's voice in his head every time he's scared, every time he's unsure.

That's the voice he heard today when Lady Harrington screamed—the voice that told him to run. Told him to be scared, and panicked, and cowardly.

And he listened.

Bobby's words ring in his ears now. Too afraid of his stepfather to take what he wants. Too scared to be deserving of all he's been given. Always running away.

He watches his stepfather yell while Reginald holds him up. His stepfather is nothing more than a gentleman grasping at viscount, coveting a life that was never his to have—resenting James *his* whole life for the title James himself never even wanted. And for the last three years since the late Viscount Demeroven passed, Stepfather's been growing comfortable and slovenly on James' inheritance. Never doing a single thing himself. Pretending he's orchestrating the viscountcy, but really, he's just drinking James' whisky and smoking his cigars, merely playing at power.

It's taken James far too long to realize it, but watching him now, he sees his stepfather is living on stolen glory. Not a single member of parliament has ever mentioned him; no one cares about him. He is a pathetic, greedy, power-hungry man, who only has power so long as James is cowering from him. His power is James' to bestow, not the other way around.

The knowledge settles on his shoulders like battle armor. James may not be ready to take what Bobby has offered—to commit to a relationship and all its ensuing pitfalls in the reality of London, to be brave and sure and bold in love. But he wants to be.

He wants to deserve the friends and family and lover he just left behind. He doesn't know if he can, if there's a life he can architect for himself that gives him Bobby—if Bobby will even have him—and keeps them all safe while making good on the title that goes with this horrible house. But he could try.

Right now, right here, in the absence of that loving life, with nothing to barter or lose, he can be brave enough. For this, at least, he can be brave enough.

"You're a piss-poor viscount, you know," Stepfather says.

"And you're nothing," James hears himself say, stepping out of Reginald's hold.

He slides his shoulders back, ignoring the screech of his muscles, and pulls himself up to his full height. And when he isn't slouching, cowering, would you look at that—he can look his stepfather clean in the eyes.

He steps forward, and his stepfather reflexively steps back in surprise.

"What did you say, boy?" Stepfather demands, his smirk falling.

This is the fight he can win. This is the stand he can take. And everything else . . . will come after.

"I want you out of my house," James says loudly, advancing again. Pride swells in his chest as his stepfather retreats, allowing James to stride out into the foyer, with its muted echo.

"Your house?" Stepfather exclaims, gesturing to the crowded foyer full of hideous paintings and busts. "Suddenly it's your house, is it?"

James looks around. He sees Reginald standing in the doorway to the kitchen, watching with bated breath. This is *his* horrible house. "This is *my* house. This is *my* title. I'm not the little disappointment of a boy you said I was when you married my mother and took her money."

"Shut your mouth or I will make you," Stepfather snaps, stepping toward James, balling his fists, going red in the face.

But James is sober, and Stepfather isn't. All it takes is a well-placed side step to send his stepfather careening as he throws a punch, the momentum of his own fist throwing him to the floor.

His stepfather lies there, winded and enraged, and James stands over him. "I want you out of my house. You have disgraced our family—tried to put my aunt and cousin on the street to slake your own ego—and embarrassed our name all over town, pretending at power everyone knows you lack. You are the disappointment, and I want you to go back to your own lands and be happy with your lot."

His stepfather tries to rise, but the drink and his own slow reflexes leave him sitting there, dizzy. "When I get up, I'll—"

"Do exactly as I say," James insists. "Or I'll cut off your stipend."

"You wouldn't dare," his stepfather spits.

"Wouldn't I? It's mine to bestow. I will arrange for Mother to have unfettered access to her dower from my father, should she wish it. She *can* go with you, if she so chooses. But she is more than welcome, and I'd say encouraged, to remain here with me. But that is *her* decision."

He hears a soft rustle from the stairwell. No one in this family will be controlled by his stepfather any longer, if that's what they wish.

"You . . ." his stepfather starts, swiping out at James' leg.

James simply kicks his wavering hand away. "Sober up, pack your things, and you'll take the horse I hired back up to the country. If you go quietly, I'll have no reason to go to the authorities about your betting and your mistreatment of my mother. She can divorce you, if that's what she wants. Lord Havenfort knows some of the best solicitors in the city, and Lady Ashmond would be happy to help her."

"You shut up about my wife," Stepfather says.

"Mother?" James calls, taking a chance.

"I'll be staying here," his mother says, her voice faint, but firm. "Get out, John. You heard my son."

James smiles and turns back to his stepfather. "Understood?"

Stepfather glares up at him, but doesn't respond.

"Reginald will be staying with me. Any of the staff who wants to return with you are welcome. Be packed and out of here by morning, or I'll call in the constable."

With that, he turns on his heel and makes for the stairs, watching in amusement as Reginald leads a flurry of maids out of the servants' hall, all of them in their pajamas and hastily tied robes, eagerly grabbing things to pack. Reginald winks at him.

When James reaches the top of the stairs, he finds his mother standing in her morning gown, staring at him with wide eyes.

"In a few weeks, we'll sell this place, and you and I will pick out a new townhouse, which you can have your run of during the year, if you like," he says, feeling a true smile come over his face. "You're welcome back at the estate as well once the season's over. But I'll decorate the townhouse, at least the first floor."

His mother lurches forward, wrapping him in her arms. "You wonderful boy," she whispers, and he feels his chest unclench.

"It took me too long," he whispers back.

She pulls away, brushing the hair from his eyes. "You are braver than me, and that is more than enough. I'll sleep in the guest room tonight, if you don't mind. And you can have the primary bedroom tomorrow, if you want."

"Would you prefer I take it?" he asks.

"I would."

"Then we'll switch. We can order anything you like, within reason," he adds as her eyes light up.

"We'll have breakfast before you go out tomorrow?" she suggests, a little meekly. They haven't dined together in weeks.

"I'd like that," he says honestly, squeezing her hands. "For now, though, I'm going to rest. It's been a long day."

"Was everything all right at the Masons'?" she asks.

James hesitates only for a moment. "I'll tell you at breakfast," he decides.

Maybe he'll tell her everything, maybe nothing. But that's tomorrow's problem. And they'll weather it together, whatever he decides.

For now, he turns and strides down the hall, closing the door to his room so he can collapse face-first onto his bed. He's taken the first step toward making things right—toward righting his own life—and that is something.

CHAPTER TWENTY-FIVE

Bobby

"You're sure about this?" Albie asks, looking across their newly refinished carriage at him. Meredith, sitting beside Albie, looks just as concerned in her beautiful new tea dress, face ringed with shiny red curls beneath her bonnet.

They've spent the week keeping him frighteningly busy with the house, and with teas, and dinners, and endless shopping. Meredith's maintained an incessant running commentary on anything and everything. Albie's attended almost no meetings with Uncle Dashiell and hasn't said two words about the ones he has—their tacit, unspoken agreement to pretend everything is normal. There's been no post, no heartfelt letters of apology, or excuse, or proof of life. And he's fine. He's perfectly fine.

And now they're watching him like he could shatter into a thousand pieces of glass at any moment.

"I'm *fine,*" Bobby insists, tugging at his collar and staring out the window to avoid their knowing eyes.

He's not technically required at this luncheon. Meredith was guest enough for Albie. But then Uncle Dashiell asked if he would accompany Beth and Gwen so he could focus on Cordelia's first event out, and how could Bobby refuse?

So here he is, lurching forward when the carriage stops outside of Stationers' Hall, heart in his throat. He's about to spend three hours in the same room as James Demeroven for the first time in a week and he doesn't know how to feel about it, let alone how to handle it.

"Well, I suppose we should—" Albie says, giving him another worried look as the door opens and an umbrella is opened for Meredith.

"Yep," Bobby says with forced brightness, gesturing for them to get out.

Albie manages to huddle under half of Meredith's umbrella, the poor door attendant getting absolutely soaked in the process. Bobby hurries across the courtyard after them, entering the bright, vaulted entryway with wet hair.

He brushes himself off and shuffles inside the hall with Albie and Meredith. Albie's smiling at just about everyone they pass, and the outer hall is packed with parliamentarians and their families, everyone milling about until the doors open into the main hall for luncheon.

Bobby stays close to Meredith, eyes flitting around the room. He should be looking for Beth and Gwen. Instead, there's a clutch in his chest at every glimpse of sandy-brown hair. He doesn't know if he *wants* to see James or not.

He hasn't been able to decide all week whether he's angry, devastated, or disappointed. Or some horrible swirling combination of all three. All he knows is his stomach has been sour since James ran away, and no amount of food, conversation, or whisky has made it better.

"There you are," he hears just as a smaller hand takes his arm.

He turns, his whole body sagging in relief to see Beth beside him, a pop of color in her pale-blue gown, with Gwen approaching behind her in a darker navy. "You're a wonder," he tells Beth.

She smiles while Gwen scoffs. "And me?"

"You're surprisingly hard to spot with that bonnet on," he returns.

She laughs and raises a hand. Bobby glances to his left and smiles at Uncle Dashiell and Aunt Cordelia as they approach. Aunt Cordelia looks radiant in a deep-blue dress. Her cheeks are still round and she gives him a smile that makes him want to wrap his arms around her and never let go.

"You look a little peaky, dear," she says, reaching out to straighten his collar.

"I'll be fine once we get some food," he assures her.

It won't fix the sleepless nights, or the gnawing unease, but sitting safely with his family, where he can't run into James without warning, will do wonders for his nerves.

"Damn," Beth mutters.

Bobby turns back to her, raising an eyebrow, and then James Demeroven appears behind Uncle Dashiell. He's in a new suit, his hair freshly cut, standing straight, his face carefully blank. Beth's hand tightens around Bobby's arm as he takes a step back. James is looking everywhere but at Bobby and Bobby feels like his stomach might make a break for his mouth.

James is right there, still so handsome, and wonderful, but buttoned up again. This is the man who ran from him, not the man who shared his bed. But oh, if the world could be different—

"How are you, Lord Demeroven?" Aunt Cordelia asks brightly.

"I'm well, thank you. And yourself? You look wonderful," James manages, only a slight waver to his voice.

Bobby forces himself to look away while Aunt Cordelia talks with James, turning to Beth and Gwen. Meredith steps into their little circle immediately and begins rattling off the laundry list of events they'll be attending in the coming week leading up to their departure to Cowes for the regatta.

Four dinners, five teas, and Albie's arranged for at least two card games. Beth and Gwen will have to join them for everything. And Bobby will simply shuffle after Meredith, from event to event, turning off his brain as best he can. He's sure he'll be miraculously out of the house anytime there's so much as a whisper of parliamentary business.

But more strategic social separation won't come until tomorrow. Today, Aunt Cordelia is inviting James to sit at their luncheon table and Bobby feels himself die a little inside.

"You want me to deck him?" Gwen whispers as the doors to the main hall open and they join the crowd shuffling forward. She takes his other arm and Bobby forces himself to smile through it.

"Maybe later. Would be a little conspicuous," he says.

Gwen nods seriously. "You just give me the sign."

Bobby squeezes her arm to his side and takes solace in her solidarity. They make their way into the room, following Uncle Dashiell, Aunt Cordelia, and James toward one of the more central round tables. The gorgeous stained-glass windows throw muted colors across the white linen tablecloths bedecked with gilded centerpieces. The dark oak paneling adds to the atmosphere, and were he in a better mood, he'd be interested in the various shields and crests mounted on the walls. But Bobby can't admire the room, not when facing the next terrible three hours of emotional torture.

Thankfully, Gwen, Beth, Albie, and Meredith make quick work of ensuring Bobby and James are seated as far from each other as possible. But that puts them on opposite sides of the table, staring at each other for the first time in a week. For the first time since Bobby bared his heart to James, and James ran away.

Ice and fire collide in his chest. He moves instinctively to grab the glass of wine by his place setting, and then retracts his hand. He's numb enough already.

Gwen leans into him on his left while Beth's hand slips into his on the right. "Want to play Spot-the-Slosh?" Gwen whispers. "First one to see five parliamentarians asleep wins ten quid."

Bobby lets out a startled laugh, earning a look from Aunt Cordelia. There's someone speaking at the podium on a dais at the front of the room. Bobby feigns attention, while nudging Gwen, who snickers quietly.

He can't quite prevent his eyes from flicking over to James. He doesn't want Gwen to punch his lights out. He wants the last week to be a nightmare—to wake up back in his childhood bed, James wrapped in his arms.

Punishing James won't give him back the magic of that week. Won't make James any braver. Won't make Bobby any more worthy of his affections. It would just make everything worse.

He blinks as James turns and meets his eyes. In the dim light, the bags beneath James' eyes are more pronounced. His face is open here in the darkened room, a flash of a more haggard reality flitting across his features. God, Bobby wants to be so angry, but when he looks at James—

James' gaze skitters to the left and his eyes widen. He rises abruptly, muttering something to Uncle Dashiell before hurrying out of the room. Bobby stares after him. Running, again? He can't even sit at the same table as Bobby now?

Not that Bobby thought there was hope for some . . . romantic reunion, but even sitting in the same space is too much? What, are they never to see each other again?

"Bobby," Gwen whispers.

He slowly tears his eyes away from James' empty seat. Gwen jerks her chin to the left. He follows the movement to the next table over and finds himself under Lord Raverson's gaze.

A sick relief pulses through his chest. Maybe James wasn't running from him after all, at least not this time. But that leaves him alone in this room with Raverson. As they stare at each other, Bobby takes in his hollowed cheeks, the way his suit hangs off his frame even when he's seated, his overlong hair. The past weeks haven't been kind to Raverson either, but Bobby has no idea why. Only that it can't bode well for any of them.

Raverson narrows his eyes, and Bobby sits up straight. He has to look impenetrable. He won't cower, not here, not now. One of them has to stand tall against Raverson.

So he holds Raverson's look until Raverson clenches his jaw and looks away. But nothing's been solved. He and James still have—

"You should go after him," Beth whispers.

Bobby flinches, that tightness in his chest turning into a pulsing ache. They still have to prevent the blackmail, somehow. But if he gets up now, Raverson will—

"I need the loo," Gwen says abruptly. A little overloud, so the table turns to look at her.

Beth elbows him. "I'll, uh, escort you," Bobby says, rising and holding out his hand. Uncle Dashiell gives him a small smile and Bobby forces himself to smile back.

He helps Gwen up and together they hurry out of the banquet hall, that damn parliamentarian still droning on from the front of the room. Bobby pushes open the door to the entry hall and follows Gwen out into the red-carpeted foyer.

James isn't there.

Bobby gnaws on his lip, letting Gwen guide him silently toward the side hall off the entry. Perhaps she really did just need the loo, after all. And at least that will give him a few minutes to calm his racing pulse. Between James and Raverson, it feels like he's been put through a laundry mangle.

He follows Gwen down the side hall—how she knows this building and he doesn't is a mystery he's too tired to parse right now—and then down a short staircase that opens onto another hall. They round a corner and find James Demeroven hovering outside of the water closets, wringing his hands, his hair mussed, eyes a little wild.

He looks up as they approach and they all just stand there staring at each other, frozen. Their tryst in the hedges flashes across Bobby's mind, images of them in bed, James' handsome face hovering over him. All those talks by the lake, holding hands while they went walking. The hours laughing and kissing. The way it felt to have James naked and wanting and—

"I, um, actually do need the loo," Gwen whispers awkwardly. She hesitates for a beat, and then squeezes his arm. He watches in a daze as she skirts around James and disappears into the ladies' room.

Which leaves Bobby and James alone, at the end of a hallway, by a set of water closets, yet again.

Bobby wants to run. Bobby wants to shove James up against the wall and kiss him. Bobby wants to shove James up against the wall and shake him.

He thought he knew heartache in school, when flings ended, when boys he fancied didn't fancy him back. But he's never known this feeling—like having his heart strangled by a gripping fist just staring at James' wide blue eyes.

Chapter Twenty-Six

James

He thought that standing up to his stepfather was the most terrifying thing he could do this season, but he was wrong. Standing in this corridor with nothing but white walls and aged wooden floors to distract him, staring at the man he loves—the man he abandoned—is the worst thing he's ever had to do.

Bobby looks just as handsome as he did that day in the hedges. His well-fitting suit hugs every inch of his muscular chest and his hair is lightly mussed from the rain outside. He is resplendent, despite the bags under his eyes, and James cannot have him.

He has expelled his stepfather, made peace with his mother, made plans to sell his terrible townhouse, and continued working night and day with Lord Havenfort to assure the passage of the Medical Act. But he hasn't figured out how to solve the problem that is Bobby.

He sees Bobby tighten his jaw, notes the way his hands are curling and uncurling at his sides, and shakes himself. The problem isn't and has never been Bobby. It's Raverson, and men like him. It's the fear that still grips at James' gut, anchoring him into unhappiness and duty.

"Didn't die on the way back, then," Bobby finally mutters.

James feels it like a blow to the chest. How desperately he's wanted to hear that voice, and how sharply painful to hear it so cold. Like their week together never happened. Like Prince's stag night never happened. Here they stand, forced back into the roles they played at the beginning of the season, reluctant partners against blackmail and nothing more.

"No," James manages, wanting so desperately to reach out and still Bobby's hands. "And your travel?"

Bobby's eyes snap back to meet his. "That's what you want to ask me?" James flinches as anger settles firmly over Bobby's face. "How was the bloody carriage ride?"

"I—"

"Awful, thanks for asking," Bobby spits. "I trust you received your belongings."

"Mr. Tilty brought them by," James says quickly.

"Good. Reliable, Mr. Tilty. Does what he says he will."

James fights the urge to sink back against the wall. He wanted to write. He wanted to explain. He's wanted the opportunity to make things right so badly, but he doesn't know how. He can't fix the world. He can't banish the threat of discovery, of scandal, of imprisonment. He can become whatever type of viscount he likes, but he can't change the way things are.

"You could have written, you know," Bobby says sharply.

James blinks back at him. What would he possibly have said? *I'm as much of a coward as you thought I was at the start of the season, and worse for convincing us both perhaps I wasn't?*

"You could have given Albie a note."

"I . . . didn't think you'd want to hear from me," he says honestly.

"That's the most ridiculous thing you've said all season," Bobby exclaims.

"What, you *wanted* an apology in a note?" he tosses back, his whole body tense—old habits. "Some vague platitude? Would it make you less angry? Make you forgive me?"

"It would have been something," Bobby insists, stepping forward. "You ran off, God knows where or how, with all your things still at the manor. Even just for Beth and Gwen's sake, you could have written."

James stares up at Bobby, incredulous. "Like anyone would have wanted to hear from me. Albert has barely attended our sessions with Lord Havenfort." And at the ones he has, Albert has been quiet and left as quickly as possible. James doesn't blame him. Albert's allegiance will always be, should always be, to Bobby.

"Oh, the world isn't all about you," Bobby says archly. "Albie and I have had to settle Meredith at the house."

James shakes his head. Even so, he's sure Albert is angry with him. "Miss Bertram and Lady Gwen wouldn't have wanted to hear from me."

Bobby opens his mouth only in time for Gwen's head to pop out of the lavatory. "You're a right prat," she says, glaring at James, curls tight against her scalp from the humidity. "And you should have written."

She disappears back into the lavatory and James stares at the door as it sways on its hinges, the breath knocked out of him. He *left*, and they still—

"No one's happy with you, but we'd all at least have liked to know you'd made it home," Bobby says softly.

James turns back to him and finds the anger gone from his face, replaced by a pervasive sadness and heavy exhaustion. He looks how James feels. He never wanted to hurt any of them, least of all this beautiful man.

"And I do deserve an apology," Bobby adds, rolling his shoulders back.

James sighs softly, his heart leaden, his mind aching, his body still tense, even a week later. "You deserve much more than an apology," he says, looking up to meet Bobby's wide eyes. "But I don't know how to give it to you."

He can see the words hit Bobby's chest, watches in regret as he takes a step backward. His own chest clenches with pain and sorrow, but he doesn't know how to fix this. He wants to, though. He wants to find a way.

"I'm sorry," he says, all he can give, and it will never, ever be enough.

"Me too," Bobby says. His eyebrows crease and he sucks on his cheek. James wants to step forward, stroke away the tension. "But I guess it's for the best, right? Solves our Raverson problem, doesn't it—we just never see each other unless forced."

James is the one to stumble backward at that, the words punching him like a physical blow. "I don't *want* that," he whispers. "I don't want it to be this way," he insists as Bobby just stares at him, looking so heartbroken James might start crying.

"Well, that's something at least, isn't it?" Bobby says, his voice rough.

They stand for a long moment, staring at each other in a shared, shattered agony. James doesn't know what else to say. Doesn't know if he wants to say anything at all. Nothing seems enough.

"We do need to get back upstairs."

Both of them jump. Gwen steps out of the water closet, her face pink, eyes a little shiny.

At least one of them gets to cry about this.

"You take her up. I'll wait a while," James suggests, glancing at Bobby before forcing a false smile for Gwen.

"Right. Good for appearances. Come along, Gwen," Bobby says, holding out his arm.

Gwen steps around James and lays her hand on his shoulder for a moment before she takes Bobby's arm. And then he watches them walk away, down the hall, around the corner, and up the stairs. Until he's alone in the water closet hallway, back where he started at the beginning of the season.

He has to find a way to fix this. There has to be a way.

CHAPTER TWENTY-SEVEN

Bobby

Bobby rolls his neck as he stands on the Havenfort doorstep. Spending the past week sitting up nights with Albie, researching and finalizing documents for the Medical Act while also going through their father's ledgers from the past ten years, has left him with a permanent twinge in his neck and a dull ache at the base of his skull.

It's been good—refreshing, actually—to work with Albie. He feels like they're finding a rhythm. The subtle distance between them is totally gone. And with Meredith finally in residence, the house feels like a home for the first time all season.

Better still, the constant, steady work has kept him so busy he's had no time to dwell on that heart-wrenching conversation at the banquet. None at all. Nor can he spare even a moment of daylight to think about the pain in James' eyes, or the way it feels like someone is permanently sitting on his chest.

The door to the Havenfort townhouse opens and Miss Wilson peeks out at him. "Oh, Miss Bertram will be pleased," she says, beckoning him in. "And Mrs. Stelm has about twelve different types of cakes all made up. Mrs. Gilpe went to market, but she'll want to see you as well."

"How are you, Miss Wilson?" Bobby asks, hoping he's not blushing.

He loves Mr. Tilty and their staff, but nowhere is as comfortable or frankly full of feminine affection as the Havenfort home. It's always like walking into a strong hug.

"I'm well, I'm well. Though I must say, Lord Demeroven's chef took me for a good portion of what I'm worth at our game of whist last night."

Bobby's heart stutters at the mention of James, but he pushes through. "I'm sure you'll take him back. James says he gets gossipy if you get him tipsy."

"Can always count on you, Mr. Mason," she says, leading him up to the sitting room.

He's kept his days so busy that he can only focus on the ache in his broken heart when he tries to sleep. And then the great expanse of his bed and the loss of heat from wrapping James in his arms comes back to him, and he tosses and turns until sunrise. He's mostly running off tea.

"I'll bring treats in a few," Miss Wilson says as she opens the sitting room door. Then she's gone in a blink, off to continue whatever business his arrival interrupted.

He shakes his head and steps into the sitting room. Beth sits in a rocking chair scooched close to the fire, wearing a well-loved green morning gown he thinks might be Gwen's. She keeps a steady rock and smiles down at her little brother, murmuring to him. It's a lovely picture and he almost doesn't want to intrude.

"Oh, there's Cousin Bobby," Beth says, looking up to smile at him.

He pads over to lean down and greet Beth with a kiss to her cheek. He strokes a finger along Frederic's little cherubic cheek too, and the baby smiles.

Beth juts her chin for him to sit in an armchair opposite her rocker. Bobby does as told, plopping down into the worn blue chair. The heat from the fire engulfs him immediately and he stretches, content to sit with Beth as long as she wants company.

"How are you?" he asks.

"Fine," Beth says, looking back down at Frederic. "We're just fine, aren't we?" she asks the baby.

But this close, there's a tightness to her eyes. And Gwen isn't here. "Beth," Bobby says.

"I'm fine," Beth insists, still looking down at her brother.

Bobby rises and quickly plucks baby Frederic from Beth's arms, ignoring her huff of protest. He sinks back down into his armchair, the warm bundle of sleeping baby tucked to his chest.

"Spill," he says, staring Beth down.

Without her brother to focus on, Beth squirms. "Everything's really fine."

Bobby just waits, rocking slightly to keep Frederic dozing. Beth sighs and slouches in her chair, her face finally losing that fake look of calm to expose an exhausted young woman.

"It's just hard, you know?" she says.

"What is?" He can think of many difficult things they're all facing now that they're back at home. And a few he's patently *not* facing as well.

"Being back. It's just—being at your manor was so . . . free," Beth admits. "Like a place out of time."

"Yeah," Bobby agrees, swallowing against a sudden lump in his throat.

It certainly felt that way to him. But he's never stopped to think about what his cousin and Beth really go through. He only ever thinks they're lucky, safe and secure under Uncle Dashiell's roof, with their own quarters and lives.

But of course it's not really like that. They aren't married, and outside of this house, they're nothing but friends. Worse, they're technically stepsisters, an uncomfortable label on a relationship that is as real as any marriage.

He's been drowning in his own unhappiness and never stopped to think that Beth and Gwen are living an equally difficult reality.

"It's just hard, to come back and attend teas and dinners and not be . . ." Beth trails off, shrugging, her eyes stuck on baby Frederic in his arms.

It bubbles up in his brain, the image of Beth holding Frederic—the yearning look on her face now. "Beth, do you want children?" he asks.

Beth blinks and then meets his eyes. "I . . ." she starts, her hands twisting together. "Maybe," she admits, shoulders falling, that exhaustion looking heavy across her shoulders.

"And Gwen?" he wonders.

Beth's face crumples. "Maybe," she whispers. "But—"

"It would be a sacrifice," Bobby agrees, seeing the bigger picture. He's been so distracted by his own problems he never even thought to *ask*.

"Even if one of us thought we could do it—could marry someone and do . . . everything necessary to have children—I don't think the other one would survive it. I don't want anyone but Gwen," she finishes, her voice hoarse, eyes shiny.

And he's gone and made her cry. "Beth," he starts, no idea how to truly comfort her through this.

Beth shakes her head and wipes at her eyes. "But I have Gwen, and my mother and Frederic and Dashiell. I'm happy, really," she adds, taking in what must be the distress on his face. "I'm just wistful, sometimes. He's really something," she says, looking back at Frederic.

Bobby follows her gaze and stares down at his little cousin. He's angelic, asleep like this. And so warm and soft, and there's a faint smell that's mildly intoxicating. What must it be like to have a little person of your very own to cuddle all day, and raise, and be proud of, and support?

"Do you want children, Bobby?" Beth asks.

Bobby slowly brings his eyes up to find her watching him knowingly. They haven't talked about the luncheon, nor that final day at the manor. He hasn't wanted to burden Beth or Gwen. Hasn't wanted to rip open his heart for them to see.

But maybe he should, given everything he's been ignoring about Beth's life. Maybe it would make her feel seen, and comforted, and like there's someone she can talk to, rather than bottling it all up. And it might make him feel better, like maybe he can sit still for a moment without the weight of it all crushing down on him.

"I'd love to have a family," he admits softly, stroking his thumb along the edge of Frederic's blanket. "But like you, I don't think I could make the necessary sacrifice. I don't think I'd be happy."

"If you could, though," Beth says, bringing his eyes back up to hers. "And the world was a different place—a better place—is there someone you'd want a family with?" Beth smiles encouragingly.

"If I could have what you and Gwen have? What Albie and Meredith have? What your mother and Uncle Dashiell have? Yes," he admits.

"Anyone in particular?" she presses.

And even though the very thought of James makes his chest hurt, he can't help but mildly enjoy her teasing. "Maybe," he hedges, watching as she giggles, delighted. "But the world isn't a better place. I don't think it will ever be a better place enough for him to want to risk it," he says, letting his gaze drift to the fire.

He wants to be so angry with James. But after seeing him at the luncheon, as broken and hurting as Bobby himself feels, he can't be. Because the world is a terrible place. All the things James is afraid of are valid. Bobby sees now that what they had at the manor was just a fairy tale.

Maybe that's what hurts more than anything else. Bobby was willing to believe until the world came for them, and James wasn't. Maybe he's better off, running before he could get burned.

He can't be mad at James, but the hurt is still there, burrowed behind his breastbone.

"What if it could be?"

Bobby blinks and looks across at Beth. "What?"

"What if the world could be a better place? What if we could *make* it a better place, for all of us?"

"I don't follow," he says, watching as Beth glances toward the hall and huffs.

"Gwen and I had planned to corner you together, but there hasn't been time and I think if I wait for her . . ."

"What?" Bobby prompts.

Beth sighs. "Look, we—we had this idea, back at the beginning of the season, and we kind of gave up on it when it seemed like you and James couldn't stand the sight of one another. We were planning to tell you both in the carriage ride home, but then James left. But I think—if you really want this, then—"

"Beth!" Bobby exclaims. "Please, what are you talking about?"

"We thought maybe you and James would fall in love, and then James would marry Gwen, and you would marry me, and we'd all go live up in the country and be . . . happy . . ." She trails off, eyes wide at what must be the slack-jawed expression on his face.

"You *knew*?" he blurts. Frederic startles in his arms, blinking up at him in reproach. "Sorry, sorry," he mumbles to the baby, rocking side to side as he brings his eyes back up to Beth. "You *knew*?" he asks, quieter but with no less consternation.

Beth blushes. "We suspected. But we'd never have pushed if it seemed like either of you didn't want—and we stopped, I swear we stopped after that horrible night at the opera."

"You were trying to trap us into marriage?" Bobby asks, dumbfounded.

"Into false marriage!" Beth insists. "You'd live with James, and I'd live with Gwen, and we'd all have the perfect cover, all the time, and it would be like it was—"

"At the manor," he finishes, the whole convoluted mess of it landing solidly in his mind while he bounces the baby.

Beth and Gwen inviting them on outings. Beth and Gwen forcing them to team up at tea-time sports. Beth and Gwen pestering Uncle Dashiell into inviting James to events. All the times he and James were at each other's throats, his cousin and Beth were waiting on the sidelines, hoping they'd fall in love so *they* could be happily in love and—

"Fuck, that's brilliant," he mutters.

"It is, isn't it?" Beth asks, leaning back in her rocking chair, a self-satisfied smile spreading over her cheeks.

Bobby glances down at baby Frederic. "But . . . God, Beth, I love you, and if I have to marry someone, you'd be my only choice, but I don't know that I could—"

"No, no, oh, Lord, no," Beth says, sitting up straight so quickly she nearly topples out of the rocking chair. "No, I . . . It's almost a perfect plan, heirs and babies notwithstanding."

"Right," he says, looking back at the baby. "Right."

"And you don't have to. I just—I thought I'd tell you, because if you do want to—if you think it could work, maybe it would be right for James too."

Bobby worries at his lip, looking down at baby Frederic, who snuffles an adorable baby snort.

Wouldn't it be perfect? The perfect disguise, the perfect charade. And the four of them, in the country, together, forever. In love, and friendship, and family. If they'd just avoided Lady Harrington finding them debauched in the hedges, maybe they could have learned about this together, saved everyone so much pain.

"Why didn't you just *say* something?" he asks, looking back up at Beth.

She smiles sadly. "It wasn't until we saw you together at the Mason manor that we even thought it might really work and then—I guess we were scared. We didn't know how you really felt about him, whether you would want him *forever.* And we wouldn't want you to be miserable just so we'd be happy. I think we both worried you would do it just to see us smile."

Bobby feels his heart break and mend and ache all at once. "You really are the best, you know? Both of you."

"The feeling's mutual," Beth says, smiling, her eyes a little watery. "And it's totally up to you. We can all just stay friends. That's lovely too."

Bobby rolls it over in his mind. "Gwen would be happy with James? In name only, but you know, at functions and parties and—"

"Did you see what a team they make at everything? She'd be delighted. And when she's being too high-strung, we can toss them together and go on a nice long walk, just the two of us."

Bobby laughs. "James really can go on about boats and fencing."

"So give him to Gwen, she loves all of it."

A strange, tentative hope creeps into his chest. It would be perfect. More than perfect. It would be a way out of an impossible situation—a way to have the happiness and safety he and James have wanted. A way to thwart Raverson and any other whispers of impropriety for the rest of their lives.

A false marriage would solve all their problems, if he and James can be brave enough to trust each other. Bobby just doesn't know if he's willing to put his heart on the line again to find out.

CHAPTER TWENTY-EIGHT

James

He stands shoulder to shoulder with Albert and Lord Havenfort, the three of them clapping vigorously. The gavel has just come down. The Medical Act has passed the Lords, and will move on to the Commons.

A surge of true pride flows through James' veins. He, James, Viscount Demeroven, has done good for the world, and his name shall forever live on that docket. It's a heady feeling.

James shuffles along, following Albert out of the hall as the lords begin to file out. He finds himself nodding to various other lords on their side of the aisle. They smile, some tip their hats, some shout greetings to him, Albert, and Lord Havenfort. He doesn't even pay attention to the other side, grumbling about government overreach.

Instead, he focuses on the blue sky as they pour out of St. Stephen's, letting himself enjoy the feeling of accomplishment. It's one he plans to become familiar with in the next few years. He's actually itching to pick Lord Havenfort's brain about what bills he thinks will be on the docket for the next session. He's eager to continue this work.

He's eager to keep building the life he's finally taking as his own.

"I cannot thank you boys—you men—enough for your help

this season," Lord Havenfort says, pulling them both out of the fray to linger at the side of the building.

James can't help but smile bashfully while Albert outright grins. Lord Havenfort rummages in his top pocket and retrieves two fat envelopes. He thrusts them at Albert and James, who riffle through them. James feels his jaw drop.

"Lord Havenfort, this is—" he starts, staring down at the packet of bills.

"It's Uncle Dashiell, James," Lord Havenfort says. James looks up to meet his eyes in surprise. "And I want you and Albert to spend this madly at Cowes. Spoil the girls, and Bobby, and have the time of your lives. Then we'll all reconvene and plan out how we're going to divvy up the shooting season."

James tries to wrap his mind around *uncle* while Albert enthusiastically agrees for both of them, as if nothing at all has happened, as if they're still friends. It's like there's something molten creeping through his chest. An unfamiliar feeling that pricks at James' eyes and requires a lot of blinking.

"I'm proud of you both, and look forward to working with you for years to come," Lord Havenfort says. "You've done a great honor to your houses."

James finds he would do just about anything to see his *uncle* look this happy again. How strange. "Thank you," he manages to say around a pleasant tightness in his throat.

"Give Aunt Cordelia our love," Albert says, slinging an arm around James' shoulders.

James hesitates, surprised, but leans cautiously into his side, smiling as Lord Havenfort winks at them and then marches off, whistling, lost in a sea of parliamentary top hats and coattails.

"Damn good show," Albert says, squeezing James once before releasing him to thumb through his envelope. "Jesus. We should pass bills more often. We could pay for the trip twice with mine."

"God, I don't even want to count," James hears himself say, overwhelmed by that warm, gooey feeling in his chest.

"How are you planning to get to Cowes?" Albert asks, bringing James' gaze up from the obscene envelope of pounds in his hands.

"I've got a rail ticket to get there for the second heat on opening day," James says, as if he hasn't been rattling off the date and time all week.

"You should come with us the day ahead."

James stares at him, shocked and unsure, but Albert simply smiles at him. Almost a little sadly, like Gwen did last week. Like—like he understands, and still wants James to come, even though he—

"Uncle Dashiell booked us all a private car and rooms to sleep in before we catch the first ferry."

"All?" James asks, that gooey warmth developing claws in his chest.

"Gwen, Beth, Meredith, Bobby, me, and you, if you want a seat. The girls would love it."

James hesitates. Two weeks of tossing and turning, of desperately trying to figure out how to make that last piece of his life—the most important one that comes with a four-letter word and soppy kisses and amazing sex—fit in with the rest of the world he's building for himself. He hasn't figured it out yet.

"Bobby would probably love it too," Albert continues.

James opens his mouth, tongue feeling swollen around too many words, then someone crashes into him from behind.

"Oi, watch it," Albert says.

James stands up straight and comes face-to-face with Raverson, glaring menacingly down at him. Up close, James can see he's lost half a stone, his suit ill-fitting and eyes a little manic. James wants to sink into the ground, but forces himself to stand tall, like Albert, who takes one look between them and pulls himself up to his full height.

"It's just one bill. There'll be others," Albert says, reading the most plausible reason into Raverson's aggression.

"Not like that one," Raverson spits.

James blinks. He wasn't— "What, did you *bet* on the vote?"

Albert nudges him, but the words are out, and the look on Raverson's face, sour and simmering, confirms it. "You cost me nearly two thousand pounds," Raverson says, his voice low but deeply threatening.

Even Albert gapes at that. "How on earth is your gambling my fault?" James wonders.

"I had a lot riding on this vote. And now you'll need to help me pay for it."

"We're hardly going to reimburse you for a poor bet," Albert says, surreptitiously plucking the envelope from James' hand behind his back and stuffing that, and his own, into his pockets while Raverson glares at James.

"Ah, but see, Demeroven's the reason I was *trying other avenues*."

James gapes. "Excuse me?"

"You told me to give up my schoolyard games, and look where it's gotten me."

"That is hardly—"

"So now I'm coming back for our arrangement. Or am I going to your daddy?" he asks James.

"My stepfather is no longer in the city," James says, superimposing his stepfather's face over Raverson's. He stood up to Stepfather. He can stand up to this pale facsimile of Raverson now. "And I don't owe you a thing."

"You'll pay. You and Mason, or it'll be front-page news the day after Cowes," Raverson says, stepping toward James.

James forces himself to stay still, which puts them chest-to-chest, Raverson's rank breath wafting over his face. He can't believe this is the same man who intimidated him in school, who's been blackmailing him, and Lord Havenfort, and Bobby all season; he's falling apart.

"There's nothing to print," James insists, forcing all the bravado he has through the painful words. Albert moves in, all three of them too close and too conspicuous.

"Oh, just because you're playing cool now doesn't mean my evidence is any less valid," Raverson jeers. "So I think you'll give me what I want."

"And if I don't?" James asks, ignoring the clench of grief in his stomach.

If Raverson is going to come after them whether they're together or not . . .

"Then maybe the two of you can share a cell at Newgate while I get fat on your uncle's money," Raverson says tightly.

"And that will fix your money problems, two thousand pounds? You don't get bruises like that"—Albert jabs Raverson quickly in the ribs, and the man flinches—"over just two thousand. What's your plan once you've run us dry, hmm?"

"You're only the first," Raverson says, rubbing at his ribs and stepping back from them, out of range of Albert's hands. "Once I collect on all my scores, I'll be the richest of all of you. They laughed at me at school," he says, looking back at James. "The second son, the never-ran. You thought I was small, but I'm not. I've gone bigger than you could have ever dreamed, and I'll have the last laugh."

"And when someone finally comes for you?" James wonders,

agog at who Raverson has become. He knew he was vile, but he never expected *this*.

"I'll have so much power no one will ever say a word about me," Raverson says, conviction, vitriol, and delusion heavy in his voice. "Have your purse strings wide open on the last day of Cowes, or prepare to get comfortable in prison."

He turns on his heel and lurches off, leaving James and Albert standing by the wall as the street slowly empties. They haven't attracted too much attention, outside of the curious looks from a few flower sellers on the street and the waiting coachmen.

"Well, now you'll have to come with us to Cowes, won't you? We'll need to come up with a plan."

James turns slowly to Albert, apologies warring in his chest, tripping up his throat. "If I'd just told Bobby before—if I'd gone to your uncle, our uncle, maybe—"

Albert reaches out and squeezes his shoulder. "Raverson being a deplorable, scheming pissant isn't your fault. You, me, Bobby, and the girls, we'll figure this out at Cowes. Meredith loves a challenge, and Beth and Gwen will die for the chance to put him in his place."

"They don't even know him," James argues, his throat tight all over again.

"He's hurting two of ours, that's all they need to know. More than that, though," Albert says seriously, taking James' other shoulder in hand so they're staring at each other head-on. "If I don't report back to Lady Harrington and promise her I showed you a great time in Cowes, she'll have my hide. I can't let my mother-in-law be my death, it would be too pathetic."

James lets out a startled laugh, something unknown letting go in his chest. "What?"

Albert turns them, wrapping his arm back over James'

shoulders to lead him to the hired coaches. "She was so worried you would be out of your mind with embarrassment, and she couldn't tease it out of you."

"She wasn't . . . upset?" he asks, the feelings of fear and panic and mortification he tamped down hard on his horse ride back from the country roaring in his stomach.

Albert opens the door for the first hired coach, gesturing for James to hop inside. James goes, surprised when Albert gives the driver the address for the Foundling Hospital.

"We're picking up Gwen; she took a shift," Albert explains as he swings inside and closes the door. "And no, Lady Harrington was only upset she interrupted you and that *you* were upset."

"We shouldn't have been—" James breaks off, unsure of how to finish the sentence in a gentlemanly fashion.

"She went snooping. Serves her right," Albert says easily. James gapes across the carriage at him and Albert laughs. "Honestly, she's seen worse with me and Meredith—a story for another time," he says. James feels his eyes widen. "Suffice it to say, she wants you to have fun for the rest of the season, and made it my responsibility. So you'll come to Cowes with us."

James can do no more than nod, watching as Albert smiles and then looks contentedly out the window. Instead of yelling, instead of demanding answers about Raverson and his bribes, instead of taking James to task for running away, he's just . . . protecting him.

That warm, soppy feeling takes over again and James slumps into the hard seat behind him, feeling dazed. Raverson's out for blood, but all Albert seems to care about is that James is . . . happy. Even after he ran out on Bobby, on all of them . . .

How can anyone ever forgive him? How can he ever forgive himself?

He has a swirling mix of grief and a massive bubble of unease in his stomach. Raverson's made it very clear he's coming after them whether James and Bobby are apart or together. No amount of subterfuge or even distance is going to stop him. Nor is it ever going to stop the world.

Bobby or not, society doesn't *want* James as he is. Will never want him as he is, no matter how much he pretends. He can be the picture-perfect viscount, but they're going to keep hating who he is at his core—all of them small-minded, and frightened, and prejudiced.

Except for Albert. And Gwen. And Beth, and Meredith, and hell, even Lady Harrington, it seems. His aunt, his uncle. And . . . Bobby.

The weeks of regret, of pain, of grief—it was all for nothing. Instead of allowing himself and Bobby to face Raverson united, happy, whole—James made them both suffer, horribly.

They can't change the world, but maybe they can face it together. All of them can face it together. He needs to make things right, right now.

He opens his mouth, unsure but willing to *start*, and then they pull up to the front of the Foundling Hospital. He follows Albert's gaze out the window to where Gwen is crouched at the base of one of the arches, talking to a little girl holding a teddy bear, lip caught between her teeth. The little girl is a tad gaunt, but wearing a fresh dress and cap.

Albert hops out to help Gwen up and James can just hear Gwen's murmured, "I promise, Beth and I will be back in a week to play with you."

The girl's eyes water. She can't be much older than two. Gwen squeezes her shoulders and then stands as a woman steps forward to take the girl's hand. Gwen waves to them both and then lets Albert help her into the carriage. She wipes at her eyes with her apron as Albert swings back into the coach and settles beside her.

Throat tight, James taps the ceiling and they lurch off, giving Gwen a moment to compose herself.

"Sorry," she says, laughing a little. "She's just too sweet."

"Lady Ashmond will take care of her," Albert promises.

"I know. She's very good with them, surprisingly," Gwen agrees. "You know, she and Thomas Parker are working on a bit of a project," she adds, looking across at James.

That pulls him from his panic. "How on earth do they know each other?"

"Oh, he's been a guest at a few of her salons," Gwen says with the most casual shrug. "She says Parker has promised to introduce her to some enterprising young men for her entrepreneurship program. I assume you are one of those young men?"

"I guess," James agrees slowly. "I'll have to call on him after Cowes."

"Good. Lady Ashmond's most excited about it. But tell me, did it pass?"

"What?" James asks, mind stalled on Thomas Parker and Lady Ashmond and Gwen's casual mention of the young men of the D'Vere clientele. All that time spent trying to keep his personal life separate from the ton, and his worlds have seemingly collided without him even knowing. What a fool he's been.

"It did!" Albert exclaims, grinning as Gwen whoops.

"Father must be pleased," Gwen says happily.

"Oh, he was," Albert says, pulling out the envelopes and handing James' back to him.

He can't help but smile as Gwen whistles. "We'll have to

make the most of the week," James says, exchanging a quick glance with Albert.

No need to mar a good afternoon with talk of blackmail, at least not more than once.

"Other than Lady Ashmond's grand plans, you're still enjoying the work?" James asks, deciding he'll have to make amends in gestures rather than apologies, for now.

"Oh, it's wonderful. I know it was Beth's idea, but I've really grown to love it. It's very rewarding. I wish I could take them all home, honestly," Gwen adds, her smile dimming a little.

"Well, maybe with the passage of the Medical Act, there will be fewer orphans," James says encouragingly. "And maybe we can get a few more doctors on staff at the hospital to help with the deliveries that do make it to the hospital, so fewer mothers die there too."

"I'd like that," Gwen says. "You have lists?"

"Absolutely. When we're back, you and I can go through them, and we can propose a few hires?"

Gwen considers him for a beat. "Yes. That would be wonderful." There's something approving in her gaze. He feels like maybe he's passed some kind of test. "Now. Cowes. What are our plans?"

"Well, we'll watch the heats, of course," Albert says. "And I know you were dying to get out on one of the boats. I figure among us"—he gestures to James—"we must know someone who could captain for us."

"I'd need a good first mate, but I could captain," James finds himself saying.

"That's right!" Gwen exclaims, looking at him expectantly.

James can't help but smile back. "Would you like to learn?"

"Yes!" Gwen nearly shrieks, launching herself across the

carriage to throw her arms around him. It makes the whole carriage rock and James feels his flush crawl down his chest and up to his hairline as she sits back. "No one would ever let me. I'm so excited."

"She's your monster now," Albert says, laughing.

But that's just fine with James. Despite maritime superstition, he can't think of anyone with as much tenacity as Gwen. She'll make an excellent first mate. "It's a deal."

"Fabulous," Gwen says, the carriage lurching to a stop as they pull up in front of the Havenfort townhouse. "Bring me an extra frock coat and linen pants. I want to be able to move."

"We'll discuss it," Albert says as James impulsively starts to agree.

Gwen rolls her eyes and hops out without any assistance. "See you tomorrow," she says excitedly before running up her front steps.

"We're doomed," Albert says.

James shrugs. "It made her happy."

"Yes, it did," Albert agrees, eyeing him as the carriage makes its way around the square toward the Mason townhouse.

James stares out the window, his good cheer rapidly deteriorating in Gwen's absence.

"Would you care to stay for dinner, to celebrate?" Albie asks as they stop outside his townhouse.

No matter how much he wants to run through Albert's house to find Bobby, shove him up against a wall, and kiss him until every apology and regret he has dissolves against his hot mouth . . . he needs to do this right, not hastily for the sake of haste. Bobby deserves more than a half-baked apology.

"No, thank you," James forces out. "I'll join you tomorrow. Need to pack, and—" He pauses, thinking.

Albert opens the door, looking back at him, giving him the

choice. It's not snogging Bobby senseless, but telling Albert would be something, at least.

"I need some time to make a proper apology."

Albert considers him for a long moment. "You're going to be good to him, make him happy?" he asks, his voice low and just a hint dangerous.

James doesn't know quite how he's going to do it, but like standing up to his stepfather, the choice is finally, ultimately, easy. "Yes," James says, his chest full. "Yes, I will."

He's not going to let anyone, least of all Raverson, take away his chance at true happiness, love, and family. Not again.

Chapter Twenty-Nine

Bobby

Sitting next to Albie as the train sways below them, light flickering through the windows to cast all six of them in swatches of greens and blues and whites, Bobby can't figure out what to do with his hands. Because across from him, James Demeroven is sitting in a most ungentlemanly fashion, leaning across the aisle to chat animatedly with Gwen, filling Beth and Meredith in on the bets they've agreed to make for the week.

He looks fantastic, in a light linen suit with blue accents that bring out the blue of his eyes. His hair is flopping adorably into his face. And unlike during their horrible standoff in the hallway the week prior, James now looks relaxed and excited. More importantly, far from ignoring Bobby, he blushed when he and Bobby first locked eyes as they got on the train.

Now Bobby doesn't know what the hell to do with himself. His conversation with Beth roils in his chest as he listens to Gwen and James bounce ideas off one another. They could all have what they want, if only Bobby can be brave enough to reach out and take it—to ask James to marry him. Well, to ask James to marry his cousin, actually, but functionally—

If it were appropriate, he might shout out the request right here, on the train, in their private car, like an undignified schoolboy. But though James blushed, he hasn't said two words to Bobby so far. Hurt and butterflies war in his stomach, pushing his heart into his throat with a burn that aches. He might combust before they arrive at Southampton.

"I was thinking, if we win all of our bets, we'd at least triple the money your father gave Albert and me, and perhaps we could put that toward expanding the children's ward at the Foundling Hospital?"

Bobby blinks and the car goes silent, all of them staring at James, who looks around, flushing.

"That's a lovely idea," Beth says softly, glancing over at Bobby. "I'm sure it would be of use."

James' smile widens and he sits up a little straighter. "And I had thought perhaps we could start a fund to house the children separately from the hospital. In a proper orphanage with lots of space and air and grounds. There must be a manor off in the country we could buy. There's a . . . community I could reach out to. Gwen said Lady Ashmond was already working with Thomas Parker."

Bobby feels his heart skip. "Thomas Parker?"

James looks over at him, almost conspiratorial. "You don't think his clientele would have interest in funding an orphanage?"

"I—I do," Bobby says. "It would be an excellent cause and a good bit of public relations."

"Wouldn't it just?" James says, his eyes bright, before he turns back to Gwen, Beth, and Meredith.

His ears are ringing. James just mentioned Thomas Parker, like it was *nothing*. All the fear and panic that drove him away mere weeks ago, and now he's mentioning the D'Vere clientele just like that? What *happened*?

"Beth and I will arrange a meeting with Lady Ashmond and Thomas Parker when we're back," Gwen says happily. "And we can discuss your roster of physicians then too."

"I think we should focus on making sure there's a few Welsh physicians. And if there are any qualified men from abroad as well, the population at the hospital has a lot of immigrants, and it would be wonderful to have physicians who spoke the language and knew their cultures," Beth says.

"Sounds like we'll need to put together an international arm of our research, then," Albie says, stroking Meredith's hair as she begins to doze on his shoulder. "Bobby, you'd be up for a trip to the Continent, wouldn't you?"

"Of course," he says. He's always wanted an excuse to go on a world tour, but his father would never have approved nor funded such an extravagance. He's not totally sure where Albie would even get the money, for that matter.

"I bet Cunningham would be willing to join, and I have always wanted a tour year, even if it's only a few months," James says, glancing over at him again.

Bobby holds James' look, full of promise. There's hesitation there too, but something has changed. He hopes it's for the better. Even as his bruised and broken heart cautions him to be careful, he *hopes*. God, he needs the next several blasted hours on this train to pass, now.

By the time they reach the Southampton station and make their way to the hotel, he's nearly vibrating with nerves and exhaustion. He hasn't formulated a plan, or a big speech, or anything useful. Instead, all he's managed to do over the past few hours is work himself up so badly it feels like his tongue is swelling in his mouth.

He hovers at the edge of the hotel foyer, barely taking in the charming wallpaper, brightly lit lamps, or towering bookshelves. It's a lovely inn, but his stomach is all knots and he's sweating.

"All right?"

Bobby jumps, turning to find James staring up at him, looking calm and collected, and how is that fair?

"Fine," he lies.

James starts to say something else, but Meredith approaches them and presses a key into Bobby's hand. "The porter's already bringing up your trunks. The two of you are in room seven."

Bobby blinks, his heart pounding in his chest. "What, both of us?"

"Uncle Dashiell only booked three rooms, what can you do?" Meredith says, eyes twinkling. "Have a good night."

She turns and saunters away, glancing over her shoulder to wink at them before she joins Albie and follows him upstairs, Beth and Gwen giggling in front of them.

Bobby and James stand there, not looking at each other. He can feel heat creeping up his cheeks as he watches the porters bring their trunks up behind the other four. He— Something changed, but he wasn't ready to— He thought he'd have the night to talk himself up.

"I suppose we should . . ." James starts, his voice tight.

"Right. I've got the key, so," Bobby manages, glancing at him before turning to face straight ahead and follow the porters up the stairs, his shoulders tense.

James bumps up behind him when they reach the top of the narrow, sagging staircase, and it's like a bolt of lightning zips through Bobby's whole body. He nearly stumbles up the last step, but James catches him, his broad hand at the small of Bobby's back.

Bobby withholds a whimper of anxiety and lust and confusion as they follow the porters down the top-floor hall they're sharing with just Gwen, Beth, Albie, and Meredith. The porters traipse into the room to leave their trunks, and neither man so much as glances at them when they come back out, uninterested in two traveling companions sharing a room. They have no way of knowing how complicated this little inn stay has just become.

Bobby stares at the cracked-open door of their suite. If they go inside—

But then again, if they don't go inside, he might spontaneously combust.

"Right, well," James says, nudging Bobby's back, where his blasted hand is still resting, calm and sure.

Bobby lurches into motion, leading them both inside, step after faltering step. He closes the door behind them and then the two of them stand at the threshold of the room. It's little more than a double bed, their trunks, a single chair, and the dark wood walls.

He glances at James, who's staring at the bed with its questionably brown duvet, his kissable, plump bottom lip between his teeth. Flashes of their week at his country estate flit before Bobby's eyes. If he could just unglue his tongue from the parched roof of his mouth, they could fix things, and then they could—

Or James could say no.

Even after his playful looks on the train, James could still say no. The marriage idea could be a bust; sometimes he, Beth, and Gwen do get carried away. James needs something concrete, something real, and maybe this won't be enough.

Now that they're standing side by side, arms brushing, Bobby doesn't know if he could bear to have James reject him, again. It might be less painful just to hover here all night—stay in the maybe, and the possible, for the rest of their lives.

James finally rips his gaze from the bed and turns to look up at Bobby. They stare at each other for a moment, all the tension of the past few hours—the past few weeks, really—hanging between them. Bobby parts his lips, and James reaches up, hesitant, his hands brushing along Bobby's cheeks.

He pauses, staring into Bobby's eyes, his palms warm against Bobby's jaw. Bobby swallows, questions pushing against his teeth, crackling along his skin. But they can wait. First, he needs to let James draw him down into a heady, desperate kiss.

His brain doesn't know what to do, his heart thudding loudly. But his hands seem perfectly fine. They slide around James' waist, curling upward to cradle his back, and Bobby leans into his kiss. The feel of his lips, the pressure of his tongue, the gentle caress of his fingers on Bobby's cheeks—perhaps he's fallen asleep on the train and is simply having another one of his wonderful dreams.

Then James pulls back, keeping hold of Bobby's jaw. Bobby blinks down at him, holding tight to his back, worried if he moves, he'll wake up. He didn't think—he didn't dare hope—he doesn't know what this means, or how to react, other than to cling to James for as long as possible before this inevitably ends, again.

But James just stares up at him, eyes wide and searching. Bobby wishes he could get his brain to form words, to ask, to understand—

"I'm so sorry," James whispers.

What in the hell is happening? James' thumb brushes at his cheek, stealing his breath with tenderness.

"I did a poor job of explaining before. And I know I hurt you, horribly. And I am so, so very sorry," he says, his voice brittle but sure. "I shouldn't have for a second made you think that you were something shameful, or that our . . . love was ever the problem."

Bobby thinks maybe he's had a stroke. "Our . . ."

"Your brother is right," James continues, smiling up at him.

Okay, he's absolutely had a stroke. "What does Albie have to—"

"It's the world that's wrong, not us."

Bobby blinks, shuddering as James' thumb brushes at his cheek again. Oh, he's crying, how mortifying. Or maybe, as James rises on his tiptoes to kiss the tears away, maybe it's beautiful. Maybe the two of them against the world is real, and right, and everything he's wanted.

"James," he whispers, trying to summon words—the right words—*any* words—through the surge of feeling and love and overwhelm that's coursing through him.

"I have to tell you something," James adds, pulling back, his hands falling from Bobby's face. He wants to chase after them.

Instead, James links their fingers together and looks up at him seriously. "Raverson's coming for us, after Cowes. He wants a thousand pounds each from you and me, or he's going to the papers."

"Shit," Bobby says, the absolute least elegant thing he could possibly utter.

"Albert is planning to convene the whole group tomorrow and we'll figure something out. But I wanted to be the one to tell you."

Bobby feels it bubbling up in him, the urge to solve the problem—to present their wild plan to end Raverson for good. "And you're still here?" comes out instead.

Because Raverson—and all that he represents—was the fear, the very reason James ran away. And now he's holding Bobby like he's something precious.

James nods slowly, looking vulnerable and scared, and yet still here, still here, still here. "Raverson is going to come after us whether we stay apart or not. The *world* is going to tell us we're sick and wrong and perverted whether we're together or not. And I'm—I'm tired of doing this alone. Better we face the wretched world together than apart . . . right?"

Joy and surprise and sorrow war in his chest, but the answer is immediate. "Yes," he breathes out. "Yes, better together, I think."

James' smile stretches into a grin as he rises on his toes to pull Bobby into another fabulous kiss—this one tinged with laughter and glory. But Bobby still has something he needs to say, now that James has bared his soul. He can be the one to fix things—really fix things. He can be the one to solve this problem.

"What if it wasn't a problem anymore?" he asks, squeezing James' waist.

"What?"

"What if we could prove to Raverson that there isn't a scandal to expose at all—that there's nothing to blackmail."

James stills, his hands going slack at Bobby's cheeks. "I told you, he'll stop at nothing. Pretending we're not . . . it doesn't matter to him."

Bobby shakes his head, pulling back to hold James by his biceps, stroking at the defined muscles still hidden under his frock coat. "I don't mean we keep hiding. Beth and I—well, actually, Gwen and Beth had a plan, and I think it's a good plan, so I'll say it's our plan."

"A . . . plan," James repeats warily.

"A way to give all of us a permanent happy ending," Bobby continues.

"A permanent happy ending? That sounds rather ominous—"

Bobby laughs, startled. "No. No, it's good—I want to marry you," he spits out, inelegant and impatient and imperfect.

James just blinks at him. "Excuse me?"

"That's our plan. I get to marry you; Beth gets to marry Gwen. If—if you'll have me, of course."

"Marry you?" James says. "But—"

"Well, marry me through Gwen. God, I'm butchering this, aren't I?" he asks, watching James' bemusement grow. He laughs a little nervously, but James hasn't pulled away. His hands are on Bobby's chest, fingers curled into his lapels.

"The plan was that I would marry Beth, and you would marry Gwen, and then the four of us would go up and live in the country and it would be like it was at my manor, but . . . forever," he says, his voice going tight as he speaks it into existence. "And then we'd have partners for everything social, and we could all live close together, and it was . . . just an idea." He peters off as James' eyes remain wide, his mouth still open.

Bobby feels his assurance fading in his chest. His fingertips go cold, worry creeping over him. What if this wasn't what James wanted? What if he doesn't actually want to be *together*, really? What if he was still thinking he'd marry, really marry, in five years or so, to produce an heir? What if—

"You want to spend forever with me?" James whispers.

Bobby's breath leaves him in a great whoosh. His heart pounds in his chest, but this part is easy. "Of course! I'm asking you to marry me. Well, marry me through our cousi—"

James suddenly drops and Bobby stumbles back, reaching out for him, only to realize James hasn't fallen or fainted. Instead, he's knelt on the ground. Kneeling like . . . *oh*.

Bobby collapses to the floor with him, his knees straddling James' forward one, hands cradling his jaw to pull him into a kiss. James laughs against his lips, his hands smoothing over Bobby's back.

"I don't have a ring," James mumbles against his mouth.

"How could you possibly have a ring? I don't even have a ring," Bobby says. Then it hits him, and he rears back. "So you—you want to marry me?"

"I thought the getting down on one knee was obvious," James says brightly.

Bobby drags another kiss from his lips and then leans back again. "Through Gwen, though. I would marry you directly if we could. Very proudly, just so you know," he says.

James' smile widens and he reaches up to brush the hair out of Bobby's eyes. "I'd marry you too. And I'll happily marry you through Gwen. We're going to kick your and Beth's arses at everything, forever."

Bobby laughs, leaning into James' hand. "We'll beat you one day."

"You can try," James says.

Bobby can't help but scoot forward into another heady kiss. And then they're half-mauling each other, Bobby grinding down on James' thigh as James works Bobby's frock coat off his shoulders. He gasps against James' lips, James' fingers tugging his shirttails out of his trousers.

He breaks from James' mouth and shifts on his thigh. They both groan, James pressed up against Bobby's hips. There's a brief moment where Bobby considers simply rutting against James until they're spent, still in their trousers. But then James tugs his shirt off and Bobby decides tonight is not for fast and hot and hard. Tonight they're . . . engaged?

They're engaged. So it should be slow. And tender. And actually on the bed.

"Up," he mumbles, standing on shaking legs.

James moans, a wonderfully rumbly sound, and Bobby reaches down to pull him up to standing. He wastes no time in divesting James of his shirt and then hauls him forward, wrapping his arms around James and leaning down to skate his lips up James' jaw. The light stubble on his face rasps at Bobby's lips and he hums.

James shivers and Bobby smiles against his cheek, and then jolts. James' tricky fingers have already worked the buttons open on his trousers, his warm palm sliding inside to—

"Off," Bobby mumbles, fumbling between them to get at James' trousers too.

James laughs and Bobby meets his eyes as he slips his hand into James' pants, the two of them beaming and panting and happy. He's so very *happy*.

"We have all night," James says softly. "Once hard and fast, and then—"

"You'll let me run my tongue over every single inch of you?" Bobby suggests.

James bucks in his hand, his own fingers curling around Bobby, who groans in reply. "Deal."

And then they're on the bed, trousers halfway down their thighs, moving together, all hands and skin and hot and pulsing. It's fast, and silly, and when they're through, they wiggle out of the remainder of their clothes and flop back onto the slightly scratchy duvet together, hands entwined. Bobby stares up at the wood-beam ceiling, unable to stop smiling.

"Do you have your own room in Cowes?" he wonders idly.

"I do, but I would think we can arrange with the girls to find a pair with an adjoining door," James says lazily, his thumb stroking the back of Bobby's hand.

"We could do that on every trip once we're married."

"Have adjoining rooms?"

"As two couples, and then we just . . . swap beds," Bobby

says, envisioning romping through Europe with James, Beth, and Gwen, sleeping beside James every night.

"That sounds divine," James says, his voice relaxed and a little blissed out.

Bobby turns his head to stare at his lover, his smile reaching epic proportions. "It does, doesn't it?"

Chapter Thirty

James

He wakes wrapped entirely in Bobby. A leg between his thighs, arms banded around his torso, head tucked into the dip in his shoulder. James lies there, feeling the rise and fall of Bobby's chest and the soft warmth of his breath over his shoulder and neck, and cannot for the life of him stop smiling. He must look like a lovesick fool.

"Mmpf," Bobby mumbles, tightening his arms. "Curtains," he adds, and James can hear the pout in his voice.

Without thinking about it, James rolls in Bobby's arms, grasping the duvet to pull it over their heads, plunging them into brown-tinged shade. Bobby blinks blearily at him, smiling.

"Love you," he says.

James feels it catch in his chest, warmth suffusing him down to his toes. "Love you too," he whispers.

Bobby tugs James in, capturing James' bottom lip between both of his own in a stale yet exultant kiss. Bobby's thigh presses up as they move together and James sighs into Bobby's mouth. He could get used to waking up like this—someone else to alleviate the morning pressure, someone to kiss, someone to love every morning for the rest of his—

"Oi, we're going to miss the bloody ferry!"

They jolt, James' forehead knocking into Bobby's cheek. They both groan. Gwen pounds on their door a few times and then they can hear her speaking to Albert, both of them way too loud for the quiet, lovely morning he and Bobby were working up to.

"I don't hear movement!" Gwen calls.

Bobby grunts, shifting to steal one last kiss. "More tonight," he promises.

"I'll hold you to that," James says, smiling as Bobby grits his teeth, throwing back the duvet.

It's a harried few minutes as they dress, searching the room for their various discarded pieces of clothing, exchanging knowing smirks. Bobby does up James' tie, his fingers lingering at James' throat, and James is about to arch into a kiss when the door clicks open.

They cleave apart, but it's only Gwen, who takes one look at them, red-cheeked and flustered, and cackles. She leaves the door open and they can hear her storming across the hall to Albert and Meredith's room.

"You owe me twenty quid," she calls into the room.

Bobby chuckles while James flushes. He lets Bobby lead him out into the hall, where Beth is already loitering in her gray travel cloak and gown, a frilly bonnet in her hands. She smiles at them far too knowingly. Gwen leans back out of Albert and Meredith's room and eyes them with glee.

"Here." James watches in mortification as Bobby passes Gwen twenty quid from his pocket. "Easier this way," he says, catching James' expression. "Not like we paid for the room."

That only makes James more embarrassed, and then a thought overtakes him that sends all that blood straight out of his face in horror.

"James?" Gwen prompts, stepping toward him, Beth right behind her.

Bobby turns, reaching out for him.

All James can mutter is "We should have asked your father first."

He didn't ask Lord Havenfort if he could marry his daughter, much less marry her so he can really marry his nephew.

Meredith steps out of her room with Albert in tow. "Ask Lord Havenfort what?" she asks.

But James' inaudible response is drowned out by the sound of Beth squealing and launching herself at Bobby, who catches her and spins her around, both of them laughing. Even his latent horror can't compete with that, and James watches them with what he's sure is a sappy, adoring smile.

He jolts as Gwen leans down and kisses his cheek. "My father will more than approve. And he won't have been expecting you to talk to him anyway, since I am my own woman and make my own choices." James slowly turns to meet her eyes, his shoulders drooping in relief. "Though, it would have been nice if you'd actually bothered to ask *me*," she says, eyebrow arched.

"It would have been nice if you would have told us you were trying to trap us into marriage!" James exclaims.

Gwen merely laughs and wraps him in a hug. He stiffens automatically, and then forces himself to relax and embrace her back. "I absolutely don't apologize," she whispers.

"No, of course not," he agrees, laughing as she giggles.

"Would someone care to let us in on the celebration?" Meredith asks.

Gwen pulls back and takes James' arm, turning them to face Albert and Meredith. Oh, shit, should he have asked Albert's permission for Bobby? Not that there's a protocol to ask a man if he can proxy-marry his brother through his cousin.

"Oh, we're going to be married, me and James, and Beth and Bobby, didn't you hear?" Gwen says with nonchalance.

Albert gapes while Meredith laughs delightedly. Albert turns to his wife, takes one look at her face, and gasps. "Did you know about this?"

"No!" Meredith says quickly, shrieking as Albert goes to nab her about the waist, laughing.

"Liar!" Albert says, tickling her.

"I just had a hunch!" Meredith squeaks. "I swear I didn't know!"

James watches them bicker, then turns to find that Beth and Bobby are already in a frantic discussion of venues and dates and decor. Everyone's happy, and eager, and elated, *for him*.

His eyes start to sting and he goes to pull away from Gwen, overwhelmed in the best way. But she doesn't let him, wrapping her arm around his shoulders.

"I promise, you get used to us," she says.

He laughs a little wetly, feeling sheepish but . . . excited. "I'm looking forward to it."

She squeezes him and they stand there, watching the rest of their motley group absolutely lose it. It gives James just enough time for his brain to catch up through all the chaos. Gives him enough time to summon what little courage he still possesses after last night.

"Gwen, would you? Like to marry me, that is?" he asks, turning to meet her eyes.

Gwen's smile stretches impossibly wider. "Absolutely. Provided we're agreed we're not really marrying . . . each other," she says, glancing toward Beth and Bobby.

"A marriage in name only, agreed," he says, laughing as she extends her hand.

He takes her smaller palm in his with a decisive shake and they beam at each other.

"I guess we'll have to figure out the line of succession," Gwen says as they drop hands, Beth and Bobby and Albert and Meredith still chattering around them.

"Yes," he says, the elation of the moment fading just a hair.

"I wish . . ." Gwen says softly, glancing again at Beth.

The image of Gwen at the Foundling Hospital gate, hugging the little girl, springs into his mind. He finds he wishes too. But he couldn't lie with Gwen, and he knows Bobby would never lie with Beth. Maybe Wristead and his wife truly are happy with a third person somewhere in their marriage, but James knows he never could be. And the way Gwen's looking at Beth? She could never either.

"I think I'd be a pretty piss-poor father, anyway," James says, pushing the words out. They're true, but it doesn't make the wistful feeling lift at all.

"Same here. Not mother material, I mean. But Beth would be an excellent mother," Gwen says quietly. "And I don't know, we turned out all right, didn't we?"

James can't prevent the snort that escapes him. "Touché."

Meredith finally gathers herself enough to begin herding them toward the stairs so they don't miss the first ferry.

Bobby's hand briefly finds his, their eyes locking. They're really doing this—stepping into the future, together. It's more than enough to chase any lingering doubts from James' mind. He squeezes Bobby's hand, and then lets him go, offering Gwen his arm.

"My dear?" he says.

Gwen smirks and takes his elbow. "Lead the way, sir."

HIS ROOM HAS a lovely view out over the Solent. Were he interested, he could sit at the picture window and watch the ships pass, or squint across the water to Lepe Country Park and watch staff set up tents along the grounds. But all he wants is to cuddle up for a nap and sleep the afternoon away.

He pokes his head out of his door. Their rooms are all in a cluster, but it's hardly as private as having had the full floor at the inn last night. Still, it wouldn't be that suspicious for him to linger in Bobby's room for an hour or two.

Of course, the moment he actually steps into the hall, Albert's door opens and he leans out, beckoning for James to join him in their suite. It's a sunny, spacious room, equipped with a fainting couch, small table, and separate bathing area. Next year he and Gwen could have a room like this, and simply swap at night. They'll get to live like married couples do, with all the benefits. How glorious.

"James."

James blinks and realizes he's just been standing in the threshold to the room, while Gwen, Beth, and Meredith sit at the table, and Bobby lies sprawled on the fainting couch. James can just see his shoes from the doorway.

Albert pats him on the back and closes the door, unconcerned. "Meredith has some thoughts."

"Always a dangerous thing," Bobby says from the couch.

James rolls his eyes and walks into the room, lifting Bobby's feet to plunk down on the couch with him. Bobby winks and wiggles his toes when his feet plop back into James' lap.

"Sorry, Meredith, you were saying?" James says.

"Well, for starters," Meredith says, after giving them all a mock-haughty look.

She reaches into a small bag sitting on the center of the table and pulls something out. Both Beth and Gwen gasp. Meredith hands whatever it is over. James glances at Bobby, who shrugs. But then Gwen slides out of her chair and onto the floor, looking up at Beth, on one—oh.

Beth nods eagerly, her face growing pink, and James can just see a tear leak down her cheek in the sunlight that comes in from the spotless windows.

"I love you so much," Beth whispers.

Gwen slips a plain ring onto Beth's finger and grips her hand. Beth beams and pushes her chair back, sinking onto the floor with Gwen. She slides a ring onto Gwen's finger and Gwen whispers something to her before pulling her in for a kiss.

James feels his chest expand and squeezes Bobby's leg. It's not just James and Bobby who get a full life together, but Beth and Gwen, now wrapped in a hug and weeping softly into each other's necks—they get their happy ending too.

"We'll do our own rings, promise," Bobby murmurs.

James feels his smile stretching across his face. "Deal."

They sit for a few minutes in contented silence, allowing Beth and Gwen to gather themselves, and everyone pretends that they don't spend at least two of those minutes kissing. How he could ever have been afraid to be honest with these people, James will never know.

Well, he does know, but now he knows better.

"All right," Meredith says finally. "Everyone up. You have rooms to carry on in later."

"My wife, the romantic," Albert says as Beth and Gwen help each other up, giggling.

Bobby stands and offers his hands to James, who takes them happily, laughing when Bobby tugs him up and into a firm hug. Bobby dips his head and presses a kiss to his neck. James shivers, zips of arousal flooding through him instantly.

"No more of that," he hears, and then Bobby's stumbling away.

Meredith yanks him over to Beth and shoves him in between

Beth and Gwen. Gwen laughs as Meredith then tugs her across the room and over to James' side.

"Some courting lessons seem to be in order," Meredith says.

Gwen snorts. "I've been through five seasons, Meredith, I think I know how to be courted."

"Yeah! I was engaged once before," Beth puts in.

"And you and Albie dragged me on half of your outings last year as chaperone," Bobby adds.

The room turns to look at James. He has the absurd urge to duck and hide behind Gwen. "I—created our initial problem with Raverson?" he finds himself saying.

Bobby groans while Gwen laughs and takes his arm. "We're three out of four, I think we can shape James up without your pedantic—"

"Courting in season, and demonstrating your happy engagements to the entire ton and to the aforementioned blackmailing slimeball, are different," Meredith says over Gwen's objections. "We must convince the ton that you are all proudly engaged, that it's been going on for a while, and that Raverson has concocted an entire slanderous narrative in his head."

"He—hasn't?" Bobby says, his cheeks going red.

"Hasn't what?" Meredith asks, turning to him, hands on her hips. She's very no-nonsense when she wants to be.

"She's going to make an excellent mother," Gwen mutters.

James coughs through a laugh, unable to meet her eyes.

"Well, I mean, I did actually . . . Raverson has firsthand proof of his claims with me. He also, ah, stole my signet ring," Bobby admits, eyes trained resolutely over Meredith's head.

"And he has proof about me too, though it was much less recent," James says. He's not proud of it, but he'll hardly leave Bobby out to dry.

Meredith and Albert look between James and Bobby, who shrug at each other. This is the bed they've both made, and already laid in. And as much as it's wonderful that they'll never need to risk lying with an untruthful or downright vengeful man again, they still have to deal with the reality of their pasts.

James glances over as Gwen holds out her opposite hand. Beth sighs and detaches from Bobby, riffling in her skirts to pull out a quid and hand it over to Gwen. Bobby groans and James flushes. Bad enough they had to explain the threat of Raverson's extortion in hushed whispers on the ferry over, but betting on the sordid details? Is nothing left to simply *be* in this family?

Gwen looks back at him, her eyebrow raised, and he can do nothing more than lift his hands in surrender. "Look, we can't all find the love of our lives on the very first try."

Gwen laughs and Beth returns to Bobby, cooing something teasing up at him. Albert chuckles and meets James' eyes.

"You'll do nicely," he decrees.

"As much as rehashing the terrible decisions that led you each to that man's bed could occupy our entire day—"

"And provide salacious details," Gwen throws in, making both James and Bobby squirm.

"It's not your mutual past with Raverson that's really the problem," Meredith continues firmly. "Raverson can only use information that doesn't directly implicate him, and as the only true evidence he has of either of your . . ." She trails off, looking to Bobby and then James.

"Ah, preferences?" Bobby suggests.

"True selves?" James counters.

"Oh, much better," Bobby says, smiling at him.

"Right," Meredith agrees. "He can only go to the papers if he thinks he has other evidence of your true desires, and, Robert, we will either get that ring back or easily make a duplicate so he can't use it."

Bobby and James exchange a glance. Well, that's frighteningly simple, isn't it?

Meredith rolls her eyes. "We'll need to remove any other remaining ammunition as well, which means the four of you need to be shamelessly public with your engagements. I want you over the top, making a spectacle of yourselves."

"A spectacle," Gwen repeats, her smile turning just a bit dangerous.

"We have permission for spectacle?" Beth asks, looking equally devious. What have they gotten themselves into?

"As I'm not worried any of you will be sneaking off to hedges with your fake fiancés, yes, spectacle. We're going to attend every single event."

The wind goes out of the room and all of them, even Albert, droop at that.

"We need it reported back to London before Raverson can get his bearings," Meredith insists. "Once it's all over the ton that you're engaged, it'll be twice as hard for Raverson to even consider slandering your names. So you'll just have to suffer through a week of parties and drinking and public soppiness. I have no doubt you're all up to the task," she says, looking over both couples.

"Oh, want to see whose engagement gets announced first? I'll bet five pounds on me and James," Gwen says.

"Dear Lord," James mutters. But the way Bobby perks up, exchanging a glance with Beth, has him rummaging in his pocket to pull out his own bill. "Ten."

"Oh, you're going to be *such* a good husband," Gwen decides, squeezing his arm before stepping away to take Beth's hand again.

"If we do this right, your reputations will be secured, we'll take down a despicable viscount, and you'll all be happily married by summer's end," Meredith says.

"Hear, hear," Bobby says, smiling at James.

James returns his smile, but something sinks in his gut. "Do you think our engagements would discredit *all* of Raverson's claims?" James asks, looking to Albert.

Albert frowns, slowly sinking to sit back down on the bed. "Probably not," he admits.

James sighs. Bobby steps up next to him and threads their fingers together.

"I don't want anyone in our community taken down because Raverson wants more money and more power, and doesn't mind destroying the men he's slept with to get it," James says.

Bobby nods next to him. "Maybe we can talk to Thomas Parker when we're back, see if we could convince a number of the D'Vere clientele to commit to speaking out, or drafting a very threatening letter?"

"That's a good idea," James agrees, glancing up at Bobby. "Cunningham's here this week, isn't he?"

"I think so," Albert says.

"Oh, we have dinner scheduled with them tomorrow," Meredith says. All three of them look over at her. "You lot have been busy with the vote and research, so I made some calls. Parker's here as a guest of Cunningham's, and I've already got them compiling a list of gentlemen they know who have had dalliances with Raverson, which they'll bring tomorrow night. And then we'll discuss who else we should connect with to get a list of men that perhaps Raverson wouldn't want coming out of the woodwork—anyone he blackmailed at school, or their fathers, who might want retribution. All of that combined should be enough to intimidate him into keeping his mouth shut, or else."

James is gaping, Bobby's wide-eyed, and Albert flops backward on the bed, a hand over his eyes.

"You really need to stop forgetting to ask for help," Meredith says simply. "We're a team, whether we're matchmaking widowed parents or blackmailing a viscount to protect our family and friends, all right? Use your words."

Bobby snorts. James' chest fills with that warm, sickly-sweet feeling again. He watches Meredith cross the room to sit beside Albert, patting him consolingly on the thigh as he shakes his head in shame.

"You ready to con the ton?" Bobby asks.

James looks up at him, glancing over at Beth and Gwen before he rises on his toes to press a kiss to Bobby's lips. Bobby steadies him with a hand on his waist, his other pressed between them, their fingers still tangled together.

"Oh, get a room," Gwen calls out.

"That's the plan," James returns as he breaks away from Bobby and sinks back down to the flats of his feet.

Bobby just smiles at him and James takes a deep breath. Conning the ton it is.

CHAPTER THIRTY-ONE

Bobby

"Lord Demeroven, dearest, thank you. I was ever so parched," Gwen simpers, batting her lashes beneath her frankly absurd lace bonnet and swishing her bright lilac skirts.

She accepts the proffered champagne from James and immediately grabs his arm, leaning coquettishly into him. Bobby's never seen Gwen in such a loud outfit by choice, but she's taking their challenge seriously. Perhaps too seriously, he thinks, as James looks woefully over his shoulder in his formal linen suit. Gwen yanks him away, going on about china patterns, and Bobby just shrugs helplessly.

James' look turns into a glare and Bobby snorts. Beth takes her drink from him and giggles. He meets her eyes and they share a conspiratorial smile.

"You do know they're winning," she says, linking her arm with his. They amble behind Gwen and James, following them toward Meredith and Albie's picnic blanket.

"I can be obnoxious," he offers, sipping his champagne as they stare out across the water.

"We can cede today to them. They need to bond," Beth says easily, looking up at him beneath her own, slightly smaller bonnet.

Her green skirt and blouse are lovely, and she looks positively delighted to be on his arm. They're not doing so poorly themselves. He raises his glass toward a few acquaintances he thinks were in Albie's year at Oxford. They're all watching them from their picnic blankets.

The whole ton of Cowes is spread out on the green grass overlooking the channel beach, an array of muslin gowns and linen suits on checkered blankets as far as the eye can see. On the water, the sailboats have lined up for the second day of races, and with clear blue skies and a cool breeze, it's shaping up to be an excellent day for flaunting fake engagements.

"Would you like to sit, my dear, or meander a bit before the race begins?" he asks loudly near a cluster of mothers.

"Your mother will be so delighted," one of them says, looking up at Beth.

Beth smiles brightly and leans into Bobby. "I cannot wait to see her. She's going to dote on him terribly."

"No, no, it will be my honor to spoil both of you rotten," he tells Beth, winking at the mothers before bowing and leading Beth away. "The letter to your mother and Uncle Dashiell must have arrived by now, right?" he asks as they finally reach Meredith and Albie's blanket.

James has sprawled down on his back, his arm flung over his eyes, while Gwen sits next to him, cheerily eating a profiterole. She pats the space beside her and Bobby helps Beth settle herself and her massive skirt.

"I expect we'll receive a very wordy letter from my mother and Gwen's father presently," Beth assures him as he plops down on her other side.

"Good," he says, pretending he's not at all afraid of Uncle Dashiell's or Aunt Cordelia's reaction. He thinks they'll be happy for all of them, but doing this in the bubble of Cowes leaves a lot of reassurance to be desired.

He looks over at Meredith and Albie, Meredith reclined

between Albie's legs, his hand resting on her stomach. "And how is life for the happily married?" he asks them.

"Wonderful," Meredith says, rolling her neck against Albie's chest to squint over at him. "Cunningham's gone to get us ices."

"It's good to have single friends at these events," Gwen says as she passes Beth a scone. "They're ever so useful."

"Lord Cunningham isn't single, dearest," James mumbles.

"Though he wishes," Bobby mutters to Beth, leaning in to sneak a bite of her scone. Meredith winks at him.

"That's a pity," Beth whispers back.

"Not all of us have fabulously clever friends," Bobby says, pressing his shoulder into hers.

"Did I hear you needed more errand men, Lady Gwen?"

They look up to find Thomas Parker standing behind them, dutifully blocking the sun while looking jaunty in his white linen suit and broad straw hat.

"Good to see you, Mr. Parker. Please join us, won't you?" Meredith says, patting the open spot beside her.

Parker sits down and removes his hat, pretending to inspect it as he passes a note to Meredith. She quickly shoves it into her blue skirt.

"A good morning?" she asks.

"Quite eventful," Parker says. "Look alive, Lord Demeroven, the race is starting."

James sits up reluctantly, frowning over at him. "Perhaps if I'd had less whisky last night, I would enjoy the sun more," he grumbles.

"But we sent you to bed with plenty of time for a good night's sleep," Parker says, sliding his eyes over to Bobby, who tries to look entirely innocent.

After their dinner and card game with Parker and Cunningham, which involved more schedule-making and planning than cards, he and James may have stayed awake all night in a drunken revel, glorying in their impending freedom.

"Lumpy bed," James says, shaking his head as both Beth and Gwen giggle. "At least Cunningham looks worse than I do," he adds.

Cunningham makes his way through the thinning throng of onlookers, carrying three ices with a grimace. His white shirt is stained with red and one of his suspenders is slipping down his arm.

"Think this will have to be the only run for ice, Lady Mason," he says, exhaustion heavy in his voice as he passes the ices to Albie and Meredith and then collapses on Albie's other side.

"Crowded?" Bobby asks.

"Absolutely mobbed," Cunningham agrees around a mouthful of his own red treat. "However, it was a useful trip."

"Did you manage to bump into Scotsman? He said he was looking for you," Parker says, nonchalant.

"I did. And he had Gladmon with him. They're both most interested in a dinner with our motley group later this week. Gladmon might be interested in investing with us too," Cunningham adds to Parker. "Seems he needs to rebuild his holdings after being taken in by a bad actor who threatened to go to his father for repayment right after school."

Bobby glances at James, watches the way his shoulders slump momentarily. Not everyone Raverson has tried to extort has had the support he and James have. They're so lucky to have their family, to have Uncle Dashiell. No one should ever have to fear the retribution of their relatives, or the ostracization of society, or, worse, imprisonment for simply being who they are.

"Scotsman and Gladmon think they might be able to set up a few other dinners for us as well," Cunningham continues, looking to Meredith. "I gave them both your card, Lady Mason."

"Wonderful," Meredith says. "I think we're all having a most productive week thus far."

Bobby catches James' eye, both of them determined. James is a little sun-kissed, a little rumpled, and entirely, thoroughly his. They're going to fix this. They're going to take Raverson down, all of them, he can feel it.

"So, Mason, what are your plans for the shooting season?" Parker asks, wrenching Bobby's gaze from James.

He turns to look at Parker, noting everyone on the picnic blanket smirking. All right, they're going to take Raverson down *and* figure out how to stop mooning over each other in public. At least, they're going to try.

"YES, PULL TAUT over there," James calls across the stern at Gwen as she expertly secures the halyard.

The choppy waters of the Solent slap against their small yacht. Bobby holds tight to Beth, the two of them being shunted around the small vessel while James, Gwen, Cunningham, and Parker capably steer them along the coastline.

Today they've learned that Gwen would make a strong sailor, Beth gets seasick, and Cunningham has never quite gotten his sea legs. Parker, however, dances along the deck as though he's been at sea all his life.

"You all right?" Bobby asks Beth, feeling like he has to shout through the wind.

They're really clipping along for a *leisurely little sail*. Gwen's not the mitigating factor he thinks James probably hoped she would be against Cunningham and Parker, who are absolutely living out stolen glory, pretending they could be part of the heat later in the morning.

"Fine," Beth yells. "Don't let go."

"Never," he assures her, catching James' eye as he swings back around them, heading to relieve Cunningham from the rudder. "Are we almost done?"

James looks between Bobby and Beth and gives Bobby a soft smile. "We'll head in. And I think the Demerovens may make this just . . . our tradition next year, yeah?"

"Yeah," Bobby and Beth say together, clinging to one another in their sea-sprayed sailing outfits. At least Beth's hoop is small enough he can actually hold on to her.

She looks like an adorably drowned rat as she peers up at him imploringly. "You promise me we won't do this again?"

"The Masons don't sail," he says. She laughs a little wetly.

Then they both groan as the boat lists, James finally at the rudder with a disgruntled Cunningham pouting beside him. Gwen makes her way over to them, holding on to the guard line with one hand.

"Oh, darling," she says, plunking down beside Beth.

"I truly hate you," Beth tells her.

Gwen snorts and takes her hand as they glide toward the first jetty at the mouth of the River Medina, just down the street from their hotel. Bobby spots Albie and Meredith watching them come in along the boardwalk, looking refreshed, coifed, and rested. He's never letting James force him out of bed before nine again.

The yacht comes to a halt at their dock and Cunningham and Parker begin tossing ropes and securing the vessel. Bobby and Gwen get Beth up to standing and James hops onto the dock. Together they pass Beth over into his arms. Gwen's snickering quietly and Bobby has half a mind to leave her onboard, but Albie gives him a look from the top of the docks and he sighs, passing Gwen over before hopping off the nauseating ship and onto solid, stable wood.

His legs sway beneath him and James has to catch his elbow while Gwen holds Beth steady.

"I suppose cruising to America might be out of the question," James says, reluctantly releasing Bobby as Meredith and Albie stroll down to meet them.

"The Masons don't sail," Beth and Bobby repeat together.

James, Gwen, Meredith, and Albie laugh. Beth huffs and grabs Bobby's hand, marching them away from their little circle. Bobby hides his own laughter and lets her tow him up to the boardwalk.

"We're just teasing," Gwen calls.

They turn to find Gwen and James close behind, Meredith and Albie having gone on to chat with Cunningham and Parker while they finish tying off the yacht.

"Well, it isn't funny," Beth says, but there's a tilt to her mouth, and Bobby can see her color coming back. "That was miserable."

"I'm sorry," Gwen says, the four of them turning to stand close against the railing at the top of the stairs down to the docks.

The boardwalk is still mostly empty this early. The yachts won't set out for another hour, and it'll be one o'clock before the first heat of the day. It's peaceful like this, just the four of them by the marina, now that they're not being pelted with sea spray and wind.

"We won't make you go sailing again. It can be a Demeroven-only activity," Gwen assures Beth.

"Hear, hear," Bobby says.

"It's still strange that you'll be a Demeroven now," Beth admits, looking over at Gwen.

"It would be pretty improper if you were about to become a Demeroven *again*," Gwen says with a laugh.

James wrinkles his nose at the thought and Beth glares at him. "Hey! I'm going to be an excellent wife. You would be lucky to have me."

"I've laid claim to you already, no need to get combative," Bobby puts in.

"Is that all you've laid, then?"

They turn together to find Lord Raverson standing just behind them on the boardwalk. His linen suit still hangs off his lanky frame, hair still slightly greasy. But it's the sneer on his handsome face that stands out the most, twisting him into something sinister in the early morning light. Embittered and desperate, and rogue.

Bobby glances at James, the two of them stepping in front of Beth and Gwen without a word. Raverson's eyebrows dance, his lips curling.

"The happy foursome," Raverson says loudly. "What a sham."

"You're the sham," Beth says hotly. "Why don't you piss off and bother someone who cares?"

Bobby adjusts his arm, blocking Beth from stepping forward. It's always hard to remember, but she does have a temper, seasick or not.

"Bold words," Raverson says coolly. "Learn those from your mother? Your line has a talent for slithering into wealth, doesn't it?"

"You will not speak another word about Lady Havenfort," James says hotly. "Go and get yourself a drink for your hangover. We're busy."

"Yes, you look it," Raverson says, a frantic energy simmering beneath his calm façade. "But not busy enough. I gave you a deadline, Demeroven, and it's tomorrow."

"The only thing you'll be seeing tomorrow is the back of our private train car, pulling out of Southampton," Gwen puts in.

Raverson looks them over, the girls pressing into Bobby's and James' backs, Bobby and James a united front before them. "Seems I'll be making that trip to see Lord Havenfort after all. I'll be taking your daddy for all he's got," he says, looking to Gwen.

"My father will rip you to pieces," Gwen spits back.

Raverson's gaze slips over to Beth, as if Gwen hasn't even spoken. "Unless you'd like to cut me a deal, Miss Bertram? I could forgo all the ugliness with your cousins and your stepfather if you'd simply . . . provide me with a living."

"Like hell," James says.

"Make an honest man of me, and this all goes away," Raverson continues.

"I couldn't make an honest man of you if you were dead," Beth says evenly.

Raverson's gaze darkens. "I see Lady Gwen's deplorable manners have spread to you too."

"You shut your—" Gwen starts.

"You're dangerously close to being thrown off the boardwalk," James says in a low voice. "Go back to your hidey-hole and pray none of this ever reaches Lord Havenfort. You've insulted three branches of his family, and he won't take that lightly."

"Well, you're leaving him no choice, are you?" Raverson says, his voice turning sharp. "At this rate, either he'll give me one of the girls, humiliating one of you in the process, or I'll take down your entire line," he threatens, stepping forward.

"Beth and I would rather shrivel up and die than marry you," Gwen says strongly.

"Shut up," Raverson bites out.

"You must be a miserable, pathetic man, if the best you think you can do is take an unwilling wife. Is it because you don't think anyone could ever love you for yourself? How sad," Beth says.

Bobby sucks in a breath as Raverson's gaze swings to Beth, bright and dangerous. Bobby tries to push Beth further behind him.

"It's not like *your* fiancé is willing, is he?" Raverson says softly, the edge of his voice able to cut glass.

"You've no idea what I'm willing to do," Bobby says, pulling himself up to his tallest and staring Raverson down.

"Just because you can only get someone to sleep with you if they're drunk or being extorted doesn't mean the rest of the world is so desperate," James chimes in. "And the normal reasons people get married are entirely out of your reach, aren't they?"

Raverson looks to James. "What, love and responsibility? Don't lie, Demeroven. You no more want a wife than you want a quick trip to the gallows. I know you."

"You don't," James says, and the certainty in his voice is something to celebrate. "You haven't grown a day since we were in school, clinging to your trinkets and blackmail because you're too frightened to face the world as a man—too frightened to take the responsibility and title you've been given and try to do anything the world might appreciate."

"Pathetic," Gwen puts in icily.

Raverson starts forward and James steps away from Gwen, blocking his path. "I've hit you once—I'm not afraid to do it again."

"Tsk, tsk. What would it do to your precious reputation?"

"Only gain me accolades from all those who have met you and found you utterly wanting," James says, and Bobby refrains from whooping.

"You won't be so confident when I go to the papers," Raverson sneers.

"With what, exactly?" Gwen asks. Bobby shifts again, trying to keep both girls behind him. "That he's happily engaged and about to receive a sizeable dowry?"

"I can prove your engagements are nothing but a sham with a flick of my wrist," Raverson says, digging roughly in his pocket to pull out a small gold ring.

That's *his* bloody signet ring. Bobby surges forward only for James to yank him back.

"You'll pay, or Havenfort will, or the whole ton will know you're poofs," Raverson hisses.

"My father won't give you a farthing," Gwen says.

"And neither will we," Bobby agrees.

"I think you're all very brave here, away from the ton, but when you get back and find yourselves plastered all over the papers—"

"See, I think it's you who will be plastered all over the papers." Raverson turns as Meredith and Albie reach the top of the dock stairs, calm and easy. "What is it you think you have to go to the gossip rags with again?" Meredith asks sweetly.

"Wouldn't be that you were seen by no less than three parliamentarians fumbling in an alley with the season's new tenor, would it?" Albie asks.

Beth nudges into Bobby's back as Gwen slowly pulls James a few steps away from Raverson, leaving the man at the apex of a triangle between Albie and Meredith and their cluster by the railing. Bobby hears a far-off curse and imagines Cunningham and Parker must be headed their way shortly too.

"I don't know what you're talking about," Raverson says easily. But his eyes have gone shifty and he's swaying on his feet.

"The newspaperman, a dock worker, and . . . how many was it again, Lady Mason?"

"I think it was three second sons of very reputable lords who know exactly what we're talking about. I'm sure their fathers would be quite displeased to find out you're planning to blackmail their sons, all of whom have perfectly respectable alibis for every encounter in question."

"But the opera singer, and the dock worker, and a few choice young stablehands would be more than happy to cash in on your offer of funds to keep them quiet. Wouldn't want your own reputation slandered in the papers. Would keep you from ever earning an honest living again, wouldn't it?" Albie asks calmly.

Raverson takes a menacing step toward him, and Albie moves in front of Meredith. Pulled up to his full height and scowling, Albie is more than intimidating enough to cow any man, much less this version of Raverson. "Take another step toward my pregnant wife, and you'll be in the channel."

Raverson stops and glares around at them. "One day, you'll slip up, and I'll be there to capitalize on it."

"It'll be your word against the six of ours, and Lord Havenfort, and his entire committee, then," James says.

"And Thomas Parker's patrons," Bobby puts in, proud to see the way Raverson pales at the mention.

"Yes, we don't take kindly to predators in our midst, no matter who you are or how well-connected," Parker's voice adds. He and Cunningham crest the stairs, a little winded, but properly menacing, backlit as they are by the rising sun.

"We've compiled a long list of witnesses who know of your nightly escapades," Meredith puts in from behind Albie.

"For a man so set on blackmailing, you've been highly indiscreet yourself," Cunningham adds.

From her pocket, Meredith pulls the list of every accusation they've been able to gather. Raverson goes red and takes two more steps toward Albie and Meredith. Bobby's not really sure which of them grabs him first, but he, James, Albie, Parker, and Cunningham make quick work of hauling Raverson to the railing and dumping him over, where he careens into the water below with an enormous splash.

He comes up spluttering, glowering up at the eight of them as they lean over the railing.

"You loathsome, horrid, blasphemous—" Raverson starts.

"It's your own fault for being drunk at eight in the morning," Albie calls over him, his voice booming across the water.

Bobby looks over his shoulder to find the splash has attracted the small number of morning walkers. A mix of gentlemen, mothers and daughters, and dock workers is heading their way. The perfect team of gossips.

"My cousin and her stepsister said no," Albie continues, overloud. "You need to accept that neither of them wishes to consort with you, and you should be grateful their fiancés only saw fit to toss you into the sea, rather than take you to task for assaulting their betrotheds."

"I—" Raverson spits.

But Albie's already turning to surveil the crowd assembling around them. "Heartbreak can do terrible things to a man. Don't judge Lord Raverson too harshly."

With that, Albie takes Meredith's arm and guides her through the crowd. Parker and Cunningham step up on either side of Bobby and James, and they quickly link arms with Beth and Gwen. They gently push through the assembled onlookers and make a quick escape, hustling across the boardwalk and up the street.

It's *over.* All in a moment.

Bobby watches Meredith pass their list over to Parker, who quickly pockets it. "You'd make a fine politician, Lady Mason," Parker says as they come to a stop a few doors down from their hotel.

"Oh, I know," Meredith says with a proud shrug.

"I could have taken him," Gwen mutters, and James lets out a startled laugh.

"I'm sure you could have," Beth agrees. "Though that's not really the impression we want to make."

"Would have been great, though," Bobby says, his eyes catching James'. They actually did it.

"Could you gents see he makes his way to the ferry?" Albie asks Parker and Cunningham. "I think he's done with his visit."

Parker nods, slinging his arm over Cunningham's shoulders. "I look forward to our meetings once we're back. Good show, all of you," he says, glancing at James and Bobby.

"Thank you," James says.

Parker smiles and flicks his thumb, sending something small and golden sailing their way. Bobby reacts by instinct, snatching it out of the air. He looks down, the initials on his signet ring glinting up from his palm.

"Thank you," Bobby says, meeting Parker's eyes.

"Secrets stay inside," Parker says seriously.

Then with a jaunty wave, he lets Cunningham turn him around to head back to the marina to strong-arm Raverson onto the next ferry out.

The six of them stand there in a daze, Beth on Bobby's arm, Gwen on James'.

"Breakfast?" Meredith suggests.

"Finally," Beth says earnestly, and they all dissolve into laughter.

James' hand brushes Bobby's as they stumble toward the hotel, their arms linked with their respective fiancées. His quick fingers snag the signet out of Bobby's palm.

"You promised me a ring," he whispers.

Bobby laughs, his chest light. "I did, didn't I?"

James' cheeks turn pink as their eyes hold for a moment, before he turns back to Gwen. Bobby takes a deep, elated breath. They're safe. Safe to be themselves, to love one another, and to walk through the world, armed not just with the support of their family, but with a community united.

All that's left to be done is to actually get married and swan off into the sunset.

. . . After they face Uncle Dashiell.

Chapter Thirty-Two

James

"Let me burn that."

James stares down at the crumpled letter in his fist. "I'm fine."

"Still," Reginald says, gently prying the letter from his hand. "Neither you nor your mother need concern yourself with him."

James watches Reginald stuff the crinkled paper into his pocket. He's right. The letter has no bearing on his life any longer, nor his mother's.

"Don't let him get you down. This is a good day," Reginald says, taking James by the shoulders.

James forces himself to nod. "Right."

"And tell Miss Wilson I expect her to be ready tonight at eight."

"I will," James promises.

Reginald grins. His plans have something to do with Miss Wilson, Thomas Parker, and a delicious meal, he thinks. Reginald squeezes his shoulders and then nudges him toward the door. James blows out a breath and heads out into the square to face the proverbial music.

What his soon-to-be ex-stepfather thinks truly no longer matters. And yet even as he hurries across the square toward his future, the weight of his past hangs heavy around his neck.

His stepfather actually congratulated him. So proud of him for *pulling one over on Havenfort*—tickled pink that James will receive a Havenfort dowry and continue the Demeroven line with Havenfort's daughter.

What utter rot. He hardly cares about Gwen's money. And there won't be an heir to the Demeroven estate. The line will die with James. He'll do the most he can while he has the title, and give as much to charity as he's able. Make it count, and then let it go.

Even if he felt a flutter of something primal and natal and desperate at reading the words *I am proud* from that man, whatever childhood disturbance it reawakened will fade with time. James is heading toward his real family—the one he's chosen, the one he's building—and he will leave his stepfather's words behind.

Distracted by the damn letter, it's only when he rings the bell at the Havenfort townhouse that James remembers why he's here, and that he should be very anxious.

Miss Wilson opens the door and immediately yanks him inside, beaming. "They're all waiting for you," she says.

James laughs, surprised, and lets her tug him through the ornate foyer and up to the sitting room. "I'm on time."

"True, you're better than Gwen. I do wish you luck with her, she's allergic to punctuality."

"I'll keep that in mind," James says, pushing down the loud laugh that wants to escape. "Reginald says he'll be by at eight, by the way."

"Oh, excellent," Miss Wilson says. "Now, enjoy." She opens the door to the sitting room and pushes him inside, whirling around to head back downstairs before he can even say goodbye.

He's immediately accosted by Mrs. Stelm, demanding his tea preference while Mrs. Gilpe pulls off his frock coat. He tries to tell Mrs. Stelm it really doesn't matter, but they're gone before he can get a word in edgewise.

And then Beth's at his side, guiding him over to sit down on the settee with her and Gwen. Bobby smiles at James, ensconced in an armchair with very pink cheeks and baby Frederic in his arms.

"Now, Mother and Lady Harrington are set on us having the reception here, but we did want your opinion, just to make sure you don't want to have the reception—"

"At my townhouse? Goodness, no," James tells Beth, accepting that he's fully part of a discussion now that was going on long before he arrived.

"Good, good," Lady Harrington says. "I'll be happy to provide linens. We kept Meredith's," she tells Lady Havenfort.

"I'm sure we have some, but that would be lovely, thank you," Lady Havenfort says, smiling over at Beth, Gwen, and James. "Albert, you'll take James and Bobby for their suits, yes?"

"Of course," Albert says from his perch against the mantel, drink in hand. "Uncle has already made an appointment with his tailor."

"And I'll go along to make sure everything fits correctly," Lord Havenfort puts in.

James blinks, having somehow missed him in the armchair next to Bobby.

It's just that watching Bobby coo down at baby Frederic is entirely distracting. It's doing all kinds of things to his chest and stomach and other parts of him, so he wrenches his eyes away, turning to meet Gwen's. Who absolutely has caught him mooning over Bobby. She nudges him and he blushes.

"And the licenses?" Lady Harrington asks.

"All settled," Albert says quickly. "Expedited, though not alarmingly so," he adds to Lord Havenfort.

"Just young people in love," Lord Havenfort agrees.

"Yes, I must say, Lord Demeroven, I haven't had the chance to congratulate you," Lady Harrington says.

And it's then that James' brain catches up to him and he realizes he probably ought to be terribly mortified in her presence, since the last time she saw him, he was—

"I was so glad to hear that you had become engaged, and happily so. Leaving schoolyard friendships behind in favor of marital bliss I think will truly be a great joy for you."

James blinks across at her, unsure how to take that sentiment. But Bobby, Gwen, Meredith, Beth, and Albert are all desperately trying not to laugh, so he thinks perhaps he's missed something. "Ah, thank you, Lady Harrington, that means very much."

Lady Harrington smiles at him and then turns to Lady Havenfort to continue planning. James slumps in his seat, catching Bobby's eye. He so wants to know what joke he's missed.

Lord Havenfort stands and claps his hands together. "Well, this seems like the proper moment. Robert, James, please come with me to the study."

Now he's nervous. He and Bobby can't even look at each other as they follow Lord Havenfort down into the foyer and around the grand staircase to his study. James' palms are sweating and it feels like his tie is trying to slowly strangle him.

They hesitantly take their seats in the two brown leather armchairs across from the desk. James fiddles with his collar, feeling Bobby's signet ring rasp against his chest where it sits on an unseen chain beneath his cravat. He glances at Bobby, who looks back, his face a bit pale. They both wince at the sound of the doors closing, and then Lord Havenfort rounds the chairs, coming to lean back against the middle of the desk.

"Uncle Dashiell," Bobby begins, his voice high.

Lord Havenfort holds up a hand and looks between them. "Will you keep my girls safe?"

James and Bobby exchange a glance. "Um, yes," James says. Lord Havenfort raises an eyebrow. "Yes," he repeats, stronger. "With everything we have."

"Will you do all you can to make them happy?"

"Of course," Bobby says quickly.

Lord Havenfort's mouth tweaks upward. "Will you agree to having my solicitor draw up your marriage contracts so that both girls are fully accounted for and provided for in the event of either of your deaths?"

"Of course!" James hears himself exclaim. Bobby jumps and Lord Havenfort looks at him in surprise. "I just—" James swallows against the rush of nerves that courses through him. "I would never—we would never—" he corrects, glancing at Bobby, "put either Beth or Gwen into a situation like my aunt faced. I'll be happy to will all of my assets over to Gwen, in fact."

Lord Havenfort smiles. "That's good to hear."

"So would I, to Beth," Bobby puts in. "Though it's obviously not . . . quite the same gesture."

Lord Havenfort looks at his nephew with soft eyes. "It's still appreciated just the same. Thank you both," he adds, meeting James' gaze. "I have only one question left."

James sits on his hands, eager to pass inspection, and eager to make Lord Havenfort proud. His is the only pride James will chase now, and it actually feels within reach.

"I appreciate what your marriages and plans to have the Demeroven property accommodate the four of you will do for my girls, and I've seen how happy it has made them. But I want to be sure you are both equally happy, and equally prepared for the life you will lead together," Lord Havenfort says, his face serious again.

Bobby reaches over and takes James' hand. James squeezes his fingers and smiles up at Lord Havenfort. This is the easiest answer yet.

"We are," James says and Bobby nods. "And we are grateful for your acceptance and your help," he adds.

Lord Havenfort smiles and James watches, surprised as he slumps against the desk, suddenly far less intimidating and far more rumpled. "Thank God. Then we're settled. We'll meet with the solicitor tomorrow, and then, my apologies, but I will release you to the clutches of my wife, my daughters, and Lady Harrington."

Bobby laughs and James feels his shoulders come down from about his ears. "What have they planned?"

"Well, we can't prove all the rumors altogether baseless without throwing the four of you the most extravagant wedding of the season, can we?" Lord Havenfort asks, looking a little bit smug.

And it's in that smile that James sees a bit of Gwen. He's going to enjoy their groomly misery, isn't he?

"I'm personally looking forward to the shopping," Bobby says.

Lord Havenfort laughs and James feels himself shrink in his chair. He really hadn't thought about the wedding. But of course, with the suit fittings, and flowers, and cards, and everything, there will be so many details to arrange. He blinks as Lord Havenfort extends a tumbler of scotch his way. He didn't even notice him pouring, too busy trying to remember what Prince actually had to do for his wedding.

"You'll survive, I promise," Lord Havenfort says, winking at him just as the doors to the study burst open.

"Bobby, we're going," Gwen says, marching into the room holding what looks like lace swatches.

"Right," Bobby says, smiling at his uncle before he hops up

and buttons his vest. He leans down to press a kiss to James' cheek. "We'll be back in a few hours," he says.

"Where are you going?" James wonders, nearly yelping as Beth appears at his side with baby Frederic.

"Dress shopping," she says, unceremoniously taking his glass before handing him the baby. She knocks back his dram and smiles at Lord Havenfort before whisking Bobby out of the room.

James sits there blinking, a squirming baby in his arms. "Um," he says, looking down at Frederic's scrunched little face.

"You'll get used to them over time," Lord Havenfort promises.

"Right," James says, smiling down at the baby. "Right, they're loud and chaotic, but we love them, don't we?" he asks.

Lord Havenfort laughs, and James looks up, blushing. Babies do something to the brain, he's decided.

"I want you to know, I would never leave Gwen in the position my uncle and stepfather left Lady Havenfort," he reiterates, meeting Lord Havenfort's eyes. "I haven't gotten a chance to tell my aunt, but it was deplorable what was done to them, and I want to apologize to her, and to you, on behalf of my family. I promise to do much better by the title, and by Beth as well."

Lord Havenfort opens his mouth—

"That is lovely to hear, and truly unnecessary," Lady Havenfort says, approaching the desk on shockingly quiet feet. Maybe that's where Beth gets her stealth.

Albert, on the other hand, plops into Bobby's vacated seat with a satisfied sigh, making James nearly fumble the baby in surprise.

"Though I appreciate the apology, it isn't yours to give, nor is it yours to atone for," Lady Havenfort says, sliding along the desk to stand next to Lord Havenfort.

"That's what Beth said," James admits. "But I still wanted to say it."

"Well, my daughter is a bright young woman," Lady Havenfort says with a smile. "All I ask is that you be a good husband to Gwen, a good friend to Beth, and be the partner Bobby deserves, and we'll never have a problem."

"I will," James promises, that gooey, warm feeling back in his chest, accompanied by something soft and needy from his childhood, like squeezing a teddy bear so tightly its head might pop off.

"I'll drink to that," Lord Havenfort says.

Albert raises his glass as well. "Hear—"

"We're leaving!" Gwen calls out.

Lord Havenfort snorts, Albert laughs, and Lady Havenfort looks up at the ceiling, shaking her head. "Well, that's my cue."

She leans up and kisses Lord Havenfort, patting his cheek before smiling at James and Albert. She presses her lips to her fingers and brushes them over baby Frederic's forehead before striding out of the room, her call of "I'm coming!" ringing around them.

They listen to the commotion of the girls, and Bobby, preparing to leave, and James looks down at baby Frederic, who has slept through it all. Clearly, he'll do well in this family. Maybe they can be the quiet ones within the chaos together over the years. Though now that he thinks about it, James doesn't find himself missing the quiet of Epworth anymore. He's happy to be surrounded by laughter and chatter and . . . love.

Albert and Lord Havenfort begin discussing next year's parliamentary agenda, but James doesn't listen, too caught up in every little movement baby Frederic makes as he sleeps. That wistfulness creeps over him again.

"Cunningham thinks there could be an amendment made,

maybe to follow the Medical Act, about standards for childcare in orphanages," he hears Albert say.

It's absurd that it's taken him this long to think of it. "How many children at the Foundling Hospital need a home?" he blurts out.

Lord Havenfort smiles, something knowing in his eyes. "I think you should speak with your fiancée about that. She may have some ideas."

HE MIGHT PACE a trench into the floor of the small vestibule. Even the marble cannot possibly withstand his nerves. Of course he's excited to see Beth and Gwen in their gowns, and Bobby in his new suit. But he wishes they could just get the ceremony over with, and the reception afterward, and head to Dover, now.

Beth and Gwen would probably kill him, given they've spent the last three weeks in a tizzy, excited and frantic in equal measure, planning with Aunt Cordelia, his mother, and Lady Harrington. He's mainly been shunted from one meeting to the next. Parker's community has come together, and their cooperation has presented numerous business opportunities none of them had previously considered. He's been having discussions with Parker, Cunningham, and new business associates just as often as he's sat with Albert and Uncle Dashiell discussing matters of parliament.

He's barely seen Bobby. And now that he's waiting to enter a church to marry Gwen, he's more than a little miffed that Bobby is late. The narrow, stained-glass window above him throws beautiful patterns of colored light across the stone floor and he kicks at them, antsy.

He's about to storm into the nave, and maybe mingle, just for something to do, when the doors to the vestibule burst open and Bobby tumbles inside.

James gapes as Bobby rights himself and closes the doors. He spins around and all of James' ire melts away in the face of Bobby, resplendent in his custom black suit, the single-breasted white waistcoat beneath his tailcoat hugging every inch of his chest. His bow tie is just a smidge crooked, and his hair in disarray from what James imagines have been a few passes through with nervous fingers. He looks absolutely perfect, and every single ounce of James is melting, fast.

"Here," Bobby says, hurrying up to him and thrusting his hand out at James.

"What?" James asks, blinking down to find a single gold band in the center of Bobby's palm. "Shouldn't those be with Cunningham's nephew?"

"I thought maybe we could do it ourselves, for real, the first time," Bobby says.

James looks up and meets his eyes. "Ourselves?"

Bobby nudges his hand into James' chest and James takes the ring, his hand shaking now. Bobby grins and takes James' left hand, gently sliding his band over the first knuckle of James' ring finger, where it promptly can't move any further.

James can't help but laugh, a slightly wet sound. Oh, he's misting up.

"Well, that's far less romantic than I meant it to be," Bobby says, sighing. "You don't have to—"

But James is already sliding the ring just over the tip of Bobby's left ring finger, where it gets stuck. Little surprise, Bobby's hands are massive compared to Gwen's. "Well," he says, meeting Bobby's eyes.

They both laugh and Bobby hauls him forward into a kiss. James reaches up to cup Bobby's jaw, holding him close. Bobby's arms wrap around James' waist, and they stay there, kissing in the multicolored light, alone in a peaceful silence, a promise made with ill-fitting rings.

A knock at the door splits them apart, and James regretfully tugs off his ring, watching Bobby struggle to yank off his own with a grimace.

"It was a lovely thought," James says. Bobby stares down at the ring.

"And it's the thought that counts?" Bobby asks, looking up to meet his eyes.

"I'll know that you wore that ring before Gwen did."

"And you wore mine before Beth," Bobby agrees.

Another knock, louder and far more insistent.

Bobby chuckles and hauls James back for one last kiss just before the doors open. They step back, not looking at each other, and Albert leans into the room.

"Cunningham says the rings have been absconded with," Albert announces.

Bobby blushes and slinks across to the door to hand the rings to his brother.

"What— You know, I don't want to know. Two minutes," Albert says, winking at James before he shuts the door.

Bobby turns to face James, shrugging. "I guess we're up," he says.

James smiles, taking the few steps to Bobby so he can reach up and adjust his bow tie. "I guess so."

"You ready?" Bobby asks, looking down at him, soft and handsome and perfect.

"I'm already in our room in Dover, taking this suit off you with my teeth," he says, delighting in the way Bobby's jaw drops.

"You—"

A knock reverberates through the door.

“Come on, let’s get married,” James says, leaning up to kiss Bobby’s cheek once before stepping back.

He straightens his jacket and steps up to Bobby’s side. Bobby reaches out and squeezes his hand. James looks over at him and smiles.

“I love you,” Bobby says.

James’ smile turns into a grin he can’t control. “I love you too.”

WHEN THEY EMERGE onto the steps of the church after the whirlwind of the ceremony, James squeezes Gwen’s hand, excited to make a future with her—one that they have chosen, and architected, and built for themselves. A life that lets all four of them be who they are, and love who they love.

Uncle Dashiell and Aunt Cordelia direct them to huddle together on the steps, Gwen and James on one side, Beth and Bobby on the other.

As the photographer disappears under the cloth, Bobby’s pinky brushes James’ and James beams for the camera. This is his life, and he plans to take every moment of joy from it he can.

EPILOGUE

Five Years Later

Bobby

It's giggles that wake them first, followed by a heavy whump and a whispered "Shh!"

Bobby smiles into James' shoulder and James groans, burrowing into Bobby and pulling the covers over their heads. "James," he prompts.

"Sleeping," James whines, shaking his head against his pillow. "Too early."

"Never thought I'd see the day," Bobby says, laughing as James taps feebly at his forearm. "Did I tire you out?"

"Yes," James mumbles, wiggling back against Bobby in a way that absolutely will not help either of them get out of bed. "The pint of whisky beforehand didn't help," he admits with a groan.

Bobby leans in to kiss the sweaty back of James' head. "Parker got you, hmm?"

"We weren't even drinking heavily, but he kept having them delivered to the table, and we were talking about the land for the orphanage, and did you know that Lady Ashmond could drink us both under the table if she wanted to?" James rushes out, his voice still a little slurred.

Bobby's decision to stay home and pass a quiet evening playing chess with Miss Wilson was clearly the better one. "I do want a full report on the progress with the orphanage," he says.

"When I can think straight," James agrees, shifting to try to get comfortable again. "Was a good night, though," he says, glancing blearily over his shoulder. "With Parker and, you know, after," he says.

Bobby leans in to steal a kiss. It was a good night. And perhaps they have been going a bit overboard. But James leaves the day after tomorrow for two months; they have a lot of romping to bank up.

"So what you're saying is if I go and handle breakfast, you'll do that thing with your tongue to—"

"Yes, go," James says quickly, all but forcing Bobby out of the bed, lest they end up tangled in the sheets long enough for either Beth or Gwen or . . . tiny eyes and ears to come looking.

"All right, all right," Bobby says, crawling out of bed and hopping across the floor to don his pajamas and a robe. "I can buy you another thirty minutes."

James' hand emerges from the pile of blankets, a duvet, and scattered pillows. He waves Bobby on and then goes still. Bobby smirks and heads out of their room, making a note to ensure that no one comes to tidy their suite today. No one need see the aftereffects of their night.

He forces himself to remain cheerful as he wends his way through the house, arms tucked up to his chest against the coming winter chill. It's always hard to have James in London, especially so close to the holidays, but it isn't as if he gets to pick the parliamentary schedule. They'll join him for the hols and new year, and then hopefully they can all return home until the start of the season.

He passes footmen Georgie and Henry on the first floor, the two of them awfully close together as they work on peeling potatoes outside of the kitchen. Perhaps there will be some shuffling of staff quarters needed soon.

He nods in greeting, withholding a smirk as they blush. They've created a haven not just for themselves, but for all of their staff as well. A place where they can live as their true selves, in love with whomever they like. As long as impressionable eyes never walk in on anything untoward, no matter between whom, it works swimmingly.

So far, little eyes have only walked in on their parents, so everything's fine. The children hardly care; it's just the mortification of it for Bobby and James. Though Beth and Gwen really take the cake—found in flagrante in Beth's tree house by a very confused little Martha. Beth still blushes every time they take the kids there.

"Daddy!"

Bobby smiles, stepping into the river-stone kitchen where Martha and Sammie are already seated around the large oak table, jam on their faces and down the front of their aprons.

"Good morning, darlings," he says, padding across the cool stone floor to press a kiss to Sammie's messy head and to Martha's cheek. "Strawberry jam?" he asks as she giggles.

"Miss Wilson said we could have the last of it," Martha tells him seriously, patting the table at her side to get him to sit down.

He does as told, noting that both children are already dressed. Martha's little flower-patterned dress goes nicely with her white frilly apron, even marred as it is now with jam. Sammie's in a simple pair of trousers and a blue shirt, covered with another frilly white-sleeved apron, equally covered in jam. His blue eyes finally blink over at Bobby and he smiles shyly. Something about mornings always makes him a bit timid, but by afternoon he'll be yelling just like his sister.

"How long until they get here?" Martha asks as Bobby reaches out to butter his own scone.

"About an hour," Bobby says, chuckling at Martha's responding pout. With her big brown eyes and curly brown hair, she's how he imagines Beth must have looked at seven, which is charming.

"That's ages," Martha exclaims.

"It's still only just daylight," Bobby argues. "Sammie's barely awake."

"Sammie's never awake before noon," Martha says simply.

"But we love him anyway. Daddy's sleepy sometimes too," Bobby reminds her.

"Of course we still love him, how silly," Martha says, reaching out to pat Sammie's head, which smears jam into his hair.

Sammie doesn't even blink, still making slow progress on his scone. Perhaps they'll have to squeeze in a bath before everyone arrives, lest Dashiell and Cordelia think they let their children run around covered in jam.

"Oh, how delicious."

"Mama!" Martha exclaims, bouncing in her seat.

Beth smiles as she comes in through the outer door to the kitchen, little Louie on her hip, still rubbing his eyes. She squeezes through, adjusting her large hoop and bumping the stack of empty crates by the door as she turns, not quite used to the new extended oval of her hoopskirt, highly in fashion and often cumbersome in small spaces. But her ensemble is casual, an afternoon robe over a simple green skirt and white shirtwaist, which makes him feel a smidge better about potentially greeting their guests in his pajamas.

"See you've gotten a late start too," Beth says, smiling at him as she deposits Louie in his high chair. "Good morning, lovelies," she adds, coming around the table to greet Martha and Sammie.

"Daddy says it's less than an hour now," Martha informs her.

"That's right," Beth says, rounding the table again to settle beside Louie and pass him a plain scone, which he clumsily begins to tear into pieces.

"Goodness, still in your pajamas, how untoward," Gwen announces as she comes through the outer door. Her ensemble matches Beth's, just in blue instead of green, and with a riot of blond curls she hasn't bothered to tame.

"We're not really standing on ceremony, are we?" Bobby asks as Gwen greets the children.

She ruffles his hair as she goes to claim her seat beside Beth. "Father absolutely won't care. Meredith will tease you, though."

"I can take it," Bobby decides, sharing a smile with Martha. "Look, Martha, Mummy has your curls today."

Martha beams over at Gwen, who blows her a kiss. "Why can't Mama have our curls too?" she wonders, looking to Beth.

Beth laughs. "Some of us just weren't blessed with your pretty hair."

"Or the patience to let Miss Wilson try it with hot combs," Gwen mutters.

Beth nudges her. "But I love your curls, darling," Beth tells Martha. "And Mr. Sammie, how are you?"

Sammie looks up at Beth with a shy smile. "Good," he whispers.

"Did you sleep well here with your fathers?" Gwen asks, winking at Bobby.

They usually swap the children every few nights, but Louie was feeling clingy last night, so Beth and Gwen kept him at Drightmore Cottage just down the front drive. Technically, it's his and Beth's house, while James and Gwen officially inhabit Demeroven Hall, but they quickly decided that Beth and Gwen were better suited to the cottage.

The children shift between both houses, so they all get a few evenings a week to themselves, but it hardly matters. They're all Mum and Dad, and the children love having two grand houses in which to play the world's most anxiety-inducing games of hide-and-seek. Martha holds the record at eight hours unfound. They nearly had a collective heart attack that day. And she was only four then.

"Does Papa really have to leave?" Martha asks quietly while Beth and Gwen pull more answers and smiles out of Sammie.

Bobby turns to find Martha looking up at him. Her little face can be so serious. "He does, but we'll write him every week, and see him for the holidays," Bobby says.

Martha's face droops and she looks back at her breakfast, no longer bubbly. "Okay," she whispers.

"But hey," Bobby says, his heart breaking for his daughter, who is absolutely Papa's little girl. "You, me, Sammie, and Louie are going to have a marvelous time here. We'll make forts, and stay out in Mama's tree house until our lips turn blue, and play all kinds of games. And your mothers will play with us. You'll be having so much fun the months will fly by, and then we'll all be in London with Papa."

"And Johnnie and Frederic?" Martha asks, looking up at him with a little sniffle.

"And Johnnie and Frederic too," Gwen says. Martha looks

across the table at Gwen. "And that means Auntie Meredith and Grandma Cordelia too." Gwen winks at Bobby as Martha's smile returns. "And, even better, you know who's going to stay the whole two months?"

"Who?" Martha asks, wiggling in her seat.

"Mrs. Stelm and Mrs. Gilpe," Gwen says theatrically.

Both Martha and Sammie yell in excitement. Louie joins in, shrieking at them with jam all over his cheeks.

"They're so excited to see all of you," Beth adds.

"Are they still thinking they'll arrange with Lady Ashmond to adopt their own?" Bobby wonders.

Beth shrugs. "Not sure. I know Mother and Dashiell could live without them, but I'm not sure Mrs. Stelm and Mrs. Gilpe want to give up their London life."

"And there's no way for it to work in the London house, is there?" Gwen asks.

"It would be much more difficult," Beth agrees. "But the Marchston Cottage is up for sale still, isn't it?" she asks, looking to Bobby.

"It is, and that's right next to the plot of land James and Parker are considering for the orphanage. It could be perfect."

"I'm sure Lady Ashmond would hire them on. They'd be excellent," Gwen says, smiling. "The best caretakers, outside of us, of course," she adds, looking around at the children and pulling a silly face.

"I know Miss Wilson would love to have them here," Beth says.

"We could have Gilpe and Stelmie here all the time?" Martha asks. Perhaps the days of serious breakfast discussion are starting to wane.

"Maybe," Beth says firmly. "Don't get your hopes up, and

don't bother them about it. They need to make their own decision about how they want to live."

"But everyone should live here!" Martha insists brightly. "Then we can all play, and everyone can kiss who they want."

Bobby snorts into his tea as Gwen turns a laugh into a cough.

"Yes, well. We're all very happy here, and that's what matters," Beth says, totally serious. She's always best at dealing with the children when they're discussing something important. Bobby and Gwen still just dissolve into giggles, even four years in to being parents.

"What's all this noise, then?"

Martha turns and squeals, spotting James leaning against the doorjamb into the kitchen. He's wearing a simple pair of trousers and a green frock coat, and now Bobby is starting to feel a little silly staying in his pajamas with company soon to arrive.

"Papa, Papa, Daddy says we can build forts with Johnnie and Frederic," Martha announces.

James smiles at Bobby and scoots in between Sammie and Martha, pulling Sammie up onto his lap, where he promptly cuddles into James, taking refuge. James listens to Martha and answers her questions, while making silly faces across at Louie. Beth and Gwen fall into their own discussion about activities and Bobby just sits there, taking it all in.

He doesn't want James to leave for two months either. Had to stop himself from asking him to stay more than once last night as they lay tangled and sweaty. But this is his job. He goes into the world for them, making laws and working with Albie to grow their fortune.

Uncle Dashiell hasn't given up hope, but even he isn't confident that a proposal to give adopted children the right to inherit a title could pass either chamber. So they've collectively decided to make the most of the Demeroven title while they have it—big swings, big efforts, big risks. They want to make the world a better place for their children, and all children, for that matter. The businesses James has started with Parker have already created a good fund, and they've time to grow it into a fortune, so their children can someday carry on their charity work, even once the titles and estates have returned to the crown.

The doorbell rings and Martha immediately jumps up, tugging Sammie out of James' arms so they can run toward the front of the house. Gwen hoists Louie into her arms and she and Beth follow them out, leaving James and Bobby sitting at the table.

"Can I just say how much I really don't want to leave?" James asks.

Bobby smiles sadly and stands, helping James up so he can wrap his arms around him. "I don't want you to leave either," he admits. "But you've work to do, and we'll be all right. Full house, and all." They hear commotion erupt from the front hall.

"Still," James says, wrapping his arm around Bobby's waist as they head for the foyer.

James leans into Bobby and brushes his fingers up and down Bobby's side as they come to the end of the hall, listening to their family chattering on the other side of the doorway.

"I'll write you terribly filthy letters," Bobby says, turning to meet James' eyes.

James snorts and then rises on his toes to press a kiss to Bobby's lips. "You'd better," he says as he pulls away.

"It's a promise," Bobby decides, taking James' hand to head into the foyer.

It's like walking into a wall of sound. Martha and Sammie, now fully awake and totally hyper, bounce around with Frederic and little Johnnie, who's not so little anymore. He's had his five-year-old growth spurt, it seems, and now looks like a mini-Albie. The four of them run among the adults' legs while Aunt Cordelia greets Beth, Gwen, and Louie. She immediately steals their youngest, cuddling him while Louie plays with her frilly collar.

Bobby's learned there is nothing quite like the cuddle of a two-year-old. Nothing quite like a two-year-old screaming either, but he loves Louie no matter what. And honestly, he'll probably be their quietest child for the duration. What have they done, inviting a little Bertram *and* a little Mason for the whole winter?

Albie and Meredith divest themselves of their coats while chatting with Uncle Dashiell, who's pulling a seemingly endless stack of presents through the front door. Frederic has a normal, respectable amount of toys at Havenfort Manor, but Uncle Dashiell clearly doesn't know how to stop buying for his grandchildren.

Mrs. Gilpe and Mrs. Stelm wave at them, chatting in the corner with Miss Wilson. Bobby smiles at them, hoping that they do end up deciding to come live nearby. They would make excellent matrons for the proposed orphanage, and he knows Gwen and Beth would love having them so close. Miss Wilson clearly would as well. And Parker probably wouldn't mind. He's getting tired of the weekly Mason/Demeroven house card games—knows all their tells, apparently.

And even though it's loud and frenetic, Bobby wouldn't want to be anywhere other than here, with his whole motley family. They're all older, wiser, and so much happier than they were just five years ago. He's looking forward to being happier for the rest of his life.

"I can't wait to come back," James says, leaning into him.

Bobby smiles and turns to press a kiss to the top of his head. "Yes. Please, hurry home."

ACKNOWLEDGMENTS

Writing *You're the Problem, It's You* on the heels of *Don't Want You Like a Best Friend* was like seeing two amazing shows back-to-back, produced by the same team, but uniquely their own experiences. And at the end of that marathon day, you're elated, exhausted, and just the slightest bit giddy. I'm so grateful to my team for getting ready for two opening nights at the same time, with such poise, skill, and genuine excitement.

To Sylvan, my wonderful editor, thank you for believing in the Mischief & Matchmaking gang. Getting to tell Bobby and James' story (and the rest of Beth and Gwen's) with you has been a dream come true. Thank you for your thoughtful notes, your laugh-out-loud commentary, and your unwavering support of Beth, Gwen, Bobby, and James on their journeys. And for your support for me.

To Allie, thank you for guiding James and Bobby (and Beth and Gwen) to the finish line with such care. Your enthusiasm, excitement, and dedication have been a gift, and I look forward to more stories yet to come to share together.

To Stacy, my fantastic agent, thank you for your guidance, support, expertise, and camaraderie throughout this speedrun. You've kept me sane, you've helped me learn, and you've made me smile. I wouldn't be here without you, and here's to many more.

To Larry, my excellent manager, thank you for celebrating each step of the journey with me. It's a long road that I couldn't walk without you. And to Devra, thank you so much.

To Wayne, attorney extraordinaire, thank you for your support, your reads, our chats, and your guidance. I hope there's so much more to talk about and to learn ahead.

To Leni Kauffman, for another magnificent cover, thank you. You captured Bobby and James' relationship so perfectly. I'll never stop being excited to see them on the shelf.

To the amazing publishing professionals who have touched *You're the Problem, It's You*, and made it the best book it can be, thank you: Erika Tsang, May Chen, Linda Sawicki, Chistine Vahaly, Diahann Sturge-Campbell, Shelby Peak, Amy Halperin, Christine Vahaly, DJ DeSmyther, Jes Lyons, Kalie Barnes-Young, Ronnie Kutys, Andy LeCount, and Caroline Bodkin.

To my beta and authenticity readers, Lovell, Kris, Zach, Becca, Lindsay, Aviva, and Stacy, thank you for your thoughtful comments, suggestions, and notes. This book wouldn't be the same without you, nor would I be the writer I am without your feedback. You're all awesome humans.

To my friends, who are unwaveringly supportive, encouraging, and loving, thank you. You hype me up, and make me laugh, and make me excited to be excited. I love you so much.

To Dylan, to whom this book is dedicated, I wouldn't be who I am without your support, love, friendship, and camaraderie. It was the best childhood growing up with you. And every year I am ever more grateful and proud to be your little sister. Being on the team with you means the world to me.

To Dani, the newest member of our Team Alban, I am so grateful to have you here with us. We're newer, better, and stronger with you on the team. Thank you, and love you.

To my parents, words can't do justice to how grateful I am to be your child. Thank you for the life I get to lead. Thank you for your love, and support, and friendship. *Thank you*.

And to you, dear reader, who has come on this journey with Bobby and James, thank you for reading. I hope you had as much fun with the Mischief & Matchmaking gang as I had writing them.

About the Author

Raised in the Hudson Valley, **Emma R. Alban** now lives in Los Angeles, enjoying the eternal sunshine, ocean, and mountains. When she isn't writing books or screenplays, she can usually be found stress-baking with the AC on full blast, skiing late into the spring, singing show tunes at the top of her lungs on the freeway, and reading anywhere there's somewhere to lean.